THE LAST DAUGHTER

BOOK ONE

ALEXIS L. MENARD

For information contact: http://www.alexislmenard.com/

Cover design by Gabrielle Ragusi

Editing by Brittany Corley

Copy Editing by Stephanie Taylor

August 2022

❀ Created with Vellum

For those who broke generational curses and forged their own fate.

TABLE OF CONTENTS

CONTENT WARNINGS

The Last Daughter is an adult fantasy romance that contains strong language and content some readers may find distressing, including violence, death, mentions of miscarriage off page, alcohol use, and graphic depictions of sexual themes.

Growing up in a clan full of ruthless killers, Ailsa knew the sting of a dagger, the bruising jab of a hammer. But no blade was as sharp as the knife-edge of their words. They were the only weapons the world could wield against her—and so the world wielded them often.

"The Aelderwood is going to eat you alive one day, Ailsa." Nikros sauntered into her apothecary only minutes after she'd set down her basket. His patronizing advice was as unwanted as his presence.

The butcher's son had been particularly smothering the past few days, breathing down her neck ever since her father left with her sisters and the other shieldmages. Nikros was built like a mountain, towering with not an ounce of warmth in any crevasse of his stocky frame. The sides of his head were shaved, forming a pale strip of hair that ran down the center of his skull. But Ailsa always found his eyes to be the coldest part about him—dark as the bottom of a lake and twice as suffocating.

She twisted the pestle against the mortar, if only to keep her hands from wringing his neck. There were very few places on this fjord that belonged to her, and this shop was her arena. If he anticipated a battle, she'd make sure he suffered the loss. "Just because I cannot breathe doesn't mean I cannot fight as good as any man this side of the fjord, Nikros. You know my father raised me in the ways of the warrior, as everyone in this clan is taught."

Her fingers were still stained black with kohl, unable to bring herself to wash the last remnant of her sister's skin from her fingertips. The darkness bled into the grooves of her callouses, where just that morning, she had painted the marks of Tyr upon their faces, the sacred markings blessed their flesh with good fortune in battle, and a swift death should the god of war demand their sacrifice. She had watched, along with the rest of their clan, as the warriors staggered into the longships and slipped away into the foggy morning, drawing north up the river to meet the king's army near the border of the sea.

Ailsa could not join her family in battle. She was not born a fighter but a healer. She saved lives; she didn't take them—a balance her family heavily outweighed on a moral scale. Marrin and Lochare, her two older sisters, had been throwing axes before they could read, clearly destined to join the ranks of the great warriors their clan was known to produce. Her people's offensive magic and ability to best any fight with spell or sword made them an invaluable asset to the king, and her clan was given much in terms of wealth and influence in return for their shields.

Ailsa had been blessed with her mother's spirit—steady, tempered, and somewhat controlled. A renowned healer, her mother was able to cure everyone else's sickness but her own. A sickness she had ultimately passed on to her youngest daughter.

"Still," he said, pacing the shop as if he were surveying her goods, "the forest wraiths get nasty this close to Yule. You should let me accompany you next time."

She paused her grinding. "Like you accompanied your jarl?"

A low grumble slipped from his throat, and Ailsa briefly lifted her eyes from her work to cast him a glance. She had an arsenal of weapons of her own, and the first slashed a blow to his pride.

"I discussed this with your father when he was gathering the clans," he bit out. "I am no warrior. My place is here, protecting the rest of the village until he returns—"

"Tell that to Egrid, Suko, and Sugrid. They were *boys*, Nikros! Yet still, they understood the call, the responsibility placed on our people to defend the king's lands from these savages plowing through our armies unlike we have ever seen in our history." Her eyes stung as she thought of how the young shieldmages stood during the last meeting of the clans, how they volunteered to fight against an unforeseen enemy to protect a land granted to her ancestors by the gods' mercy alone. "Even they had more honor growing inside their bones than you. But yours are hollow, barren of anything desirable. You shamed the name of your family and your father, Nikroth, the day you decided to stand for nothing."

She spat the words like they were laced with hemlock. Nikros rolled his shoulders back, taking a defensive stance. "I am following my jarl's orders. Your father agreed my place was here." It took him only two strides to approach her desk, resting the whites of his knuckles on top of the rugged varnish. "We both agreed my place was here with *you*."

Ailsa scoffed. The sharp breath stirred the thistle seeds in her cup. "What are you saying? My father decided you would stay to protect me? Don't fool yourself. I can look out for myself."

"No." His round face shook while his black eyes locked on her face. "We had a different arrangement."

Dread curdled in her stomach. "*No.*"

His lips pulled into a crooked smile. "He already promised you to me. We both decided there was a fair chance our armies would follow that of the sea clans, and he didn't want you to be left alone, husbandless, and lose your status. Without a husband, you will lose the support of the clan and the only thing left for you will be this pathetic excuse for a shop. Your family name means nothing now, Ailsa. Through our union—"

"No," she repeated. Her steps retreated from the work-bench, fingers finding the fire poker behind her back. It was still hot from when she stoked the flames just moments before. He'd been pursuing their union for years, but Ailsa knew he didn't care for her. Not in that way. Nikros was appealed by her blood, not her heart. "My father wouldn't give me away without my consent, especially to a spineless man like you."

"I've already received your dowry."

"Keep it. I don't care."

"It has been decided. I have witnesses–"

"Fuck your witnesses," she hissed. "If my father dies on the battlefield then his bargains and his promises die with him."

Nikros scowled, the only warning she was given before he leaped over her workbench in a stealthy pounce. His meaty hands reached for her shoulders to shake sense into her stubborn body like he had done so many times before when she rejected him. But Ailsa was prepared this time for his unwanted advances.

She swung the iron so swiftly he barely had time to flinch, the orange tip scalding him in the temple and scorching the shaved skin above his ear. Watching that hideous grin fall was almost as satisfying as his wails, but Ailsa wanted to teach him a lesson. She needed to make a point. Twisting her wrist, she sent a blow to the side of his knee, followed by a thrust of her palm to his nose so hard, cartilage cracked against her palm.

He staggered backward, knocking entire shelves off the wall where his weight flailed about, sending vials crashing to the floor. The air was saturated with warm spice and the sound of broken glass, and her footsteps approaching his vulnerable figure crunched the echo of stray shards. A few burns and a broken nose were far less than he deserved. But sometimes, the worst wounds always hid beneath the skin, and she hoped she'd hurt his ego enough to leave a scar.

Ailsa shoved the pole against his throat, crushing his windpipe as she pinned him against the wall. "You cannot protect yourself, much less me. I would rather die than unify with you and leave our clan in the hands of a pathetic excuse for an Ostman."

He choked on a laugh. His words were raspy as he spoke. "Your mother was only a few years older than yourself when she passed. How much longer will you wait to settle down, to plant your roots, and start a family? You're running out of time. You know this, and your father knew it before he left. Be with me and you can live out the rest of your days in security and comfort, knowing you will be cared for and protected."

Ailsa answered with a heartless smile of her own. "I've been dying my whole life, Nikros. You cannot scare me with my own death, nor will I be intimidated by the number of years marked on my life thread. In fact, I'd use my last breath to tell you exactly what I'm going to tell you now." She leaned in closer, smelling the foul breath panting from his pale lips. "Fuck off."

He pushed her away with a mere thought. He was a trained shieldmage—the last shieldmage. He should have joined the rest when the call was placed to defend her homeland. But the magic was wasted on the man before her. He only ever used it on his work—and her. "You'll regret this, Ailsa. There's no other man who will take a woman like you and tarnish their family line."

"Get out," she muttered, returning to her work as if nothing had ever happened. "And don't come back, or I'll have my wolf tear your balls from your shriveled sack and tarnish *your* family line. I will not show you mercy again."

He left with haste, cradling the last fragments of his pride. But his final truth hung in the air, poisoning any satisfaction she may have felt at that moment. Because despite his cowardice, he was still right. No man wanted her, fearing she would bear an heir with the same hereditary condition plaguing her mother's family line. And even with the promise of death, the daily struggle of living like she was in a perpetual state of drowning, her loneliness festered deeper than any sickness.

He chose his words with intent to cripple, used them to lash the place she was most vulnerable. They cut deep, hurt worse than she'd ever admit. But she'd never let him see her bleed.

The bitterness veined deep in her heart, stealing the energy she required to work. She locked up and returned to her longhouse on top of the hill overlooking the village of Drakame, taking a stalling glance at the mouth of the channel. Home wasn't quite the same anymore. Being greeted by the eerie quiet wasn't the sort of welcome she looked forward to. The rooms were a little bigger without her family, more space to notice their absence. It was like this every time they left, whether to raid or to scout new lands. The jarl never let her join the plunder. His reason was always the same.

"Every warrior who joins the raid must contribute their share. You cannot keep up with us, dóttir. Our enemies are ruthless, and I cannot afford to watch out for you." He would tell her.

"If I cannot fight for my clan then perhaps I don't belong here," she would reply.

His hazel eyes would settle over her, the lines around his lips tighten in a frown. *"Being an Ostman is not in what we do, but in who we are. Not all battles are fought with iron and steel, some are fought in our hearts and our mind. You, my dóttir, are perhaps the greatest warrior of us all."*

She smiled, because he never lied to her, and every time he said the words, she believed them a little more.

Ailsa begged to be on that boat leaving the harbor this morning, even knowing how it would end for them—for her. She spoke true to Nikros. She did not fear death. But she *did* fear dying alone. She dreaded that extended agony her mother endured, the slow suffocation until her breath was stolen forever.

She could sense it coming, like the winter season teasing its entrance on a fall breeze. It seemed everyday she felt a little worse. The herbs worked a little less, the weight sitting on her chest a little heavier. Fate had its hands around her throat, ready to squeeze the life from her. But as she looked out into the channel, knowing in her bones her family was never coming back, she could only wish it would be mercifully soon.

Her hands slipped to her neck, pulling out the chain tied to her mother's ring beneath layers of flax and fur. The ring had been passed down for generations just like this home, her mother's line the original founders of Drakame. Her fingertips caught the rune marks engraved along the thick band, a language long forgotten and impossible to decode.

"Please," she sighed to the heavens, to the weavers of

destiny if they heard the pleas of mortals. Her voice now scratchy from swallowing tears. “Please, just take me soon.”

There were fates worse than death. Lives not worth living if given the choice. And if she had no role left in this world, if the last of her days were to be spent beneath a cold man like Nikros and know happiness only in the form of a sham, then it didn’t truly matter if her life thread was cut now or later.

She gripped the ring a little tighter, letting the runes press lines into the soft skin of her palm. But if there *was* a reason to fight, if she still served a purpose in this quiet, water-faced village, somehow claim the title of jarl to protect herself from unwanted vices, then perhaps…

“Perhaps not yet,” she whispered. Her eyes shut as the sun dipped low, sinking behind the hazy line of the horizon. Her heart still beat, her breath still flowed, and while she lived, so her hope for something more still survived as well. And she swore she heard fate whisper back.

Not yet.

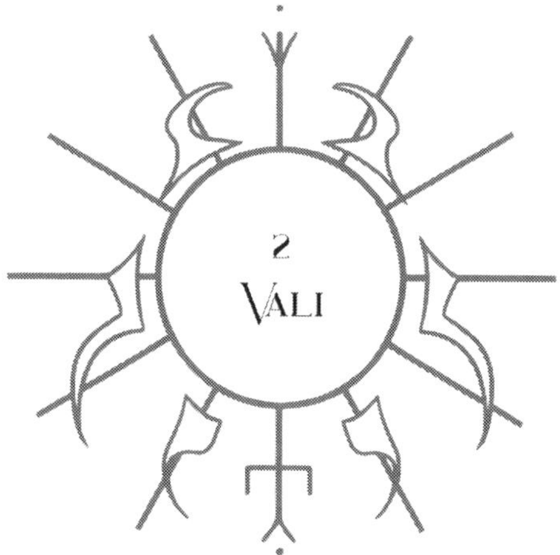

2
Vali

Cold apathy washed over Vali as he watched the sea beyond the isle litter with boats. More men, more fighting, more senseless death at the expense of pure stubbornness. He had killed so many mortals this past week he was starting to feel like a god. The thought made his skin betray a rash of chills.

Vali had sent his demands to the mainland with the last Ostman, a prisoner from the previous battle when his legion had overtaken this smear of land floating in the North Sea. The mortals his men encountered were savage, skilled in their fighting and organized in their approach. They showed no fear when his soldiers docked the ship and raided the coastal kingdom, like the heathens were practically starving for a fight.

But half a century of searching mottled the mind into a mass of desperation, where little else mattered to Vali and his crew besides completing their task. Nearly a thousand days at sea only exacerbated the hunger. They were too close to their objective to grant these men a reprieve. Too close to getting what they came for and going *home.*

His commander approached from the side. Her face hardened as she counted each shield lining the hulls. Seela had a heart big enough for them both, yet he had witnessed the slow fade of her spirit, turning her compassion into something more calloused. "You requested a man, and they have brought an army."

"Did you expect anything less of the heathens?" Vali spoke without breaking his gaze on the boats spilling their crew into the shallows. Had their weapons been of formidable strength, they would have been a match to be reckoned with.

"When your dreams called you to this flooded map of a realm, did they tell you of these Ostmen and the resistance we would face?" she asked.

Vali shook his head. The writers of fate had a nasty habit of only providing him with pieces of the picture, or in this case, the name of a single man.

Ledger Locharsson

"No," he answered her. "Would it have made a difference?"

Seela said nothing, but he knew she was already regretting what had to be done. There were always innocent bystanders caught in the crossfire, pawns in a larger game unwittingly used for a greater purpose. Only after a time did she ask in a tight voice, "We're going to kill them all, aren't we?"

"If we must," he said on the tailwind of a sigh. "Do not have pity on the heathens, Commander. If they're hiding the lost power from us, then they decided their own fates." The stakes were too steep to falter on the downward slope of death. The reward too great to let anyone stop him now. "Get me a horse and open the gates. I'll try to parley with their speaker, first. But if Ledger isn't here, or if he hasn't brought what I've asked of him, be prepared to strike."

"But Vali, what if—"

"That's an order, Seela. Do not argue with me on this, or do you forget who I am?" he spat. Even as the words left his lips, he knew he would pay for them.

She scoffed a mirthless laugh. "You know, sometimes I wish you could feel shame like the rest of us," she whispered so only he could hear. "But then I am grateful your conscious was ripped away long ago. It will make it easier to live with yourself when this is finished." She turned sharply on a heel to carry out his *orders.*

He closed his eyes and swallowed her words, letting them awaken something painful in his throat. Seela knew Vali better than anyone, but what she didn't know was that he *did* feel shame. In fact, he clung to it like a lifeline, like it was the last thread holding together his morality.

But when shame collides with anger, monsters were born.

VALI WAITED in the middle of the stretch of land that separated the vehement sea from the stronghold behind him. The band of brutes stood in an unrelenting wall of shields, only separating for a moment to allow three men to pass through. He dismounted as they approached.

The three men stopped several paces from where he stood, and the proximity allowed Vali to discover that two of the men were not men at all, but women. Any hint of a feminine physique was tucked away beneath armor vests and golden chain mail. Their wind-burned faces were marked with black paint, an intricate design bleeding across their scowls.

"You did not comply with my demands," Vali said. The Tether was not here; he would be able to feel it if it were this close. The man leading the trio shifted on his feet, widening his stance.

"It is not a request if you do not detail what exactly you are looking for," he said in a voice too casual to be afraid. "We have taken much from the Saxons. You'll have to be more specific."

Vali smiled beneath his hood. "I am no Saxon, and I have no interest in the riches you steal from this world. You are the man they call Ledger, are you not?"

"Aye, that is my name."

"You are from the clan, Drakame."

Ledger's eyes shifted to one of the women at his side before returning to him. "What do you know of my clan?"

Vali brought his hands in front of him, folding his fingers between each other. "I know that the rest of your kin will perish for Drakame's secrets. Those behind you may not know what I'm after, but you do, heathen. You have stolen something from the gods, something that does not belong to you. Do not waste your breath, *Ledger the Liar.* Your falsehoods will only kill you faster."

"I will let the gods be the judge of my integrity," Ledger replied, lifting his chin an inch higher. "If I am as guilty as you claim, if I have indeed stolen something from our gods, then I will perish in combat."

Vali's grinned widened. "Trial by combat? I believe that's fair. Unfortunately for you, Ledger, you chose the wrong adversary to pass your judgement. I was born solely for revenge and redemption, and I will not leave this realm until I seize them both."

Ledger's face paled, further faded by the overcast sky stealing the color from a vibrant realm. His gloved hand went toward the hilt of his sword, unsheathing the steel in a languid motion. "This realm? Who are you, demon?"

Vali's smile fell. His blood roared as his magic primed beneath his skin. "I am precisely what you believe I am."

Ledger swung the blade without a precursor of his intentions, aimed for Vali's exposed neck. He wore no armor, only a dark green velvet tunic beneath a heavy cloak—the rest of his riding gear of equal refinement. But before the blade could meet the base of the hood concealing his marks, he intercepted its trajectory with a bare grip.

Ledger's eyes widened as Vali wrapped his long fingers around the sharpened metal and pulled it free from his grasp. His mind was the only weapon he needed here, the power in his veins sharper than any steel, and he used it to still the heathen in place while thrusting the sword into Ledger's chest. A strangled sound escaped his painted lips as the man folded over his weapon; his knees buckled as he collapsed against the earth.

"Guilty," Vali spat. It was the last word the liar would hear.

"Faðir!" *Father,* one of the women shrieked in the old language. Vali's gaze shifted to her. They were a family, his daughters, no doubt as guilty as their predecessor.

The other woman didn't even flinch, unhooking the axe at her side to avenge her father's death. Vali thrust out a hand in her direction, sending her flying off her feet. She landed hard on her back, and Vali coaxed the remaining air from her lungs with the twitch of his fingers. She would suffocate until he gave the air back.

And he would *never* give it back. These heathens liked to steal, but he could take as well.

"Let her go, swine—" the remaining daughter was on him in the blink of an eye, using her dagger to slash at his face. No fear in her eyes, no blanching, just anger and hatred and a heinous amount of ego.

Vali ducked before her dagger hit his temple. Not that it would have cut his skin. His movements were more out of the reaction than defense. As he stooped, he spun, twisting around the woman while she staggered forward. He snatched the thick blonde hair trailing her back, forcing her face toward the sky and exposing the vascular area of her neck. He used his fingernail to draw a line across her throat, the skin flayed open beneath his touch. He pushed her dying body to the side, stepping over the father's corpse to mount his steed. A strangled choke forced him to look over his shoulder, to verify the woman he left for dead was truly dying.

Her cheeks were bruised, lips stained blue, and the whites of her eyes were bloodshot. But the Ostman was standing, her arm trembled as she pointed his way. Curious, he watched her, wondering what she was trying to say.

A breath later, Vali felt something warm dribble down the thin lining of his tunic. He pulled back the fold of his cloak to find his shirt now soaked with blood, sourced by a hole over his left pectoral growing larger before his eyes.

He looked back at the woman, now on her knees, yet still focused on the last moments of her final command. Vali smoothed his coat, hiding the damage to his attire and closing the wound she created with a smooth of his hand.

"So, there is magic in you heathens." He smiled down at her. She collapsed against the dew beaded grass, her mouth gaping open as if to string him with curses.

"It's a pity you went for my heart, Lady Ostman." He knelt, closing the distance between them as he closed her parted lips with a finger beneath her jaw. "Because I do not have one anymore."

From the back of the shield wall, arrows fired. They whistled a soft cry through the air and arched high above the battleground, and Vali watched their trail break through the misty morning. Before they descended upon him, he held up his hand and disintegrated the futile arrows into the same ash their shafts were carved from.

These mortals were playing a losing game with him, but he would humor them in their efforts. And they would lose everything in their gamble against a power greater than they.

Just as he had.

3 Ailsa

On the seventh day following the departure of the longboats, the bordering clans arrived in Drakame. The arrival of Yule had snuck upon her regardless of her feelings on celebrating. But holidays were always a good distraction, almost as efficiently diverting as work, and Ailsa dove into both to take her mind off the empty fjord and the solemn quiet of her longhouse.

They should have been back by now. The Isle of Farroe was only a day's journey, even when the sea was at its most unfavorable conditions. Instead, the skies were barren of trouble, soothing the spirits of the tide in a harmonious relationship. Any hope she had left of seeing them again, dead or alive, had been slashed by the cruel whip of time.

The occasion called for a scarlet floor-length gown tied at the waist with a silk sash. The wide neckline revealed her sunken collar bones and the assortment of gold necklaces adorning her neck. The fitted sleeves hugged her shoulders and belled at the wrist, and she decorated her forearms with rows of arm rings that gleamed in the playful light. Gatherings such as these were the only occasions she showed her status through her appearance, and tonight Ailsa felt like true royalty.

The last thing she wanted to do was feign her composure with a fine gown and painted face, to see her clansman for the first time since her family—their families—floated away in their own casket. But appearance was intimate with power, and her gown was as much of a statement as a fashion choice. Tonight, the Riverland chieftains would decide their next move against the demon army who killed her family, and she needed a seat at the table. She would not lose her home and her reputation like she lost her family.

"Ah, the princess of our water-logged kingdom has arrived!" A coarse voice called from across the gathering hall as she entered. Ailsa rolled her eyes but smiled. Only her favorite artisan could get away with calling her such a thing. Ziggy rose from the head of a long table; each fist held a half-full tankard. "Ailsa, you are too radiant to belong to this world. Come join your lowly clansman for an ale. Gods know you deserve a few pints."

Ailsa paced down the aisle formed by two rows of benches. The room suddenly hushed their drunken conversations. "Later, Ziggy. I need to keep my head clear for what's coming. Don't drink all the good mead until then."

"No promises," she winked. When Ailsa neared her chair, Ziggy snatched her forearm and pulled her close. "Do not fret about the vote. You know you have my family's support, as well as many others."

"Do I look like a woman who worries?"

Ziggy gave her a wide smile, missing several of her front teeth. "No, child. You look like your mother."

A small grin played across Ailsa's lips, and she snatched one of Ziggy's cups and drained it before the old woman could protest. She slammed it back on the oak varnish, now slippery with sloshed ale.

Ziggy cursed under her breath as she stared at the bottom of the cup.

"Ailsa!" A familiar voice called from the banquet hall doors. The afternoon sunset spilled behind the voice and darkened his figure. But her heart knew the sound as well as her memory.

"Erik!" Her feet broke into a run, charging toward the boy who filled her childhood days and finding the man he had grown to become. His arms wrapped around her waist and lifted her into a spinning embrace. She buried her face in his neck, smelling sea salt on his skin and the winter breeze in his hair. The fur lining his cloak was chilled from traveling, but his arms felt like the warmth of coming home.

He set her gently on her feet, stepping back to assess her full body. "Odin's eye, Ailsa, you're even more… well, you look… How are you? How have you been feeling?" His lips pulled into a charming smile that crinkled the corners of his muddy eyes. His blonde hair, like bundles of grain warmed by the sun, was braided at the sides and pulled half up with the rest spilling down his shoulders.

"I'm as well as I can be, I suppose. And me? Look at you! You've must have grown an entire head taller since I saw you last." Erik's father had moved his family three years ago when his following grew large enough to rival his chieftain's. Instead of fighting over the land her mother's line had maintained for the past several centuries, Erik's family and his supporters left the fjord in search of lands beyond their continent. Where less competition existed for the riches offered from the earth.

"Jarl Erik," Nikros approached from the eastern wing of the banquet hall. "I believe you're the last to arrive. The rest of the chieftains are waiting for you in the gathering hall in the back of the banquet."

Erik's smile faltered as the butcher interrupted their banter. His lips tightened in a polite grin instead. "Thank you, Nikros. Impeccable timing, as always. You always did find me when I least wanted to be found." He snuck a wink Ailsa's way.

"Not difficult to notice you when you're spinning my betrothed like a spider ensnaring a gnat in its web." He crossed his thick forearms to reveal an iron hammer strapped to his side.

Erik opened his mouth, raising his hands in defense, but Ailsa cut him off. "Oh, piss off. Your brain has been replaced by a turd if you think I'll ever bond with you. I meant what I said the first time. You have no claim over me."

The bastard colored a shade of red Ailsa didn't believe was natural for skin to turn. "I will have you, Ailsa, with or without your permission. Either way, your father has already promised you to me, and you dishonor his wishes—"

"Do not speak of honor when you have none of it. Only a fool speaks of things he does not understand." She stepped between the pair of men; aware the room had silenced all light conversation. "Besides, I have the approval of our current jarl to break the vow of the former one."

Nikros flung his head back with a joyless laugh. "Drakame has not voted on a new chieftain, Ailsa. What jarl did you get this approval from?"

"Myself." She sneered, her hands gesturing wide to herself.

A bench screeched as the butcher stood suddenly from his seat. "It'll be a sunny day in Helheim before I support a woman as my chieftain. My son should be given this honor; he has contributed his life, sacrificed Valhalla to stay and defend Drakame from this unknown enemy, and he's already had the blessing of the former jarl to add to his support. Not to mention he is the last remaining shieldmage!" Nikroth pointed at his son while devouring the attention of anyone who would listen. "He is well admired by many in our clan, established a business to grow his wealth, and he has proved himself to be a valuable source of stock in our trade deals—"

"Well, if those are the requirements, perhaps Ziggy should be jarl," Ailsa pointed her chin in the direction of the drunken potter, who lifted a newly filled tankard in agreement. "Face the facts, butcher. If I were a son instead of a daughter, this clan wouldn't even question who would assume leadership. The spot falls to my father's last of kin, as the spoken law states."

"How do we know you are his kin?" The butcher shrugged. "You don't have his magic, his health, for all we know your mother ran off and—"

His accusation was interrupted by steel sliding free of its sheath. Erik was at her side with his blade half drawn. The candlelight danced along the polished metal. "Finish that thought and I'll remove your hollow head from your fat neck," he threatened.

"You wouldn't have time to lift your blade," Nikros hissed, unbolting his own weapon in his giant fist.

Ailsa swung between them to tame the fire in their fight, recalling Erik's temper and how it only took a small spark to feel the burn of his rage. If she didn't stop him now, things would get bloody. "Enough! All of you," she said, turning over her shoulder to look back at the butcher. "My father claimed me as his own, and that should be enough for you not to question my blood. As for my claim as jarl," she raised her chin as she'd seen her father do, "I'll be dead in a few years, as your son loves to remind me. You can vote on a permanent chieftain then. But I am the Jarl of Drakame, and if anyone else has a problem with it, they can say so now."

If they could blame her illness, then she was allowed to use it to her advantage. A quiet settled over the hall. Nikroth and his son were now matching shades of purple, but even they did not challenge her further. What the butcher failed to understand was that power came in many forms. Sometimes in strength and following, sometimes in wealth. In her case, it was respect.

She was loved by this village, healed every person in this room at least once in their lifetime. From children who nearly drowned in the bay, the hunters attacked by the forest wraiths, to the babies she birthed nearly every full moon now. She had touched each person in this room in some way. And few semblances of power were more influential than personal friendships.

"Come, Ailsa. Let us take our place with the rest of the chieftains." Erik sheathed his sword with a forceful thrust, glaring at Nikros as he strode down the narrow aisle to the back of the hall, Ailsa leading the way.

THE CHIEFTAINS SAT around a massive oak table; five seats filled for the five clans founding the Riverland nations. There were other, smaller clans who attempted to break from the original territories. Then there were the clanless who roamed the wilderness and followed their own moral law, trading the protection and support of Drakame and her sister territories for freedom from the gods' law. But their populations had not gained a significant following to compete in world matters, and so the responsibility fell on the five individuals sitting around the blood-stained table.

Much had been discussed in this room, from the overthrow of the previous Wicked King Maxon to the fate of the wraith-whisperer Jomeer, who was rumored to have called the forest spirits and cursed the land with withering darkness, making it almost impossible to traverse the woodlands at night without feeling the claws of the tree spirits.

Her blood was not the only one bruising the varnish of this meeting place, but Ailsa was not privy to the other sacred decisions which happened beyond the doors that now closed behind her. She sat beside Erik, Jarl of Eurkame, a territory named after the one it was born from and the one who had founded it. She assumed Eurik had fallen in battle as well, leaving his son to inherit the virgin lands far west of her fjord.

The rest were Lattimer of Rutbrok, Gunner of Lisandria, and Rollo of Bristrak. The trio waited for them to claim their seats, shooting pointed looks at her. But if they objected to her presence, they kept their mouths shut.

"Several new faces," Lattimer led the meeting due to his seniority. "Unfortunately, we do not have the time to settle you into your new titles. A survivor from the battle has reached the king, and I have traveled from the high city of Rutbrok to share his words. Riverland is waiting for our next move, but I fear we are out of options."

"Speak first of our enemy," Gunnar spoke. "Let us understand who is strong enough to wipe out an entire army of Ostman. For centuries, the gods have ensured we were the most feared, most infernal creatures in this land, and now some of our strongest men and women have been slaughtered by a faceless foe." He spat on the dirt padded floor. "If King

Orin does not gain control of this problem, he will lose the regency he fought as his rightful claim."

"And if he does not stop these invaders, there will not be a regency to lose," Rollo said at his side.

Ailsa stole a glance at Erik, who met her stare, wondering if he was thinking the same. Invaders who did not come to conquer or control, only to destroy. How long would it take until they reached her shores? Until they brought this war to the mainland and extinguished the North Kingdom—erased their empire from history. How could they stop an enemy who had no motivation beyond their bloodlust?

Lattimer nodded a slow, deliberate movement. "This faceless foe has been identified, though none believe the words of the boy who survived."

"They think he embellishes the truth?" Erik asked.

Lattimer snorted. "Saying his truth is embellished is like saying nightmares are adorned with demons."

"And what demons adorned his nightmares?" Ailsa asked, finding her voice. Lattimer's attention flickered to hers. He wore his age in his eyes, half a century of life behind the mossy color in his gaze.

"Demons from another realm," he mumbled in a tired breath. "The boy was found tied to the hull of a longship; his entire fighting arm dismembered. When he finally found the strength to speak days later, it was of creatures with stone faces, whose magic could cut through a man without lifting a finger and skin that could not be broken with a mortal blade."

A chill swept through the room despite the hearth's blazing light against Lattimer's backside, creating a shadow around his frame that swallowed his features.

"Did he say anything else about them?" Erik asked. "Surely

there is a way to kill these demons. They are made of flesh and blood, the same as us. If they can bleed, they can die."

Lattimer shook his head, turning to pace the perimeter of the circular table. "No. Only two survivors have come out of the battles with these demons, and both have spoken only of the slaughter our people faced. The gods are either testing us or purging the world of their creation."

"Then we are either failing miserably or following their will," Rollo murmured into his mead.

Ailsa slapped her palms on the weathered wood, exasperated and tired. "Do we have any other information besides the fact our enemy is terrifying and invulnerable?" she asked. "I find it hard to believe the survivor tied himself to a boat and rode the sea to Rutbrok just to warn us of our impending doom."

"Aye, Ailsa. The young warrior mentioned one more thing." Lattimer placed both hands on the table and leaned his weight against it as he looked her dead in the eyes. "They spoke with a chieftain before the battle. Your father. They offered a chance for peace should we return something our kind stole from them."

"*Stole*? Ostmen do not steal! We claim what is rightfully ours through fair fights or trade. What would we need from demons?" Erik countered.

Lattimer shrugged and pushed off the table. "That is all the boy said before he died. That the demons had a particular interest in Ledger Locharsson. Do you have any idea why, Ailsa?"

Ailsa chewed her lip in thought but shook her head. If these creatures were indeed from another world, how would they have taken anything that belonged to them? Surely there was no way to cross realms, and she was certain no one from her clan had the means to try. But then, why was her family name singled out?

Her father did not lie to her, but that did not mean he didn't keep secrets.

"We should try to contact our enemy again," she said. Rollo and Gunnar made sounds of disapproval, but she continued. "We cannot survive another attack. We have one shieldmage left to pass on the power, and Nikros can barely wield his magic. Rollo, your clan alone cannot support our relationship with the English kings. We need warriors to defend the lands they surrendered to us—"

"King Rupert is our puppet," Rollo dismissed her. "He won't have the bollocks to push against us now, not when the only reason his kingdom isn't sleeping in a marsh is because of the gold and silver he vowed to trade in return for our withdrawal."

"But if you no longer have the men to enforce your notorious reputation, there will be nothing to stop Rupert from pushing back." She motioned to the map in the center of the table. Rollo's lands sat to the south, near the bordering Saxon territories and the wealth of land beyond it. They had fought and conquered the majority of the map for the past five centuries, but all could be lost from them if they placated their current enemy with the remainder of their forces. "The Saxons are scared, not foolish. If we are to keep our boundaries where they are, we need to keep your men within defending distance."

"I agree with Ailsa," Erik spoke at her side.

"Of course you do," Rollo spat.

Gunnar spoke before she could counter. "I agree with Jarl Ailsa as well." Her brows raised at his support. "This is not a fight we will win with force. We need to send someone to speak with these brutes and settle this debt. Otherwise, they will burn the world down in search of what they lost."

"And who will go?" Rollo threw his hands up, his drink sloshing from the deep pit of the tankard.

None of them spoke, each waiting for the other to offer a better alternative.

Ailsa sighed deeply, stirring the heavy fluid in her chest and triggering a noisy exhale. It was an obvious choice. One she chose quickly, without the chance to think of the repercussions. Before her fear silenced her courage. "Clearly, these monsters have an issue with my family. I don't know why, but I intend to find out. Send me."

"*Skide!*" Erik swore. "Like Hel, you'll be the one to face them—"

"I'm the least intimidating of anyone here, Erik. Surely you must agree it would be better to send someone who appears as frail as I am, obviously not a threat, to speak of peace with our enemy." She touched his arm, feeling his own fear tense the corded muscle solid beneath his hot skin. "This is what I'm supposed to do. I can feel it. It is time for me to do something for this clan, something that will echo the worth my family has brought this fjord for generations. Perhaps I was born for this, and the gods allowed me to live this long for this purpose alone."

She rationalized her thought process as she explained it to Erik. In a way, she was taking fate into her own hands, and if this led to her end, so be it. It was an ending she would decide for herself, not sit around and wait for. Even if dread was slipping its icy fingers around her heart. "Our lives have always been decided by the gods. Now we must have faith. And if they ask for my life, I will place it in their hands with my gratitude," she said.

Erik did not meet her gaze, only stared ahead with a scowl that could spark a wildfire with its intensity. He hated when she talked of her mortality like she was expendable, when she used it to get what she wanted. But she longed to have a strong ending to her fragile life, to serve her clan as her family had done before her. And perhaps this way she could see her family again. To die in battle would mean an afterlife with warriors. It was the only honorable way to die.

Lattimer nodded. "I feared there was only one way ahead, but you have given us another path, Ailsa. Let us hope this will lead to our salvation."

Ailsa agreed with a slow nod, but inside her chest threatened to cave. She was not immune to fear as her father had been. She felt her nerves like they were a hot iron in her flesh, a thick smoke in her lungs.

She stood hastily from her chair. "Have someone prepare a longboat and send me the written coordinates of our enemy's camp. I'll leave at first light."

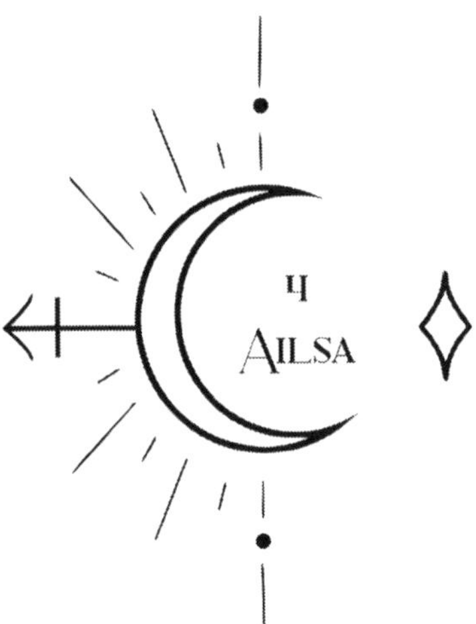

"Let me come with you," Erik spoke softly from the doorway of her longhouse. He lounged against the frame as he watched her pack.

She took a long puff from her pipe, settling the anxiety that consumed the space in her lungs. Each breath made it a little easier, the ache more bearable. "You have a clan to lead, Erik. I am not your responsibility, nor should I be."

Her bag was filled with the basics: a few changes of clothes, her blade, an extra pipe, and a sack of herbs. Her mother's ring now back around her neck, the one token she would take to the grave. Whether that was a hole in the ground or the sunken depths of the sea, a piece of her family would be with her until the end. Their presence was all she needed to make peace with her decision; their blood in her veins assured her she had the strength to face this.

Gunnar had agreed to arrange a small crew to take her across the North Sea, where she would then board a separate vessel to approach the enemy camp. There had been a brief discussion concerning if someone would join her, but she refused the idea. Her solidarity acknowledged she had no fight with the demons, and she did not want them to think she was afraid. Respect was earned, not given, and she would demand it with her very presence.

"I'm replaceable, Ailsa. I have three younger brothers who would kill to have my place." His hands settled on her shoulders as she tied her bag. "Literally, I must sleep with a blade beneath my pillow. They are that ambitious."

The mental image brought a small smile to her lips. "Don't pretend you are not promised to someone yet. Don't insult me by avoiding the truth. You are too powerful and too handsome a man to not have kings trading their castles for your place beside their daughters."

He was quiet as his fingers slipped from her skin. The smallest gesture spoke volumes. "It was not my choice," he muttered.

"It doesn't matter, Erik." She turned to face him. "You should not be in my room, begging to board my boat, when your hand and your heart—" He broke her words with a kiss, his fingers gently tipping her chin to meet his staggering height. His tongue brushed the seam of her lips, but she did not give him admittance. She broke their connection, despising the distance it created. "—are spoken for."

"I speak for my heart, Ailsa. As do you."

"My life was spoken for the day I took my first breath." The one that wheezed and gurgled, the one that *tainted* any pursuit of her hand. Had her father not had his magic and the ability to choose anyone he wanted despite their clans' arguments, her mother would have met the same fate. He was too powerful to challenge, and he wanted only his beloved.

But she had no one like her father. Everyone had too much

to gain without her, and it was better this way. Her condition should not be allowed to pass on to anyone else, the curse it was, and Erik deserved to have a fleet of offspring. She did not deserve him, and he did not deserve her.

"Will you still deny us, Ailsa? Even when this may be the last time I will ever see you again?" His hands skimmed her skin like she was feverish to the touch. She shuddered, wanting nothing but to collapse into the heat of his embrace and indulge the fantasies that pestered her nightly dreams.

"Why admit I want something I can never have?" Her voice was strained through the grief tight in her throat. Her hands clutched over her chest if only to hide the way her heart still beat for him.

"Because I adore you," he whispered, kneeling on the floor to catch her gaze. "And because I see right through you. I see what I know to be true."

She shook her head, defiant and decided. "You see what I want you to see."

"Ailsa," he breathed. She looked away from his gaze. The desperation in his eyes made her heart swell and she could not afford to burst. She wanted to leave this life behind, not take it with her.

"Will you come with me to our old spot? I want to look over the fjord one last time." She tied her bag shut and set it on the bed until she needed it, ignoring his plea with a subtle change in subject.

He sighed disapprovingly but nodded. "Of course."

They climbed to the highest hill bordering the inlet, pausing frequently to settle the aggravation in her chest. Erik pulled her most of the way, supporting her weight with effortless strength. Regardless of his help, she was still weak and trembling when they made it to the top. It took her a time to settle her heart, which was currently racing like a thousand horses across an endless plain.

"This was a bad idea," he muttered as she leaned against the smooth face of a boulder. "Calm down before you cause a rockslide with your hacking."

Her fingers made a cursing gesture, but she smiled through the stars exploding behind her field of vision. She coughed into the sleeve of her gown, the one she didn't care enough to change out of even though it was an added weight. "Never tell a woman to calm down," she managed to say. "It is a quick way to get murdered."

"Good thing your hacking cannot kill then, or I would be afraid." He offered a piece of cloth he had torn from the edge of his tunic.

"Thanks," she gasped, snatching the rag from his hand to catch the scarlet-tinged fluid loosened from the deep holds of her trunk. He turned away and gave her space, knowing she hated when people stared or hovered over one of her fits.

Erik waited on the edge of the drop off, his feet dangled over the edge when her body finally acclimated itself to the altitude and the exertion. Ailsa sat beside him, resting her head on the edge of his shoulder, the fur from his cloak warmed her cheek like an intimate memory.

This cliff side had all but marked the edge of her world, been the line at the end of her life's map. From here she could see the moonlight illuminate the channel, the black water nipping the shore near her village. Lanterns speckled the hilly landscape between the cliffs where her clan gathered for a feast that could feed thrice the number of revelers, and music floated into the clear night. Her feet hung over the jagged edge, swinging to the lyrical sounds of the lyre.

A western breeze skimmed the sea and ascended the rocky cliff side to where they sat together, wrapping Ailsa in salt and ice. Erik draped the border of his cloak around her shoulders, feeling her shiver, and she burrowed into his side, pretending for a moment he was still hers and the fates had not torn them apart.

"Why did you offer to go?" he asked after a time.

She closed her eyes and breathed him in, savoring the heady scent as it caught in her throat. "I don't belong here, Erik. My family is dead, my only marriage prospect is Nikros, and I can literally feel my life slipping away with every breath I take. If I don't get out now, I'll die sitting over the same view, watching everyone else leave and *live*. It is not in my blood to accept anything less."

He sighed against her temple; the gentle wave of his chest rocked her head in a soothing sway. "If you want to leave so bad, then leave. You want to live yet you're walking right into a den of wolves."

"My going means someone else doesn't have to, and if I can save one life then perhaps my time here meant something," she replied.

"You mean something to me, is that not enough?" he asked. The question bit off a piece of her heart, letting something harder fill its place.

She sighed against his chest. "No, it isn't."

He shifted uncomfortably next to her. Her candor hurt him

worse than he'd ever admit, but it was the raw truth. She loved Erik deeply, and he had loved her once as well. Even now, she could still see his love pour out for her unfiltered from his gaze. But it was not the love her father had for her mother, who would have traded his soul with the fates for one more day with his *sváss*.

If it was not a love that rewrote the stars, it was not a love worth having.

"If we were meant to be together, Erik, you would not live across the world, and I would not be sick. There would be nothing standing between us, *nothing* to keep you from me." He opened his mouth in defense, but she settled his guilt with a light kiss upon the stubble of his cheek. "I do not fault you for choosing your family over me all those years ago, so do not fault me when I choose myself over you."

"That's not fair, Ailsa. You do not understand the position I was in, what your father—"

"What do you have against my father?" She withdrew from his touch like a reflex, her words spat from a bitter place. "Was it not your own father's greed that forced you to travel an ocean away just for a position of power? Mine had nothing to do with you leaving."

His hand drifted across the pointed blades in her back. Her skin seemed to hug her bones and sink into the hollow places where the fat never stuck. His touch only outlined the edges of her insecurities, traveling each peak and valley like it was a conquest. He would overthrow her heart if she wasn't careful. "I will not speak ill of the dead, but if you knew the truth, Ailsa, you would not defend him so blindly. I would have given him anything for your hand—"

"You speak as if my heart were something to trade. But if

you truly loved me, Erik, you would have done something as simple as stayed."

Erik's breath inserted sharply, and she felt his body go tense next to hers. She knew she was crossing a line with him, but at this point she didn't care. "You're a fool, Ailsa," he murmured, "and you'll die alone because of him."

She scoffed. The harsh breath blew a white cloud from her lips. "Maybe so. But you will live a life you settled for. Which one is more dishonorable in your opinion?"

He stood suddenly, leaving her to sit alone on the edge of the cliff. For a moment, she feared he would push her off the side. But instead, he stroked the crown of her head with his hand. "I will live as half a man because you stole the other piece of my heart. And if I see Ledger Locharsson in the afterlife, I will kill him a thousand times over for spurning me of a life with you."

She waited for him to walk away before standing and facing the channel, stealing a private moment with the view she used as a medium to manifest her dreams upon. The last time she would sit by on the side, watching the boats leave and return, hoping one day she might do the same and witness the world her people described in their raids and their adventures.

It was her time, she felt it in her bones.

"Erik?" She phrased his name into a question. There was something on the horizon, flames glittering in the veil of darkness. The sight so eerie she wondered if her eyes were playing tricks on her. "Do you see that?"

"What?" he asked, coming to stand behind her. She pointed in the direction of the lights. The quick insert of his breath informed her he could see them as well. "Strange," he mumbled in her ear. "There are no more boats left to arrive."

"That isn't a longship," she observed. Even from a thousand

meters high on the cliff face, she could see the obscured outlines of the boat approaching, the fires on its deck further illustrated the shape of the vessel, nothing she had seen before on this inlet.

Panic closed her throat, speeding her pulse in her ears until she could hardly hear Erik barking orders at her. She swallowed the lump in her throat, shoving down the chaos building in her chest and willing her heart to slow. "Erik, do you have your horn?"

"*Skide!*" He cursed as his hands ran over his tunic. "No, I must have left it in the hall with my blade."

"Then you need to go, you need to get back to the village as quickly as possible," she looked at him with wide eyes outlined with fear. "I'll follow you, but I can't keep up if you are to get to them in time. You must leave me behind."

"Absolutely not," he said, snatching her by the arm and pulling her back toward the unmarked path.

"You sentence my people to death, Erik! If that is the same enemy that struck down our fathers, then you leave all those below with no warning and no chance." She yanked her arm free of his grip. He turned back to face her with a vicious scowl, the moonlight forming deep shadows around his eyes. "I know this path like I know the woods, I can navigate it with my eyes closed. Go, Erik, or there will be no hope for my clan!"

His breath heaved beneath his cloak as he glanced from her to the drop off, the decision tearing his soul between his head and his heart. In a voice that broke he said, "Please, be careful, *elskan mín*."

My love.

A smile struggled on her lips, already numb from the frozen breeze and the fear of losing everything she had left, the little it was. But the words she wanted to say stuck to her lips, and she was unable to release them. He turned away, swallowed by the mist curling against the coast before she could return his affirmation.

Her last chance to tell him she would always be his slipped away like the fog on the breeze.

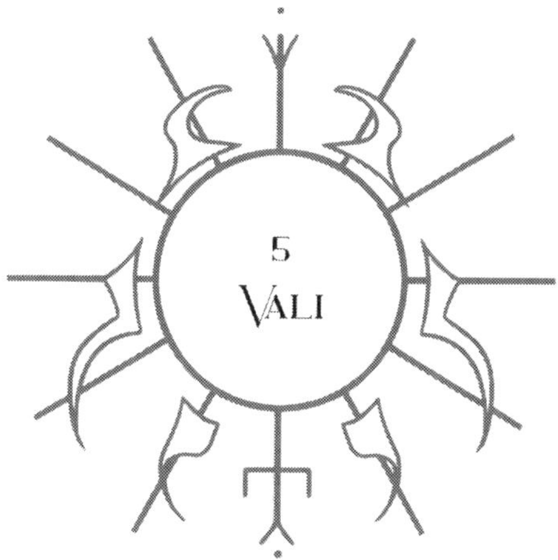

"Music.

Songs of an ancient time spun like flakes of frost in the thin breeze, meeting the ship Vali led through the channel. Strapped to the mast, now closed to allow his magic to float them along, was the last survivor of the Ostman's army. With the right kind of motivation, Vali was able to persuade his captive to show him exactly where the man they called Ledger once resided.

The spirits of Midgard whispered the name for a reason, and he had little doubt the heathen was hiding the artifact somewhere deep within this rut in the land. The closer the ship drew, the more the hunger inside him gnawed into a feral starvation. A lifetime of patience and hope crushing disappointments—it was all coming to an end.

"The ship cannot proceed any further. Shall I release the boats?" Seela appeared beside him. His commander walked with a grace that gave her the essence of a stream.

Vali leaned against the shroud attached to the pale wood of the quarterdeck's edging, eyes peering into the distance to assess the party they were about to crash. His lips tipped into a wry smile. "Always so quick to attack, Commander."

"It always ends the same with these brutes. Might as well get right to the point and save time." She sighed. Her breath was tired. Vali could tell by the way her shoulders fell slightly as she released her frustration. She had been at his side since the beginning, and the constant disappointment was wearing her thin.

"Not this time," he spoke confidently. "This is it, Seela. I've seen this place in my dreams. The place between the stone curtains, parting to invite us inside the heart of the land. The magic in my marrow is reaching, and I feel the Tether calling back." He adjusted the leather gloves shielding his fair skin from the freezing cold plaguing the north country. "But you may have the men in position for a show of force."

"As you wish." She slipped away and began clipping his demands.

He hadn't bothered to shield his ship from sight—there was little point. He took down hundreds of the heathens within an hour. A small village would be no conflict, and as long as they did as he asked, there would be no reason for them to fear him. He would take what he came here for and leave.

The music broke into a hushed silence. The lights in the townhomes flickered out, shrouding Drakame in darkness. Vali made his way down to the main deck, his heart full of a hope that bordered on desperation. The ship slowed to a halt; the anchor dropped to settle them in place.

He leapt over the starboard, landing in a dingy that fell into the water in a swift dive. And Vali stood. One foot lunged against the seat as if he were weightless in the balanced boat and pushed the vessel the rest of the distance into Drakame's harbor.

6

Ailsa

Ailsa made the trembling climb down the steep cliff side, cursing her poor footing and the beautiful gown that caught on every serrated surface. Her hands were white and numb from the freezing night, which seemed to drop in temperature every minute she stumbled through the dark. She hardly felt the torn calluses bleeding from her anxious grip, leaving a crimson mark on every ledge she traversed.

The moist air found her lungs as she made her way closer to the docks, ignoring the frigid marsh water that seeped through the vulnerable places in her shoes. With only the beams of the full moon to guide her, she followed the sounds of distant shouting. The village was dark, light from the feast snuffed out when the vessel floated an obvious distance from the docks. It stopped some ways away in the small harbor, the shallows not allowing the great ship to come any closer.

The chieftains were gathered at the docks by the time she made it down the cliff, where she leaned against the back of the fisherman's cottage to catch her breath, remaining concealed by the shadows formed by the torchlight lining the harbor. A lone man stood at the top of the steps of the pier, but the hood adorning his head darkened any defining detail of his face. She could only see he wore a dark green cloak that hung to his knees and embroidered with gold so flawless the torchlight transformed the leafing into a living blaze. His posture was one of casual charm, asserting he wasn't threatened to face an entire village alone.

The figure was tall, masculine appearing. His cloak was tailored to fit his broad shoulders perfectly, tapering in at the sides to flatter his narrow waist. He placed both hands on his hips, revealing no sheaths and no weapons, just long legs made of lean muscle and curiously tight pants. She'd never seen clothes like these, not even the ones described in the stories her father told her of the English men.

Lattimer stepped forward, facing the stranger several strides from the bottom step. "Are you the one who has brought war to the North?" A simple question loaded with accusation; the man shrugged off the weight of it.

"I did not *bring* the war, Ostman. I *am* the war. Your kind has stolen something that does not belong to you, and I want it back. Return the Tether and we will leave these shores clean and bloodless." Ailsa thought his voice sounded like the sea, calm on the surface yet full of peril, pulling her deeper like a riptide. He could drown her world with his tongue alone.

"What does this *Tether* look like? Where did it come from? Who stole it? You ask for something of which we have no knowledge of and refuse to explain—" Lattimer's words were cut off with a strangled sound. He clutched his throat to find a breath. The man's only movement had been a clenched fist.

"It is not my problem if you are all too foolish to understand a basic demand. I will do your gods a service and purge this world of your ignorance," he hissed. Lattimer fell to his knees, his shaved head falling over as he continued to struggle. "Does the name *Ledger* mean anything to you, heathen?"

Ailsa's own chest seemed to starve for air as she watched him, hardly hearing her father's name over the thready pulse in her ears. Had her father followed his ambition too far? Could he have been involved with creatures of myth and fallen into the misfortunes of one their own legends? She had no way of knowing, but that didn't ease the tension pulling her heart into pieces. One thing was for certain, her people were promised certain death if this man's power was as omnipotent as it appeared.

"Enough!" she shouted, emerging from the back of the cottage and feeling as much uncertainty as her body betrayed with its quivering.

The man surprisingly listened to her and let go of his invisible hold on Lattimer, evident by the man gasping a hungry gulp of air. Erik's jaw jutted in disapproval; his eyes flashed a warning she did not heed.

"He is not the one you need to speak with. I am," she said.

"Ailsa," Erik growled through gnashed teeth. "Go back to the hall. This does not concern you."

She did not look at Erik, her gaze fixed on the stranger standing on her pier. His hood turned toward her. The torchlight kissed his lips and revealed a foreboding smirk, the kind that made her want to see what else hid beneath his cowl.

"Who are you?" he asked, his voice rising a level in genuine curiosity.

She swallowed, forcing back a choke. His eyes were a mystery beneath the hood, but she felt them burning into her flesh, forcing a thin sheen of sweat to drip down her back despite the cold. "I am Ailsa, daughter of Ledger, Jarl of

Drakame." She sucked a breath which felt more like a shiver. "Who are you?"

The man's gloved fingers stretched, his shoulders rose with an impatient sigh that made her take an involuntary step back. He reached for his hood, sliding it back to reveal his face, his hair, his *slanted* ears.

Her eyes widened to absorb every detail. The man had hair like the wings of a raven, glossy and black as her darkest dreams. His eyes were a clear gold like they were formed by Freya's tears, dripping a warmth that contrasted the chilling way he glared at her. There was a glow from his pale complexion that competed with the darkness surrounding him, skin that had never been marred nor burned, flawless and untouched. He rivaled only the sun with his glory, stole the light of the stars with his existence. The most dangerous thing about this man was not his power but his presence, a treacherous combination of contradictions that seduced before it destroyed.

"Odin's fucking eye," Erik mumbled.

"You're..." she shuddered, suddenly awestruck by the man uncovered before her. "You're an elfin."

7
Vali

She was not terrified as he revealed himself, not as he had hoped. Instead, she seemed drawn, transfixed—her gaze on him, fascinated. Despite the fact he had nearly smothered her kinsman in front of her, she stared in unashamed interest.

He assessed her in return with an equally critical eye. The woman named Ailsa, another daughter of his mark, was clearly not a warrior like her deceased family. She wore a tattered gown, a deep shade of red that flattered her olive warm skin. It hung on her thin body, exposing her thin frame composed mostly of bones and little muscle, her skin sinking in the hollow places and sharpening every edge of her body. Her hair was a dull shade of deep brown, unlike her family's pale heads.

Raven feathers braided into each side of her skull and flowed down to her waist in soft waves. It was the only soft part about her, as her eyes were a fierce cerulean, reminding him of the sky before a storm. She had little paint on her face, unlike the other men before him, only a thin black rim around her eyes and blood red on her lips.

This woman was not a warrior—but she was a fighter. There was a strength not in her flesh and bone, but somewhere deep within her spirit. Her thin shoulders relaxed under his scrutiny despite the rapid rise and fall of her chest. She did not fear him, and something about her tempered approach made him even more irritated.

"You're one of the fae," she repeated.

"Yes," he said. He made his way down the weathered steps, closing in on her. She planted her feet in the sandy earth, the unmovable meeting the unstoppable. "An astute observation, Jarl Ailsa."

"Stop right there! Don't go near her." A man with bleached hair pointed his blade at Vali.

"And who's going to stop me? Certainly not you, Lion-heart." Vali cocked his head at the heathen, pausing his advance only to stare him down. The man glanced at Ailsa wearing his concern plain on his face. Vali smiled, perceiving he cared for the woman. This would be all too easy.

He turned back to her. "I said what I meant. Hand over the Tether, and I will leave as quickly and quietly as I arrived. Do not, and I will destroy everything you see before you."

Her stoic expression never faltered, but her hands fell to her chest, wrapping around a thin piece of metal. A ring. "Please," she beseeched him, her voice so soft it tamed something violent in his blood. "Just tell me what this *Tether* looks like and I vow to you, I will find it."

Vali thought for a moment, considering he had never personally seen the Tether with his eyes, only what he'd heard from the legends and the witches. It was one of the reasons he never described the Tether to the Ostmen, because he didn't actually know himself—but they didn't need to know that.

But he felt it. As soon as this woman stepped across the black sand, his flesh had all but begged him to get closer.

Pulled him closer into her orbit as if she were a star. "Come here, heathen."

"*Sváss*." The chieftain at her side used a term for lovers as a threat. But she didn't look at him, only strode toward Vali until she was so close, he could see her tremble. See her bleeding fingers fidget with the ring until it was coated in blood.

"Who's ring is that? Your own?" he asked her.

She shook her head. "It was my mother's. And her mother before her. It's been in my family for generations."

Something must have sparked awareness in Vali's eyes, because the woman flinched and took a guarded step back. Clutching the ring until it was hidden from his sight. He matched her retreat with a single stride, keeping the distance between them to a minimum. "Give it to me," Vali said.

"No!" she shrieked. "This is all I have left of my family. You will not take this from me as well!"

"Your *family* stole this power from the gods, and now it's time to give it back," Vali said. It wasn't the woman who pulled him, it was the ring inside her fist. It had to be.

"Just give it to him, Ailsa!" The chieftain to his left threw his arms up in exasperation. "Do not be selfish like your father and keep what is not yours. If he wants the ring, then let him have it."

"And what will you do with it?" Ailsa's gaze on him was murderous. "There is nothing in this ring besides memories. You are mistaken, and I will not bet my heirloom on your false discretion." She was protective of this artifact, as if her life depended on it. Almost like she had no choice.

"You know something, don't you?" the man argued. "There is a reason that same ring has been passed down the original shieldmage line. You're sentencing us all to death because you want to keep your family's power over us all! So no one else will be able to challenge the *Jarl of Drakame*."

"Erik, this isn't the time. Calm yourself before you say something you will regret." The bald chieftain rose, finding his breath again. But Erik ignored him, boring his glare into the woman.

"You're letting this demon warp your opinion over me," she snapped, the light in her eyes dimmed. "No one told me they were searching for something until tonight when we met with the chieftains—"

"If your father would have told us the truth about your line, Ailsa, none of this would be happening! We could have returned it before they slaughtered our families!" Erik threw his sword on the soft ground, his bronze skin now tainted pink and shaking with unrestrained rage.

Vali took an observant step back, letting the exchange unfold between the two.

"He never said anything about this ring, nor a power bound inside it. You must believe my family has nothing to do with this! That I had nothing to do with this." But the crack in her voice made Vali wonder if even she believed her own claim.

Erik stepped towards her, pointing his finger at her chest. "My father is dead over whatever your family has hidden on top of that hill! Over a game of power!"

"And my whole family is dead! Am I now the enemy? If this ring is indeed the Tether, is the blood of our fallen on my hands because I was ignorant, Erik?"

"You should have done *more*," he seethed. Vali watched as the woman visibly recoiled, her stormy eyes now cloudy with hurt.

"Aye," she muttered. "I never was enough for you."

Vali cleared his throat, returning their attention back to him.

She smoothed a hand over a cheekbone, smearing a rim of black paint that was now wet from a single tear. Quicker than he'd ever seen a mortal move, she ducked and swiped the discarded blade from the sand, thrusting it from her chest as the blade pointed toward Vali. "If you want this ring, demon. Come and take it," she spat, each word laced with hatred.

Vali regarded her statement, assessing her anguish behind the mask this *Erik* had stripped away with his accusations. His lips curled in a smile, a genuine one. Oh, he liked this woman very much. She had witnessed firsthand the consequences of facing him, had seen it with her own eyes as he strangled the bald chieftain. But here she was, pointing a sword too large for her tiny frame at him, and not a lick of fear in her eyes.

"Fine," he said, shrugging. "Have it your way."

"No!" Erik flung himself between them. "No, fight me, not Ailsa. I'll fight this trial in her place."

Vali rolled his shoulders in frustration. This wasn't about the fight, it was about conviction; he could easily kill them both without breaking a sweat. She wanted to defend what belonged to her, even if it killed her. This man was robbing her of that honor. "Interesting you should care about her well-being now, considering you just stabbed her in the back." He waved his right hand, sending the other three chieftains waist high into the wet sand, ensnaring them.

"But if you want to die with her, so be it."

This man had no honor in him if he let his temper attack the woman he cared for. He was a hot head, a match easily burned when struck. And Vali felt no pity for the man as he boiled his blood.

8

Ailsa

Erik's screams ripped through the night and sung across the fjord. She had never heard a sound so agonizing, so full of torment. A sound that would haunt her nightmares every time she closed her eyes. The elfin was hitting her where it hurt the most, understanding the deepest wounds were not in flesh and bone but in the soft places of the heart by burning Erik alive with an invisible heat and no promise of dousing the flames.

"Stop!" she gasped. Her arms stilled and the cumbersome weight of the sword fell from her hands. Her blood roared in her ears; panic-stricken fear raced her heart to a speed she was not competent to tolerate. She fell to her knees beside Erik as he writhed, but his skin was feverish, so hot it burned her with a skimming touch.

"Please," she wheezed, fear making her breaths noisy and thick. It shamed her for this male to hear her weakness, witness her desperation through the tears wetting her cheeks, see the pain she endured as every breath was a battle of its own, one that left her smothered and stole her strength.

"Stop!" she screamed. Erik's wails were softer now, quieting. Her hand found the necklace dangling across her chest, a wave of fresh anger sourced the remaining strength left in her body.

"*Lètta*!" she shouted, this time in the old language, and the world stopped, obeying her command.

There was lightning in her veins, a terrible light surging through the lifelines of her nerves and arteries, climbing until it surged through every inch of her flesh. She tasted metal, smelled burning ash, and the crack of Thor's thunder clipped through Erik's shouts, silencing them completely.

Ailsa shut her eyes against the force wracking through her body. This must be death, she thought. This must be what it felt like to have her soul ripped from her body, to be separated from her bones and taken to the dark realm of Helheim. There was no pain, only blinding light, and a heat that brushed against her skin and burned her center into a hearth. Her breath evened and her heart slowed to a normal rate. She opened her eyes, expecting to see the cadaverous face of Hel calling her away, but instead found an even stranger scene.

The elfin was halfway across the harbor, lying face down in the sand before slowly pushing himself up into a seated position. His face found hers, and the brilliant gold of his eyes darkened with shock.

"Your skin," he said in a voice filled with awe. She looked at her forearms, now exposed as her sleeves fell around her elbows. Written across the soft skin beneath her arms were the same runes that had marked the ring. They shimmered a luminous orange before fading into black, like hot metal inside a forge cooling into shape. The burning across the midline of her throat ceased, and her fingers felt scratches raking down her neck and beneath the neckline of her gown. More runes written there as well.

Erik was unconscious, unaware of the event that ceased his agony. His chest rose and fell in a labored rhythm, and Ailsa was satisfied he was well for the time being.

She, however, was not in such a position.

The elfin stood hastily to his feet, sand falling in a filthy haze from his cloak. He crossed the beach in lengthy strides to where she crouched like a hunted animal with no place to hide. With the others, he used his magic, but with her, he used his hands.

"What did you do with the Tether?" he shouted as his fingers wrapped around her throat. She opened her mouth to defend herself, but the elfin thrust his thumb into her hyoid bone, closing her airway so she couldn't speak. "You are a snake, just like your father. Do you have any idea what you've done?"

Just when she thought her lungs would shrivel from lack of air, a blur of stormy grey fur broke them apart. Ailsa fell into the sand, watching as Ivor attacked the elfin, biting his shoulder until a crimson gradient spilled across green velvet.

"Ivor, stop!" she shouted at the beast, terrified he would kill her wolf. The elfin cried out as her teeth ripped through his shoulder joint, twisting and shaking her giant head.

With a savage sound, the elfin threw her to the side with an unseen force. Ivor shrieked as she hit the ground. He eyed the wolf where he threw her some feet away, his fingers assessing the damage she created while his face twisted in pain.

"Well, this night just keeps getting more interesting," he grunted as he sat up, still cradling his shoulder and the arm that hung loosely out of socket. "Animal teeth cannot penetrate elfin skin, nor a metal from your realm. But perhaps this isn't just a wolf," he shot her a murderous look, "like that wasn't simply a ring."

"What are you talking about?" Ailsa asked in a whisper.

Ivor crouched, already back on her feet with her fur raised, and teeth bared at the elfin in a discernible warning. The male pursed his lips and blew a breath that strengthened into a gust, brushing against the wolf and shimmering her fur with silver starlight. Ailsa watched as the wolf whimpered, slowly retreating as the glimmer became blinding, until everyone still conscious on the beach had to shield their eyes from the light.

When the glimmer dimmed, Ailsa looked upon her wolfhound once more and found a woman instead.

"Just as I thought." The elfin struggled to his feet, his upper lip curled back. "A wolven."

"Ivor?" Ailsa could hardly speak. There was too much going on at once—Erik still incapacitated, the chieftains swallowed by the earth. Her hound was now a woman, and a fae wanted to kill her with his bare hands. She looked desperately at Rollo, Lattimer, and Gunnar, but they regarded her like she was something to be feared—or caged.

The naked woman was curled into a ball, rousing slightly, as if she were just waking up from a long sleep. Ailsa ripped off Erik's cloak as he remained unconscious, forgetting the elfin as she staggered towards her and covered her exposed body with its heavy weight.

"Ivor," she repeated, shaking her dark skin until her eyes fluttered open. Confusion struck her brow, and she peered up at Ailsa with the same frosted gaze that stole Ailsa's heart all those years ago in the wood.

It was her—*Ivor*. Somehow, the beast had shifted into a person. Her hair was a gradient of black and grey like the wolf's hide, her skin a rich umber like the clans in the west. She wiped a hand across her face, each finger lined with a black nail that was sharpened like claws—and shrieked when she realized she was in her true form.

"It's okay, Ivor," she said, smoothing a hand down her silken hair. Ivor relaxed, but the fear in her eyes remained.

"I'm... sorry." Ivor managed to use her voice for the first time. Ailsa, too stunned to hear her speak, could only nod in solace.

A hissing sound prompted her to turn around from where she hovered over the wolven. The elfin male was attempting to put his arm back in place with little success and growing more annoyed by the second. His hair was disheveled, sand coated the right side of his cheek and dusted the elegant coat she admired. For the first time since he arrived on her shores, he appeared uncertain.

But this offered Ailsa no comfort, for she knew a frightened, injured animal was more dangerous when it was desperate. She stood and approached him, holding the ring with both quivering hands.

"You said if I gave this to you, you would leave. So, take it and be done with us!" she said. The elfin ran a hand through his wavy hair, combing it back out of his face. His features appeared even more striking, more lethal.

"That was before you rendered the ring useless," he said in a voice wrenched with bitterness.

"What are you talking about?"

"You, Ailsa, are the Tether." He stepped towards her, tentative. Every stride was calculated and methodical, one she mirrored to maintain the distance.

"That's impossible. I have no idea what that means—"

His chest rose and fell, steeping his anger. "It means the darkness that was bound to that artifact, the magic that has the power to shape the past and the future, raise the dead to life again, to start wars between gods, the power that has been fought over for centuries, has leashed itself to you."

Ailsa felt her heart drop somewhere in her toes. She shook her head so vigorously the braids against her scalp came loose. "No, that's not *possible.* I'm not even a shieldmage! Why would it bind itself to me?"

The fae stopped in his tracks, his eyes running over her like he was trying to figure out the same thing. "I do not know, but the power *accepted* you as it's home, and it cannot be undone. Not by me, anyway." He reached out and snatched her with his good arm. His hand cold through the fabric of her sleeve. "So, I guess I'll have to take you instead."

Ailsa laughed, but it was an empty sound. "I'm not going anywhere with you."

"We made a deal—bring me the Tether and I would leave your village alone. You *are* the Tether now. I have over a hundred men on that ship in your harbor. Imagine what a hundred of me can do to this quiet little *skide* hole you call home. I can either drag you with me through the flames or you can walk away willingly and keep your people safe. Make your choice."

Ailsa glanced at Erik, who was starting to groan awake, then the chieftains who had nearly dug themselves out of their ensnarement. She then looked back at her village, knowing the lives of hundreds were locked behind closed doors, waiting for her sentencing. They were the future of the Riverlands, and the future was hers to write or erase.

"Fine," she whispered.

A voice attested over her shoulder. "I'm coming."

"Why would you think I would allow that?" the elfin asked.

"She… is sick. Needs someone to help… take care." The wolven spoke as if every word were a fight and she was losing.

"And you do?" he asked.

Ivor nodded. "I've watched."

His face turned to stone as he regarded them both before cocking his head to the side in the direction of the docks. "Go, get in the boat. We leave now."

"Will you allow me to at least take my things? I have herbs and medications. I won't survive a few days without them." Ailsa's voice sounding pathetically small. It did nothing to soften the elfin, only seemed to make him hate her that much more.

He clenched his teeth and nodded, and she felt his eyes watch her every step up the hill.

She returned with extra clothes for the wolf—Ivor, who was still wearing only the heavy cloak. With her bag over her shoulder, she set her course to the docks. Ailsa looked toward Lattimer before she reached the steps, ignoring the elfin who had grabbed her arm to yank her along faster.

"Lattimer," she said. He finally looked her in the eyes. "Tell Erik I'm sorry. Tell everyone I'm sorry, but I'm going to make this right. I promise."

He gave a solemn nod and pressed his fist over his heart, saluting her departure in quiet respect. The rest of the chieftains motioned the same. Their act brought tears to her eyes, and she turned her head before anyone could see them fill into fat drops and spill down her cheeks.

She boarded the boat and stared at the receding image of her village until her tears blurred the inlet beyond recognition. Somehow knowing in her heart, she would never see Drakame again.

9
Vali

Ailsa and her wolven were dangerously quiet as they boarded the ship. He maintained a close eye on them both as he barked orders at his men, insisting they depart with speed. Seela challenged his frustration, her own eye carefully testing the fragile hold he had on his breaking point, just one wrong look away from unsnapping his wrath upon all of them.

"Get your filthy fae hands off me!" she scolded behind him as his officer, Sorrin, attempted to escort her below deck. He turned to find her thrashing in his arms, the pain in her eyes replaced with rage. They stared him down with an anger much like a crevasse of ice, colder the further he dwelled. Her hatred was bottomless.

Vali crossed the distance in only two strides, unsheathing the small dagger at his hip that was forged from the gold beneath the dwarven mountains—the only kind of weapon that could be used against his kind. He bound her hands together in front of her waist with the magic in his mind and pressed the sharp edge of the blade against the bounding pulse in her neck.

"Do not ever speak to my men like that again, or I swear to

the gods below, I will cut your foul tongue from your filthy mouth so you never speak again," he said, applying a whisper of pressure with the knife against her skin. Her eyes glanced at the metal now reflecting the light of the moon, her breath blew harsh against his wrist.

"I come here *willingly*. Do not treat me like I'm your prisoner."

"You are the definition of a prisoner, Jarl Ailsa. Having to threaten the lives of an entire village does not mean you come on your own will."

She struggled against the invisible bonds around her wrist, aware every fae on this ship was watching her. Their opinions of her would be defined by this moment alone. Meaning this was a power struggle, and he would not let her win. "Let me go," she demanded.

"No," he seethed. "You will be locked away until I need you again. You are dangerous, not only to everyone I command, but to yourself."

Her lower lids brimmed; his face so close to hers, Vali saw the moonlight in her tears. She said, "You have already taken everything from me. Will you take away my freedom as well?"

He traced the tip of the dagger up her neck, stopping just below her jaw. She swallowed as the blade nipped the soft skin beneath, her breath turning fast and shallow. The runes written along her skin flickered like a flame against the wind, fighting to come alive.

He dropped the blade immediately and took a guarded step back. The power inside her was triggered by the most extreme of emotions, and he needed to tread carefully so it was not activated once again. She was lucky she was weakened on the shores, or the power may have drawn enough strength from her to clear the entire cliff side. Or worse—bind to her permanently.

"What would you say to a truce?" he asked. Her brows danced with doubt, and he explained. "We have a long journey ahead, and I cannot have you fighting tooth and nail every step of the way. What will please you enough to agree to comply?"

Her eyes locked on the blade in his hand, and she bit her bottom lip in quick deliberation. Then her scowl bled into a wicked smile and the light returned behind her eyes. "I have only three demands. If they are each met, I vow my companion and I will not be the cause of any trouble."

"Name them."

She cleared her throat and gestured with her eyes at her still bound wrists. Vali sighed and released her for the time being. With a satisfied nod, she spoke. "First, Ivor and I will have a private cabin. We will *not* stay in a holding cell. We are not your prisoners and you do not command us."

Vali nodded and motioned for her to continue.

"Second, we will be allowed to roam at our leisure. I have waited my entire life to leave my home and see the world, and I'll be damned to Hel before I stay below deck the entire way."

The first two demands were surprisingly simple, but he had a strange feeling she was saving the worst for last. She wore a clever smile like it was a priceless jewel.

"Lastly," she said, "I want to kill you."

The disgruntled voices of his men were interrupted by Vali's dry laugh. He would have guessed this was her ultimate motivation all along, his blood in payment for the lives of her family. It was never wise to bargain with someone who had very little left to lose. And he expected nothing less of a Ledgersdóttir.

"I will grant you one try, Jarl Ailsa. Does this appease you?"

"One try would be all I need." She practically beamed like the moon with delight. "But I want three. One for each life you took from me: my father and my two sisters."

Vali grimaced with displeasure. This was going to be very uncomfortable, seeing as his right shoulder was barely hanging onto his arm. But he already needed extensive medical attention for the wolven bite, so he might as well get this over with.

"You have a deal. Three jabs, then you belong to me."

Seela pushed her way through the crew gathered around them, but Vali did not look at her. His eyes were on Ailsa and the way she seemed to flip a switch with the simple opportunity of stabbing him to death.

"Captain, you cannot be considering this mortal's demands. She has no place to request anything at all!"

"Shut your mouth, or I'll demand your throat next," Ailsa spat. The commander's eyes widened at her brazenness, the coil before her strike. Vali stepped between them both before Seela threw the mortal overboard.

"Enough," he said. "Seela, I have wronged this woman in the eyes of her culture, and we shall settle this once and for all so we can move past it." He extended his arm and offered the golden dagger. Ailsa accepted it gingerly, palming the hilt. Her eyes admired the craftsmanship of the gilded handle like it was a work of art.

He stood in the center of the deck and outstretched his arms, wincing at the pull of his injured soldier. "Do your worst, heathen."

Her fingers gripped the handle with the confidence of an assassin, and he very much dreaded the bloodlust that filmed her gaze and the sureness accompanying her strides. She was on him before he could take a guarded breath. The blade sinking into the hollow part of his stomach.

"For Marrin," she muttered in his ear as he doubled over. Agony ripped through him as she pulled the blade from his stomach, but his face remained unchanged. Without hesitating, she pierced his right lung with another perfectly placed blow, slipped expertly between his ribs like she had done this a thousand times. The air rushed from his chest in a sharp hiss.

"For Lochare," she said. He fell to his knees as the hurt began to steal his strength. She paused before the final blow, tilting his chin with a single finger beneath his jaw. And as he looked up at her, his breath ragged and teeth clenched, he found the anger in her gaze was gone. Inside their dark depths was a pain as great as the one bleeding inside him.

She was a fearless combination of fight and fear, of rage and regret. There was a hurt set in her gaze every time it washed over him, only broken by fleeting moments of warranted anger. She was a warrior spirit trapped inside a fallacious body, one broken by a condition that rattled the air inside her chest.

She was deceivingly dangerous, and he thought she was undeniably beautiful.

The muscles in her jaw feathered to hide the tremble, and her grip on the dagger adjusted. Vali only nodded, encouraging her to finish this. To fill the void of her grief with his blood. She needed this, and he would give it to her. If only to selfishly relieve him of an ounce of his own guilt.

She raised the dagger and let it fall. But Vali felt nothing because the blade sunk into the left side of his chest, where his heart should have been. "For my father," she whispered in a voice so smooth it was almost a consolation to his pain. Her hand slipped from the shaft of his dagger, the splatter of his blood hidden in the crimson of her gown.

He had half a mind to let her stab him again, as the last one missed its mark through no fault of her own. But he only pulled the knife from his chest with a groan that heaved from his stomach, spitting up a mouth full of blood in the process.

He sat back on his heels and breathed through the pain pulsing from all the places she tore him apart. The floorboards beneath his knees were slick with his blood, the smell of metal floating on the crisp night breeze. Ailsa stared down at him in horror, not perceiving how he was still alive despite the lethal blows she delivered.

"Just as I thought," she said. "You are a monster."

Vali stood to his feet, his knees shaking. The magic in his blood currently spilled across the deck and prolonging the healing process. He heaved a long sigh and looked up at the moon, unable to witness the way she was looked at him. The acknowledgment of his worst fears was written plain across her face.

"No, Jarl Ailsa. I'm much worse."

10
Vali

"Is there no one on this damned ship who can realign an arm?" Vali seethed as the elfin healer fumbled with his joint like he was tearing off the thigh of a roasted chicken. For hours he had been poked and prodded, pulled and tortured by every healer on board. But magic was useless on a wolven's bite, and his people were not skilled in a wound that required mundane practices. Not when the wolven were driven out of the High Branches long ago.

"*Hel take me,* if he doesn't shut up soon, I'm going to cut his arm off myself," a soft voice mumbled across the quarter deck. His eyes shot to the source of the sound, finding the mortal woman leaning against the wooden edge, her head bent low to hide her words. But he could hear even her softest giggle from across the ship—an irritatingly pretty sound. Ivor smiled in reply.

"I thought we agreed no more stabbing," he muttered in her direction. Her cheeks flushed slightly; aware she had been caught.

She pushed off the side of the boat and crossed her arms. Vali noticed she had changed into a new gown, one that was black as pitch and flattered every sharp angle of her body. She wrapped a leather belt around her thin waist with an iron dagger tucked into its sheath. The blade did nothing to protect her here; she was nothing more than a snake with broken fangs. Her only venom her words.

Her eyes assessed his bare chest and traced the runes painted across his skin, tracing his own markings. Her gaze left hot trails as they lingered over the holes she left in him, already starting to heal. She then locked on the broken skin covering his deformed shoulder girdle. "I can reset your arm." She cautiously added, "if you'd like."

"Why would you help me?" he asked, wary of her assistance. She'd most likely twist his arm to further his misery.

"Because although your wailing was satisfying at first, it has become quite annoying, and it is personally offending me to watch your healers repeatedly butcher their attempts." She reached out and slid her chilled fingertips over his collarbone without waiting for permission. He stiffened; the uninvited touch sent an iron rod down his spine. The pads of her fingers palpated the deformed lining of his muscles, not so gently nudging the space where the ball and socket separated.

"Relax," she mumbled, her lips so close to his ear while he sat in a chair, which did nothing to help him loosen. He did not enjoy his enemy so close, so intimate. He found himself wrapped in her spice, a mixture of scents simultaneously earthy and floral. "It is really a quick process, but it will hurt. A lot. I will countdown so you can prepare." She covered the arch of his shoulder with her palm and folded his arm into a sharp angle with the other. "All right, brace yourself in three—"

In a simple motion she pulled his arm midline and the bone snapped into place, shooting stars across his vision and a pain through the joint worse than the original blow. But the agony ceased as quickly as it began, leaving him only time to yelp.

"Why didn't you count?" he gingerly rolled the sore muscles in his shoulder to return his arm back to its former function.

She scoffed and walked back to where the wolf was still standing against the shroud, his skin still cold where she touched him. "Because I hate you."

"You're a healer?" he asked, ignoring her insult and how matter of fact she phrased it.

She sighed, growing frustrated with him. Making it plain she had no interest in small talk with her family's killer. "I own —used to own an apothecary. When your entire family descends from shieldmages, you find plenty of opportunities to mend the body in creative ways."

She turned her back to him and stared across the sea. The sun was rising over the eastern horizon, bruising the sky with deep blues and magentas, piercing the darkness with the first rays of morning. Taking the hint from her posture, he stood and strode down the steps leading to the main deck, ending all further conversation.

He would need to make it a point to avoid her. The woman would soon be brought to the gods, and she would most likely die to unbind the power latching itself to her soul. He could not allow himself to pity her or her situation. She had done this to herself, and he had a job to do.

"Vali." Seela stepped in his path. "I would like to speak with you about the girl."

"Her name is Ailsa, Commander. Might as well say her name, she's going to be with us for a while. What about her?"

Seela's face betrayed a flash of irritation before returning to its passive coolness. "You let her walk all over you. If she is the Tether as you said, and I do not doubt your claim, then shouldn't we keep her locked away? What right does she have to be making demands?"

Vali stepped closer to his commander to private their conversation. "Ailsa nearly blasted me apart on the shores of Drakame. Surely you saw the power inside her from the ship?" The commander nodded. "Some of those heathens had magic, but not like the one we witnessed. It is better to keep her happy, to let her feel like a guest instead of a prisoner. If she loses control for a moment, if we anger or frustrate her, the power inside her could be unleashed and bind itself to her permanently. And what then? Whether we like it or not, she has the upper hand right now."

Seela jutted her chin higher. "I will not serve the woman who tried to kill you."

Vali shook his head and laid his hands on her shoulders. "You serve me, and me alone. You have been brilliantly loyal for so long, Seela, and we will all be rewarded soon enough. This is a test like all the other trials we have faced together, and we will find a way to endure like we always have. But until we reach Alfheim, keep your eyes on the water. I have a feeling the way home won't be as easy as when we left."

She bowed her head. "As you wish."

He squeezed her delicate shoulders and continued toward his quarters that lay in the back of the ship, desperate to get a few hours of sleep and unwind this night from his mind like a tangled thread wrapped around a spool.

VALI SLEPT THE MORNING AWAY. By the time his eyes opened, the sun was high above the world, heating his cabin into a furnace. He threw on a loose linen shirt over the light leather breeches that stuck to his skin and popped open a new bottle of mead they had scavenged from the island. His tongue felt as heavy as his thoughts, and he needed something strong enough to tend to them both.

There was a doubt that corrupted any sense of satisfaction at finally discovering the Tether. He had been searching for the past half century, yet only recently had the wraiths spoken to him. The fates did not weave their threads into a meaningless pattern. There were motives for their methods, a way for each present of a story to line up seamlessly with the past. This seemingly unexceptional woman had been sent the Tether, the power had to have chosen her for a reason. And if it wasn't a divine intervention, he didn't know what else it could be.

His own destiny had been woven into the tapestry of time from the beginning of his life. He was bred for this purpose, and this purpose alone. To deliver the Tether to Odin and save his world in the process. This power was tied to his fate as much as it was tethered to Ailsa's soul. As much as he hated to admit it in his mind, their destinies were woven together, each sewn into the same embroidered fate, each from entirely different spools of stringing.

His men were hard at work manning the mast now inflated with air, angled in such a way to catch the northern breeze and sail them against the wind to the Edge of the World. He fell effortlessly into their rhythm, assisting the soldiers turned sailors with the strength of his magic freshly restored and eager to help. The labor took his mind off the state of everything, a much-needed distraction from the woman who had taken room and board inside his head.

"Sorrin," he called to one of his officers. The male with pure white hair pulled low behind his head stopped his work and nodded in acknowledgement. "Did our guests recluse to a cabin for the day?"

"Just the wolven, sir. She's in my old cabin. I moved in with the mates below."

Vali chewed his cheek in consideration. "And the other woman?"

Sorrin pointed above their heads. He followed his gesture to the peak of the main mast. "She's in the nest. Been up there all morning. We were just about to send someone to check on her, but no one is willing. We… don't heal as quickly as you do."

"Don't bother yourselves," he muttered, rubbing the sore spot on his rib. "I'll do it."

11
Ailsa

The sky was cloudless, a flawless blue stretching as far as her eye could see and beneath it the same endless stretch of waves leaping and receding like bobbing mountains made of ocean spray. She peered through the gilded spyglass, trying to catch a glimpse of their destination, but the Great Sea spanned the entire width of the realm, lining the world in a cerulean frame.

Ivor retreated inside their cabin, finding the motion of the boat too disorienting to remain on deck, and Ailsa could hardly stand the sounds of her retching to remain in the cabin. So instead she climbed to the tallest mast and stared at the sea, finding a piece of comfort in being some place other than her longhouse or the Aelderwood. Even if it was with a bunch of outlanders.

Her black gown attracted the sun. The coarse cloth was hot to the touch, sending a trickle of sweat beading beneath her smock. She brushed the thick wave of hair hanging low down her back over her shoulder, letting her skin breathe and the sun dry her neck.

"What are you doing up here?"

The quiet lull of the waves was broken by the same fae who had disturbed everything else in her life. Ailsa did not turn to look at him. Instead, she rolled the spyglass between her fingers as she leaned against the wooden railing.

"Can a girl not enjoy the view?" she hissed.

In the corner of her eye, she watched the elfin lean his hip against the side in a casual posture, like they were friends or something. "Your neck is seared."

"An astute observation."

He made a sound that reminded her of a pig. "You should go inside. Your skin is too fair, and the sun is much stronger over the sea. You'll be blistering by high noon."

"And why would you care about my skin?" She met his stare finally. He looked like he belonged on the sea, the way he sat on the edge without fear of falling to his death, the way his loose shirt inhaled the breeze like the mast beneath them. His sleeves were rolled up around the thickest part of his forearms, too casual compared to the elegance of his face. It almost made her forget the monster waiting behind the twitch of his fingers.

His eyes dropped to her chest, ignoring her question. "Do you feel different? After becoming the Tether, do you feel more powerful than you did before?"

She ran a careful assessment over herself but shook her head. "No, I feel nothing. I'm still weak, and I'm still drowning." But that night when the power latched to her, she recalled how briefly she felt *good*. For the first time in her life, she breathed easy. But the sensation was fleeting, a transitory tease of what life was like without soggy lungs. That power surging beneath her skin, running along her veins. It must be what he felt like all the time. The thought made her heart murderous with envy.

She wrapped her hand around the beam and leaned against

the smooth grains. Her gaze looked through the thin fabric of his shirt, the material sheer enough to see the black lines painted across his own skin. Rune marks, similar to hers. She noticed the pink, healing flesh covering the holes in his chest. "Did I at least hurt you?" she asked.

He nodded. "Very much."

"Good."

His gaze fell down her skirt, tracing the embellishments burned into the rough fabric. "I hope you know I did not come to this realm to kill your family, Ailsa. I think in time you'll understand why I needed the artifact, why I went to such extremes to find it."

"I do not care for your reasons, nor do I want to spend any time with you to figure them out." She crossed her arms and pretended to be interested in the never changing horizon. "You've ruined my life and you don't even care. Why should I be anything but indifferent to your cause?"

He was quiet, letting her seethe in quiet and dispel some of her anger before speaking. "Have you ever done something wrong for the right reasons?"

"Of course, but those reasons never resulted in genocide."

The elfin sighed and paced the perimeter of the nest. "I'm not saying my reasons justify the lives I've taken."

"Then what *are* you saying, Captain?" she snapped, growing tired of this petty dance. If he was trying to gain her pity, he was wasting his time. She felt nothing but hatred for the fae who killed her father, nothing but ice in her heart. "Do you know what it is like for me? To see your face every time I turn around, to feel the ghost of your hands around my throat and imagine my family's last moments being something similar."

He was quiet, but the boards of the nest groaned as he

paused his pacing. "I imagine it must be quite torturesome for you to look at me."

She pushed off the beam to look at him. To *really* look at this male who had unknowingly ruined and saved her life all at once. Up here, away from his men and his commander where she finally got him alone, he was vulnerable. Different. Showing a side of him he allowed her alone to see, the male beneath the angst. And there was a softness there she didn't see before when she was blind with rage.

"Did you kill them?" she asked. "Were you the one who took their lives?"

His eyes met hers, steady despite the shame he tried to hide behind the pretense of apathy. "Yes. Your father and two sisters approached before the battle. They all three attacked me, and I ended them."

She took a trembling breath, swallowing back the wave of nausea rising in her throat. Of course, they would attack first. "Did they die well?"

The question visibly caught him off guard by the way his head slanted, but he recovered just as quickly. "Your father died like a king—completely fearless in front of his army. Your sisters..." He looked somewhere off into the ocean, brows rising at the memory. "They were even worse. They died like a fire, refusing to be snuffed out."

A faint smile drifted to her lips. Because even though this fae had killed her family, he spoke of their deaths in a way that was akin to respect, even dignified. War was brutal, death was certain, only honor validated them both. She wiped away a tear before it ran down her cheek.

"I appreciate your honesty, but you will never gain my forgiveness."

"I do not ask for it."

"I will find a way to kill you."

"You're welcome to try." His face remained expressionless, but his words carried a tone of amusement.

She nodded with a tight jerk of her chin and followed his gaze to the gradient of blue. "Where are we going, and what will you do with me?"

"We are going to my home, Alfheim. The highest realm in the High Branches, the land of the elves. As for what we will do with you," he rolled a rope in his hands and sat on the edge of the nest, "that is not up to me."

The Tree of Life was the pillar of the heavens, connecting all nine realms and allowing passage between them. In the canopy of the tree lay the fae realms: the elves in Alfheim, the dwarves in Svartalfheim, and the giants in Jotunheim. Under the fae realms stood Asgard, where the gods roamed and ruled. Beneath Asgard was Midgard, the mortal realm. And in the lowest realms, the tree extended its roots into Vanaheim, Helheim, Muspell, and Niflheim.

She had wanted to see the world, and now she was going to see all of them. The fates, for once, had shown her threadbare life a stitch of mercy. Never had she experienced a mercy so cruel.

The elfin paused and dangled his feet over the edge with only the rope as his lifeline. "You know, you've never asked me my name."

This made her grin, even against the sorrow pushing past her eyes. "Don't need it. I have plenty of names for you. Trust me when I say you do not want to hear them."

"Are you always this unpleasant?"

"I could be much worse. Consider this a mercy you do not deserve."

His sigh faded into a laugh, and the sound made her throat

dry. Demon or fae, he should not be allowed to make such a beguiling sound. Not when he nearly killed her with those hands that snatched her gaze every time they smoothed nervously over his thighs.

"Why are you here?" she asked.

He shrugged and said, "It is my ship. I can go where I wish."

Her brows narrowed. "Then start wishing to be far away from me."

She shoved hard against his shoulder and pushed him off the edge of the nest. The elfin released a sharp cry of surprise as he fell back, regaining his orientation the next moment and swinging back to the main deck. His feet kissing the floorboards like he had meant to fall that way all along. His grace was both a thing she admired and despised.

He looked up at her from below and threw her an obscene gesture with his fingers, and she stepped away from the half wall as a frown pulled her lips. He was not torturesome to look at—not even a little bit. And for that reason, she hated him even more.

12
Ailsa

Days passed, and still they sailed on what seemed an endless stretch of ocean. She didn't realize the sea was so vast, consuming the world with the extent of its unexplored reaches. Ailsa spent time sitting in the nest of the mainmast, enjoying her time alone and watching the fae from an eagle's perspective.

Their magic was different from what she had seen from their captain. It came in spurts for the sailors, exhaustible, utilized almost exclusively during the day. They could manipulate the breeze and the tide, sometimes entire groups of them working to influence a favorable combination, pushing them further toward an unforeseen destination.

She also watched the elfin. His name was Vali, as she heard his commander often speak so affectionately. She approached him often, and Ailsa wondered if they had something *more* going on behind his captain's cabin door.

Ailsa had not made a point of it, but she noticed the commander came and went from his quarters at her whim, never knocking or needing an invitation. A pang of jealousy gnawed at her heart, not because she envied them *together*, but what they seemingly had. Freedom with another person she had lost so many years ago. Her loneliness was like a brand, never letting her forget.

Their last night in Midgard was noted with a feast on the main deck. Fire pits encouraged drinking games around their blazes, musicians pulled out curious instruments Ailsa could only guess were created in the fae lands. Soon, the night was filled with song and mead, making her feel at home for the first time since she left it.

But Ailsa kept her head around the elves. She didn't trust the pointed eared creatures or their magic fingers. Instead, she watched them get drunk. The alcohol loosening their lips around her, their guard lowering significantly. She marked her first victim with the offer of a full tankard.

"Evening, Officer." She approached Sorrin, whose round face was already flushed and perspiring.

His throat bobbed with a hard swallow. "Evening, Miss Ailsa. To what do I owe the pleasure?"

"Do you need a reason to enjoy the pleasure of my company?" She gave him a coy smile. "I was hoping you would tell me a little about your homeland. I'm intensely curious about Alfheim. You must tell me everything."

Sorrin's eyes drifted off behind her, looking for a way out. "Oh, it's a lovely place. Sunny, warm, once quite safe. I'm sure Captain would be a better source of information—"

"Who is Vali to you, Sorrin?" She stepped closer. Sweat beaded across his lip. "Captains are not referred to as 'my lord' and no one here has the bollocks to look him directly in the eyes. No one besides you."

A nervous laugh escaped him, and he sipped his mead at a stalling pace. "He's our captain for now, and in other realms he is other things… titles."

"Titles?" Ailsa inquired. Titles that only changed when they entered new realms, new jurisdictions. This Vali was a conundrum indeed.

"I... um... I need some water, I'm afraid. Let's finish this conversation later."

"No, wait!" she pleaded, but he was already halfway across the deck, disappearing into the crowd. Ailsa leaned against the edge of the boat, deflated from defeat. Ostman were much easier to get the drunken truth from than elves.

"There you are," a voice purred behind her. Ailsa turned to find Seela stalking toward her spot in the corner, where Sorrin had abandoned her in a fevered sweat.

"Here I am," she replied, waving her hands unenthusiastically. "Need something?"

"Rumor has it you're good with a lyre."

Ailsa had played the songs of her home in her cabin during moments of boredom. The crew must have heard the music through the thin walls of the vessel. "And?" she replied harshly.

Seela licked her lips. "And we were hoping you would show us some of your people's music. It was lovely that night we sailed into your harbor."

Ailsa's face winced as she scoffed. "I'm glad we could entertain you before you came to slaughter us."

Seela frowned. "Do you see a bunch of murderers around that fire, Ailsa?"

Her gaze fell behind the elfin toward the men draining a barrel, the beaming grins of comrades with skin warmed by weeks of sailing. There was a kind of joy present on this deck she hadn't witnessed in a very long time. So long, the reunion was uncomfortable, unsettling. A kind of warmth only reminding her of how used to being cold she had become.

Seela dipped her head to catch her gaze again. "Fifty years

we've been searching. Every single day, waking up with a new hope only to have it crushed the next. It has been a long journey to find what you carry, but we are finally going home. And we mean to honor their deaths, Jarl Ailsa, and all those who died as a retaliation for the fight over the Tether. If you truly do not wish to play, I will not pressure you. But consider it." Seela offered Ailsa another cup of mead, and she warily accepted. "I think some of us would be *very* interested in hearing your song." She winked and spun on her heel before Ailsa could ask her meaning.

"Seela?"

She looked back at her. "Yes?"

"I want to know what's going to happen to me." She looked down into her cup, avoiding the elfin's violet gaze. "I do not want to be led like a pig to the slaughter. You all owe me this."

Seela nodded slowly. "In time. I vow it. Sometimes remaining ignorant is safer."

Her father must have reasoned the same to keep a family secret so large from her. If this was the safety ignorance offered, she wanted none of it. "Tell that to my family."

Ailsa turned away from her and watched the crowd gathered around the mainmast, a makeshift stage created from mead barrels and dining tables, while draining the contents of her cup. Patience was a virtue she never claimed to master. But Seela's tentative agreement was a step in the right direction.

Things had settled between her and the fae in the past few days. They were just so damn *happy* and kind to her. She had tried her best to maintain her grudge against them, but it was difficult to think of them as monsters when they were so familiar in nature and heart. So like the people she cared for on the quiet fjord. Even harder to believe them a bunch of cold-hearted murderers.

Over a decade ago, her father had executed one of their own during a raid gone very wrong. Her cousin let his arrogance cloud his judgment, and his selfish decisions had cost the lives of many clansmen, death the only fitting punishment for his crime. His immediate family had been furious with her father for weeks, but eventually they made peace with his decision, understanding it was not personal but necessary to prevent something worse from happening in the future.

Could she also find peace with a change of perspective? Was forgiveness possible through understanding one another better?

Her gaze drifted to the male leaning over the upper deck's ledge, watching the revelry from afar. He brought a pipe to his lips, drawing a long breath and holding it, before letting white smoke spill from his mouth. Vali looked as lonely as she felt despite being among his own kind. She hated him, hated who he was and what he had done. How he left her alone in this realm over a ring. Every time she looked at him, she saw her father and her sister's faces. And yet each day that passed, it hurt a little less, their faces a little dimmer.

As if feeling the weight of her gaze, Vali's eyes shifted to her. Ailsa looked away quickly, unnerved she had been caught and cursing quietly under her breath. She leaned away from the firelight to hide the flush heating up her throat. Almost involuntarily, she glanced back at him a few moments later, finding him still staring down at her. The smallest of smirks plaguing his arrogant lips. A small torture to witness.

Perhaps not forgiveness, but a tolerance could be found. She decided to abandon her brooding and threw back the rest of the contents in her cup, finding enough courage at the bottom to confront the elfin male.

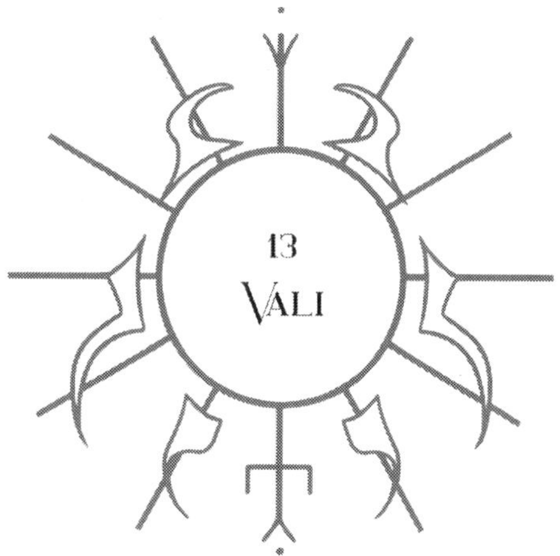

13 Vali

Watching the crew celebrate was a reward Vali didn't feel like he had quite earned yet. Although this journey had been far longer than any of them had anticipated, it didn't feel as though it was close to being finished. So many unknowns still lurked in the future. So many ways all of this could go wrong, and he'd been alive far too long to be anything less than a pessimist.

He felt her stare before he caught it. The little heathen stood off to the side, watching his men as closely as he was. Poor Sorrin had made the mistake of giving her an inch of kindness, and she took advantage of it as much as she could, trapping him into conversation. But Vali supposed the old fae didn't mind. He had daughters at home he hadn't seen in decades, and he imagined he must have seen some of their spitfire in Ailsa.

She looked away as soon as their eyes met, so fast he almost missed them. For someone who wanted him to stay away from her, she was having a difficult time keeping her eyes to herself. A fact he simultaneously found annoying and yet became increasingly more comfortable with.

His attention lingered on her after she looked away. She was nervous tonight, knowing they were about to leave Midgard, and he couldn't blame her. It was the first time she had shown a sliver of vulnerability since joining the ship, and his observation only made her writhe. Aware he now had a foothold beneath her skin, he stared until she couldn't stand it anymore. Which wasn't very long, seeing how she slammed her ale back with an impressive forte and started toward the stairwell. Vali took a breath and mentally prepared himself for what would follow.

"Why are you being such a recluse up here?" Her voice announced her presence. Ailsa stood to his left; her arms crossed with an unreadable look on her face. "Shouldn't you be celebrating with the rest of the crew?"

He simply shrugged and looked back toward the stage. "There is nothing for me to celebrate yet. The crew have done their job, but I have not completed my task."

"But you found the Tether."

"I found *you*," he replied dryly. "Do not expect me to be happy the Tether came with a sharp tongue and an affinity for stabbing."

"If I didn't know better, I would think you were disappointed I am the Tether."

"Disappointed is not the word I would use." Maddened was more like it.

She didn't respond. The only sound was her steps as she perused behind him, walking the width of the upper deck. Vali, not enjoying having his back to her, turned around to find her staring out at the sea. Something she often wasted her time doing. Sometimes for hours—not that he noticed.

"Why do you stare at the waves so much?" he asked. It wasn't like the scene ever changed.

She sighed and leaned her hands against the rail lining the deck. The full moon draped her in silver light, washed away her warm skin tone and darkened the shadows around her eyes. "At first, I was thinking of a plan to escape."

"Oh?" His brow arched, suddenly intrigued. He breathed another long drag from the pipe still warm in his hand.

"Aye. I was going to take one of the little dinghies and row back to the North Sea. Until I remembered your spare boats aren't like longships and probably wouldn't survive the waves going home." She chewed the inside of her lip. "And I don't exactly remember the way."

"You've never been this far from home?"

She shook her head. "I've never been anywhere but home."

Vali scoffed and started to pace the upper deck himself. No wonder she was stubborn. A heathen who had never experienced anything except the safety of her little village was even more of a liability. "Is that the only reason, then? You don't know the way back?"

"No," she said, turning around to face him. Vali realized it was the first time he'd seen her appear defeated. Not even when he dragged her from the shores of her fjord. Her gaze was low until she lifted her thick lashes to look at him. "I packed my things and told Ivor the plan. But just when we were about to commit, I stopped. Because I realized… I do not want to go back."

Vali stepped closer, intrigued by why she was sharing this with him, admitting her treasonous plans. "Why? What could possibly be behind you that is worse than anything that lay ahead?"

She crossed her arms defensively, closing off. "A fate worse than death, not that your immortal soul would ever understand."

"Try me, Jarl Ailsa," he said, taking another drag of his pipe.

She sighed against her arms woven tight against her chest. "When you killed my family, you left me alone. Claiming the title of jarl was my only form of defense, and even that is weak compared to a fat butcher's ambition."

Not quite following, he thought over her words as he strode to where she leaned against the railing. If she objected to him standing beside her, she made no move to leave. "By the way you responded to fighting me back in Drakame, you do not strike me as a woman who requires defending."

Ailsa suddenly turned her head to look at him, like she was seeing him for the first time. "That's not…" She shook her head and returned her gaze to the mast above. "It's not that simple."

"I hope not," he replied. "Fat butchers will be the least of your worries when we leave this realm."

"Are you speaking of yourself?"

Vali laughed and leaned his hip against the wooden edge. "You have it all wrong. I am the only being in all the realms you do not have to fear. Because I am the only one who will protect you at all costs."

She faced him then, dark eyes swimming with disdain. Her arms were still crossed in front of her, pushing up her chest and tempting Vali's gaze to fall lower. "You will not harm me?"

Why did she think he wanted to hurt her? Hel, he couldn't harm her even if he tried. His flesh wouldn't allow it. "Of course not. I will do everything I can to keep you safe. You can hate me all you want, Ailsa, but you can trust me as well."

She offered a reluctant nod in place of a reply while rolling her bottom lip through her teeth. The pads of her fingers tinkered with a loose strand on her sleeve, and from their closeness, Vali noticed her skin prickled with chills.

He asked, "Why did you come up here? Did you not insistently request to be far away from me?"

Her eyes narrowed on him. "Perhaps I am studying my enemy up close so I may learn his weaknesses and take him down where it hurts the most."

He nodded slowly, pretending to consider her response. "Cunning, I'll give you that, Jarl Ailsa. But allow me to save you some time: I have no weaknesses."

"I disagree. If you can bleed, you can die."

"Are you still on this killing me business?"

"Killing you is my only business," she said with a wicked smile. "And I have a lot of free time these days."

Vali took a small step back, growing more concerned the longer she grinned at the idea of bleeding him out. "For a small heathen, you are quite scary."

A laugh burst from her lips, one she tried to hold back but ended up coming out obnoxiously loud. Her giggles suddenly turned sharp as the air she sucked in whistled and wheezed. The amusement in her face fell into a bracing wince as she caught her breath.

"Ailsa?"

He stepped toward her, but she held a hand up to stop him, turning slightly from his sight as she started to cough in a fit of strangled sounds. Vali didn't know what to do besides stand there and gape, feeling helpless as her coughs turned wet.

After a few minutes, her chest finally slowed its breathing pattern to a steady rate. With her back still to him, she wiped her fist on her gown, but Vali noticed the smear of blood on her wrist. "Are you well?"

"I'm fine," she said, sounding breathless. Slowly, she spun to look at him again. Her eyes were red around their dark centers. Her cheeks damp from wiped tears. "You asked why I stare at the sea. Because for the first time in my life, I am looking at something new. Different waves, different faces, different sunrises and sunsets. You obviously take for granted the life you live, the breath in your chest, the power between your fingers. And I think that is why I hate you the most." She wiped her lips with the back of her hand. "Because you have everything I do not."

Her evaluation of him made something hot burn beneath his skin. "Do not presume to know me or what I value."

Her face lit with an amused smile. "That would be assuming you have values at all, and I do not believe you do."

"What would a heathen know of values?" he asked, stepping forward again. She mirrored his advance, meeting him somewhere in the middle.

"More than a monster."

He laughed, and it was a true sound that made her flinch. "If I am such a beast to you, then why are you standing so close?"

She lifted her chin to meet his glare. "It's a small ship."

So he was beginning to notice. Before he could respond, another voice joined them on the upper deck.

"Vali, the crew are requesting your—" Seela began, trailing when she noticed their standoff. "Am I interrupting something?"

"Nothing at all." Ailsa looked past him at his commander and smiled. "He's all yours, Seela. I'm going inside for the night. Goodnight, Captain." She spun on her toes so fast, her dark hair smacked him in the chest.

Only when she disappeared down the stairs did the tension in his shoulders fall. *Values*. He snorted. She had no idea what he held near, heartless or not. The things that burdened him, that shook him awake every night—all the reasons he couldn't celebrate. How could a simple woman from a simple place ever understand the weight he carried?

"Vali—"

"I'll be down in a minute," he bit out. And Seela, knowing when he needed space, retreated to give him all he needed.

Whatever things Ailsa cherished now, whatever she valued in her heart, those would change. Journeys such as these had a habit of changing people along the way. And he almost regretted the woman he stole from the shores of Midgard would not be the same as the one he would give to the gods.

That fire in her fight would soon be reduced to cinders, and he'd be the one left standing in her ashes.

14
Ailsa

Ivor's rich complexion was tinged with green when Ailsa finally made her way inside. A combination of shifting for the first time and the motion of the boat had wreaked havoc on her stomach. The wolven looked up from her sickbed for a brief moment, then rested her head back on the pillow.

"Do you need anything?" Ailsa asked. She ran a hand over her forehead, still cool to the touch, but clammy. Ivor shook her head, pressing her lips tight. "I brought you some water and some food, just in case you change your mind. I also have some fresh ginger I can put in a tea to help the nausea."

"Thanks," she groaned.

Ailsa threw herself on the bed next to the wolven and rested her eyes. "I'm just glad to see you talking. You had me worried for a while."

She didn't reply for the longest time. A silence stretched between them, and Ailsa thought she had fallen asleep until the small mattress shifted next to her.

"I didn't know how to shift," Ivor said quietly. Ailsa peeked her left eye open to look at her as she continued, "My family warned me against shifting, said we were in this realm as wolves, and we would stay here until Fenrir made it safe for us to be known. I never knew how to shift into my human form, so I could never tell you who I truly was."

Ailsa slipped her hand into her friend's, squeezing it gently. "Why is it dangerous to shift?"

"The wraiths, Ailsa. I smelled their presence constantly in those woods, lingering in the shadows of the trees. They see everything, whisper between themselves. If the wolven were seen in your area, Fenrir's enemies would hunt us down. Possibly hurt your people as well." She pressed a hand to her mouth, waiting for an isolated wave of nausea to settle. "The god was chained to an unknown island somewhere in Midgard because Odin resented his power. The Norns claimed the wolf would be his ending. But his bonds were broken by the love of a mortal woman who discovered his prison. It was said Fenrir could shift, and when he did, he mated with the mortal who then bore his offspring, the wolven."

"The gods in Asgard are still searching for Fenrir, as they believe he will destroy the worlds. The wolven used to hide in the Highest Branches with the fae, as the gods did not disturb the godless fae or the giants who antagonize them, but we were driven out by a darkness that descended upon the upper realms nearly a century ago. Now they are free to hunt us down, and if they do, they will torture us until we share Fenrir's hiding place."

Ailsa's voice lowered to a whisper. "And do you know where he hides, Ivor?"

She paused before answering. "All wolven hear his call on the fourth night of midsummer, the anniversary of his imprisonment. He reminds us he is there, watching, waiting to take his revenge and make a new world, one safe for his offspring."

Ailsa had never heard this tale of Fenrir before, perhaps

because the storytellers did not know the true fate of the Great Wolf, or perhaps they were protecting the wolven from anyone searching for them. She could imagine the slaughter that would ensue, the reward the gods would give for finding such a beast. "Yet, you still came on this journey to the Highest Branches where the gods reside and on a boat full of fae who know exactly what you are. Why risk yourself?"

Ivor sighed. "Because you saved my life over a decade ago when you found me in the woods, after my pack had been killed off by a group of hunters. And you are my family. I will follow you to the end."

Ailsa smiled, her heart warm because all at once she gained another piece of family. She was suddenly not so alone anymore. "I'm glad you're here, *systir*," she said.

Ivor's response was interrupted by the violent shift of the ship. Voices raised outside of their cabin, the starlight outside the small window on the wall now sunken beneath the waves. She sat up from the bed and attempted to steady herself against the rocking floor beneath her feet. The pitcher on her bedside table crashed to the floor, soaking the lining of her leather shoes and sprinkling glass shards across the room.

"Ivor, stay in bed. I'm going to see what's going on," she said. Using the furniture pinned in place, she pushed herself to the door.

"I should come too, just in case—"

"Clearly you haven't broken in your human legs, much less your sea legs. Rest, Ivor. I'll be back soon." The wolven made a sound of protest, but reluctantly agreed. Ailsa threw herself from the room, meeting the violent beginnings of a sudden storm on the other side.

Black clouds plastered a dark canvas across the sky, the moon and stars disappearing behind the walls of a fierce squall. She smelled the rain in the torrential wind, turbulent against the waves and forcing the spray of whitecaps over the edge of the vessel. The ship groaned. Everywhere she looked, things were breaking, ropes snapped, sails tore against the force of nature.

A thick fist snagged her arm. She turned to find the face of one of the inebriated officers, now sobered by impending danger. "Get back inside!"

"I can help!" she shouted above the beating wind stealing her voice. Ailsa had never been on a ship of this size, but the mechanisms were similar to the longships she was taught to manage. Even though she never left home, her father made sure she could sail, fight, and take care of herself. She would finally use her lessons in a way that mattered. "Release me, Sorrin!"

His grip only constricted, pushing her back towards her cabin. Before she could argue, a sound disrupted the chorus of waves crashing against the hull. The raspy sound of a throaty growl made the world quiet for a beat, and the officer paled as his eyes caught something behind her.

She turned and found the face of a serpent. His massive head lifted from the water, jaws parted to reveal several rows of serrated and salivating teeth. Lightning veined the sky behind the beast, reflecting the luminous emerald green of its neatly folded scales. His head must have been the size of their ship, able to consume the great vessel in one jaw-stretching bite.

Jormungand.

She knew the tales of the serpent encircling the world, lurking beneath the depths of the Great Sea and guarding the edges of Midgard. But they were only tales, and this beast before her was very, *very* real. The beast croaked another bone splitting sound before its head dunked back into the ocean, a great wave produced in its wake.

The swell hit the side of the boat, lurching the vessel and tangling the masts in a mess of canvas, wood, and rope. The elves had already sprung to work, using their magic to catch the broken ropes flapping wildly in the salty gusts. But they were unable to maintain control of their power as the wreckage slipped free of their enchanted fingers. The world was too disorienting, the air moving too quickly to aim the enchantments properly, and without the daylight to fuel their power, they were running out quickly. The ship was tipping, and if the crew didn't take back control of the vessel, they would surely be swallowed by the sea—then by the beast.

"It senses you, Ailsa!" Sorrin shook her back into focus. "You have to get inside and maybe the serpent will spare us all."

Another male Ailsa did not recognize joined them in the center of the lower deck. "Use her! If there was ever a time to test the power of the Tether it is now! Make her destroy the beast!"

"She could destroy this realm if the power in the Tether feels threatened!"

"I'll take my chances," the male replied. He yanked Ailsa from Sorrin's grasp and pulled her toward the edge of the vessel. She tried to twist her arms from his grip, but the sailor was unnaturally strong. He pushed her in front of him, pinning her against the side by his hips so she was forced to look over the boiling sea.

He displayed her to the beast like carrion for the crows. Like bait.

"Let me go!" She writhed against him, but it was futile. There was no outmatching this male pressed against her back. The waves near the boat foamed as the serpent slid beneath the water's edge. Her skin was suddenly fevered, the marks across her forearms burned as hot as her fear.

"What are you doing?" A distinguishable voice boomed behind them, anger as familiar as the night she first experienced its wrath.

"Captain, we must use her to kill the beast, or we have no hope of ever making it out of this infernal realm!" Her captor tensed; his body went rigid as if he were frozen in place.

"Let her go," the elfin hissed. There was a moment of disobedience before the male complied. His arms fell limp at his sides, and she pushed away from the edge.

Falling to her knees at the expense of the ship's lurching, she crawled to the staircase leading to the upper deck, holding on to a post so she could regain orientation. The thrill in her heart would not be soothed, not when the beast was still somewhere beneath their ship, scratching the casing with its scales —looking for her.

"Did I order you to use the mortal woman, Thoriel?" The elfin held his sailor by the throat, the man's eyes bulging from his skull while the sea beat the hull behind them.

"No, my lord, I just thought that—"

"I didn't hire you to *think*. Do you know what you have risked in reaction to your own pathetic fear?" The elfin squeezed his neck until his knuckles turned white. "I should toss you to the serpent for your disobedience."

"No!" Ailsa shouted, unable to fathom anyone fairing a fate in the jaws of the sea snake. He had only acted out of self-preservation, and that in her mind was not enough to receive death as punishment. "Let him go! We have enough to worry about without killing each other."

The elfin's gaze flashed to hers for a moment, considering her as she clung to a wooden post as if trying to understand why she would defend a male who forced her against the beast. He released the soldier and spat an order at him, before turning and offering his hand to her.

"I am *not* going inside, in case you were going to order such a thing," she sputtered the words. Her lips now numb from the icy water spraying over the sides of the vessel.

"Yes, you're too foolish to do anything rational." Yet despite his disapproval, the side of his lips curled into a subtle smirk. He pulled her to her feet. "It would be better if I tied you to the mast."

His words struck an idea, and she took off toward the mainmast before useless rationality made her hesitate. The elfin followed her like a loyal shadow as she climbed the ladder, skipping rungs as she raced to the top. Her flats faltered on a slippery step, and she stumbled, catching herself with an unsteady grip.

"Are you mad, Ailsa?" Vali said below her. She grinned the kind that showed teeth. She was quite possibly mad, and her lungs were sore from the excitement, but this was the most alive she'd felt in years. Maybe ever. She recovered her rhythm and pushed to the top, her soaked gown clinging to her legs every step of the way, but never slowed her pursuit.

Once in the nest, she found the loose rope that dangled to the deck below and pulled it up.

"Ailsa—"

"Thoriel was right. You need to use me. If the beast wants me, then let's bait him into a snare," she said. Turning to him, she held up the frayed end of the long rope. "When it comes up from the sea, help me get its attention. When it attacks, we jump."

"We jump?" he asked, clarifying. "You haven't thought any of this through, have you?"

"There!" she shouted while pointing toward a spot in the rolling waves that had begun to bubble. The elfin stepped behind her, flush against her back. He placed his hands on either side of her waist, his palms emitting a golden light that attracted every eye with its brilliance. It surrounded her, warm and shielding the wind still shredding their sails. Beautiful magic she didn't know a creature like him was capable of. It almost distracted her from the beast now setting its sight on the nest.

"Ailsa…" he warned behind her.

"Wait for it," she commanded, and for some reason, he listened. One hand clasped the rope, the other his wrist, the hum of his magic vibrating beneath her touch. She waited for the beast to lunge. The serpent coiled, then decided on its attack.

"Now!"

The elfin wrapped his left arm around her waist and pushed them both over the shallow half-wall bordering the nest. His other hand grabbed the rope to hold them up. Ailsa wrapped her body around the rope, leaping with him as he pushed against her back. He clung to her as much as he clung the corded line, his fingers dug into the soft part of her stomach. His desperation palpable in the way he held her against his hard chest.

Wind scorned her ears as they fell, a sharp tug of the rope bruised her fingers as their slack ran out. They swung beneath the main mast and toward the quarterdeck, timing their release just right to land near the bow with Ailsa sprawling and the elfin gracefully landing on both feet. On her back, she looked up to where they once stood, the serpent's jaws wrapping around the nest in a sickening crunch as the pointed beam pierced its palate. Blood rained from the broken mast, spilling down the white canvas in scarlet streaks. The momentum of his body leaping towards the main mast sent it arching over the vessel, landing in the ocean on the other side, its scaly tail landing with a loud splash. But the sea remained undisturbed.

The elfin heaved a sigh of relief and turned towards her, offering his hand to help her up. "That was brilliant, Ailsa. But gods below, don't ever use yourself as bait again."

Lightning streaked the silver storm behind him. The sheer power of its light made her wince. Through the slits in her eyes, she saw a burst of energy strike the foremast, splitting straight through the beam. The fractured mast groaned started tipping towards them.

"*Look out!*" she shouted, but he did not hear her above the moaning of the wood as it fell, nor the sounds of the storm. She stood and rushed him, pushing him back and over the railing where they fell to the lower deck. The broken foremast narrowly missing them both.

She landed forcefully on the flat plane of her back. The air rushed from her chest, stolen from the fall. Her throat shut in on itself, and she couldn't take a breath no matter how much she needed it.

"Ailsa!" Above her golden eyes looked down, the only color alive left in the world. She clawed the wet skin exposed from his torn shirt, desperate for a drop of their life.

Vali only panicked; his lips parted as his eyes searched for an answer coded somewhere in her struggle. He placed a frozen hand on her chest, as if he were able to command the air to find its way inside her.

"Turn her on her side!" Ivor commanded, appearing out of nowhere. The elfin did as she said, and Ailsa curled into a ball to let the blood pool across her lungs. Her nails scratched the weathered floorboards of the deck as she used every ounce of her strength to focus on the hardest inhale of her life.

Sweet relief flooded her chest as her airway finally obeyed, letting in a strangled gasp that sounded more like a choke. She coughed in a fit after that first breath, spitting crimson that washed away in the harsh rain.

"I've got her," Ivor spat above her head. "Go manage your crew, fae filth. Get us away from the beast before it finds the strength to come back."

Vali did not listen to her, nor did he move right away. Only when she had taken several full breaths did he stand slowly, and she heard his footsteps run off to somewhere far from where she coiled.

Ivor drug her back to their cabin, concealing the storm behind a closed door. And she held Ailsa as she breathed, her tears hidden in the saltwater streaking her cheeks.

Only then did Ailsa let the void take her, falling into a deep sleep.

That night she dreamed of a blind crow.

15 Vali

The sea settled after he and Ailsa baited Jormungand into its own undoing. They didn't kill the monster, but they had injured its pride enough for it to sink into its home and nurse its wounds. Her plan prevailed, buying them time to escape the heart of the storm and continue to the Edge.

Repairs were already in progress, the crew using their magic to seal the sails. He did not worry about the ship nor crossing the border of this realm in its weakened state, but another thought troubled his mind—the reason for the damage. Ailsa had not emerged from her cabin since the wolven drug her inside, and he was resisting the overwhelming desire to check on her.

But she was not his to worry about, and he remained in his chair, drowning away his impulses with the help of his commander.

"Are you all right, Vali?" Seela sat in his cabin, assisting him in draining a small barrel of barely good mead. "You look like you haven't slept for three summers."

Vali shook his head, clearing his thoughts of the mortal woman who had enthralled him on a level he was uncomfortable with. "I'm fine. Have the spirits sent you any word of home?"

"Not a whisper. I don't know whether that is good news or bad."

"They have been silent for me as well. I haven't heard anything since that woman boarded this ship."

Seela sipped audibly from the tankard before setting it down in her lap. "Perhaps they are afraid of her."

"I'm afraid of her," he admitted, matching her drinking pace. "Jormungand gave us no trouble when we arrived, yet almost tore us apart to get to her. There will be more to fear than sea serpents when we leave this realm."

Her lips pinched, souring his expression. "Perhaps those with Aesir blood are simply drawn to the power inside her the same way you are, Vali. Even monsters can descend from gods as you know all too well." She leaned back in the leather armchair, worn for long conversations such as this one. "No, Vali. You are not afraid of *her.* You are afraid of what she makes you feel."

He spit half a sip of mead across his desk, specking his papers with dark brown stains. "You mean frustration? Irritation—"

"Attraction, intrigue—"

"Enough! You're going to make me ill," he mumbled. Though her marks were not far off. But there wasn't enough ale in this world for that conversation. "She is a thorn in my side. Nothing more."

"Yes, and I was born yesterday." Her lips puckered in disbelief. "Do not lie to me. I see the way you steal looks at her when you think no one's watching. Just remember, I always am."

His fingers played with the flame from the candle, feigning disinterest. "I prefer you better when you're my commander."

"But I'm of better use to you when I'm your friend." Her gaze on him softened significantly. "We've been together for more than fifty years, Vali. You cannot hide from me. But you need to be careful. I've seen that look in your eyes before, and we both know how that ended."

"That is wonderful counsel, Seela. Save it for when I actually need it." His hands smoothed over the map of the Tree of Life, outlined with the paths twisting through the branches. The sea would transition into shallow rivers once they passed the way to Asgard, and they would follow the streams feeding the High Branches all the way to his home.

Seela sighed and shrugged one shoulder. "Look, I completely understand. She is quite pretty when she isn't being so disagreeable. And her wolven..."

"Seela," he groaned. He needed her to stop talking.

Her laugh was like a spring of joy, filling the room with its light. "Relax, I'm only teasing because it is refreshing to talk about something other than the Tether. Besides, she doesn't even like you."

"Impossible. Everyone likes me," he said with a tilt of his chin.

"Not when you kill their fathers." Seela stood from her armchair and took a moment to study him, and he ignored her concern like the rest of their conversation. "I'm worried, Vali. I fear the sea serpent won't be the only beast that senses her magic, and the worst is still ahead of us."

"We can only give her to the Aesir and pray it is enough."

Her eyes traced his chest, as if she could still see the heart behind the cage of his ribs. "It is never enough."

Vali knew this to be true. The gods were known to be fickle with their side of a deal, his father the worst of them all. But after the mess he had made, after all he lost, this woman and the power inside her was the only chance he had left at redemption. There was nothing more important, nothing to stand in his way.

He watched his commander leave the room, a little of her light leaving with her. Seela had been by his side since they were old enough to train for this mission. But unlike him, her participation had been voluntary. He was the only tortured soul on this ship who had no choice but to be here, whose destiny was written as clear as the runes on his skin.

Vali the Heartless would become *Vali the Redeemer.* He would be written in the Halls of Alfheim for his services. His history was being decided each day, and he would make sure the Nine Realms remembered him as someone worth celebrating.

He stood from his chair, the legs sending a harsh sound across his cabin, and left to check on his one last shot at redemption.

"WHAT ARE YOU DOING?" he asked.

Ailsa was still resting. Her face softened under the guise of sleep, the tension often set in her jaw relaxed and left someone more youthful in her place. Ivor laid her bare beneath layers of blankets, her dark hair combed neatly in gentle waves across the ivory pillow. He watched the rise and fall of her chest, the simple motion lulling him into a trance.

"Her breathing treatment. She usually smokes it, but I've seen her father do this after one of her more vicious fits. She has been ignoring her routines with all the excitement, and her lungs have borne the consequences."

Ivor was burning a combination of herbs wrapped in

incense paper and blazing on one tip. It was a delicious smell, opening his senses immediately, familiar but unplaceable. Lavender, eucalyptus, a mention of mint, the heady spice of cedar. He realized then it was Ailsa's smell, the scent she wore like a perfume.

The wolven swirled the smoke around her head, creating twisting silver tendrils that fell and kissed her skin. He watched them both in quiet observance, leaning against a darkened corner far from the bed.

"You look at her like she is a wounded animal," she said. Vali glanced at her, tearing his eyes from Ailsa. "She hates when people do that."

"What ails her?" he asked.

Ivor shrugged, continuing to spread the incense over the sleeping woman. "I've heard her family call it *The Drowning.* But no one knows exactly. It is a condition she only shares with her mother's line. Manageable, but she gets sick very easily. She's lived much of her life in isolation, as her father was too afraid to let her go to foreign lands with their strange diseases."

"Her mother has passed, I am assuming?"

Ivor nodded, placing the burning paper on a wet towel next to the bed. "She died when she was a few years older than Ailsa now, around her twenty-ninth year. It was before I came around and they never spoke about her much."

Vali sat on the leather couch sitting beneath the cabin's lone window. Ivor arched her brow in his direction as he made himself comfortable. "So, she's alone? No husband or partner?"

"She has me," the wolven clipped. "But no, she was not wed. No man wanted to *weaken* their family line seeing as her condition is hereditary, and her father was very particular about the men who came around his daughters."

Vali's breath sang between his teeth. "Like there is anything to weaken in the first place." The way she faced him on the shores of her home, the look in her eyes when a sea monster was staring back—she was viciously brave. Terrifyingly so, even if her bravery bordered on reckless.

"For once, I agree with you," Ivor mumbled as she rolled up the rest of the herbs. "Why are you here?"

He bit the inside of his lip, pondering the same. "I wanted to make sure she was all right. She must be kept safe and *alive* until the gods are able to unbind the power from her. If she dies, it loses its Tether, and could be lost for another century."

The wolven snorted. "Of course, the *Tether*. I should have known your motives were purely selfish."

He replied with a dry laugh. "I've spent most of my long life searching for this, Ivor. I'm not letting her out of my sight. Too many have died for this moment to let her slip away."

Ivor slammed the rolled pack on top of the dresser with impatience. "And what of her life? Do not pretend this will end well for Ailsa."

He surrendered from the disdain in her gaze, knowing her hatred was validated. But this was no longer something he could control, and he would not add Ailsa to his already long list of things to be ashamed of. "I do not know how it will end for her, but it was not my choice to bind the power to her. She sealed her own fate, and I will not alter my own plans because of it."

Ailsa roused in her sleep, catching his eye. Her skin tone had warmed from sitting in the nest the past few days, turning it into a deep tan that, combined with her dark hair, made her appear all the more exotic. The delicate arches of her cheekbones and the point of her nose were slightly burned, providing a kiss of color to her flawless complexion. At any moment now, she could stir in her dreams and the sheets might fall a little lower. The thought sent his imagination reeling.

Vali smoothed his palms down his thighs and stood, suddenly feeling the need to do anything but remain in this room. The smoke from the incense was starting to make him lightheaded. "Just tell her when she wakes… tell her thank you for me. For what she did today. It was completely ridiculous and reckless, but she saved us all."

"You're welcome," Ailsa mumbled. A smug smile pressed across her lips. Her eye peeked open, and she trapped a giggle forming in her throat. Vali's cheeks colored, realizing she had been faking her slumber this entire time.

"Oh, good," he said flatly. "You're awake."

"Any more monsters I need to slay for you, Captain?" She stretched, and the blanket fell slightly from her shoulders, revealing an expanse of honey sweet skin that did not help the blood clear from his cheeks.

"Plenty to come, Jarl Ailsa." Before he slipped out the door he said, "We'll be coming up on the Edge soon, so if I were you, I'd get dressed and meet me on deck."

16
AILSA

The Edge of the World was a place where Midgard met the void between realms, where the Tree connected them all and filled the space with its cosmic passage. Every man, whether it was their shift or not, lined the edges of the ship. Ailsa and Ivor stood near the front, meeting Vali and Seela as the pair stood on either side of the dragon figurehead, daring the way ahead.

The sun had not risen despite the moon setting. The sky was darker than she'd ever seen before, more stars numbered above, and she felt so close to the cosmos she could feel their starlight warm on her face. The ocean stilled into a glossy black mirror, reflecting the constellations so precisely Ailsa couldn't tell where the water stopped, and the sky began. They were no longer sailing—but flying.

"Ailsa," Seela whispered. Her silver hair practically glowed in the moonlight. She beckoned to join her near the bow, giving them both an extensive view of The Edge.

About a hundred meters from where the ship drifted, the still ocean was disturbed by a great fall, a turbulent force of water rushing over the end of the world and into an abyss. Ivor dug her nails into the wooden flesh of the boat, her eyes widening as they looked upon The Edge of the World.

"That's not what it looks like, is it?" Ailsa muttered to the elfin commander. Seela smirked.

"You mean a giant waterfall that will most likely reduce this ship to splinters should we traverse over its edge? That is precisely what it is."

"Then why are we sailing *toward* it?"

"Relax, Jarl Ailsa. It is much easier to show you than to explain with words."

"Show me what exactly?" she hissed. But Seela was looking beyond her now, and Ailsa had no choice but to watch helplessly as they drew closer to the fall, clinging to Ivor and the railing in a vain attempt to prepare herself.

The elves whispered behind her. Their voices were soft yet joined together to form a dull roar. She could not make out their words, only that the language was cryptic and vaguely similar to the ancient language of the gods.

She turned to see Vali standing in the middle of the deck, his lips muttering the same words as his companions. But he was separated from the fae lining the perimeter. And while the other men were still, his hands were outstretched, palms facing the sky. The skin beneath his linen shirt glowed, the inky runes she skimmed just days before with her fingers now shining like molten gold.

He was mystical, standing there in an ethereal glow, dark hair tousled gently by the building breeze. How such a beast could survive inside a cage as beautiful as the one containing Vali was lost on her. Eventually, a monster would have to scratch or blemish its enclosure, revealing a hint of the kind lying inside. But with him, it wasn't so. He was perfect on the outside, completely unscathed by the dangerous soul festering behind his faultless complexion.

The wind picked back up, combining with the violent sound of rushing water falling from the face of the earth and rumbling against the quiet. She dared one more look to the horizon, the glossy top of the sea now churning over the jagged rocks mutilating the face of the Edge.

Her wide stare glanced at Ivor, but the wolven had already shut her eyes, refusing to watch for another moment. She clutched the railing and hung her head as if she were going to be sick.

"Seela, we're going to go over the Edge! Have you fae completely lost your minds?" she all but shrieked over the roar of the ocean falling into space beyond them. But Seela appeared to be in a trance, her gaze remaining fixed and motionless. Even Vali was now glowing like a torch in the night and similarly distracted.

Ailsa only had time to betray a small squeal as the ship groaned, slightly tipping forward. She used both arms to clutch the handrailing as the boat met free air, her view now completely swallowed by a realm of nothingness.

There was a splitting snap like lightning, and the sky above them and below bled into crimson. From black to red, the world bathed in a bloody filter until fading into a spectrum of colors. Each time she blinked they came into clearer focus—the outline of the river, the shades of green forming a landscape, the muted grey sketch of distant mountains.

Her mind reeled with explanations, how in the few blinks of her eyes they had fallen seamlessly into a different place, a different realm entirely. The air was lighter, laced with a humming sensation she could only articulate as pure magic. A small star above burned light across the river lined by wilderness on each side. Wherever they had landed, they were no longer in Midgard.

The realization struck Ailsa cold in the heart. She gripped the handrail when her head started to lighten, the skin over her knuckles stretching against the tension and blanching white. She heard someone call her name behind her, muffled like she was under water, before her knees gave out. The vibrant world glazed over as the back of her skull hit the deck and stars clouded her vision, darkness tailing their brilliance.

"AILSA, WAKE UP!"

Ivor's voice was followed by a gentle shake. Ailsa's eyes fluttered open, and she found herself back in her cabin, the back of her head throbbing obnoxiously. She groaned, sitting up, and gingerly touched the tender spot.

"What happened?"

"You passed out after we crossed over, and Vali carried you back to the room."

Ailsa blinked Ivor into better focus. "Vali *carried* me? You let him touch me?" The idea of the elfin with his hands on her body, her face against his chest. It was enough to make a part of her heart twitch with an annoying flutter.

"Never mind him." Ivor waved the thought away. "We docked twenty minutes ago. Everyone's waiting for us to get off. I've already packed our things."

"We've docked? Where?" she asked, throwing her legs over the side of the bed. Forgetting Vali with the promise of seeing land again.

"Oh, as if anyone told the wolven! Enough questions. Let's go see for ourselves."

Ivor carried both their bags, as Ailsa was still feeling dizzy from the fall. The elves regarded her with not-so-subtle amusement as she crossed the ship to the docking port, and she paid careful mind not to touch the sore spot on the back of her skull. Sorrin stood near the gangplank taking stock of the wares being toted off by the crew, while Seela and Vali stood off to the side. Feeling the weight of her stare, his eyes found hers.

"How's your head?" he asked, crossing the width of the ship.

"Fine." Ailsa looked past him to gain a glimpse of where they docked. A heavy mist settled over the landscape, obscuring the details. "Where are we?"

"Everywhere and nowhere, all at once." He spread his arms wide, gesturing to the milky world beyond. The forest green cloak he wore flared at the bottom and skimmed the top of his leather boots, gold leafing threaded over the shoulders in an immaculate design. He replaced his sea attire with unnervingly tight pants and a black tunic. The neckline was cut into a deep V, revealing short-lived peeks of his bare chest and the hard lines defining him. "We are still in the Lower Branches. The river from the trunk of the Tree thins into smaller underground springs where it feeds into the Highest, so we are unable to travel by ship from here. The wells supplying the Tree and all the Nine Realms flow through these rivers, and we will follow them until we reach the fae realms."

"On foot?" Ailsa replied dryly. It was difficult to climb her humble cliff side, much less trek the wilderness of the World Tree. There were tales of monsters who roamed the Realm Hidden Between Realms, and with little but Vali to protect her, she felt more exposed out here than she did in the Great Sea.

"It is not a far journey—a few days at most. We will take our time and rest as often as you need."

"You mean as often as we *can*." Seela approached their small group, her lavender eyes falling on Ivor as she spoke. "Not even I want to be in the wilderness of the Lower Branches longer than necessary. It is said the Tree speaks to those who walk between worlds, and it is not kind to those who listen."

"Well, the heathen should be just fine then," Vali muttered before reaching into a fold in his coat. He pulled out the gilded dagger she had used to stab him and offered it to her. "Take it," he said when she did nothing but stare.

She tentatively reached for the dagger, now sheathed in a holster with leather straps. "Why are you giving me this?"

"Just in case you need it. I cannot leave you defenseless."

Ailsa flipped the weapon in between her fingers, testing the weight. "And you trust me not to use this on you?"

This made him smirk, and she despised that no matter what she said, it always seemed to amuse him. "I'm counting on it, Jarl Ailsa. If anyone can discover how to put me out of my misery, it'll be you."

"What do you mean?" she asked. But he had already turned his back to her, his commander at his heels.

"Strange, those two. Always together," Ivor muttered.

Ailsa nodded. "Do you think they're..."

"*Together*? Definitely not."

"How do you know?"

Ivor dipped her chin, her umber cheeks warming into copper. "Because Vali is not her type. Let's go before they leave us behind."

Ailsa scoffed and flipped a heavy wave of her hair over her shoulder. "And forget his precious Tether? I think not."

Ivor carried both their bags over her broad shoulders. "You

and Vali seem to be warming up to each other. He used to look at you like you were injured. Now he looks at you like you're a meal. He even smells different."

"What are you talking about?" Ailsa laughed off her concern, but Ivor's face remained hard as stone.

"Everyone has a scent, *systir*, and they change depending on a person's intentions. I can tell when someone is friend or foe by the hostility they emit through their smell alone. When Nikros was around, I could sense his lust for you, as well as Erik's desire and your father's bloody ambition. Your sisters were always joyful and liberating. Vali initially smelled like something rotten and musty, like vengeance but fouler. Now, he smells... like the first blooms of spring. A scent I am unfamiliar with."

Ailsa shook her head and stepped up to the gangplank, taking in a sight no mortal had ever had the privilege of witnessing. Even shrouded in mist, the Realm Between Realms was too beautiful for the finite words in her mind to articulate. There was a mystery here that was searching, reaching for her. Like she was always meant to find this place.

"Perhaps the elfin just took a bath, Ivor." Ailsa failed to see the significance in the way someone smelled. Besides, there was no going back now. She'd been at his mercy since the day he threatened her people. At least helping him kept them all safe from his wrath, made him return to his world and keep him out of her own.

"I'm warning you, Ailsa. His objectives are changing—"

"His objectives do not matter. Like he said the other day in the cabin, he needs me alive to carry this power, or I would probably be dead on the shores of Drakame. I have nothing to fear from him but his golden glare."

Ivor tugged her back from the plank, pulling her close.

"Intentions and motivations always matter. Do you value your life so little you will follow him without question?"

Ailsa swallowed, her throat suddenly bone-dry. "What choice do I have, Ivor? I can't go home now. We must see this through. Besides, I have a plan when I see the gods."

"Oh?" Ivor's brow arched. "What did you have in mind?"

She turned to face the wolven as the last fae filtered from the deck. "If I live after they take this power, I want to be healed. If I die, as Vali is inclined to believe, I want to see my mother again. I want her and my family forever in Valhalla together, even if they must drag her out of Helheim themselves. If I'm forced to do this, I'm going to get something out of it myself." Her name was called somewhere on the grassy shore, beckoning them to hurry. "Besides, I'm getting what I've always wanted."

"What is that?"

Ailsa looked out into the Realm Between Realms and smiled. "An adventure."

THEY TRAVELED IN A COMPANY, with Vali leading the way and Seela bringing up the rear. Like Ailsa, they were each armed, even Ivor had been given a small blade she strapped around a muscular thigh. The fae pulled carts of supplies using their magic, resorting to manual labor when the drain became too much. She watched as Sorrin pushed off one of the carts, clutching his lower back as a grimace struck his fine features.

She quickened her pace to catch up to him. "Sorrin? Are you all right?"

He straightened quickly and walked it off as if nothing had

happened. "Oh, Miss Ailsa, of course. I'm just fine. Don't fret over me, my backside just isn't used to this kind of labor now that I'm nearing my second century."

Two centuries! He looked no older than his early thirties. The fae, to her annoyance, had eternal beauty going for them as well. "Nonsense. Come find me when we stop. I have something that might help if your special elfin skin will let it penetrate."

He sighed, noting the decision in her voice, and halfheartedly nodded. Sorrin had unintentionally nuzzled into a softer place beneath her heart, reminding her of Obrecht, the blacksmith back in Drakame. It was hard to imagine a warrior past the steel gray eyes that pinched every time he laughed at her endless teasing, or the bone white hair always neatly combed down his back. He was endearing to her and her only companion in this company, besides Ivor.

He kept his promise a time later when Ailsa's audible breathing prompted Vali to break the line. She found a nearby tree to prop her weight against while Ivor brought her things.

"Pipe?"

"No, just the oil will be fine. Thank you," she managed between breaths. They had traveled into a dense wood. The fog was heavy here, so thick the light only filtered through the frayed canopy of the trees, revealing only a few meters deep into the edges of their camp.

She massaged a drop of oil across her sternum, feeling the effects with every rise of her chest. Sorrin coughed uncomfortably and pretended to be engrossed by the foliage.

"I'm fine, Miss Ailsa. Please, I'd hate to use up your herbs—"

"Lay on your stomach."

"Pardon?"

Ailsa's lips twitched. The fae were much different from

her people. They were modest despite their loose tongues, and each male seemed to take a personal offense when she brushed them unintentionally. In contrast, there was little of her clan she hadn't seen, being the only healer on the channel, and she had stripped in front of Erik too many times to count.

But they were similar in that they liked to keep secrets.

"I'm just going to spread a tincture I've concocted from a special blend I discovered a few years ago. Trust me when I say I have plenty of experience in healing overworked bodies." She gestured to the carpet of grass, and he obeyed. But she felt the eyes of his subordinates watching them as she lifted the back of his shirt and spread the oil base across his skin. Her thumb traced small circles against the muscles that tensed beneath her touch until he finally relaxed and melted against her bewitching hands.

"Are you happy to be going home, Sorrin?" she asked.

The elfin tensed again. "Happy does not quite do my heart justice. But yes, we are all very much looking forward to seeing Alfheim again."

"How long has it been?"

"A little over fifty years, I believe. I've spent a third of my life on this adventure."

Her fingers pressed into the spaces lining his spine, and he squirmed. "Anyone special waiting for you?"

This made all the tension in his body melt away. "Yes, my daughters. I left when they had just turned the quarter of their first century. They'll be nearing their third quarter now, and I cannot wait to see what they've accomplished while I've been gone."

She wanted to ask of their mother, but thought it better to save that conversation for another day. "Why did you leave? It must have been a good reason for you to leave your family with no idea of when you'd return."

"Because I believe in Vali. I believe in who he is and will serve him until my dying breath should it come to it. My daughters understand, and if they did not before, I'm sure they do now."

Ailsa paused her work and sat back on her heels. Sorrin was a good man. She could sense the genuine spirit that clung to him like an aura. To her, Vali was a monster, a murderer who had brought his men from a distant realm to slay her countrymen and steal the last years of her life. But to a male like Sorrin he was worth leaving behind his family, his entire life.

Who is Vali to demand such loyalty?

Sorrin pushed up to his knees and sat beside her in the cool grass, somehow sensing she needed a lift. "We are sorry for what happened between the elven and your clansmen. Your people were innocent and simply caught in the crossfire of something much bigger."

"And what of me? Will I be another nameless soul that was simply caught in the crossfire? Will I have to die as someone else's martyr?"

He released an uneasy breath. "I do not know, Jarl Ailsa. These things have never happened before in our history, we do not know—"

"You are a terrible liar." She spat as she stood from her seat in the grass and wiped her hands clean on a towel hanging from her waistband.

"What? I'm not... I only mean—"

"How would you feel if it was *your* daughter?" she interrupted him. "What if it was one of your own in my place? Would you escort her to her own grave? You all know something I do not. I hear the whispers when I pass, the pointed stares, the condescending smirks from your *captain.* I'm nothing but another casualty of your cause, and you won't even tell me what that is!"

"Keep your voice down," he warned, his finger raised to his lips. "The woods are listening, Ailsa."

"At least *something* is listening to me."

"What's going on over here?"

Ailsa's shoulders fell at the sound of his voice. She tidied the rest of her herbs into her bag and drained the rest of her canteen before answering him. "Just helping your officer with his injury."

"How benevolent of you," Vali said, his voice tight. "I'm sure you had no ulterior motives."

"None whatsoever," she replied tersely. His hand gripped her forearm as she turned to leave them both. She glared back at him, and he matched her look with an equal fierceness. "Let go of me."

"What is your problem?" he asked, voice deep like a growl.

"My *problem?* You aren't seriously asking me what I could possibly be upset about!"

Vali squinted his eyes, as if trying to peer into her mind. "This is hardly the time or the place to discuss the things you want to know, Ailsa." His grip on her was strangling now. "I am asking you, *please,* to drop the subject for now. When we are in the fae realms, we will be safe to speak of it."

"And you will tell me everything?"

He nodded only once. Ailsa sighed, frustrated. But the look in his gilded gaze was brimming with something she had not seen in them before.

Fear.

He was threatened by these woodlands, of who or what the

trees spoke to regarding the travelers beneath their lacing branches. She couldn't fight the way her eyes shifted towards the blackness lingering behind the scattered trunks, feeling the triggering sensation of being watched. She twisted out of his crushing fingers, now cutting off her circulation, and set her jaw.

"Fine," she whispered. Because she had never seen him afraid of anything, and if a fae with his power feared the forest, then she would be wise to as well.

And Vali never asked for anything, much less used the word *please.*

He relaxed then, seeing she finally grasped the seriousness of their situation. Ailsa was a simple woman from a simple place, where nothing was life or death, and the most danger she'd ever been in was when she'd gone cliff diving when the waters were still frigid from the spring melt-off.

"Well, if you have enough breath to banter, then you have enough to walk. Let's go."

She scowled at the back of his head and pulled the strap of her bag up higher on her shoulder. But just as she took a step to follow him, a sound slithered over her shoulder.

They know. And they are coming.

Her steps paused mid-stride; an icy chill swept down her spine. The voice was clear as if someone had spoken right beside her. "Did you hear that?" she said. Vali spun sharply on a heel, her eyes wide on him.

"Hear what?" he asked.

"The voice," she said, turning around to stare into the edge of the woods lined just a few strides behind her. But there was no one there.

"What did it say?" Vali's words were slow, careful.

"They… they know. And they're coming," she repeated.

He stepped silently behind her, reaching a hand around her waist to unhook the strap holding her blade in its sheath. "Who, Ailsa?"

She didn't know, but she didn't have to. The trembling of the earth from a hundred hooves answered him instead.

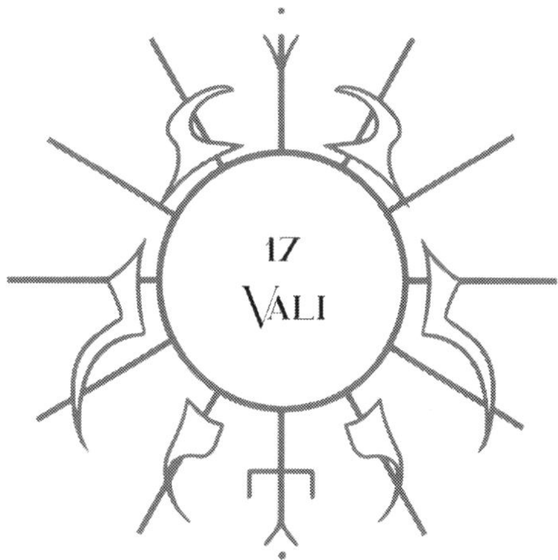

17 Vali

If dread was a sound, it would be the approach of the Vanir. Vali stepped away from Ailsa, unsheathing the longsword at his hip. The screech of blade against sheath echoed across the camp as his soldiers did the same, falling into a staggered line. He pulled the woman close behind him, shoving her into Seela's arms, who appeared with the wolven trekking behind.

"Watch her," he said in a loud whisper. "And if things go south, take Ailsa and run. Do not let the Vanir know about her." He then lowered his face to the mortal, who was clutching the gilded dagger against her chest.

"What's happening?" she asked.

"The Vanir have been tipped off about our arrival. Ailsa, this is imperative." His eyes shifted to the trees, and he lowered his voice so only she could hear. "You *must* not let them know your secret. No matter how frightened you are, no matter what you see, stay in control. And if Seela tells you to run, you must promise me you'll run as far as you are physically able."

She gave him no stubborn reply, but nodded slowly. And even as he warned her, the markings on her throat flickered awake, burning gold and then a fiery orange. His own flesh was triggered, his magic lurched beneath his skin to connect with the source of her own. She felt like a bottomless well and his power was parched.

"Are they…looking for me?" She craned her neck to mutter the words into his neck. He dipped his chin in a nod. "How will you find me if I run? What if I get lost in there forever?"

He reached for her arm to calm her, skimming her shoulder with a hesitant palm before drawing back. Her skin was warm, pleasing, and the magic beneath it shuddered through her flesh. "I will always find you, Ailsa. There is no place in the Nine Realms or the space between too far for me to find you."

Something about his words made her markings dull into black, feeling safe again, leaving the runes seemingly burned into her amber skin. He followed the runes down her neck, wondering how far they crawled down her chest, until Vali's gaze caught on the ring dangling on a thin silver chain. The ancient code of creation still engraved in the metal.

"Can I borrow your ring?" he asked.

"What?" she said, her voice sharp enough to make him wince.

"I might be able to trick Njord. Perhaps he will take it and spare us all."

Ailsa's hand covered it from my sight. "You asked for it once, and the answer is still no. Why should I help you anymore than I already am?"

The earth was humming now, the Vanir were so close. Becoming desperate, he placed his hands on top of her shoulders, feeling her bones sharp beneath her skin. She flinched at his touch. "Ailsa, there are worse hands you can fall into than mine." Vali licked his lips, seeing the doubt still narrow in her gaze. "And because this time I am *asking*."

With a sigh that heaved her shoulders into his palms, she

swatted his arms away and turned her back to him. He thought she would refuse again until she motioned to the clasp. "Take it, then. Before I change my mind."

"Thank you, Ailsa," he whispered into the shell of her ear. His hand brushed her hair to the side, disturbing the scent locked in their strands and hitting him with her aroma. With the quietest of breaths, he breathed her in like a long drag, letting her smell poke something inside him that had been neglected for far too long. As his fingers fumbled with the tiny clasp, he skimmed the chill bumps crawling up her spine.

With the ring now in his hand, still warm from her body, Vali took several deliberate steps back, nodded to Seela, and left them behind. He found his place on the front line and waited for the Vanir to spill out of the mist.

Three black boars with their riders emerged first, the rest concealed so Vali was ignorant of their number. Clad in a deep blue that reminded him of the deepest part of the ocean, the leader of the Vanir, Njord, pulled his beast to where Vali stood in front of his men while he dismounted without a word, removing his helmet in a languid movement.

The god smiled through a long white beard that covered his chest. "Well, if it isn't *Vali the Heartless*. It's been so long, dear friend."

"So long I must have forgotten we were friends."

Njord laughed. The bristling sound echoed even through the blanket of mist. "It has taken you so long to complete such a simple task, Vali. Surely you didn't mean to keep your people waiting in their oppression—"

"It is not your concern what I've been doing or what I've done," he spat. Njord took a step forward, disregarding the longsword poised at his side.

"Considering you have what belongs to the Vanir, I'd say it

is very much my concern. Word is you're going home, and that would mean you have the Tether."

His eyes narrowed on the god. "And do you mean to stop me from completing my task?"

Metal clipped from inside the fog, and the dread in Vali's stomach faded into an aching fear. The god only shrugged. "I don't care what your task is. I don't care if you need it to save your people. I will not give away Vanirian power just so you can use it to barter your freedom."

"And if I do not give it to you?"

Njord's brows rose on his structured face. His blue eyes sparkled with interest. "Then I will take it back by force."

Vali looked back at his men, feigning deliberation. With a theatrical sigh, he reached into his cloak and pulled out Ailsa's ring. He stored a bit of his magic inside the vessel, hoping it was enough to fool the god of wind and sea.

"What is this?"

"It is the Tether. I found it in the far reaches of Midgard." A half-truth.

"Midgard? What was it doing there?"

This time Vali scoffed. "Hel if I know. Do you think I'd go to Midgard if I didn't have to?"

Njord mumbled something in agreement as he fumbled with the ring. He traced the runes with a long finger, trying to decipher the meaning. "What are these runes? I've never seen anything like them."

"They were written from the forbidden language of creation, the knowledge from Gullveig's power. That is the only explanation I've been able to rationalize. I believe these markings keep it contained as it waits for its master to take it back."

The god smiled and spun the tip of a sharp edge on his

thumb. "Nice work, Vali. It seems you're not as useless as your father claims you to be."

Vali tried not to wince, but he was not expecting the blow to his pride—nor was he expecting the blow to his heart.

Njord had tossed the ring and, in the same motion, manifested a blade in the same hand. He thrust the sword through Vali's chest, just to the left of his sternum. Vali had no time to react, only endure the terrible squeeze of his muscles as they tensed around the metal in his chest. His throat filled with blood and spilled from his lips in a strangled gurgle.

"I bet you don't even feel this, do you?" Njord whispered in his ear as he twisted the blade. "You are an abomination and a liar, not worthy of the blood in your veins."

A tiny gasp broke through the sound of his choking. Through the dark haze filtering his vision, he saw the god turn his gaze to the sound, a slow grin creeped across his lips. Vali fell to his knees as Njord pulled the sword from his chest, a shiny new object stealing his attention.

Ailsa stood partially concealed by the furthermost soldier, watching the scene unfold with a front row view. If he had time to be angry, he would have burned her to ash with his rage, but anger was not the feeling that consumed his suffering thoughts.

A panic unlike any he had ever felt before struck his core, delivering him new strength. He scrambled for the longsword he dropped and jumped to his feet, slashing the god's back before he could get anywhere close to her.

Njord screeched in a painful surprise, arching his back as the blade lacerated the soft, unarmored skin over his shoulder blades. He turned back to Vali with a fresh anger fueling his fight, giving Ailsa the time she needed to flee.

"Go!" he shouted at her when she stood there, paralyzed by

either fear or concern. Her eyes glistened like starlight as they connected with his, stealing one last look at his tortured soul before turning on her back heel.

He didn't look away until she faded into the mist.

Go!

Vali sprinkled the ground with blood as he spat the command. Ailsa did not want to run, she wanted to fight. She wanted to stop the bloodshed and the slaughter, the wasted death following the Tether like a crimson shadow. But most of all, she wanted to reach inside herself and pull out a cord of the power stretching beneath her flesh and let it sing for them.

She *wanted* to help him.

Ailsa slipped away from Seela when the elfin was adjusting the strap of her weapon. It was only a moment, but it was all she needed to slide away unnoticed. She rounded the border of fae who noticed her too late to react and stood just on the edge of the front line, allowing a clear view of Vali and the intruders.

He had not earned her trust, and because of this she took her safety into her own hands. Her people worshiped the Vanir gods, sacrificed and built altars in their name. For thousands of years, they placed their lives in the hands of the same god she saw before her, and she saw no reason to run and abandon them now based on the unjustified words of an elfin.

But everything changed when she saw him skewered on the god's blade.

He made a final, desperate attempt to steal back the god's attention. His movements were clumsy and staggered, each step requiring an energy of which he had been depleted. But he stood on graceless feet, his inky hair draping over a bleeding scowl, and fought back to buy her more time.

So, she did the only thing she could do for him—she ran.

The mist was a thick fog concealing anything more than a few feet in front of her face as she broke through the hazy wall surrounding them. She took a few practiced strides before finding her footing among the thick ropes of roots sprawling the earth and sprinted between the trees, dodging pale trunks only seconds after they came into sight.

She ran until her hair and dress were damp with dew and her heart was beating blood faster than she was conditioned to tolerate. When her lungs demanded she pause, she claimed one of the countless ash trees and sucked the air down, her chest starved. The wood was deadly quiet inside the obscurity of the mist, the sounds of her labored breaths exaggerated by the silence.

Another sound broke the quiet, a hiss before a splintering thud. Her reprieve was shortened by an arrow piercing the flesh of the trunk beside her. Ailsa stared at the arrow, her eyes widening with dread, and darted in the opposite direction.

Voices muffled close behind her, following her every turn and outmatching her pace. She willed her legs to run faster but they screamed their refusal, her bones eventually turning to stone and weighing down her strides. Her foot caught on a reaching root, and Ailsa tumbled through the fog.

She landed hard on her stomach, her palms and cheek

grazing a web of tangled roots. The dagger in her hand clattered somewhere beneath the haze. Ignoring the burning pain from the scratches marring her skin, she pushed off the ground and continued to scramble. The voices nearly upon her now.

Her dress snagged as she crawled, and she looked back to see one of the Vanir soldiers, his armor the same color as the god who stabbed Vali, but his face was hidden behind a silver veil. He stabbed the fabric of her gown with his sword and pinned her to the earth while a second soldier appeared from his shadow. This one with an arrow cocked in her direction.

"What do you want?" She kept her voice from trembling.

"Come," he only said.

Her palm slipped over something cold, as if the forest itself had slid her only weapon right beneath her fingertips. "What did you do to them?"

"The elves?" He scoffed, finding her concern humorous. "They will die. As you will if you do not listen, mortal. You do not belong here. This mist will swallow you whole and never let you out."

"I'm not going anywhere with you," she spat. The soldier reached down to snatch her arm but met the sharp edge of her blade instead.

He staggered back with a cry of surprise, tripping over the meshwork of roots. Ailsa used his distraction to pull her skirt through the sword pinning down her dress just as the second soldier set loose his arrow, nipping the exposed skin on her shoulder. She shrieked as it cut deep.

"That was a warning," the archer warned. "The next one will not miss."

Ailsa clutched her shoulder and pinched the skin back in

place, feeling warm blood seep between her fingers. "Kill me, then. Either way, you won't take me back alive."

The first soldier was back on his feet and pulling his sword from the earth. "Or I'll just cut off your limbs so you cannot flee or fight. I like that option better."

"I'm not sure," the second said, his arrow not dropping from the aim on her heart. "She made a compelling request."

The fog stirred behind them as they argued her fate, spitting out a single male who charged with a longsword carved high above his head. With a wild cry that shook the foundations of the Tree, the steel-eyed fae cut through the first soldier. The Vanir fell where he stood.

The second had time to release the arrow formerly intended for Ailsa, and it sank into the elfin's side. He staggered from the shot and mist curled around his legs.

"Sorrin!" she cried. Her hands scrambled for her dagger as she stood. The arrow did not wound the elfin greatly, for he was already recoiling his fighting arm to strike down the archer.

But Sorrin was too far, his charge would never meet the soldier where he stood. The second arrow left its quiver, and Ailsa could only watch as the Vanir pulled it against the taut bowstring. The soldier waited until Sorrin was coming straight for him, a clear view of his chest, before releasing the tension in the string.

A visceral scream tore through her body as she watched the arrow sink into the space above his heart. The anger boiled her blood hot, the runes marking her skin itched as her rage burned impossibly higher. She gripped the smooth hilt of the dagger against her palm—and let the power do her bidding.

She was on the soldier in a blink, her blade sheathed into the side of his throat. He uttered a choking cough as the hilt burned hot beneath her palm, the skin around its neck necrotizing and sloughing into ash. His arms went limp, the bow clattered to the ground as his knees buckled beneath the weight of his body. She pushed him off her blade, horrified at the sight of the Vanir withering away before her eyes, a deed committed by her own hands and the strange power breaking through her temper.

As the soldier slumped to the earth in a procession of clinking mail, a painful wheeze slipped beside her. The sound distracted her from what she had done and quenched the fire in her bones. The runes turned black once more.

"*Sorrin*!" She ran to his body now lying across the uneven terrain. The arrow still jutting from his chest. His eyes rolled lazily across her face as she placed his head in her lap, stroking his cheek with a bloody thumb.

"You are all right, Jarl Ailsa," he whispered. A small smile flickered across his lips.

"Thanks to you," she said. "How did you find me?"

"Simple. I just followed the trouble. It seems to follow you wherever you go," he grinned. But his eyes fluttered like he was falling asleep. "Njord ordered them to follow you into the mist, and I trailed behind them to make sure you were safe."

"But why? Why did you trade your life for mine?" *Because I am the Tether.* The only reason any of them were trying to protect her.

"Because if you were my daughter," he corrected her thoughts. "I'd hope someone would do the same."

Ailsa held back a horde of tears behind her eyes, and she shook her head at the elfin. "But your family... You were so close to seeing them again. No power inside of me could have been worth giving them up."

"Then *make* my sacrifice worth it, Ailsa. Make sure your

father, your sisters…" His breath caught in his throat, and he coughed back a wet sound. "All those who gave their life today. Make sure they did not die in vain."

"But how? I don't even know what I'm tethered to!" she argued, but her fight was silenced, feeling cold fingers cover her trembling hand.

"Trust Vali." Sorrin offered a tired smile.

Ailsa shook her head. "I hate him."

"No, you don't," he said. And although she wanted to protest, to remind Sorrin how much Vali had taken from her, she knew better than to argue with a dying man. He squeezed her hand gently in his own before speaking again. "Don't waste your days holding grudges. Hatred and anger drain us of precious moments, rob us of waiting joy. You have a good heart, Miss Ailsa, use it to see the best in others, even if they hide their goodness far beneath the surface."

"But the good could never outweigh the bad, Sorrin. It's too much—"

"Adversity is the heat that forges the strongest bonds. Good luck. And tell my girls I'll be in the Light that surrounds them for eternity."

Ailsa held him until his breaths turned agonal and the life finally faded from his eyes, stroking his face some time after he passed. She pulled his head into her stomach and grieved him, letting her tears fall like rain into the earth and water the shrouded forest with her mourning. Only when she was drained of her grief did she slip from beneath his body. Ailsa hated leaving his body behind with the Vanir, but she had no choice. He belonged to the Tree now, and if she did not want to follow him into the afterlife, she needed to find her way back to Vali.

Trust Vali.

She would honor Sorrin's final wish, even if it went against every instinct in her body. And although he was a murderer and a whole host of unsavory things, he was all she had left. He was the only one who cared even a fraction of her life for the time being. As much as she hated to admit it, they shared a common goal—and now a common enemy.

She stumbled into the never-ending mist, hoping beyond the boundaries of her faith she was walking in the right direction. There were no landmarks marking the way back to Vali, only the desperate tug of her heart propelling her forward.

AFTER SEEMINGLY HOURS OF DRIFTING, Ailsa collapsed against a tree and pulled her knees into her chest. Her breaths were labored, a sharp whistle partnered each inhale. The blood on her hands was now sticky from the fog. A bitter cold from the dampness clung to her skin and seeped deep into her bones, and her leather shoes were starting to fray against the rough terrain.

She was scared, tired, starving, and hurt. She was lost in a completely different realm far beyond the only home she'd ever known. Her wolven was gone, the last family she had missing to her because of her impulsiveness. But she was too lost on her own, wandering aimlessly through the misty borders of the Tree of Life, to have the opportunity to think of anyone but herself.

Thoughts of her cliff side came to mind as she sat there against the ash tree, weeping tearless cries as the memories of

Erik and Ziggy—even Nikros—rushed through her mind. How simple her old life had been, where she never had to kill anyone and gods and fae were just words spoken over a bonfire after a late springtime feast. How ungrateful had she been for her boring life, thinking simplicity was insignificant.

This is what you asked for.

"Fuck you, forest," she answered the trees. "This is *not* what I asked the fates for when I said I wanted an adventure."

What you want and what you need are not one in the same.

"Oh, and I need *this?"* She gestured around herself.

You have great power within you, Ailsa Ledgersdottir. Stop standing in your own way.

Ailsa sighed and rested her head against the smooth grains of the trunk. She had officially hit rock bottom, arguing with a forest.

If you need help, ask for it.

She released a wicked laugh. "I need help!"

But the forest did not answer this time. She kicked a root with the heel of her flat and muttered a curse. "Some *help* you are."

A bird cawed in response.

This sound did not come from her mind, but from the canopy. Ailsa peered up at the branches linking above her and found a crow perched on the lowest limb. Its eyes bashed out, bleeding from the sockets and reminding her of the one she had dreamed of all those nights ago after fighting the sea serpent.

"A blind crow," she whispered in awe. The black bird cocked its head at her, cawed another obnoxious call, and suddenly stretched its wings to fly towards a distant branch still visible in the mist. The crow did not fly away, but peered back at her, as if waiting for her to follow.

She wiped her cheeks now stained with blood and salt and stumbled to her sore feet. Together they traveled through the mist draping the forest, and her hope redeemed a little more with every step.

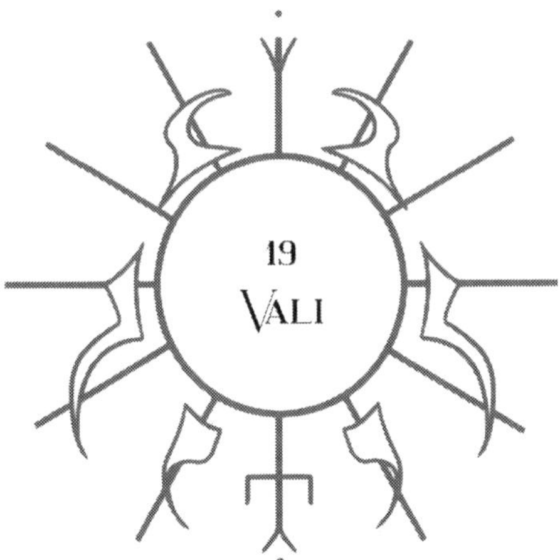

19
Vali

Vali stood over the remains of his crew; their bodies mixed with an equal number of Vanirian soldiers. He surveyed the waste. The blood of his kin now saturated the earth, stretching the width of the small clearing. The last thing he remembered were Njord's men following Ailsa into the mist, and the god shoved the hilt of his sword into Vali's skull, knocking him unconscious.

He awoke to the smell of open wounds and the stinging taste of copper on his tongue. The entire realm settled back into a quiet peace, as if hundreds of lives had not been ended in the last hours.

Vali sank to his knees and wailed into the quiet, disturbing the agonizing peace that irritated him beyond real words. He should have seen this coming, should have anticipated that the Vanir would try to stop him. He should have traveled smaller, taken an off-route path, set up a diversion. He should have done *anything* to prevent this.

He should have prevented this.

"This does not bring me satisfaction, Vali," a voice crept from the fog behind him.

Vali's knuckles blanched as he clenched his fists. "It didn't have to come to this."

Njord sighed. "No, it didn't. If you would have returned the Tether—"

"The Tether is not mine to give away!" He stood to his feet and spun to face the god. Njord faced him alone, his riding beast somewhere far behind a layer of haze.

"That's right, Vali. It isn't yours to give. It belongs to the Vanir, and the sooner you return it, the better. You are thinking about yourself and your people, but giving the Aesir the Tether will affect all the Nine Realms." Njord took a step back. "And you know this."

Vali said nothing, and Njord turned from him to disappear in the direction of Vanaheim. "You know where to find me when you change your mind, Vali."

He spent the rest of his time counting the bodies, naming each one in a specific prayer to the heavens, where the fae returned as rays of light. A small spark of hope flickered when he felt the pull of the Tether, his own magic catching her like a scent in the breeze. Ailsa was still out there, Seela and the others were not counted amongst the dead, and all was not lost just yet.

If there was still Ailsa, there was still hope.

"ODIN'S FUCKING EYE," he heard spoken through the mist. Foul words spoken by a voice soft as silk in sunlight.

Through the pale fog, her figure emerged, a dagger weakly hanging between her fingers, and her shoulders slumped from exhaustion. Ailsa's dress was torn, a crude slit ripped up to her upper thigh and flashed her legs as she walked. Her eyes were bloodshot from crying, her cheeks still damp from tears. They filled again with a kind of relief he never thought she'd regard him with.

"Vali!" Her voice broke. He realized it was the first time she'd ever said his name, and to hear it so affectionately sighed from her lips made the bleak day a little brighter.

She threw herself against him, wrapping her arms around his neck. He stumbled back, startled, but quickly caught her embrace. The events that transpired were heavy on his mind, and he didn't have the energy to question her advance or the implications of her body pressed against his chest. He simply held her back and let himself remain blissfully ignorant of how much her touch did something unexplainable inside him.

"I never thought you'd be happy to see me," he said.

"You try wandering a sea of mist for hours, believing you'd never see another soul again. You'd throw yourself at your most hated enemy as well."

"Thank you... I think."

She was thinner than she appeared. His hands discovered how much her clothes hid the way her skin hugged her form into tight curves. Her hair had fallen out of the tight braids she liked to weave, leaving messy, damp waves trailing down her back and skimming his arms now locked around her small waist. She smelled like a battle all on her own, and he wondered about the horrors she faced in this forest.

He pushed her back by her hips to look her over. "Are you all right? Are you hurt? You're covered in blood, Ailsa, gods below how are you walking—"

"Just a little is mine. Most of it is Vanir. And..." she flinched.

"And who?"

She bit down on her trembling lip. "Some of the blood is... is Sorrin's."

The name made the grief return. He had hoped for the best when he didn't see the officer's face in the field, but Ailsa's tears told him his worst fears had come true. "I'm sorry, Vali. It's my fault. You told me to stay out of sight and I didn't listen. He followed the Vanir who were chasing me—"

"He did his duty." Vali placed his hand beneath her chin to direct her gaze back to his. He could see the guilt plaguing her heart, the guilt that was rightfully his to bear. "This battle was unavoidable, and it is likely that Sorrin would have met his end even if he would not have gone after you. It is not your fault, and I certainly do not blame you for his death. Now, where are you hurt?" She motioned to her shoulder, grimacing as he gently skimmed the exposed flesh with his fingertips.

"That's a nice slice. May I heal you?"

"I'm fine. It's only a graze." Her eyes drifted to the hole in his chest, now gradually sealing shut as the day wore on. "How are you? Last I remembered, you were impaled."

"It's only a graze," he grinned, echoing her stubbornness.

Her stormy eyes widened at him before a graceless giggle slipped from her mouth. "Did you just make a joke?"

He smiled. "I'm heartless, Ailsa. I never joke."

She tamed her remaining bits of laughter with a firm hand across her mouth. She cleared her throat and took a deliberate step back, realizing how close she'd been standing. "I still hate you," she said, reminding him as much as herself.

"As you should," he replied. "But perhaps, just for tonight, you can hate me a little less." His hand reached for her without thinking, like his head was no longer in control of his body.

She glanced hesitantly at his outstretched arm. "I need to know who you are." The words came out slow. "I will not continue another step of this journey without knowing what I will face."

Vali swallowed a large breath, dissolving his resolve. If the Vanir were after them, gods knew what else they would face on the road to Alfheim. The Tree already knew his secrets, it seemed. "I will tell you everything you want to know."

Satisfied, she nodded and accepted his hand. He pulled her in the opposite direction of the clearing where the bodies still piled, venturing deeper into the forest where they could rest for the night and search for their companions in the morning. The sun was setting, and the fog was patching thicker in some places. He needed to set up their camp before it swallowed them completely.

He laid out his cloak for her on the lumpy ground and started a small fire with the remaining kindle of his magic, and once she was comfortable, he finally spoke.

"They call me Vali the Heartless. I am the future High Lord of the Light Elves and the bastard son of the Aesir god, Odin."

20
Ailsa

"You're a *god?*"

Vali shrugged off her astonishment. "Technically I'm only part god, or a demigod as most like to call me. I have no following, so I'm not a true divine."

Odin's fucking eye. The semantics hardly mattered. Ailsa had stabbed the son of the Allfather. Three times, in fact. Her head fell into her palms. "I am so going to Hel now."

A low sound escaped from his lips, a laugh that originated from deep in his chest. "Wish you'd been a little nicer to me now, don't you?"

She lifted her gaze from their burrow in her hands to glare at him. "You forget I still have your blade, Vali. If I've already ruined my chance to please Odin, then I have nothing left to lose by stabbing you again."

One of his brows jumped, like the idea excited him. "Always such a heathen."

"Better than a filthy fae," she replied. Or a half god—whatever in Hel's name he was. "What's the son of an Aesir doing so far from Asgard?"

Vali propped his arm on his knee as he sat against a fallen

tree. The flames in the fire between them lowered by the slight of his hand, dancing to the motion of his fingers as he waved them absentmindedly. “Do you know the story of Baldur?”

Ailsa nodded. She knew the legends of the gods by heart. Her father taught her the stories of Odin’s son, Baldur. He was a favorite among the gods, unable to be harmed by anyone or anything in all the Nine Realms until Loki deceived the goddess Frigg into sharing the only element that had not sworn an oath of protection against Baldur. Loki tried to play off his deception, but his act of jealousy could never be undone.

The gods were devastated when he died. It was said Baldur’s wife’s heart literally burst from sorrow and the Aesir were unable to speak through their suffering for weeks. When Baldur could not be taken back from Hel, they took revenge on Loki. But Baldur’s death was the harbinger for the end of the Aesir. Their only chance at defeating Fenrir was now lost in Helheim.

Ever since, Odin has searched for a way to retrieve him from death.

Vali spoke across the fire where he lounged against a fallen ash tree, his arm propped over his knee. He rubbed the cracked blood stain over his chin, wiping it clean, before speaking of a side of history she had not heard before. “My mother was High Lady of Alfheim during those days. She was there when they gave Baldur to the sea and burned his body with his wife on the funeral pyre, as many beings attended his cremation. She once told me Odin’s pain was like a brand on her heart, she could never forget how the god was tormented after losing his favorite son.”

“You must not have been born yet.” Ailsa winked. Vali

snorted and pretended to nudge a log in the fire, but she thought his cheeks colored an endearing blush.

"Technically, no, I wasn't. But to be honest, I've never even met Odin."

"You've *never* met your father? But you're one of the Aesir!"

Vali shrugged. "I was not born to be his son. I was conceived solely for revenge and redemption. He never claimed me as his own, nor do I have a place in Asgard."

When his silence replaced an explanation, Ailsa spoke for him. "You said you would tell me everything, but if you have changed your mind, I will not fault you." She could tell when a man was retreating. Her father looked the same way when she asked him about her mother. He would grow quiet, look anywhere except her eyes, and now Vali was doing the same. He wanted to keep the truth buried deep within his heartless chest.

He shook his head and finally met her stare. "Alfheim used to be a bright, beautiful realm. The elves lived and reigned there for centuries using the Light to source their magic. It was a harmonious relationship between the elves and the land, and the dwarves lived beneath the mountains in their own realm of Svartalfheim. A parallel, yet slightly darker world mirroring the one above it. All in the fae realms prospered during what was known as the Golden Age. Until the rise of Gullveig."

"Gullveig? You mean the seeress?"

"She is a witch," Vali spat. "She was one of the Vanir who discovered a dark magic called *sedir*."

Ailsa's memory triggered at the word. "I know of sedir. There were seers who came to Drakame and claimed they could practice dark magic. The last one was named Jomeer and my father had her burned before she could taint our lands with her darkness."

The elfin nodded. “Yes, he was wise to burn her. Sedir is not evil on its own, but it can be used to both tell and shape the future. There is a kind of knowledge in its power that was forbidden by nature long ago, and those who practice sedir must be careful of how far they dwell into its secrets.

“Being one of the Vanir, she taught them her magic, which is consequently how Freya became a seeress herself. But when Odin heard of this power, of this forbidden knowledge that could be used to change the rules of fate and time, it greatly appealed to him. He took the witch while she was traveling between realms and brought her to Asgard.

“While she was there, he tried everything to get her to find a way to save his son Baldur, but the witch refused. For changing the future was easier than rewriting the past, and it could threaten the very fabric of the universe if she attempted such a thing. Odin in his fury burned her, but she would not die. He burned her three times and three times she rose from the ashes, but after the third time, her power was gone.”

Ailsa squirmed, realizing where this story was heading. “And where did her power go?” she asked.

Vali shrugged. “No one knew. She claimed it was lost, but the gods knew better. They believed Gullveig had hidden it somewhere, tethered it to something until this world ended and the old gods fell. Only then will she be safe from Odin and free to use her power again.”

Ailsa chewed on her bottom lip, mulling over every detail and carving each one into her memory. Before she could inquire for more, Vali gestured to a dent he had padded into the earth, his hand outstretched over the hole, pulling water from the soil and into the formed basin.

“Thirsty?” he asked.

She nodded enthusiastically. Her hands were about to dip in the clear water before she hesitated. “You go first,” she said.

“Are you afraid it's poisoned or something? I can assure you I would’ve tried that before my monologue.”

Her expression soured. “No, I was just trying to be nice.”

His mouth twitched into a smirk. “I don’t believe you. Drink, Ailsa.”

She rolled her eyes but complied, not hiding the sighs of pleasure that escaped her as the cool water slipped down her parched throat. Each time she dipped her hands into the basin, Vali filled it to replace what she took.

“You don’t suppose you could make a hole big enough for a bath, do you?” she asked as he drank his own fill. He paused mid-sip to stare at her like she had grown a second head. “I’m joking!” she said, laughing at her own humor. “Well, sort of.”

He licked his lips and thought for a moment. His eyes carefully roaming over the tattered bits of her dress and the blood and dirt caked into her skin. He then tore off his own shirt, revealing the runes painted across his chest that Ailsa remembered well. She subsequently recalled what his bones felt like beneath her fingers, the warmth of his muscles against her palm. The sound of ripping fabric distracted her thoughts from running wild.

“What are you doing?”

He dipped one of the pieces of cloth into the water and held it out to her. She took it tentatively from his hands. “For you to wash,” he said.

“You didn’t have to destroy your shirt over it; honestly I was jesting.”

“I’m not. You look terrible. It will do us both a favor.”

She threw the soaked cloth at his head, nailing him in the ear. “Ass.”

He peeled it from his face, his expression delighted by her reaction. "Don't be ungrateful," he said, tossing it back.

This time she kept the cloth, using a dry piece of his shirt to wipe the dampness once she had cleaned. She used their drinking bowl to rinse her face and her hands, turning the clear water a rusty color.

Vali leaned his head back as she washed herself, the firelight warmed his pale skin and danced along the symbols brushed across his chest and down his arms. She was caught by the sculpted planes of his chest, how his muscles tensed and relaxed with every breath, emphasizing the deep striations carved into the side of his ribs. They were so well defined she could count them, but instead followed the dark hair dusting his abdomen, a thin trail leading beneath his belt, the ridge pressing against his pants. He was exquisitely proportioned, a perfect combination of muscle and man.

"And now you will be shirtless the rest of our journey," she observed out loud.

He opened his eyes and peered over at her. "Does this offend you?"

Ailsa thought for a moment about her reply. There were a hundred different ways she could approach this question, like it was a test he was giving her. She let her gaze fall back to the basin as she dried her hands, cocking a shoulder passively while she said, "It does not."

She noticed the elfin smile out of the corner of her eye. "Would you like me to fix your dress as well? I'm not good at tailoring, but it will help keep your legs covered."

She shook her head. "It's fine. It's actually easier to walk in now. Unless…" Her brows rose half an inch as she asked him, "Unless my legs offend you?"

He sucked in his cheek to prevent the grin pulling at his lips. "Definitely not."

Ailsa ignored the way the confession made her heart squeeze and skip a much-needed beat. She cleared her throat and picked up his cloak off the cold earth, crossing around the fire to drape it over the fallen tree.

She sat down next to him and waited for the elfin to finish his tale. "So, I am assuming this Gullveig witch woman's power is now tethered to me?"

"The very same," he said

"And what do *you* have to do with it?"

Vali stretched and cleared his throat, preparing for another speech. "When Gullveig lost her power, the Vanir were furious with Odin, and war broke out between the gods. As I'm sure you know from history, the Aesir-Vanir war came to a stalemate, and the god's arranged a trade of hostages. Frey and Freya, who are the same deity in truth, went to live in Asgard while Hoenir and Mimir were sent to Vanaheim.

"Odin made Frey ruler over Alfheim without my mother's knowing. He took over the realm, passing down the magic he had learned in Vanaheim and spoiling the souls of the elves who lived there. The elves are creatures of Light, because it is what our power dwells from. But this power made their magic dark and lifeless, splitting our people into two sides: the Light Elves and the Dark Elves. Sedir in Alfheim was slowly destroying the realm, and my mother was desperate to save her people and the fae worlds.

"She prayed to the fates, and the same night she had a dream. She would bear a son of Odin who would take back the darkness and use it to raise Baldur from the dead. She told this to Odin, who with his all-seeing eye saw she was telling the truth and vowed if their son returned the power of Gullveig to him, he would remove Frey from the land and restore the realm to its former brightness. She agreed and they conceived me, and I have been trying to fulfill her vision and restore my mother's land. Alfheim is the only home I've ever known, and why I call myself fae, not Aesir."

Ailsa was quiet when he finished. He told the story like it wasn't his own, and truthfully it wasn't. It was a tale concerning him, but not about him. His life had been decided before he took his first breath.

Her eyes drifted across his bare chest and followed the markings spilling over his chest, down the corded edge of his shoulders. "And the runes on your chest? Are they the same as mine?"

He shook his head and touched the spot where she stared. A point of insecurity she didn't understand until he explained. "Odin wrote them himself when I was barely a few hours old. They tell of my destiny and bind me to my purpose. Runes have the ability to protect as well as harm and weaken, and mine keep me on the path mapped out for me. If I take a step out of line, Odin will know. And he can end my life as quickly as he ordained it."

"You mean you have no choice?"

His neck constricted with a swallow. "Fate is very difficult to fight, especially when an entire realm depends on me to do what I was born to accomplish. The marks on my skin remind me of this. But I hope, one day when I return the Tether and Odin releases me from this duty, I can begin my life and choose a future for myself."

Ailsa released a long breath in place of a reply. Beside her sat a man not unlike herself, whose fate was written for him, who did not get to choose his destiny. The desperation and rage he unleashed when she took the power in the Tether, the slaughter of her family, the loneliness she recognized in his eyes, they were the product of a universe of expectations all placed upon the shoulders of a single man. And she realized, for the first time, someone else understood the weight of the world. Someone else knew the strength it took to carry it all.

He was not a monster. No, he was not barren of remorse like he had first shown her. She did not recognize him from nightmares but from a spirit she knew in her own bones.

Ailsa set her chin on the bony parts of her knees and tucked them close into her chest, trying to trap the tears even as they escaped. Vali traced her arm with a fingertip before his hand fell back in his lap. "I'm sorry, Ailsa. When I came to Midgard I was fraught and failing, and I let my despair destroy hundreds of lives—including yours." His voice was heavy, quiet as a breath. "As you have seen today, I thoroughly understand your loss. And I see their faces every time I close my eyes."

She turned her head and looked at him. The elfin stared into the flames, unblinking, his eyes a clear gold that shone like a cloudless sky in winter. She reached over and grabbed his wrist, smoothing her thumb over the top of his hand. "I don't know if I'll ever forgive you, Vali. But I understand, and I..." She cleared her throat to hide the tremor. "I do hate you a little less."

He shook his head. "I do not deserve your forgiveness, and I will not ask for it. But thank you, Ailsa. If all else fails, I was very glad to meet the fiery Jarl of Drakame."

She laughed and shoved him aside, the tension melting between them. "Don't speak so soon," she warned. She then remembered something she had been too afraid to ask before. "Are you really heartless?"

He shifted in his seat to face her, gently taking her hand and bringing her palm flush over his ribcage. She felt for a moment. His warmth penetrated the chill inside her bones, the soft skin contrasting the firm muscle of his chest, the stillness where a heartbeat should be. She locked eyes with him, her hand pressed between his body and his palm for far too long, before pulling away. "How?" she asked.

He scoffed and sat back against the tree. "*That* is a story for another night. One I do not wish these trees to hear."

She smiled at the canopy. "The trees know me now, and we are friends."

"I am concerned about the company you attract."

Ailsa pulled the cloak over her shoulders and settled against the log, feeling increasingly comfortable the more she learned of the man with eyes like sunshine. "I will help you as much as I am able, to fulfill your calling and restore your home. Even if it costs me everything."

"Why would you willingly pay that price after all I've done to you?"

A good question, one she was still figuring out herself. There were two sides of her heart constantly warring, and in the middle was an impasse named Vali. His first impression battled what she learned this past week, who he was when he stood on her shores against who he was now sitting beside her. And though she missed her home and the faces of her old life, they felt like ghosts—stories of a distant time. In front of her was an adventure, an opportunity to make her mark, and if not in her world, then someone else's.

She stared into the satiated flames as the elfin waited for her reply. "I only agreed to come on this journey to save my people, to protect them from you. But as I learn more of the threat on the worlds and the one on your own, I think perhaps I was supposed to help you. I've been sitting on a cliffside for the past twenty-six years doing *nothing* while everyone was experiencing life beyond the fjord, and it is my turn to leave a legacy, to make the world better than I left it." Her eyes fluttered shut against the pull of sleep. "I will help you because my world does not need me, and yours does. And because one of us deserves to be free of our fate."

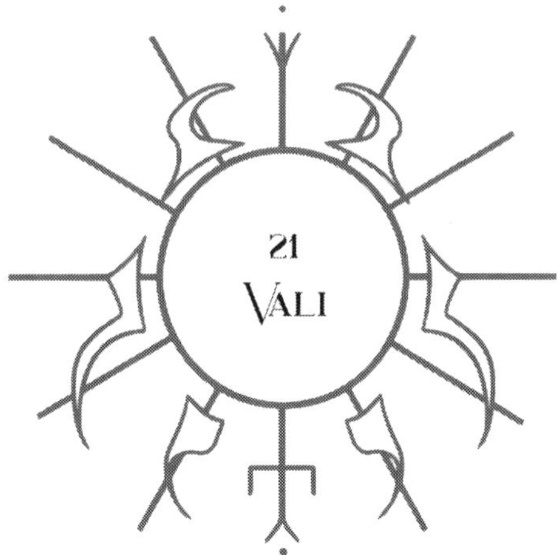

21 Vali

Vali deeply regretted tearing apart his shirt.

Any warmth left in the Between Realm followed the sun when it set. Each time he fell asleep, the fire dwindled. His shivers shook him awake until his efforts became futile. Ailsa reclined next to him with his cloak draped around her delicate shoulders, and he listened to the steady rhythm of her breath like it was a chorus, a secret song without words that seemed to speak to his emotions all the same. Guilt ate away the remaining fragments of his dignity. One of them deserved to be free of their fates, and it wasn't him.

Ailsa stirred in her sleep, and he stiffened as she brushed him. It didn't take long until her head was propped against his shoulder, her body unconsciously searching for a better cushion than the hollow fallen tree. He swallowed an agonized moan and beat his skull against the callused trunk.

This was *wrong*. Despite how unpleasant she was in the beginning, she had shown herself to be witty, smart, even quite charming. She was arrogant to the point it was mildly attractive.

Worst of all, she was warming up to him, tugging at his

mask of apathy and nudging the dormant spring of his self-conscious awake. For the first time in decades, he felt bare, flayed open like a fish by her devastating smiles and the compassion she showed him so openhanded. When she looked at him now, she was looking straight through him.

And the problem was that he *didn't* despise it.

No.

His mind repeated the word until it was a mantra. Until it convinced his flesh to reject the sleeping woman curled against his side and focus on what she carried instead. The salvation of his people, the knowledge to raise gods from the dead and the power to start wars between them was stored within this fragile mortal woman. And she slept peacefully, ignorant of the significance of what she carried.

He peered down at her, studying her profile and the way her lips fell naturally into a soft smile. Even disheveled and covered in mud, she was an exquisite little creature. She stirred again, her dreams realizing she was too comfortable. Her thick lashes fluttered awake.

"Vali?" she whispered.

He inhaled a steadying breath, losing a bit of his resolve each time she said his name. "Go back to sleep, Ailsa."

"You're shaking." She sat up slowly and unwrapped the cloak from her shoulders, reaching a corner of the wool over his left arm. "Put this around you."

"Ailsa, this is—"

"Warm? Comfortable?"

"I was going to say inappropriate."

Her head turned up at him, and he became acutely aware of how close their faces were. "Oh, sweet Vali. If this is what you fae consider scandalous, I'd hate to see how you'd react to my clan's romantic advances." She patted his leg. "Take the cloak, I'm going to find a flatter patch of ground—"

"Come here," he snapped. She made a pleasing yelp as he reached his arm around her waist and pulled her against him, the cloak tightly wrapped around them both.

"See? Isn't this better?" She rested her head beneath his chin.

No. No. No

"Yes," he gritted out.

She laughed at his misery but was lulled by the steady motion of his chest and quickly fell back asleep.

Vali, despite the situation, slept better than he had in years.

"Look at them. Beside themselves with worry, these two."

Ailsa's eyes flew open. Ivor and Seela stood across from them on the other side of the lifeless fire, their arms crossed and wearing matching looks of disapproval.

Vali was dead to the world, his head cocked back against the log while an adorable snore snuck from his barely parted lips. She nudged his ribs gently and roused him awake. His head snapped to attention when he finally sensed their presence, not bothering to hide his grimace as he noticed his commander, and Ailsa took it upon herself to remove herself from his chest.

Seela's brows rose impossibly higher when she saw his state of dress. "Is there something you both need to tell us?"

Vali rolled his eyes as he stretched. "Relax, Seela. It was cold, and we had one cloak."

"It was *cold?*" she clarified. "Ivor and I have been walking the wood for the better part of the morning while you two snuggle in the misty lands of the Tree, all while our dead kinsman water the forest with their blood only a half a day's march away and your reason to ignore it all is because it was *cold?*"

"Seela," Ivor spoke behind her. "Let us just be glad they are alive. Just a few minutes ago you were belligerent—"

"Yes, Ivor, I was terrified something happened to them *both.* But clearly those sentiments were not returned."

"Of course, we were worried about you and the... and Ivor." Vali said. "But I was *impaled,* Seela. I could barely walk another step, much less keep searching for you. I knew through our bond you were alive, and I know you are more than capable of handling yourself. Besides, I did not want to push Ailsa without her herbs."

Ailsa smiled inwardly at this admission. Her lungs felt better than they should have, considering the activity of the previous day. The air and the water here were medicinal, so pure she felt recharged with every breath.

Seela seemed to cool off, her arms falling slack to her side. But Vali continued, "I am sorry if it appeared like Ailsa and I were unconcerned, but that is not the case. I searched for your face, Seela. I looked at each body in that field to make sure it wasn't one of you three. Don't you dare tell me I don't care, not after all we've been through."

Seela's face crumbled, and she turned her face to wipe her cheeks. Vali approached her and embraced her in a tight hug, one that made Ailsa turn away, feeling like she was intruding on a private moment. She heard him whisper something to the commander before stepping away.

"How are you, Ivor?" she asked the wolven as she wrapped her arms around her waist. "I'm sorry I abandoned you yesterday. I wouldn't forgive myself if something had happened to you."

"Think nothing of it, *systir.*" She squeezed her back. "I am well and whole, and so are you." Her head dipped low to skim her ear. "But we *will* discuss what happened here."

"There is no need." She stepped out of the wolven's arms. "It was nothing, I vow it." Ivor was not convinced as she ran a trained eye over her tattered skirts.

"I hope you're right, Ailsa."

THEY TRAVELED in an uncomfortable silence for the next few hours. Their fae companions promised Alfheim was only a day's march up the Highest Branch, but they conveniently forgot to mention the literal incline of said branches.

Ivor with her long legs helped Ailsa traverse over steep ledges, where the forest dropped off into a rocky hillside that extended as far as she could see. Even with her lungs in their best shape, she was forced to fall behind to apply her oils. This leg of the journey proved to be the most difficult task of her life.

Her stomach rolled, gnawing on itself as she consumed nothing but the spring water trickling from the split in the rocks. Vali ignored her, as did Seela. The pair walked together several paces ahead of them, but she caught him looking back at her every so often. His indifference still stung deeper than she wanted to acknowledge. The male she had spoken with last night had disappeared with the arrival of his commander, and they were back where they started.

Her distracted strides caught a pile of loosely structured rocks, and Ailsa's footing slipped as they gave out beneath her. The rippling sound of stones sliding from their settlement prompted her group to turn around. Ivor's eyes widened as she watched her slow fall against the boulder's edge, her body sliding off the slippery surface.

"Ailsa!" Ivor shouted, but she had already landed hard on her backside. "Are you all right?" The wolven peeked over the ledge and looked down at her. Ailsa stared up, miserable, but gingerly climbed back to her feet, her pride injured far worse than anything.

"Fine. Just help me up," she said, much harsher than intended.

Ivor pulled her over the boulder's edge as she found a better foothold. Seela and Vali were climbing down to meet them, but their eyes were looking beyond her. She turned to see what had stolen their attention away from her embarrassing fall.

Below them now were miles of misty wilderness stretching far into the distance. They made considerable ground despite the grueling uphill climb, and Ailsa was rewarded with a view of the branching landscape that stole what little breath she could keep in her chest. But dark clouds were shifting across the sky, carried by a cold wind. She smelled rain, listened as the sky rumbled with gravelly thunder, and watched as dry lightning flashed within the ominous cloud wall now coming their way.

"Vali, we cannot be out here during a helstorm. We need to find cover," Seela spoke. Ailsa looked at him, but his eyes were locked on the impending storm.

"How much longer until we reach Alfheim?" she asked.

Vali shook his head. "At this pace, hours at the very least."

"And the storm?"

He sighed, looking at her at last. His gilded gaze unnervingly anxious. "We just need to go. Hold on to one of us, Ailsa."

She snatched the wolven's arm, and the group started back

up the jagged hillside. Vali led the way, pulling her up while Ivor assisted her steps. This technique was more effective, and they made it to the top of the stacked boulders quicker than they would have before. But the storm was nearly upon them, and there was still no sign of civilization in sight.

"The river is just a little further, come on!" Vali shouted. Ailsa took long, rhythmic breaths as she ran after him, the increasingly violent gust at her back a plain reminder she had no time to pause if she lost her breath. Lightning streaked the sky and split the earth, sending a tremor beneath her strides. But the sounds of the storm were interrupted by an intense flow of river water, competing with the soft whisper of heavy rain now falling in sheets of ice.

"Get in one of the boats!" Vali commanded. He stood on the bank and gestured toward a broad canoe that could easily fit several families. He stayed behind on the sandy shore to push them into the river's powerful current, and they were swept away as soon as the hull scraped off the shallows.

Ailsa sat near the back; her hand held out to help him board. But just as he reached for her, lightning struck near the shoreline, blinding them both with a brilliant light and a deafening crack.

"Vali!" she called over the ringing in her ears. But the elfin was thrown back dazed on the shore, his body unmoving, his chest did not rise for air. Each second he didn't move, they drifted further away, and she panicked to think of him being left behind and consumed by this storm. She unclasped his cloak from her neck and kicked off her poor footing. Ivor and Seela had no time to question her motives, nor stop them from manifesting, before she leapt into the river.

The water was an unfeeling type of cold, so deep was the chill her flesh was numb at first touch. She submerged, her head dipped below the surface for a beat as needles combed against her skull. A thousand knives jabbed her skin, and each time she stroked the water to reach the river's edge, they stabbed her again.

The voices from her companions were silenced by the endless ringing in her ears. Her blood froze into slush, deadening the nerves controlling her limbs. Every move was heavy and clumsy. Her body did not belong to her, nor could her mind control it. But she set her gaze on the elfin still motionless in the sand and pressed on, her heart beating stubbornly against the ice in her veins.

Vali was still unconscious by the time she reached him. Beads of rain kissed his face and rolled off his skin, and his eyes were closed as if he were simply dreaming. She pressed a freezing hand to his cheek and tried to rouse him awake.

"V… V… Vali," she stuttered as her teeth knocked against each other. But no matter how hard she shook him, he did not open his eyes. His chest did not heave. His body remained completely limp.

He was dead.

"N… No," she stammered. Her pale fingers skimmed the rune marks over his chest as if searching for a way to bring him back. There was one technique she remembered from training with the healers in her homeland, and even that was a long shot, but it was *something.* She tilted his chin with her left hand and pinched his nose with the opposite, and reverently brought her lips to his.

She breathed into him, letting the air from her crippled lungs flow easily into his own and lift his chest. She broke away for a moment and let it fall, allowing his body time to consume the air before she breathed into him once again. She did this several times, watching his chest rise and fall like the waves in the sea.

"Come on, Vali… Please," she cried. Her tears were hidden in the rain, but each one that trailed her cheek left a mark on her heart. His journey could not end here. She wouldn't allow it. Not when they still had so much left to accomplish, when she was just starting to understand him.

She shook his shoulders so hard, his head tossed against the sand. "Do not leave me alone with this! I need you, Vali." Her skin tingled and burned until she was no longer crying, but glowing. The runes painted on her skin now a lustrous orange that contrasted brazenly with the darkening storm.

Try again. A little voice whispered in her mind. And she reached down, tipped Vali's chin with a single finger, and placed her lips upon his. She breathed a long, full breath, one that was followed by a groan against her mouth.

She pulled away promptly and found his eyes fluttering awake and his chest moving on its own. "Vali!" she cried.

"What?" He blinked up at her, dazed and disoriented. The rain was still unyielding around them, and she helped him sit up so he could speak without drowning. "Ailsa, what happened to you? You feel like ice, and your lips are blue!"

"Aye, and you were dead and now you're not!" She wrapped her arms around his neck in a clumsy swing. "You were struck by lightning, and you weren't breathing. I jumped into the river and swam back to the shore."

He untangled himself from her arms so he could look her in the eyes. His hands braced her shoulders. "You *swam* in the River Irving?"

Her body released a violent shiver, one that chattered her teeth noisily. She nodded.

"You risked your life... For me." His voice could barely say the last words. Ailsa only bit a numb lip, realizing he was right. But she had only acted in the moment. There had been no thought of herself when she saw him lying there, helpless in the claws of a mighty storm. Only that she couldn't imagine going the rest of this journey without him now that she knew what was at stake. Before she could reply, his commander thankfully intervened.

"Vali!" Seela approached behind them; the boat beached further down the river. "What happened? The lightning struck and—"

"And I don't remember anything after that, but I think I died." His grip on her shoulders tightened. He stared at her with a kind of wonder she couldn't explain. "And Ailsa brought me back."

"Impossible," Seela whispered. Thunder crushed the sky behind them, and she glanced at the storm. "The weather is getting worse. We need to go before the wind picks up."

Ailsa nodded and slowly stood despite the protest of her flesh. Vali held her by the small of her waist as she staggered toward the boat, her legs heavy and throbbing. It took all her focus to maneuver the simplest of movements. Once they pulled her back into the boat, she collapsed across the seat. Ivor followed her with the cloak, one side still dry, and covered her in an attempt to seal the few ounces of heat still trapped somewhere beneath her skin.

Vali sat on the seat across from Ailsa, watching her as Seela manned the push pole, guiding them down the river and away from the creeping storm. Ailsa shivered until she couldn't, until the pain in her body demanded she remain as still as possible. Her eyes burned and her head felt like it was still swimming in the icy waters of the Irving, she just needed to...

"Don't fall asleep!" he ordered her. Ailsa peeked her eyes

open and wanted to obey, but the ache behind her eyes could not be challenged. She was tired. So very tired from saving him. She felt her actions justified a bit of rest.

The sound of his curses was a mumbled lullaby, shushing her to sleep.

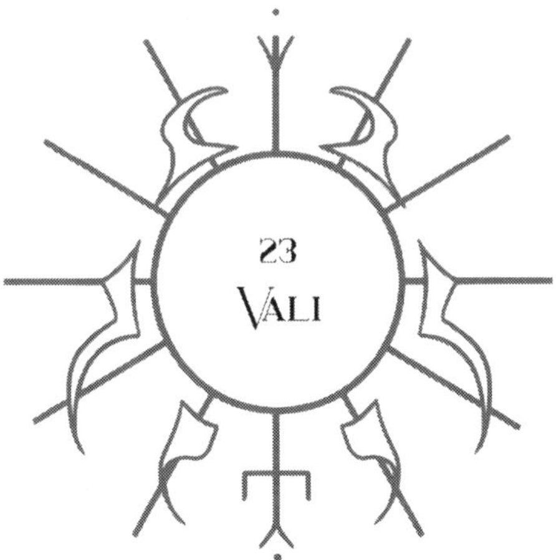

"Come on, Ailsa, stay awake for me," he groaned while shaking her shoulder. But the woman was long gone, submitted to her exhaustion and the cold. "We need to get her inside, near a fire and out of this rain. Take us a few miles down this river and we'll bring her to the closest hall we can find."

"Vali," Seela said softly. "The nearest hall is—"

"I *know* where the nearest hall is, Commander. But we have no choice."

"She may yet live if we build a shelter and wait out the storm. It isn't wise to risk seeking a giant's help if we do not need it," she said.

He stood and faced her, his glare informing her the decision was not up for debate. "She will *die* if we do not get her warm soon. There is nothing in Jotunheim a larger risk than the consequences of her death. Or have you forgotten the purpose of our mission?"

"No, I haven't," she scowled. "Have you?"

He balked at her question, turning to sit back on the boat seat rather than answer her ridiculous retort. "We will go to

Jotunheim, and they will help us. Drieger loves it when people are in his debt."

Ivor looked up from where she was hovering over Ailsa. "Jotunheim? As in the land of the giants?"

"The one and only," Seela replied dryly.

"This is the *only* option?" she asked him.

Vali nodded. "It is the nearest realm besides Asgard, and no one but the gods can use the Bifrost to gain entry to the Aesir's homeland."

Ivor's shoulders fell at the sobering realization, and she looked down at her freezing friend, considering her like she was already dead. And for what Vali knew of the giant's love for the Aesir, she might as well be if they discovered his true lineage.

Vali pushed them along down the river with his magic, assisting Seela and speeding up their arrival as Ailsa's fair skin turned a terrifying shade of blue. The storm was crawling behind them now, but the realm of Jotunheim was unpredictable. The sky could erupt in a blizzard while the sun was shining a warm day, and the river could rise and flood the mountain valley in a flash.

The order of life did not matter here. There were no laws for nature to follow. This was a realm of chaos and powerful giants that hated the Aesir more than they hated the land they were bound to. The river prevented the giants from going anywhere near Asgard or Midgard, but those not intimidated by the Irving could come and go at their leisure.

Lights flickered near a mountain's base. And as the sun set behind the towering peak, Vali noticed the lights were the glowing windows of a hall, surrounded by small homes dimly lit against the harsh landscape. He docked them quickly, taking care to push the boat to the other side of the river for safekeeping, and carried Ailsa to the hall of Drieger, the Frost Giant Lord.

GUARDS SURROUNDED them on all sides as they were escorted from the gatehouse to the Lord's lodging on the top of the hill. Faces peered from shadowed terraces as they walked the streets, watching the strange procession make the long climb up the unpaved street.

Ailsa whimpered in his arms, and he held her close, trying to give her a fraction of the body heat he still contained. Her pulse against his skin was slow—but steady. She would make it if the giant agreed to help her, and he anticipated giving the giant anything he wished for just a moment by his fire.

The great hall doors swung open and admitted their entry, and Vali led the group past several long tables toward the throne dominating the room. The seats lining the dais were vacant, but the torches behind them were lit as if the room was expected to soon be occupied.

"Wait here," one of the guards ordered before he disappeared behind an olive-stained tapestry.

Vali's arms were starting to prickle from holding Ailsa the entire trek through the village. The tattered remains of her gown seeped cold river water against his bare skin. But she was so peaceful against his chest, and every time he shifted his hands, she whimpered like it was a painful experience. She was only suffering because of him, and so he endured the pain, hoping it stole a portion of her misery.

The tapestry parted once more to reveal the displeased face of a giant Lord. He was followed by three women, one his wife and the other two slightly younger. Vali assumed they were his daughters.

"Who disturbs my family during our dinner?" Drieger sat on his oversized throne. The giant was not much larger than Vali, but he towered over them from his platform. The Frost Giants were beautiful beings with lavender skin and hair that ranged from a deep red to a soft blue. Drieger's was somewhere in between, the torchlight pulling auburn.

"Lord Drieger," he beseeched the giant, "my name is Dane, and I am one of the fae neighboring your realm in Alfheim. My group was traveling when we were chased by a helstorm. One of our companions fell into the River Irving, and she will probably die if I do not find a place to accommodate us."

"And you come to Jotenheim seeking… shelter?"

"Please, sir. This was the closest hall, and she is running out of time." Vali shifted Ailsa's body just enough to reveal her bruised lips and skin, her coloring resembling the giants. The woman behind Drieger's throne flinched, and she whispered something into his ear.

The giant swatted the woman away. "What is an elfin doing with a mortal?"

Vali stiffened, not expecting the question. But his wit was not as sharp as his tongue. The longer he went with his mouth hanging open, the less of a chance anything intelligent would come out. "She's my… She's… well… She is carrying—"

"His child," Seela spoke behind him. "She's carrying his child, which is why we were traveling from Midgard to Alfheim in the first place." Vali swallowed and discovered his throat to be dusty. Of all the excuses his commander could have conjured, *that* is what first came to her mind?

The giantess's green eyes widened in despair, and she spoke again in the ear of her husband, her whispers louder than before. He waved at her again before speaking. "Fine, fine, if it pleases you, Skiord." He sighed before looking back at them. "My wife has taken pity on your human, Dane. Bring the woman to my wife's chambers and she will take care of the rest. Meanwhile we will find food and rooms for the rest of you."

"Thank you, Lord Dieger, you are most generous." Vali bowed his head, if only to hide the flush of his cheeks. "And I vow to repay you in any amount you deem worthy."

He grunted. "It is my wife you should thank, not me. I only agreed because she wouldn't let me live it down for the next seven moons. As for payment, I would like to finish the rest of my meal in peace before it grows cold. You have one night here, elfin. I do not wish to see any of you in the morning."

Vali nodded again, wary of the ease with which the giant offered shelter to a stranger. But he followed the giantess into the wing breaking from the hall, which carved deep into the mountain. She led him to a windowless cavern where a firepit warmed the room. Furs lined the floor leading to a steaming pool—a natural hot spring.

"It's safe for her?" he asked, nodding to the heated water. Vali was leery of rewarming her body too quickly. The giantess only smiled.

"Yes, we will warm her slowly. She is not the first to have fallen into the river, and I have used the spring while carrying all my children. I assure you it isn't too hot for a babe, even as early as she is." Vali cleared his throat again, unsure of why the topic was making him so uncomfortable. She continued, "My girls are getting some spare clothes from their wardrobes, and they'll return to help me clean her up. You look exhausted, Dane. Go, take care of yourself and let me care for your human."

Vali muttered his thanks and placed Ailsa on a bench before turning to leave. Her daughters filed in the room as he left, but he lingered outside for a moment to make sure they weren't going to do something conniving—like eat her.

"Where am I?" Ailsa's voice mumbled as they undressed her. Her old gown sinking to the stone floor with an echoing flop.

The giantess spoke with a genuine kindness. "Jotunheim, my dear. You fell in the River Irving and scared your lover half to death."

Vali cringed and could only pray Ailsa wouldn't expose his lies. Perhaps the giantess lady would think she was merely confused in her state.

But Ailsa replied, "Oh... Oh! Aye well, he scared me first."

He let loose the breath he was holding and smiled despite their situation. He pushed off the wall and ventured back to the hall, feeling certain his human was in good hands.

24
Ailsa

The most beautiful woman greeted Ailsa when she finally awoke. Her eyes sparkled like gemstones mined from the heart of the world. Deep emeralds surrounded by light violet skin. She was told the Frost Giants were enchanting but couldn't have fathomed this level of beauty existing.

Her daughters dressed Ailsa in a long, green smock with a matching sheer robe. They shoved a hot mug in her hand for her to drink as they braided her hair, their nimble fingers making quick work of the wet strands. The youngest one ran a finger down the slope of her nose, studying the contour of her face.

"So pretty," she said with a beaming, front toothless smile.

"Sorry," her mother said. "She's my inquisitive one, and she has never seen a human before."

"That's all right. I've never seen a Jotun before." She tapped the girl's nose with her own finger. Or an elfin, or a god, or a whole sort of other creatures for that matter. "Thank you for everything. I don't know what would have happened to me if you hadn't taken us in. I hope we weren't too much of an inconvenience."

"It was my pleasure; I rarely get to entertain guests anymore. The winter brings harsh weather to Jotunheim this close to the border. But I'm sure your sweet Dane would like me to return you to him now. He was quite fraught over you both."

"Both?"

"You and your child."

Ailsa blinked twice. "Where is this man of mine?"

Because he had *so* much explaining to do.

SKIORD BROUGHT her to a great room that reminded her of the gathering hall of Drakame, though this one was much grander and built from solid stone. The roof was thatched with cedar beams and straw, and the jewel-colored theme marking the territory's symbol continued to the tapestries and the rugs.

Vali sat at a long table alone, balancing a bare bone between his plate and his finger, when Ailsa and Skiord entered the room. He jerked from the table as she came into view, sending a harsh screech from the bench.

"Ailsa!" He beamed a smile that warmed the coldness left-over from the river. She couldn't recall what the giantess had called him, though he apparently was going by an alias here. Instead of guessing, she used the nickname she unofficially entitled him the first day they met.

"*Sólskin!*"

Sunshine.

His smile wavered as she said it, but he reapplied his mask before Skiord noticed. He took her hand and placed a kiss on the inside of her wrist, making a real show of his affection.

Those soft lips lingered over her pulse, tasting the racing beat that only sped faster the longer he saturated her skin. His eyes fluttered shut, as if she tasted of ecstasy, and he was relishing her like an after dinner treat. "Thank the Light you are all right. I can't put into words how relieved I am to see you well. Lady Skiord—"

"I know," the giantess smiled. "And you are welcome, Dane. But Ailsa needs to rest now, so I would recommend bringing her back to your room as soon as she finishes eating. I'll have a servant come by in the morning to see off your group." She stepped behind Ailsa and patted the back of her shoulder. "It was lovely meeting you both, and good luck with the rest of your pregnancy. It will be hard, but it is worth every second of suffering."

Ailsa only flashed her teeth, unable to form a real smile. Not when the queen's words reminded her of a worthy suffering she would never have. "Thank you, Skiord. I will never forget your kindness."

The giantess left as Vali led her back to their room. Their *single* room.

"They believe we are together, Ailsa. What was I supposed to do, ask for another room? They'd suspect I was lying then." Vali argued.

As much as she hated the idea of another night of close quarters with him, this time would at least include a real bed. "Fine, but the first time you touch me, you're sleeping on the floor."

"You weren't so offput by my touch last night," he said, smiling.

Ailsa wanted to slap the gratification from his face. "Do not flatter yourself. I was trying to help you."

His smile only stretched. Golden eyes shifted up and down her figure. "Are you feeling generous again tonight?"

She reached for the nearest couch pillow and flung it at his head. "Keep it up and you will sleep outside in the snow!"

"You're overreacting." He yanked his shirt over his head, tossing it over the back of a chair to make himself more comfortable. His belt went next, ripping it from his trousers and allowing them to hang several very agreeable inches lower. *Odin's eye*. There were certainly parts of her that were overreacting, but definitely not her logic. The room was suddenly stifling.

Ailsa cleared her throat before speaking. "Oh no, apparently I'm *expecting.*" She gestured widely to her hips.

Vali wiped his face with his palms in exasperation, the tips of his ears turning pink. "It was not my plan! Seela was the one who came up with the whole idea."

Ailsa slumped in a fur-lined chair near the blazing hearth. "I knew it. She hates me."

This made a sudden laugh spill from behind his lips. "I'm sorry, what did you say?" he asked.

"Seela. It is clear she hates me."

"Because she told the giants you were with child and saved your life?"

Ailsa shut her mouth. Vali explained their trouble with the lord and how Seela had thought of the idea in the spur of the moment. An idea that ultimately grabbed his wife's attention and spared them all a lot of grief in the end.

"She does not hate you, Ailsa. She is just protective of me."

"Are you… *together*? Because if you are, then you are definitely spending the night with the rug."

The elfin threw his head back and laughed, falling into the

seat across from hers in the process. "Me and Seela? Absolutely not. She's my *Hjartablód*."

Ailsa thought for a moment, deciphering the combination of ancient words. "Heart's blood?"

"Yes. The fae have two kinds of mates, bonds that bind us for life. One is a *Fraendi*, a life mate. But when elfin go into battle or missions like ours, we usually have a *Hjartablód*, a blood bonded, to keep us safe. We can sense each other for miles, feel each other's pain and take it away, heal each other with our blood even if the other is on the brink of death. It is an ancient, sacred practice for the fae."

She suddenly felt very juvenile. "Oh."

Vali's gaze fell to the fire, his posture one of complete ease. Strange, since he was so rigid against her last night. "Seela has been with me since I was a child. She knows everything about me, and I know her. She knows the dark parts of my past and only wishes to not see specific history repeat itself."

Ailsa was about to ask why any of that would matter at a time like this, but he interrupted her with a shake of his head. "Look," he sighed. "I'm sorry for how things transpired with the giants. But they were our best option to save your life. We are leaving in the morning, and this will all be null as soon as we depart Jotunheim."

Ailsa took a long sip of her tea, remembering the stories she heard as a child of the Frost Giant's realm. The winters were harsh, sometimes locking dwellers inside for months. "And what if something happens and we're stuck here? What will we tell them when my stomach doesn't grow?"

Vali's face scrunched. "Liars are punished most severely in Jotunheim. It won't come to that, but I suppose if by a miracle it does, I will just have to get you pregnant."

Ailsa spat her tea before she choked on it. His words triggered something deeply rooted in a bad place. Memories flashed in her hindsight—a bundle beneath a tree, how the wolves howled when she bled into the forest, Erik leaving on the boat—and the mug in her hands slipped to the floor as they consumed her. Wells formed behind her eyes and leaked hot trails across her cheekbones.

"Ailsa?" he asked, his voice softer. He leapt off the bed. "Gods below, I'm sorry. I'm an ass. I wouldn't really force you to go through with such a thing. It was a horrible, tasteless joke."

"You don't have to apologize," she said, wiping her cheeks. "It wasn't what you said, it's just…"

He knelt in front of her chair, his sunset eyes searching hers. "It's what?"

The words spilled out of her before she could catch them. "I was pregnant once."

She had never told another soul about this, not even Erik, the father of her unborn child. She stared into the fire unblinking, letting it sear her eyes and dry her tears. Vali sighed and took her empty hands in his. "Come." His voice was quiet, yet commanding.

Hollow of fight, she let him lead her to the large bed, barely feeling his fingers delicately pull the robe from her shoulders. He didn't say a word as she slipped beneath the sanctity of the heavy quilts. Wordless as he laid on top of the covers next to her. Vali only waited, testing her boundaries with him. He was close but made no move to seize the fragile fortress of her heart she protected with guarded words and thick skin.

"I was only nineteen," she said. "When I was growing up, the older women used to warn me about taking my contraceptives religiously, that I would be selfish to have a child and pass down my condition to them. They said I would ruin a man's family line should I mate with anyone, and if I truly cared about their sons, I would stay away from them." A long breath streamed through her lips. "And then I met Erik."

"Lionheart?"

She rolled her eyes, but a smirk plagued her mouth. "Aye, the man you nearly killed on the beach. We grew up together, but one day he kissed me on a dare, and we were inseparable ever since. I thought we were in love, and I gave myself to him. The very next day his father decided to leave Drakame, and he took his sons and traveled half a world away. He wrote me a letter saying he couldn't stay with me. He had chosen to follow his family and wished me the best. I found out I was pregnant two months later, and he was long gone."

Vali was quiet for a breath before he said, "I think I'm going to travel back to Midgard one day and finish boiling that man alive."

Ailsa laughed despite the pain in her chest. "It's not his fault. We were young, and I was foolish to think a man like him would stay with someone like me."

"Someone like you?"

She shrugged beneath the blankets. "Sick. Worth, among my people, is based on strength and following and influence. The only worth I offer is my dowry."

"But your mother was ill, was she not? And your father still chose to be with her."

"My father was a shieldmage. He could quite literally do whatever he wanted because he had magic. And magic only exaggerates strength, following, and therefore influence. He cared for my mother with a love that was pure and true, and nothing would have stood in his way to have her."

Vali propped himself on his side to look at her better. She

turned her face on her pillow to meet his gaze. "What happened to your baby?" he asked.

She took a steadying breath and for the first time, she let her secret fly free from the cage of her heart. "When I realized I was with child, I was overcome with grief and guilt. Whatever happened, my body rejected it, and I buried its little body beneath my favorite tree in the Aelderwood. The tree Erik and I had our first kiss beneath." More tears spilled from the corner of her eye. "Sometimes I think it knew I didn't want it, and it claimed its own life in the womb. No matter what I tell myself, it always feels like my fault."

"You did this alone? Gods below…" he cursed. "It wasn't your fault, Ailsa. None of it was."

"There is nothing you can say that I haven't already told myself."

He reached for her cheek and caught a tear before it reached the pillow, rubbing the drop between his fingers. "Sometimes words sound different coming from someone else. Sometimes we need to see ourselves through another person to remind us what we truly look like. You've done that for me, and I wish to do that for you. *It was not your fault*, Ailsa. Fate is crueler to some than others. Do not add to your misery by being cruel to yourself as well."

He was right. She had told herself the same thing for the last seven years, yet when he said the words, something lifted beneath her skin. Vali knew guilt, experienced the power shame had on a person's perspective, like a broken spyglass that skewed how the future and the past appeared when looked through. Perhaps she could stop seeing herself through that remorseful filter. Maybe begin liking the woman in the mirror who knew pain and rejection, and still loved herself fully despite them both.

She offered him a smile in gratitude and a silence stretched between them before he spoke again. "This sickness… does it claim your people quickly?"

Ailsa nodded. "It always feels manageable until one day it isn't. None of the women in my family live very long. Most die in their thirties for some reason. My mother was the quickest of them all, and I fear I will beat her record." She stared up the rafters, wondering if things would have been different in those days if she had a mother's guidance. "That child was my one chance at having a legacy, to have a part of me live on after I died. But perhaps it is better this way, and the sickness dies with me."

Vali shook his head, making the bed creak. "You know, the rivers in Alfheim are known to be sources of miraculous healing. I don't know if they could heal you but…"

"I won't get my hopes up, but I'll try anything," she mumbled.

"Good," Vali said. "But you must promise me something."

"What's that?"

His eyes traveled over the quilt outlining the harsh curves of her figure, and her toes curled under his inspection. She despised how her body was beginning to react to him and his gilded attention. He said, "If you drink from the river and are healed, you must find someone who places your worth in who you are, not in what you can do for them."

Ailsa fought the stupid grin that wrangled itself on her lips. "In other words, don't go back to Erik."

"Exactly."

She rolled her eyes but smiled. "I don't think that is an option I even have at this point." She took a deep breath and felt her lungs fight back. "Would you mind if I had a smoke before bed? My chest is feeling a little tight."

He gestured to the dresser at the other end of the room where Ivor had left her bag of herbs. "Of course not. Bring them over here so I can see how you mix them. Just in case I need to know one day."

Ailsa eyed him carefully, but retrieved her herbs without saying anything. She found the bundle bag and spread it along the top sheet, dread rolling over her heart. Her stash was getting low. She had only prepared for a few days across the Great Sea, not an epic journey across the Nine Realms.

"You're running out." He read the look on her face. She nodded solemnly before mixing half a dose of her usual to ration the rest. He watched her crush the herbs in her pestle and sprinkle it into the pipe Ziggy had crafted for her many winters past.

When she was through, she slipped beneath the covers and faced Vali, who was still lounging on top. She reached out and pressed her palm where his heart should have been, checking to see if it had somehow grown back. The male she was speaking to seemed too thoughtful to not have one.

"What happened to your heart, Vali?" she asked quietly.

The elfin stared at the ceiling to avoid her gaze and ran a hand over a long, jagged scar marring the runes across his skin. "The first and last woman I loved stole it."

Ailsa's brows kissed. "Like literally stole it?"

"Yes. She was working for a witch who knew about my mission. They believed if they cut out my heart, stabbed it, and burned it to ash, then I would finally die and could not fulfill my destiny. But the runes Odin burned into my skin protect me from death until I succeed in bringing him the Tether."

"Why bring him the Tether if it will only make you vulnerable after? Wouldn't you *want* to live forever?"

"It's not really living if your life is always controlled by someone else."

Ailsa slipped her hand from his bare chest; her own heart beating like a war drum. The easiness of touching him was startling, more pleasant than it should have been. Her palm hummed where she touched him—the rest of her skin suddenly envious, wanting to know how those vibrations would feel everywhere else. She tucked her palm into her chest instead. "Who was this woman you loved?"

He shut his eyes and shook his head, as if dismissing the thought of her. "Someone who loved gold and glory more than she loved me."

Ailsa found her heart aching for him. "I'm sorry, Vali." She meant it. "I bet she's somewhere furious, realizing all she had to do was lock you outside during a thunderstorm."

Laughter burst from his chest. The sudden jovial interruption made her jump, pleasantly surprised he could even make the sound. "Technically, I didn't die, and I probably wouldn't have if you would have waited."

"Oh, so now this is my fault?"

"Of course not!" His voice was sharp, obnoxious in the intimate quiet of their room. "I only meant that the fates must have planned for you to save me all along. Perhaps they just wanted you to kiss me—"

"That was *not* a kiss!"

"Could have fooled me, Jarl Ailsa." His brow arched elusively. A challenge. One she wanted to claim and win. If he thought *that* was a kiss, then he had no idea what she was capable of. Perhaps she needed to show him.

Ailsa rolled on top of him, pinning him to his back. Their bodies were only separated by a wool blanket and limited clothes. Her legs fell into a straddle around his waist, pressing her hands on either side of his face to look down at him. The humored look in his eyes tempered, falling instead on her lips as she parted them in a plea for attention.

"Oh, sweet Vali," she sang above him. Her hair falling over her shoulder to skim his cheek. "If I kissed you, there'd be no fooling."

She couldn't move as he reached his arm toward her face, his fingers tucked a loose wave behind her ear. His callouses rough against her hairline. "Prove it," he said. His voice glacial slow, eyes dark and hooded in a trance. The power between them suddenly shifting, and she didn't know if she had surrendered the upper hand. Not until he muttered, "Please."

Ailsa let the plea pull her near until her lips were inches from his. Their chest brushed in the space between them, rising and falling in anticipation of the other's next move. She'd never been this close to him voluntarily. From the proximity, she noticed the flecks of orange in his eyes, the black rim of his iris. Waves of juniper and pine rolled from his body, blocking her last thread of sense.

"Do not move," she demanded.

His eyes shut; throat convulsed with a hard swallow before he jerked his chin in a nod. The room utterly silent besides the crack of a dwindling fire. Ailsa ducked her head, placing a light kiss upon a cold cheek, feeling it contour as he smirked beneath her graze.

As she pulled away, his eyes snapped open, pupils wide with curiosity. She sat up straight, still seated on top of him, and reveled in the way he was reduced to a mass of complicated desires beneath her. With a smile of her own, she asked, "Do you understand the difference now?"

"Clear as rain," he replied through tight lips.

She rolled off his hips, falling back to her side of the bed with a bed shaking flop. "Good."

He shook his head, clearing the flush settling over his face. "You're going to kill me one day, Ailsa. If not with a blade, then with your mouth."

"Then you will die a lucky elfin."

He smiled before asking, "I was curious as to why you brought me back to life, however, seeing as you hate me so much and vowed to find a way to end me."

She shrugged as if it were obvious. "Because if you die, it will be by my hands. No one else gets to harm you but me."

He nodded his approval as he chuckled. "I can accept that."

Her head fell to the side to look at him. "You should do that more."

"What?" he asked.

"Laugh. It's nice to hear." And his laugh was a melodic sound, one she never tired of hearing. He had a smile that touched his whole face, pulling the corners of his eyes into creases. It was rare, but when he laughed, she caught a glimpse of a different Vali. His best kept secret, one he didn't share with just anyone. "Besides, it's a nice reprieve to the grating sound of your voice," she added to maintain the ambiguity of their bond.

"I suppose I can grant you some relief in that way." He slid his arms over his head and beneath the pillow, his thick lashes dusted shut. "Goodnight, Ailsa."

"Goodnight, *Sólskin.*"

VALI WAS SNORING MINUTES LATER. Sleeping just an arm's reach away, his noisy breathing became quite loud, keeping Ailsa awake the rest of the night. And although she could have pushed him on his side to silence the beastly groans slipping from his parted lips, she decided against it. He was in a deep slumber, and she couldn't bring herself to disturb him.

At some point, he flipped on his stomach, his arms and legs sprawled and taking most of the bed. She curled into herself to avoid touching him despite the will of her flesh to reach out and stroke his face like the giantess child had done to study her own. Her heart was pulled into a battle of contrasts. She wanted to hit him if only as an excuse to touch him. To hate him yet want to know his deepest, darkest history. She was repulsed by her fixation on her family's killer and the way she didn't even blame him anymore.

Her father used to say sometimes in battle there was no good side or bad side. What was right and what was wrong changed with a simple shift of perspective. And by spending a short time with her enemy, she'd learned he was not a monster after all.

His face was softened by sleep, dark hair tousled from his restless head constantly shifting back and forth on the pillow. The worries constantly setting his jaw disappeared, a tenderness replacing the tension, tempered by the bliss found in his dreams. He was so beautiful to her, and his beauty was just another thing she wanted to despise him for—but couldn't.

She dared herself to move a silky strand that had fallen over his eye, a movement that challenged her to follow the sharp edge of his jaw and the curve of his chin. She traced the outlines of bones and the planes of his face. Her fingers halted their exploration before meeting his lips—his snoring silenced.

Without warning, his jaw opened, and he bit her curious

finger, holding it hostage in his mouth. Ailsa betrayed a small yelp of surprise at the sting of his teeth. Vali opened his eyes and his lips curled into a smirk.

"What are you doing?" he asked in a garbled language. A smooth tongue flicked the pad of her fingertip as he spoke. She yanked her hand back, but he bit down harder and prevented her escape.

"You had a fly on your face," she muttered.

"Liar. Try again."

Ailsa glared at him and huffed a frustrated breath. "You're just *so* handsome and irresistibly touchable. I cannot seem to keep my hands off of you." His laugh loosened his jaw enough she could slip from his bite, her skin retaining the lines of his teeth.

"Yes, it is a curse I must bear."

"I don't know how you manage to get out of bed each morning."

He flipped to his side, his face too close to breath normally, without smelling his rich scent that reminded her of pine trees in deep winter. "Admit it," he murmured. "You like my face."

"What—" she said, but she was cut off by his fingers threading through her hair, pushing the wavy strands from her face so he could run a knuckle down her temple and smooth a thumb over her cheekbone. His palm was warm, smoothing across her skin in a way that felt like a question.

"You have particularly sharp features for a human. They're almost fae-like," he said.

"I suppose that is a compliment coming from an elfin?"

He ran the tip of his finger down the slope of her nose. "Just an observation. No, you're obviously not fae, even the giants could tell at first glance you were human."

Ailsa's heart drooped with disappointment. "Because I'm so plain?"

Vali flinched. "Plain? Is that what you think you are?"

"I feel plain among beings like fae and gods and giants."

He scoffed, bringing his hand beneath her chin before leisurely running his thumb over her bottom lip, stretching its plumpness. "I think you are the least plain being I have ever seen."

Blood rushed to Ailsa's cheeks and other gullible organs deep within her core. His eyes set on her lips, hooded in the half-suspended space of sleep. The rough callous of his thumb skated against the smoothness of her lip, a pleasing variation of sensations.

Vali nose flared with a forced breath, jerking back as if having a sudden realization he was lingering over her lips far too long. He cleared his throat and all but jumped out of bed, leaving an empty space next to her that felt much larger now that he was gone.

"We should start getting dressed to leave. It will be morning soon and I'd rather not see Drieger in case he's changed his mind about owing him." He sat in a chair and pulled on his boots.

"Aye, good idea." She found the dress the giantess had donated to her and glanced at Vali.

He cleared his throat. "I'll go find Seela and Ivor while you change. Meet us in the hall when you're finished."

"Okay," she said quietly.

Ailsa was grateful when he finally left the room, somehow finding the breath she lost under the spell of his touch. A troublesome feeling wormed its way into her gut, and she couldn't place the reasoning as to why she felt this way. Perhaps Vali had unnerved her with his prodding, or perhaps it was only unnerving because he stopped. Either way, she buried the uneasy sensation sticking to her stomach like a warning.

She changed, gathered her things, and left their room. With the click of the latch, she shut away the intimate memories and budding emotions that were forbidden for her heart to feel for such a male. When she felt strong in her convictions, she turned and left in the direction of the hall.

Until blackness fell like a curtain over her eyes as pain erupted in the back of her skull—receding only when she fell into a world of oblivion.

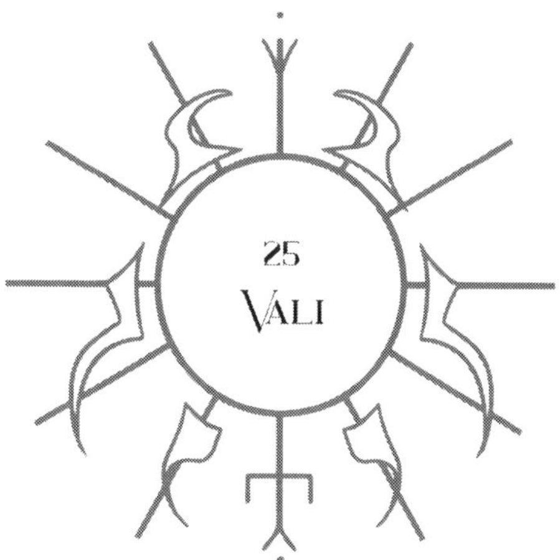

Vali and their companions waited in the hall. Seela looked at him hard, noting the flush edging his skin long after his fingers left the heat of Ailsa's lips. Gods, he wanted to kiss her, and if he hadn't reminded himself of who she was in that moment, he would have. It had taken every ounce of his willpower not to turn his head when she grazed his cheek, to taste the breath caressing his skin. But Ailsa was not just another woman he shared a bed with. She carried stipulations the size of his realm. Her lips were not his to claim. They never would be.

But that didn't soothe the covet in his flesh. Nor did it help him forget the way she sat over him, looming with those deep blue eyes and brandishing smirk. Just the memory of her heat on top of his core made him hard as iron, the feel of her thighs squeezing his hips. It made him wonder if she had wanted him too, if she also thought to remove the barrier of the sheets and feel her weight on his length, rub all her soft places where he was hard. To really kiss him. Why else would she touch him while he slept? How could anyone look at him like that and not feel *something*?

"What's taking her so long?"

Seela tapped her foot impatiently as they waited. Dawn was peaking over the valley, spilling a new sunrise through the frost-covered windows with a glaring light. Vali sighed, feeling her exasperation and resisting the urge to find out for himself.

"Ivor, will you go check on Ailsa?"

The wolven nodded and left in the direction of their room. She returned a few minutes later, her strides quick against the floorboards. Vali stood, sensing the urgency in her steps.

"She isn't there," Ivor said. Her voice was rigid as the muscle in her jaw. "When did you last see her?"

Vali ignored her question. He was halfway down the corridor leading back to their room before she could finish. The bedroom was empty, her bag gone, but nothing else was amiss. There were no signs of a struggle, the windows were frozen shut with a thick layer of ice, and he could still smell her cedar oil lingering after a recent application.

"She hasn't been gone long. I left her just before I knocked on your door, so maybe twenty minutes?" he said.

"A lot can happen in twenty minutes," Seela mumbled at his shoulder. "Can you feel her still?"

He had been so consumed by his panic, he had almost forgotten. The pull he felt from the Tether was so consistent it felt natural at this point. But when he focused, he could feel her, even as it weakened as the seconds ticked. From the dwindling tug of her magic, he guessed she was slipping further away.

"Someone has taken her." He could barely utter the words. They were so close to leaving unscathed, and a moment was all it took to snatch her away. He smashed the nearest table with the heel of his boot, cursing his own carelessness.

"Vali, calm down," Seela said. But he was already pacing the floor, his hands tearing through his hair.

"I need to speak with Drieger. This whole situation reeks of giant. He must have found out who we were—but *how?*"

Seela stepped in his path and thrust his sheathed sword in his hands. "We will figure out the why and how later. For now, let's get her back."

Ivor stepped in front of the commander to look Vali in the eyes. "I will never leave her alone with you again. You worry about what's inside her, but I am the only one here who cares about *Ailsa.* Your negligence will cost her everything!"

Seela pushed her to the side with a forceful shove, but Vali made a motion to stop her. "No, Seela, she's right. This is my fault." He turned to the wolven. "But know this, Ivor. There is no one in the Nine Realms who cares more about Ailsa than I do, and I will do *anything* in my power to get her back. Next time you question her well-being or my intentions, remember my words."

He stormed out of the room to hunt down the Frost Giant Lord.

"Drieger!"

Vali scourged the length of the corridors leading from the hall, his strides devouring the plush rugs lining the floor. There was no question in his mind the giant lord had something to do with her disappearance, and he would shout his name throughout his home until the Jotun showed himself.

"Dane?" Skiord stepped out from a private room, rubbing sleep from her eyes and appearing as if she had just woken.

"Where is Drieger? I demand to see him *now.*"

"He left early this morning to visit his brother—"

The elfin growled, releasing his rage with a savage, unintelligible shout and a punch to the cavern wall. His hand throbbed, distracting him from the pain in his chest throbbing against his ribs like a heartbeat.

"What is the meaning of this!" The giantess was clearly appalled at his behavior, but he was too desperate to care for her judgement. He shook his bleeding hand to beg Skiord for her mercy once more.

"I need to go after him. He's taken Ailsa, and I don't know what he has planned to do with her. Please, Skiord, may I borrow a horse?"

"I don't know, Dane, we don't have many horses as it is—"

"Look at me!" he shouted. With a placating sigh, she did. And Vali let her see every ounce of fear, every inch of despair blown wide in his gaze. "I *need* her. I cannot lose her."

The giantess sighed and stared up at the ceiling. "Whatever my boorish husband has done or what his plans are is beyond me, but I will make it right. I will grant your request, but the rest of your party must remain here. That is my collateral, so you will return with my horse."

Vali practically deflated with relief. "Thank you. Where are the stables? And where did you say he was headed?"

Skiord set her jaw with an expression of distaste. "I'll show you to the stables. As for where Drieger went," she rubbed the back of her eyes wearily, "you just need to hurry. Thrym is not a giant you want your woman around."

26 Ailsa

It was bright when Ailsa woke. The gentle shaking of a carriage nearly lulled her back to sleep. Ailsa first noticed it was freezing cold, her breath coiled in a white cloud in front of her face, prompting she was outside. She sat up from where she was stuffed into a corner, finding herself in a metal wagon with bars lining the roof. Through the top of her cage, a clear sky draped over the world and a new morning sun had just risen over a reaching mountain peak.

She banged on the iron wall, a thin layer of ice falling as she knocked. No one answered. She sat on her knees and tried to see over the solid black wall of her cage but gained no hint of her kidnapper, only the quiet sound of hooves pressing against soft snow and the squeaky groan of rusted wheels.

"Hello?" she called out. But yet again, no response. She settled back into a corner and squeezed her elbows into her side to conceal her last bit of warmth. But the metal at her back pressed a chill down her spine.

They came to a stop a few minutes later. Ailsa tensed in anticipation, pulling her knees into her chest as voices manifested beyond the wall to her left side.

"You think this will work, Drieger?"

"Wait until you see her, Thrym. The Aesir won't let this one go."

The side opposite to where she crouched swung open on squealing hinges, and Ailsa was met by two Frost Giants. One of them eyed her closely, then turned to the giant with a striking resemblance. "Freya is as good as mine."

"All in good time, brother. Let's see how *Vali* reacts when he realizes I have his little mortal."

Thrym grunted. "Get the human inside before she catches her death. What did you say her name was?"

"Does it matter? Get out here, girl!"

Ailsa could only glare at them both as she unfolded her limbs and stepped out of the cage tentatively. A large hall stood behind them, but this one was different. The flags marking the entrance to the hall were colored crimson and grey, and the giant Thrym was dressed in similar colors, clashing with Drieger's mossy tunic.

"Where am I?" she shuddered, trying to hide the cold tremble in her bones that resembled fear. She glanced around, but the landscape was barren. This place was nestled deep into the valley where even the trees did not have a place to root themselves.

"Let's get her inside and chain her to the whipping post. If you are right about this Aesir, it won't take him long to get here. Gather the surrounding Jotun."

"What do you want with him?" she asked. The giants considered her as they moved to grab her. She darted from their advances. "What do you want from the elfin?"

Thrym snatched her forearm in his massive hand and squeezed until the pain made her knees buckle. "Don't worry, little human," he sang in her ear. "Vali the Heartless is just going to do a little job for me across the rainbow bridge."

"And if he refuses?" she hissed.

"If he refuses?" Thyrm cocked a dark green brow at her. "I will make you both suffer."

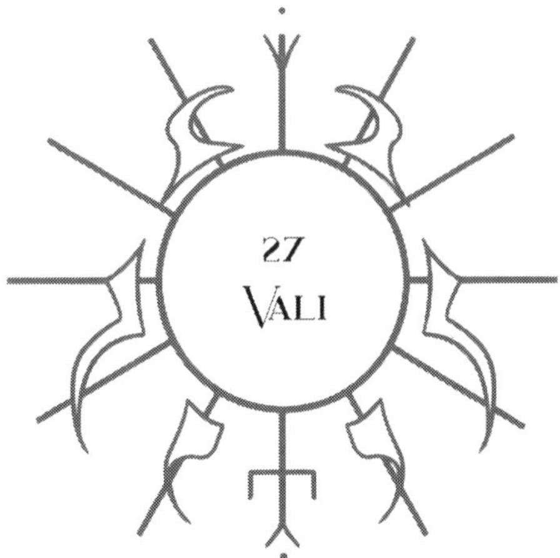

27
Vali

Vali pulled his cowl high over his ears, just enough to block the freezing wind tearing around his body as he rode deeper into the valley. Drieger's prints were still marked in the fresh snow that must have fallen as they slept, guiding him through Thrym's territory.

The pale mare flew down the winding path. The farmlands bordering the giant's hall were a blur as he stood in the saddle to aid their swiftness. He dropped from the horse as it neared the mouth of the hall, where a similar steed was pulling a metal cage.

He saw the world in a bloody filter, his rage dominating his inclinations. The scent of iron curbed the taste of copper against his palate; his fingers ached with a desire to hurt. Guards waited for him outside the open hall doors, but he threw them aside with his magic, not giving them a chance to lift their own.

"Vali!"

Ailsa was chained by her wrists to a beam in the center of the room, surrounded by giants who had seemingly just arrived judging by the icy slush melting from their boots. Her braids were snagged, and her gown was stained with wet spots like she had been drug through the snow, but she otherwise appeared untouched. The look in her eyes wrecked him, and he was grateful he didn't have a heart to feel it break.

"Ailsa, are you hurt?" he asked, approaching her. He was immediately stopped by an invisible wall.

"Not too close, *Vali*."

He forced himself to take a steadying breath. "What is the meaning of this, Drieger?"

The giant appeared from a distant shadowed corner, his fist occupying a large ale. "Did you really think I wouldn't know the kin of my most hated enemy when it showed up on my door? You may look like a fae, but your eyes give you away. Though I am curious as to why you are traveling with a mortal."

"I told you why," Vali spat.

"Yes, you also told me your name was Dane. An obvious lie that forces me to question all your other claims. Do you even care about her at all? Or is this another crafty Aesir trick?"

The room filled with judgmental whispers, but he ignored them. "Of course I care about her. I would not have sought help from my *most hated enemy* unless I was truly desperate."

Thrym stepped from his place on the dais on the opposite side of the room, forming a triangle between him and the giants, and Ailsa sat in the middle. "I wonder if she is even with child. Maybe we should give her a check, just to be sure—"

"Touch a thread on her dress and it will be the last time you use that hand," Vali warned as he unsheathed his blade. A strange urge beckoned him to protect Ailsa as if she were a selfish acquisition. His anger spread through the metal, an extension of his body, setting it on fire as he pointed the blazing sword at the giant.

Thrym shot his hands up in defense as he chuckled. "All right, I think we learned the answer to *that* question. Though she is pretty, I have no interest in your human, Vali."

"Then why is she in your hall?"

"Because I want something from the Aesir, and I need your help to get it. Our dear Ailsa here is just providing you with some necessary motivation."

Vali lowered the weapon, and the flames died. "If you want something from the Aesir, I'm afraid you threatened the wrong one. The gods of Asgard do not recognize me as one of them, nor do they care if I require their assistance."

"Just hear us out," Thrym said. He paced around the platform supporting Ailsa. "We mean to steal something from the Aesir so we may use it as leverage in a deal. I plan to propose to the goddess Freya, but I would like to be reassured she will not refuse."

"How romantic," Ailsa mumbled.

Thrym glared at her. "This object we take must be precious to them. Something they cannot live without."

Vali shrugged. "Like what? Their mirrors?"

The giants crowding the room delighted in his response, but Drieger shook his head. A flicker of excitement flashed against red eyes. "Not mirrors, Vali. Mjolnir."

It was Vali's turn to laugh now, and he did so like the heartless monster he was. "You want me to steal Thor's *hammer*? I'm pretty sure he sleeps with the damned thing."

"Then wait until he bathes! Do what you must, Vali. Only gods can cross the Bifrost. You are one of Odin's sons, are you not? You alone, out of all of us, have access."

Vali paced the floor and passed a hand through his hair. Ailsa watched helplessly as he attempted to think of a better plan, but the giants were right. He alone could enter Asgard, and he alone had the ability to steal Mjolnir. And even he could not fight this many giants alone, no matter how much anger fueled the power in his veins.

"Asgard is a two-day journey there and back. How will you assure me Ailsa remains safe while I am away?" The way the giants looked at her, he didn't trust them for a second. An odd territorial feeling rose within him, despite his lack of claim on her.

Thrym thought for a moment before responding. "We will lock her in the dungeon and give you the only key that opens it. There is a slat we can pass her food through and a bucket she can waste in."

"Odin's fucking eye," Ailsa cursed at the very thought.

Vali's gaze softened on her. She was a hostage being used against him, forced to be a prisoner among strangers while he left her to travel a world away. He turned to Drieger. "May I speak with her about this? In private."

"This is all my fault," he muttered when the giant's footsteps slipped out of hearing range, leaving them alone in the underground prison. "I shouldn't have left you alone for a moment in Jotunheim. Gods below, will I ever stop being an idiot?"

Ailsa snatched his elbow to cease his pacing. "Probably not," she said with a small grin. "I'm jesting, of course. You are not an idiot, Vali; you have the entire Nine Realms working against you. Something bad is bound to happen eventually."

"How are you so calm about this? You're going to be alone in a giant's dungeon!"

She placed her hands on top of his shoulders. "Relax. It

wouldn't be the first time I was kidnapped by strange men. I will be fine. It is *you* who I am worried for."

He shook his head. "I do not deserve your concerns."

"You still have them. Are Ivor and Seela still waiting at Drieger's?"

He nodded. Her hands shifted from his shoulders to the back of his neck, and his hands ached with the need to touch her back. "You looked like you were going to murder every giant in that room just now."

"And I would have if they hurt you. Still considering it, actually."

Her lips pressed into a hard line and her eyes sparkled like sapphires in the low torchlight. He wished he could see inside her mind. To know what she was thinking. She probably still thought him a monster, a man with bloodlust dominating his every impulse. "That seems a bit excessive, Vali."

"I will not apologize for keeping you safe—"

"Then don't." She interrupted him. Her eyes lowered nearly as much as her voice—a lush and sultry pitch. Her pretty upper lip curling over her teeth. "Because I liked it."

The sharp insert of his breath prompted her to look at him again, and her cheeks colored a lovely shade of pink. She spoke again before he could appease her embarrassment. "And I know it's only because you're protecting what's inside me, but I still appreciate what you've done and what you will be forced to do in Asgard."

It is not the only reason. The thought was intuitive. But he locked away the words behind the seal of his lips, only nodding in reply.

"Be careful," she whispered. "The days will be dark without you, *Sólskin*."

Hearing her name for him broke the fragile plane of his

willpower, and he wrapped his arms around her thin waist while burying his face into her neck. She smelled like her oils, like the forest—a dangerous essence of earth and wildflowers matching her stallion spirit.

"The nights will be dull without you, *Stiarna*." Starlight, he called her, for reasons still unknown to him. All he knew was it fit her, and it made her smile against his cheek. He pulled back to gaze into her eyes, to make sure she heeded his words. "Take this time to rest," he said. "Remember what you carry. The giants are equal to the gods in their power, and I would not wish for *you* to fall into their manipulating hands. Do you understand?"

"Aye," she said. Their faces lingered in a space too comfortable for enemies, too close for friends. Her cheeks glistened in the dull torchlight, wet from tears she wiped away with a stealthy swipe. "Now go. The sooner you leave, the sooner you come back." She dropped her gaze to his lips for a heartbeat before looking away, focusing on the single cot on the floor. "But Vali?"

"Yes?"

"I can't believe I'm even saying this to you," she shook her head smiling, "but please don't leave me here. Come back for me."

He lifted a hand under her chin, tilting it an inch to look up at him. "There's nothing in the Nine Realms that would keep me from you, Ailsa."

Her smile fell as he said the words, sensing a forbidden message behind them, searching for a deeper truth he could never speak out loud. The seriousness of their situation suddenly snapped him back into reality, to a world where he was Vali and she was the Tether. Where an entire realm depended on him to follow his calling. He turned away before he did something he regretted. And after last night, his self-control was particularly vulnerable.

When the giant unlocked the cell, he left without sparing her another glance. The sight of her tears stimulated something uncomfortably vulnerable inside him, and he swallowed it before it carved an Ailsa-sized foothold in his mind.

This time apart would be beneficial, he decided. He needed space to settle these feelings festering inside him like a weakness before they manifested into something more crippling. He could not afford to let her threaten his conviction. Not now.

Not yet.

"One moment, Vali," A voice followed him as he was leaving the dungeon stairwell. Thrym emerged from the shadows and offered him the single dungeon key. "I want to warn you just in case you get any ideas. If I see even the slightest bit of force from Asgard, I will blow apart those dungeon locks and squash your human like a grape."

Vali turned slowly to face the giant, staring him dead in his crimson eyes. "And if I return and hear you have even looked upon her in a cruel way, you won't have to worry about the gods. I will be the Aesir who ends you. Take care of her, Thrym, or I will take care of you."

He left the giant's territory, the hole in his chest a bit larger than before.

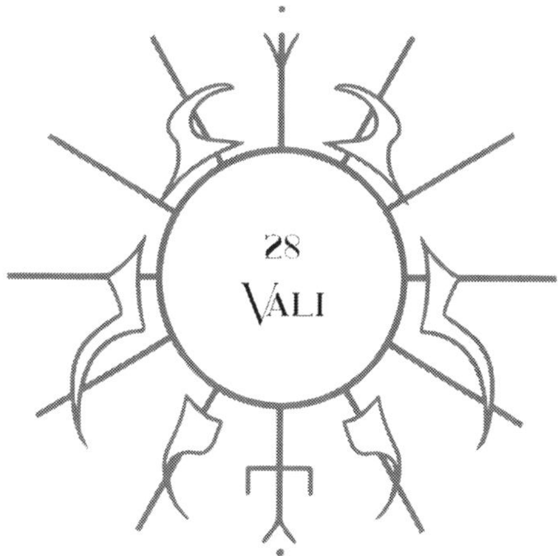

28
Vali

Vali did not stop to rest or eat. He traveled back to Drieger's and returned Skiord's horse, knowing the beast would never cross the river in the shallow boat. Seela was raging when he returned, furious he left her without a word. Her anger did not quench when he explained the giant's bargain.

"This mortal is becoming more trouble than she's worth," she mumbled as Vali pulled their boat back to shore. "We should have tried to transfer the power ourselves. The ring was much easier to carry around."

"Like she asked for any of this! We were perfectly happy in Midgard before you fae came along and murdered everyone," Ivor muttered.

"If she would have kept her hands to herself—"

"Enough, Seela." He was tired and stretched thin, and their constant fighting was draining him of patience.

"Do you not agree?" the commander asked.

"What does it matter?" he asked. "What's done is done. We cannot go back and change the events in Drakame. Whether we like it or not, Ailsa is our responsibility. And I'm tired of you speaking of her like she is a burden."

She didn't answer right away. Her silence spoke loud enough. "Oh, Vali," she whispered. The tone of her voice demanded his attention, pity in her eyes. "Don't tell me things have changed. You can't do this now. Not when we're so close."

"What do you mean?" Ivor's voice was tight behind her. She searched Vali like he was hiding something. Her nostrils flared with a large breath. "Are you saying—"

"Gods below," he moaned. His hand was on the bow of the boat, so close to sailing away from this uncomfortable conversation. "Yes, I care about Ailsa, but not in the way you think, Seela. It is purely platonic."

"You're lying! No wonder your scent is different." Ivor yelled at him. "Things have been changing since the day we boarded your ship. Your intentions, your feelings, everything about you has transformed into something worse. Something more deceptive."

It took every last ounce of his willpower not to set the wolf on fire. Glaring at her, he said, "I am not the only one who has changed, I assure you. Do not assume to know me, wolf."

The wolf sneered, barring her teeth. "I know you, Vali. You're a heartless beast who wouldn't know compassion, even if it bit you on the ass." She took a step closer, crowding him. "How could you possibly care for her? You killed her family. You kidnapped her from the only home she's ever had. You ruined her life—"

"Don't you think I know that?" He spun to face her, one move of his index finger away from snapping her neck. But Ailsa would never forgive him if he killed her wolven, and he had already added enough to her pain. "You are right about one thing, Ivor. I am heartless. I have one purpose in this life, and I will complete it. Neither god nor giant nor anything else in creation on this Tree will keep me from delivering the Tether and saving my home. Especially not a pretty little heathen." Ivor slammed her mouth shut, her response replaced with a scowl. "Enough of this. I am going to Asgard, and I will return as soon as I have the hammer. Keep an ear out for any news of Thrym or Ailsa, Seela."

"Of course, Vali." Seela embraced him before he left to whisper in his ear. "Remember the vow we made to each other in the forest?"

He nodded against her temple.

"I will never judge you for your choices, and I will support you until the end, as long as you are always honest with me. I will keep my promise, as long as you keep yours."

Vali slipped out of her embrace with a sigh. Whatever this affectionate feeling he had for her was, it must be forgotten. Ivor was right. He had turned her world upside down, taken everything from her and gave her nothing back but grief. He couldn't take something as precious as her heart, not when he had nothing to offer her in return. Vali had committed so many crimes against Ailsa, but caring for her would be the worst.

He spared no time when he reached the opposite side of the river, gathering his small bag of supplies and his blade, and started the long trek to Asgard. It was a day's ride to the dwelling place of the Aesir gods, and he was making the journey on foot. But he would not stop for rest until he saw the wall surrounding the divine realm. There was enough burdening his mind to distract him from the fatigue of his body.

THE SUN SANK at his back and rose to meet Vali the next morning as he neared the realm of the Aesir. The first morning rays of light struck the opaque stones composing the wall and glared a thousand colors across the landscape. A tangible bridge formed from the fragmented light.

The Bifrost.

"It's been a long time, brother," Heimdall spoke as he broke from the treeline and reached the edge of the bridge. "Will you finally enter Asgard?"

When Vali was young, he would travel to the Lower Branches without his mother knowing just to steal a glimpse of his father's domain. Even from the concealment of the wilderness bordering the god's realm, Heimdall could see him. The guard could see a hundred miles in any direction, hear the grass grow and the time pass. But he never questioned Vali, just let him look upon the Aesir stronghold before sneaking back to his home.

Seeing the watchman dressed in fluorescent white robes was a welcoming sight. The sunlight made his skin sparkle, nearly matching the paleness of his hair and the white staff in his hands. His eyes were gold, like Vali's, but so were his teeth. He was a fellow son of Odin, his half-brother, and the only one who considered him one.

"Yes, Heimdall. I am ready to enter Asgard. Will you tell Odin I am here?"

The watchman waved a dismissive hand, a sheen of golden light trailing his path through the air. "He already knows. He watches you, always."

"Wonderful," he replied dryly.

"He has been in particularly good spirits the past few weeks. Would that have anything to do with you and your mission?"

Vali swallowed against a dry knot in his throat. "Nothing gets past you, Heimdall."

The white god howled a deep laugh into the clear sky. "It's good to see you, Vali. You belong here with the Aesir. Demigod or not, you deserve to sit amongst the gods and be worshipped as one after finding the Tether."

Vali tried not to wince. He had no interest in joining the Aesir or becoming a god. He was fulfilling his calling to be rid of it, not for a title, and certainly not for Odin. He *belonged* with the fae, with his family.

"We shall see," he only said.

The watchmen nodded knowingly and stepped aside to let him pass. Vali was accepted by the Bifrost as soon as his feet stepped across the spectrum, the refracted rays of light establishing beneath his boots. No matter how he felt about the Aesir or Odin, he was powerless against his admiration for Asgard. The beauty of this realm was rooted in every aspect of its functioning, from the bridge to the twelve halls splitting the massive realm into the stronghold it was known to be. The wall built by the hands of a deceptive giant, impregnable and unscalable, was as much of a masterpiece as it was a fortification.

Heimdall escorted him along an extended, paved path broken up by several staircases. Asgard was built on a mountain towering over the rest of the twelve territories dividing the realm. Odin's home stood proudly at the crest, so high it could be seen over the wall. His open-air palace was lined with gold roofing and marble columns. The land here was the most fertile in all the Nine Realms. Every inch of the landscape was covered in thick greenery and flowers, the colors of the richest jewels.

It made him think of Ailsa trapped in a dark dungeon, and how she would have loved to see this view.

"Gods below," he muttered to himself, shaking his head to clear the face of her phantom. Heimdall snuck him a curious look but did not comment.

"I'll bring you to the Well of Urd. The gods have already held their council, but Odin lingers there often, watching over mankind in the waters."

"And we will avoid the other gods in the process," Vali spoke the unsaid.

The watchman shrugged. "Best if no one knows you're here unless Odin wishes it to be known."

"The Allfather is still ashamed of me?"

Heimdall sighed. "Shame is not the word I would use. Don't let them get to you, Vali. Leave the past in the past."

They continued the endless path to a sprawling garden. Every kind of plant, tree, or flower grew across the miles of tended fields stretching below Idun's hut. Her golden apple orchard stretched across the main strip, lining the way to the well. Heimdall lingered near the goddess's home, letting Vali approach on his own.

Odin was leaning against the stone border, studying the images floating beneath the surface. His patched eye was to Vali, but the god knew he was there by the way his shoulders stiffened. He took a moment longer to finish the vision before pushing away.

The first thing Vali noticed about his father was his youth. The immortal fruit of Idun's tree kept the gods young, and Odin appeared no older than himself. His golden hair spilled down his back, matching the color of his sight. His eyes were the only thing Vali inherited from the god, and he was grateful for it. There was nothing else he wanted from him.

"Vali," Odin smiled. "How good it is to finally meet my long-lost son in the flesh. You look well. Strong."

Vali said nothing. He did not move or return niceties. Odin laced his hands behind his back and paced around the well, his pale blue robes skimming the trimmed lawn. "I know you must think poor of me, what your mother must say of my absence in your life. But know I couldn't leave Asgard even if I wanted to, and I could see you were doing just fine without me."

Vali let loose the heaviest of sighs. "We really don't have to do this, Odin. I'm sure you saw what happened and why I am here. Will you spare me the breath and just tell me if you will help or not?"

Odin didn't answer at first. He sat on one of the empty benches and gestured for Vali to follow. The elfin took the seat at the edge of the bench to claim as much distance as possible before Odin spoke again. "I used to watch you, but ever since you found the Tether, my sight of you has been obscured, and I am unable to see past Gullveig's runes. She protected her power since the beginning, which is why she was so difficult to find in the first place. I see you sometimes, but then something gets in the way and the vision cuts off. You've been on quite the adventure these past few weeks."

"That is the understatement of the century."

Odin was quiet for a long time, and Vali listened to the breeze slip through the orchard. He finally asked, "Where is it?"

"Jotunheim."

Odin cursed under his breath. "And why did you go to Jotunheim?"

Vali rubbed his face warily. If the power was protected from his all-seeing eye, that meant he didn't know about Ailsa. Somehow, the idea comforted him. "The Tether is bound to a human soul, not an artifact. We were traveling and she fell into the River Irving. I had no choice but to bring her to the closest hall or she would have died, and I would have lost the Tether."

The god stared somewhere beyond where they were sitting, considering his words. "Do the giants know?"

"No, but we risk them finding out every second she is there. They are holding her hostage until I steal Mjolnir for them."

"What do they want with Thor's hammer?"

"To bargain with in a marriage proposal to Freya."

Odin groaned, rubbing his forehead like this conversation was giving him a massive headache. "Forget Ragnarok, Freya is going to kill us all if we agree to such a thing."

"Then don't. Find a way out of it, as the Aesir always do. It is not my concern how you get the hammer back, only that you let me take it. Otherwise, your power will remain in Jotunheim."

Odin tapped his long fingers against his chin. "Will you bring her to Alfheim after?"

"I vowed to return the power to my land. Frey can bring her with him when he leaves the fae lands."

Odin stood and approached the well once more, searching for the answer to his doubts. "I think you should go back to Jotunheim, slay the beasts, and take back what is ours, Vali. That is what any son of mine would do."

"I am not Thor," he spat. "I do not have a hammer that can crush a giant's skull in one blow—"

"You have more power in your pinky finger than Thor has strength in his entire body." Odin cut him off. "You slaughtered the humans without a second thought, and now you show weakness to giants?"

"I had an army to face the mortals. I am but one man in a realm of monsters who could squash her before I draw my blade. What would you have me do?"

Odin shrugged. "Let them. Let the power tether to something else and then search for it again. But I will not let the giants try to manipulate the Aesir. Especially not for Freya."

Vali was seething, hot blood burnished his veins. "I've never asked you for anything, and the moment I do, you say no."

"Your request is foolish."

"Foolish? Yes. I was foolish to come here." He stood to leave, and the god made no move to stop him. Vali laughed a heartless sound before turning back to his father. "She brought me back to life, you know."

This sparked the god's interest. He looked at the elfin over his shoulder and Vali continued, "I was hit by lightning in a helstorm, and she brought me to life with Gullveig's power. You want to keep your beloved son in Helheim? Fine. But the key to his revival is in Jotunheim and you're about to throw it away for gods know how much longer because you do not want to take away your child's favorite toy."

"How dare you speak to me—"

"If you let her die in the hands of giants, I will not search for the Tether again. I will not let you abandon that woman and continue on like it never happened. Kill me for all I care."

Odin was facing him now with an arched brow, his hands on his hips and snarl across his lip. Everything before this had been an act. How Odin really felt about him was obvious in the here and now, the way he was looking back at him like he was his greatest disappointment.

"Thor is getting drunk with Tyr in his chambers. I will

speak with Loki about retrieving the hammer, but you may have to wait until he falls asleep. You may use Njord's' old chamber, since he demanded to go back to Vanaheim, and meet me here tomorrow morning. I'm sure between the gods, one of us can figure out how to get us out of the mess you've made."

"Thanks for your help," he said bitterly, turning to leave.

"But Vali?" His steps paused and Odin continued, "I promised your mother I would remove Frey from the fae realms should you succeed. But if you fail, if you think for a moment you can keep Gullveig's power from me or try to use it against me, so help me, Vali, you will regret the day you defied me."

"I have no interest in your witch's power—"

"Then what are you interested in? What is your endgame in all of this?"

Restoring his realm, fulfilling his calling, becoming the man his mother wanted—needed—him to become. All his motivations now seemed superficial and shallow. He was only here because of choices made for him, his life predetermined by a single dream. His immortal life was meaningless, and his father knew it. Men like Vali were easier to control when they had nothing to live for.

He left without giving Odin an answer.

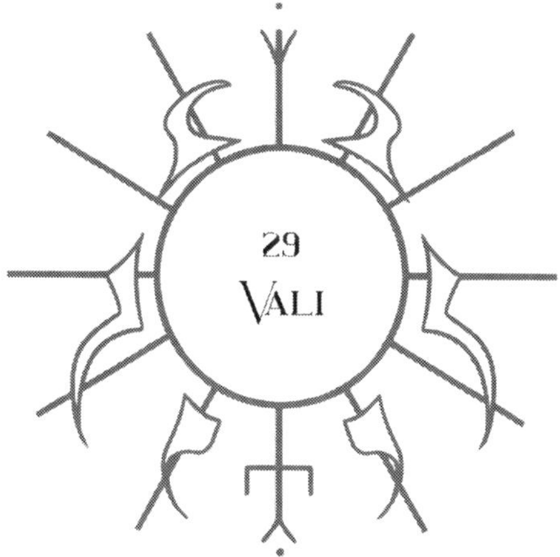

"Can you show me to Valhalla?" Vali asked Heimdall, who waited near Idun's cottage in the garden for him to return. Odin remained behind, consumed by the well and the visions which intrigued him.

"What business do you have with slain mortals?" the watchman asked.

"Not business. Questions. Particularly for a man I recently killed."

Heimdall nodded toward the eastern wall. "I'll show you to Gladsheim where Valhalla stands, though I have to warn you, it might prove difficult to find a single man. If the human you are looking for is not there, he may be in the fields of Folkvang, lying to the west."

"Not Ledger," he muttered. There was only one place in the afterlife a man like him would go. He followed the god toward a large field that stretched miles in each direction. The twelve sections of Asgard were each as large as the fae realms by themselves, each spreading across a different branch to carry the weighty foundation of many worlds inside a single realm. The Hall of Valhalla stood at the end of a field, where Valkyrie perched on top of rooflines made of shields. The winged maidens stretched their wings in the waning rays of the sun, no battles in Midgard to require their services.

Over five hundred doors lined the halls stretching to the east and west, and Ledger now resided behind one of them. Only those slain in battle went to Odin and Freya, and although the goddess had first pick over the slain warriors, he couldn't imagine Ledger belonging to anyone but Odin himself. Even from his brief introduction, he knew the man was destined to reach Valhalla.

The ground was bloody as they crossed the fields, evidence a great battle had just taken place. The warriors fought in the afterlife to train against the inevitable rise of the giants at the end of the world—the day the Norns predicted the gods would fall. Their eternity was filled with fighting that could mangle but not kill, the ultimate heaven for any true, gritty heathen, and a great feast was held at the end of each battle.

Music slipped from behind a pair of towering double doors, informing Vali this feast was already in progress. Heimdall left him to return to the Bifrost, and the elfin pushed aside the doors leading to the revelry.

The smoky smell of roasted boar hit him immediately—boar mixed with the heady odor of blood, sweat, and grime of satisfied Northmen all sitting around long tables and boasting about their daily kills. Their conversations hushed as Vali passed, noting the sight of the elfin and his fae appearance, nonverbally questioning his intentions.

But he ignored their silent queries. He was too focused on scanning tables, the hundreds of so that were there, for the face he met on the island in the North Sea. Ailsa did not resemble her father, though she had his mouth. The first time she scowled at him, he noticed the similarity.

When it was clear there were too many heathens to comb through, he turned to a man with fiery red braids. "Do you know a man called Ledger Locharsson?"

The man peered over his rack of ribs, his left arm missing from the day's fight, yet he appeared not to notice. "Who's asking?"

"The one who sent him here."

"That's not an answer."

"Do you really care?"

The man squinted at him precariously before turning to assess the tables behind him. He pointed toward a few tables over. "There."

Vali locked eyes on his target. Ledger appeared exactly how he did when the battle maidens carried him home. His straw bleached hair was cut short around his skull, a graying beard braided down his chest with the tip now dipped in blood. His fists were filled with meat and mead and speaking obnoxiously loud over the other raised voices competing throughout the hall.

Vali crossed the length of the room and sat on the bench across from Ailsa's father. The man lowered his feasting hands when his brain recognized the man sitting in front of him.

"We meet again, Ledger the Liar." Vali smiled pleasantly and poured himself a drink.

The man only grunted. The warriors next to him suddenly became interested in other topics of conversation. Ledger licked his fingers of leftover fat. "To what do I owe the displeasure of seeing you again?"

"I want to know something about your family."

His breath sang sharply between his teeth in a scoff. "Fuck off."

"It's about Ailsa."

Ledger crossed the table in a blink. His fist reached for Vali's throat. The elfin stopped his hand with a firm catch of his wrist just an inch away from his neck. Ledger used his free hand to grab a nearby sconce and swung hard to strike him in the temple. Vali hissed as the weighted pewter candlestick cracked over his skull. He twisted the man's arm by his wrist and slammed him against the table, pressing him down by his shoulder. "I thought the fight was over?" he asked the Ostman.

Ledger laughed beneath him. "Fighting never ends in Valhalla, that is what makes it paradise." He squirmed beneath the elfin until Vali finally released him. "What do you know of my daughter, swine? Has something happened to her?"

The elfin took a stalling sip of rich malt before replying. "We should speak of it somewhere else."

"Is she…" He swallowed the rest of the words.

Vali shook his head quickly. "No. She is alive, but I have reason to believe she could be in danger."

"And why do you care about my Ailsa's life?"

The elfin grimaced. Fathers were not on his good side as of late, and he anticipated Ledger wondered about his motivations as much as his own father did. "Let's go outside."

Ledger looked regretfully at his half-eaten plate, but eventually nodded.

"HAD I known you were one of Odin's sons, I would have died with a smile on my face," he finally said after Vali explained the events leading up to his entrance at Drakame. "To be slain by an Aesir god is all an Ostman could ask for in the end."

"I am not a god," he reminded the man. "Godhood requires a following and ceremonial duties, and I have neither."

"Aye, but the other men don't have to know you're not an official *god*. I still have a reputation to keep around here." Ledger unstrapped the axe at his side and stood across from a training dummy. He led the elfin towards the training grounds, which lay empty beneath the cover of night. The bloodlust of the fallen warriors now sufficiently satisfied for the rest of the night, only to return with vengeance in the morning.

"You Ostmen and your reputations," he shook his head. "Ailsa told me you were highly revered as a shieldmage." He sparked the conversation with a subtle fact.

"My daughter speaks to *you*?"

"Yes, right after she tries to stab me."

Nodding in approval, Ledger pitched his axe at the wooden man across the throwing field. A streak of gold followed as his magic increased the weapon's momentum, shattering the dummy at the end of the field. "Only shieldmages come from Drakame. My clan was respected and feared, unchallenged in most political disputes. Our magic made us invaluable to the king, and we were paid well for our support—and to keep my family's line from claiming his throne."

"You didn't want the throne?"

"I didn't say I didn't want it. But our ancestors made a contract with the throne long ago, and Ostmen are nothing if they do not honor their word. Even if the decision was made long ago by people in different situations… different ambitions." Ledger stepped in line with an undamaged dummy and picked up a spear.

"Why are shieldmages only from Drakame?"

The man faltered with the spear when Vali asked, before

throwing it clean through his sparring partner. He sensed he just prodded a sensitive place.

"Why are you asking me about Drakame? I thought this was about my daughter," he asked, rolling another spear in his palm.

Vali picked up a dagger the length of his forearm from the arsenal of weapons lining the table behind them. "We're getting there. Answer the question, Ledger."

He tapped the tip of the spear against the ground in careful thought. "They've been in my family for centuries. I am a direct descendent of the first shieldmage. And from him, the line branched throughout Drakame. Those born with the power must remain in our clan to practice their gift. If an Ostman breaks that code, they are executed. That is the law. The gods blessed our line with magic—"

"Is this what you truly believe or what you've been told to say?" Vali was skeptical the gods would give humans magic. It went against the laws of their realm, throwing off a carefully constructed balance. In the fae realms, magic and life were one and the same. It was a give and a take. A relationship. But these heathens had no bond with the earth or the life inside it. And it was difficult to believe the gods would share their dominion over life in Midgard with their patrons.

"It is as I said," he gritted through clenched teeth. "A gift."

"From whom?" Vali arched his brow.

Ledger squinted his small eyes, their hazel nearly black in the gloam. "Why does a fae concern himself with the magic of mortals?"

"Because *my* mortal was given a power that should not have fallen into her delicate hands." His palm gripped the steel.

"Your mortal?" Ledger scoffed. "My Ailsa does not belong to you. She discovered the Tether by accident—"

"I don't think she did. I don't think it was by chance at all that the ring was passed down through her mother's line. I don't think the wind whispered your name without reason." He flipped his wrist, and the blade gleamed in the starlight. "But do you want to know the most damning evidence of all?"

The man sucked his teeth. "What?"

"Centuries ago, when your great grandfather was dubbed the first *shieldmage,* the witch Gullveig was traveling the Nine Realms and was at the peak of her popularity right before Odin took her as his personal seeress. I wonder, perhaps, if your family called on the sedir witch to give your clan an advantage."

"I've never heard of Gullveig. And we do not practice *sedir.*" Ledger spat the word like it tasted bitter on his tongue.

"Is that why you burned the seeress who came to Drakame?"

"How do you—"

Vali interrupted his question with a boastful grin. "Ailsa likes to brag about her father. She's told me much of your history and the events leading up to my arrival in Midgard. But I wonder if you deserve an ounce of her admiration."

Ledger's eyes dropped, unable to hold his gaze. Shame was reclusive, never enjoyed being seen. Vali knew this well. Ledger spoke quietly, "I never deserved Ailsa as a daughter. She was too kind to belong to me, too forgiving. She should've had her mother, and I would have traded places with Astrid in a heartbeat so they could have been together."

Vali agreed with him but said nothing. His silence was condemning enough. "Ledger, I did not come here to torment you in the afterlife. But if you know why Ailsa was chosen to bear this burden, it might help me anticipate the danger waiting for her in the shadows. There are dark forces competing against the Nine Realms. You and the rest of the fallen fight to train for Ragnarok, but the end might be closer than we realize."

The chieftain tossed his spear back on the table, suddenly not feeling the urge to destroy. "Even if I did know why the Tether latched to her, what would you do about it? You said it yourself, you are no god. You cannot protect her."

The elfin spared a glance at the dummy before hurtling his spear across the field. The weapon blasted through the center of its chest, and the target and the blade both splintered into pieces, littering the earth with their shattered remains. He turned to face Ledger, who only offered a grim expression.

"I can manage," he said. His head cocked toward his not so indirect display of strength.

Ledger stroked the tip of his beard, still matted with someone else's blood. "You must promise me you will not tell Ailsa what I'm about to say. I do not want her to be ashamed of me… of our family."

"It's a bit late for that."

A muscle feathered in the jarl's jaw. "Promise me, Vali."

The elfin placed a hand over his chest to feign loyalty. But he had no intention of keeping this man's secrets—especially from Ailsa.

Ledger looked off into the distance, where the evening sun was still brushing the blanket of nightfall. His chest rose and fell slowly before he spoke. "Our magic did not come from gods. It was not a blessing or a gift, but from an arrangement with the Volva."

Vali's posture stiffened at the mention of the witches. The Volva were more than just average seeresses. They were powerful beings skilled in sedir, called by all kinds of beings in times of crisis. Some believed they were followers of Gullveig, but those claims were disputed when the Volva continued to roam long after the witch disappeared. Legends said their blood magic could bless or curse, but not much else was known about them concerning where they lived or whom they learned their craft from. The mystery only added to their menace.

"My ancestor was Bjorn Bloodblade. He was known for being a merciless warrior and a fierce Ostman warlord. Before we conquered England and before Riverland had a king, Drakame was struggling to compete on the world stage. Despite the riches he accumulated on his raids, there was still conflict concerning who should lead the clans into war against the Saxons.

"Bjorn had two brothers and three sons, and the competition for the first Riverland king was a toss between any one of them. He was a successful warlord but had no consistent following, as people didn't like him much. He was… detestable. His bloodlust was disturbing even among our kind." Ledger picked at a crimson spot caked into his wrist casually as he continued. "It is unclear if he contacted the Volva before or after he murdered his family—"

"Wait," the elfin held up a hand to pause him. "I feel like you're skipping over a very climactic part of the story."

The man glowered. "If you care for the gory details, I will indulge you. The night before the vote, he gathered his family into the gathering hall. He placed a poison in their ale and killed all three of his sons and his brothers, though his youngest brother had been suspicious and chose not to drink the ale. Bjorn was forced to personally end him."

"He killed his entire family for a position?" Vali winced. And they called him the monster.

"Aye, but this wasn't just a position. This would set up the line of whomever sat on the Riverland throne, and he wanted to be the one who established the North kingdom, as our enemies would come to call it. But what he did was not accepted well by the other clans, and they were threatening to exile him. When Bjorn realized he had made a grave mistake and exhausted all his other options, he sought assistance from the Volva. He needed an advantage that would make him invaluable to his people again.

"The witch agreed to help him, but she had a price. She would touch our family with the Blessing of the Berserker and give us a power on the battlefield outmatching any foe we faced. This blessing would remain as long as our line continued, but there was a catch. The women who were born into our family would face a short life. This was to balance the protection the blessing gave the warrior, to weaken our family just enough we could not create an empire of battlemages. Our daughters started dying younger and younger, from either illness or from battle, until we were barely producing heirs. We kept the blessing to Drakame, unified with only those in our clan so that the blood spread to as many of our followers' families as possible. But once the original line ends, the blessing will die with it."

"The line ends with Ailsa?"

Ledger put his mouth beneath the spout on a barrel perched on the table, letting the mead flow into his mouth directly from the tap. He wiped his lips with the back of his hand. "She was supposed to marry a shieldmage. His lineage to our common ancestor is weak, but their union would have continued the line. I already paid her dowry—"

"His name wouldn't be Erik, would it?"

The man frowned and shook his head. "No. I forced his family away when I saw Ailsa and Erik becoming too close.

Erik's family has never shown evidence of the blessing, and I needed to make sure Ailsa joined with someone who had the blessing in his blood so it would be passed down."

Vali was pacing the field. His mind was fumbling with the pieces Ailsa and her father had given him to connect their stories. "But Ailsa claimed Erik and his family chose to leave. He wrote her a letter stating he wished her well."

Ledger shrugged. "I made Erik write that letter. Sent him and his family away with enough gold to fund the five clans combined. His father would have castrated him if he refused me."

Vali stared at the man long and hard, trying to understand how a woman so considerate and caring could come from a long line of selfishness. Then he remembered what Ailsa told him, the agony she faced after losing not only Erik but her child—all because of her father's ambition to maintain their pedigree. "But she was in love with him! You made her think Erik did not want her."

"She was nineteen, elfin. Hardly old enough to know what love is or what is good for her. Besides, I would not want my daughter with such a man. Erik's temper outmatched even that of his father. He might have deceived her into believing he was genuine, but I saw the darkness inside him. And for the sake of the blessing, she must be with Nikros."

If Vali had not already thrown his spear, he would have used Ledger as his personal training dummy. His hands itched for something to skewer him with. "*Blessing?*" he seethed. "You think what Ailsa endures is a blessing? One you arrogantly want to pass on to the other women in your line just so your clan can preserve their magic?"

He staggered away from the elfin as Vali crossed the

distance between them, his strides hungry. "Well, when you put it that way—" he stammered.

"There is no other way to put it!" Vali grabbed the nearest hammer and swung it towards the man's temple, narrowly missing his skull. As Ledger ducked, he tripped over his own boots, falling on his arse before him. Vali towered over him, clutching the mallet. "You don't deserve Valhalla. You don't deserve an afterlife among the honorably slain. There is no honor in misleading your daughter and asking her to bear the curse of your ancestor's mistakes."

Ledger's face flinched as the elfin reared back the hammer, ready to let it fall on his head. But Vali hesitated, lowering it by an inch even as his breath heaved heavily with hatred. "Why did you burn Jomeer?"

The man's face twisted with confusion. "Jomeer? I burned the witch because she came to Drakame uninvited and threatened to tell everyone the truth about our magic."

"Why?" he hissed. "Why would a witch travel all the way to your quiet little clan just to threaten you?"

But Ledger only tightened his lips, denying the elfin any further information. Instead, he asked his own questions. "Why are you here, Vali? Why do you care what I've done to my family?"

"Because I need to know!"

"*Why?*" he screamed. The single word echoed across the barren fields of Asgard, similarly constant inside his head as he asked himself the same.

In the heat of the moment, the answer sparked, and knowing the truth he unleashed would never leave this hall, he let it fly free from the cage of his tongue. "Because I am the reason Ailsa is alone. I am the one who ended her family line and practically forced this curse upon her. And for some reason, Ledger, I *care.* So if there is a way to take this burden from her, I vow to you and every star above listening to us now: I will find it."

Before her father could respond, Vali brought down the hammer and split open his thick skull. Hot blood spewed across his face and painted the field, but did nothing to soothe the anger in his flesh. Ledger was sprawled limp beneath him. It would take him all night to heal from an open head wound, and Vali left him there to be found in the morning.

His confession rocked something inside his spirit, an acknowledgement to both himself and the universe he would be forever marked by Ailsa in a way that ran deeper than the marks on his skin. He cared, but that was not the worst of it. He cared for *her,* even when he knew he could not.

He made the long walk back to Idun's garden, feeling the ghost of his heart beat an ache across his chest.

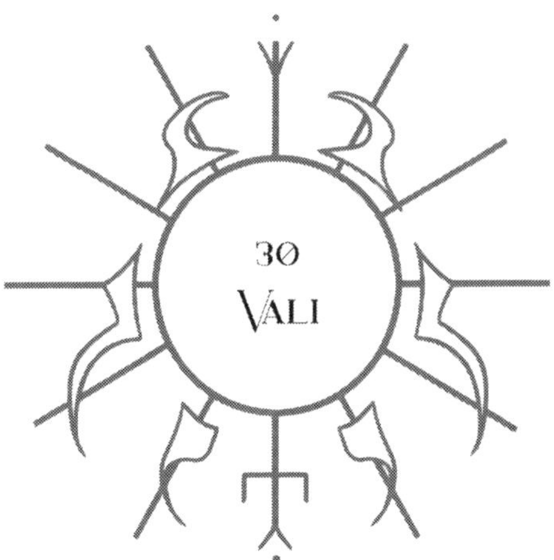

30
Vali

Thor's hammer sat on the edge of a bench near the well, unguarded.

Vali approached the well, struck by the solacing solitude found beneath the orchid canopy sprawling like fingers above him. He lifted the encumbered weight of the hammer, and as his fingers slipped around the stumped handle, bolts of incredible energy surged through his fingertips. Mjolnir was larger than his head, inscribed with protective runes, enhancing the enchantments molded into its metal.

The weight on his shoulders lightened significantly despite the bulky weapon. He had confessed something tonight that had shaken off a dusty place he had ignored for decades. Awoken by a new motivation, one with a steeper stake and a harder fall. He cared for Ailsa—not because she was the Tether or because she held the key to the salvation of his realm, but because she was Ailsa. The distance should have tempered this feeling inside him, but it only made him more desperate to return. He wondered if this feeling in his chest, this hollow ache in his lungs that was insatiable by air alone, if this was what it was like to miss someone.

"What are you doing here?" a quiet voice spoke behind him. Vali startled and looked over his shoulder to see a small woman draped in a silver robe. The sun had not yet risen, and the shadows beneath the cowl concealed her face.

He held a breath as she neared the well. "I was just leaving," he said.

"Something troubles you, Vali the Heartless. Something beyond your usual burdens."

He laughed at her blatant understatement. "I don't need a seeress to know I'm completely screwed."

"Then maybe a seeress can help you with something else?"

Vali turned to face her. The woman dragged a long finger through the water, the ripples glowed beneath her touch and illuminated the plain features of her face. He asked, "Who are you?"

"They call me Skuld," she said without looking.

"The Norn who writes the fates of the future?" he asked in a voice light with interest. "Can you tell me my own?" She was one of the three Norns that stood around the Well of Urd, her two sisters representing the past and the present. One of the most powerful beings in all the realms, even more so than the gods, because even the divine could not control them. Even gods were at their mercy.

The Norn gave him a sad smile and shook her head. "Fate is not predetermined. If our legacies were written before our actions, how would we feel accomplished for our successes or take ownership of our failures? I can help you see your potentials, nothing more."

"What potentials?" he said. "I have nothing beyond what others have decided me to be."

"Oh, Vali," she said, clicking her tongue. Her lips twisted in a wry grin. "I have spun your life's string through many eras. I have woven and untied it from many other threads, left some to join new ones. Your thread is simply a small string in the complex web of all that exists. A long one, I admit, but still just one. You have many connections still to be made and some to be broken. Some to be cut for good, one to be braided."

He thought of Ailsa and their time coming to an end. He would deliver her to his mother soon, and she would give him over to Odin. The thought made him want to heave his ale. "Whose life string am I braided with?"

The Norn stared into the well and smiled. "That is still to be decided. Choices to be made."

"So, you really can't help me with anything." He scoffed and stood from his seat on the bench while he mentally willed Mjolnir to shrink in his palm. Once the hammer was small enough, he slipped it inside the inner closed pocket of his cloak.

"You believe your life's thread is already sewn into the tapestry of time. You make choices like your fate is decided. I am here to tell you it isn't, Vali. There are infinite outcomes to your life and the threads that align with it. Whoever has decided what you will do or who you will become does not have the power to do so. You are the weaver of your own fate."

He paced to the opposite side of the well and looked inside the murky depths. The Norn wrote symbols on the surface, her eyes reflecting scenes in the water he could not see with his own. "I see your future change, even now as you realize your power over your life," she said.

He gripped the stones lining the edge of the well. "Is she there?" he asked, his voice sounded small across the well's opening.

The Norn smiled again. "She is now."

Vali swallowed nervously, afraid of the truth weaving itself into his future. "For how long?"

"That is for you both to decide."

He blew a harsh breath, disturbing the water. "Can you at least show me a way to help her from what she carries? Or break the curse on her body?"

"The curse is not her body but her blood. She will need to accept who she is in order to be healed. But the end of her thread does not cut off because of an illness." Skuld spoke in a hushed voice. "It is by betrayal. Or greed. Or love. These are the potentials."

"Are there no potentials where her thread weaves on?" The world around him seemed to darken. The starlight snuffed out until he felt the darkness suffocating his senses.

"You are asking the wrong question."

It took all his willpower not to strangle the answer from the Norn, but he thought better than to threaten the performer of his future. "Can I change the potentials?"

She nodded approvingly. "Yes." Vali sighed and ran a hand over his weary expression. "Does this displease you, Son of Odin?"

"I feel like I'm going to make the wrong choice." And nothing about Ailsa felt like a choice. Not her fate, certainly not how he felt about her.

She rounded the well and placed a cold hand over his, ceasing the tremble that had manifested with his confession. "Fate is not carved into stone, Vali. If you do not like where your thread is stitched, then rip it out and start a new path. Because I see a potential for you that is very possible should you do something so simple as choose it."

"What potential is that?" he asked.

"Happiness."

Four days.

It had been four days since Vali left her in a dungeon in Jotunheim, taking the key with him. The giants had been decent hosts, leaving her alone for the better part of the day. She was able to get one of the guards to bring her a pack of cards, courtesy of the gambling games her keepers let her engage in when she convinced them to let her play.

She passed the other lapses of time with sewing. Ailsa had never been particularly crafty with a needle and thread when it came to garments, but she was working on a project to keep her mind busy. Otherwise, she would think about Vali and the trouble he could be facing. He told her two days, and he wasn't the kind of man to lie. Not about something as serious as his time.

She missed him. This throbbing in her chest rivaled the kind she felt when she watched Erik sail away, but this was worse. Erik had known how she felt and rejected her, something she learned to accept. Vali was ignorant of her feelings for him, as was she before he departed. Even now, days later and after plenty of time to be alone with her thoughts, she wasn't quite certain. But her heart seemed to know things her head did not.

She had nothing to gamble with but her words. The giants were easily amused by her sharp tongue and baited by her insults. After only a day of sitting in her own company, she felt anxious, needing something to do. She found the fabric of their clothes were rich and fine despite the living conditions in the valley and decided to work for the materials of her new project.

"I see from the state of your cell my guards are inept at cards." Thrym sauntered down the steps of the dungeon while she was deep into her work, surrounded by rolls of black silk and spools of golden thread.

Ailsa set down her needle and rolled her shoulders free of stiffness. "I think they just feel bad for me now, seeing as I've been stuck pissing in a bucket for the past four days."

Thrym leaned against the bars and surveyed the mess of her cell. "I'm sure your elfin will return as soon as he is able. I did not give him an easy task."

"Or he left me here," she said with a sour face. "Maybe he realized I'm more trouble than I'm worth and used this as an opportunity to dump me on someone else."

The giant threw his head back with a barking laugh, and it was a pleasant sound to behold. His lilac skin practically sparkled in the torchlight. "Trust me, my lady. No male, fae or giant, would forget a woman as lovely as yourself. He would be the greatest fool in all the realms to leave you in my hands."

She couldn't conceal the blush creeping in her cheeks. Even though the Jotun had imprisoned her, he wasn't as cruel as he made himself to be on the first day. He had even agreed to get her supplies should she win them off his men. She enjoyed his banter, and he wasn't offensive to look at either. "That's very kind of you, Thrym."

"What are you making, anyway?" He jutted a chin toward the bundle in her hands.

"It's supposed to be a shirt, but I'm a terrible seamstress. I'm not sure if I should just change it into a large handkerchief at this point." She held the tunic by the shoulders, watching the uneven cuts reveal themselves.

"A bit large for you, don't you think?" he asked.

"It isn't for me."

The giant made an 'O' shape with his lips. "So, it *is* for the elfin."

"I don't know," she confessed, dropping the poorly made shirt from sight. "I should probably just scrap it. It's a terrible idea."

"What do you mean?"

Ailsa could not believe she was about to confide in a giant. Where was her wolven when she needed her? Ivor would definitely agree this was a mistake, would have talked her out of it. Perhaps she was waiting for someone else to confirm her doubts. "In my world, when a woman wants to show a man she is interested in pursuing him romantically, she makes him a piece of clothing. Usually a shirt. But I don't even know if I'm that interested in Vali or if he would return the sentiment. I could be making a fool of myself and not even because this shirt is hideous."

"I'm confused," the giant shifted against the bars. "I thought you were already together. You *are* carrying his child, after all. And the way he reacted to your kidnapping, it seemed like he was quite taken with you."

She let the silk slip between her fingers as she remembered the way he looked at her that day in the cell. The way he called her *Stiarna* and how her toes curled into her flats when he dug his nose into her neck, the way his husky scent clung to her for days after like a taunting ghost. How she wanted nothing more than to rub her fingers over his lips and taste the salt in his words that seemed to burn through her like an open wound.

"It was all an accident," she admitted. "Our meeting, what's inside me, our entire relationship. Hel, he even killed my father and my sisters before we met. It's all been very fast, and my logic is trying to keep up with my intuition. My head says I'm being foolish while my gut says this is right. I just don't know which to listen to." And every day that passed was less time she had to figure it out.

The giant mulled over her words for a moment before opening his mouth again. "Vali nearly slaughtered my house when he saw you in chains, and I was genuinely afraid of his wrath. This tells me he is the kind of man who is more comfortable showing his love through protecting than physical affection. Very common in us violent types, but he cares for you nonetheless."

Ailsa shrugged one shoulder and folded the shirt over a crossed arm. "I'm just afraid that this… child is the only reason for our connection. That when I no longer carry it, he will not be interested in me anymore."

Thrym shook his head in contempt. "Give him the shirt, Ailsa. If he rejects it, you will be hurt. But if you do nothing and never find out how he truly feels in return, you will be alone. And loneliness is much worse."

She nodded solemnly before breaking her glum with a small grin. "Aye. I would say you're right about that. Thank you, Thrym. For a giant who kidnapped and threatened to crush me, you aren't so bad."

"The Jotun are completely misunderstood creatures." He winked. "Do you need anything else for your garment?"

She looked over the shirt with a disappointed frown. "No, I believe it is quite past the point of fixing. But I wouldn't mind playing a round or two to pass the time."

"Clean up your cell and give the extra scraps of fabric to my guards. I'll bring down some ale so we can all have a few rounds," he said.

Ailsa did as he asked, later finding herself sitting with her knees against the bars and sliding cards beneath the grate. Thrym slipped her a cup of golden ale through the small window used for her dining tray.

"All right, no more gambling," she said as she sorted the deck. "Just bragging rights and the eternal embarrassment of losing your own game to a human."

"Ailsa?"

A hoarse voice snuck through the dungeon, stilling her hands. She looked toward the stairwell to see Vali, his cloak caked in mud and dripping rainwater. His dark hair shone like spilled ink, wet from the storm pouring outside the dungeon's vented windows. It waved messily down the back of his neck, flipping around each side to hug his nape. His brow arched with interest as he watched her shuffle the cards.

She cleared her throat of the girlish squeal forming there. "Well, look who finally decided to come back from Asgard."

Thrym and the other guard were already standing, sensing the game had ended before it even began. Vali did not answer, only tossed his cloak to the nearest guard, the key to her cell in his right hand.

"The hammer is in the inside pocket," he murmured to Thrym as the giant crossed his path. When the Jotun found what they were looking for, the chieftain ordered them to clear the lower floor. But not before offering her an encouraging wink.

Then they were alone.

"What took you so long?" she asked, crossing her arms as he unlocked the cell. The hinges groaned from being used for the first time in four days.

"I'm sorry," he said wearily. "I had no horse and had to travel the whole way on foot. Then the river flooded when I arrived in Jotunheim, and I had to hide in a tree until it receded. I think I've slept a whole three hours in the past two days." He looked exhausted. His golden eyes were lined with deep shadows, the whites now an irritated red. He smiled at her anyway.

She gave him a tight nod. "Well, I suppose that is a sufficient excuse to be late."

"Not that you missed me much with all the company you seemed to have." His statement came out like a growl as his eyes shifted toward the stairwell.

"I was gambling for supplies." She stepped an inch closer to him, smelling the rain on his skin. Gods, his scent made something shake inside her, a sleeping piece of her waking at the call of his presence. "I had a project I've been working on, and the Jotun are quite generous when it comes to card games."

"Oh?" he matched her step. "And what have you been so diligently working on?"

"A shirt," she said. Words suddenly seemed too complicated to file into full sentences. "For you. For the one you tore apart. For me."

She noticed his cheek concave as he bit the inside of his mouth. "And where is this shirt? You made. For me."

Ailsa's composure finally crumbled with misery. Why did she even mention the ugly thing? "You must promise not to laugh. My father attempted to domesticate me, but he was a poor tutor when it came to tailoring."

He placed a hand over his chest and said, "Cross my heart."

She shot him a glare before pulling the shirt out from beneath her pillow. She could hardly look at him as he unfolded the shiny material and held it against his body, evaluating the shirt on his frame.

"Is this silk?" he asked.

"Aye, it's not the kind of fabric I'm used to working with at home. Usually I use wool or flax, but this material was so fine and delicate, stitching was a tedious job. And I didn't have your measurements, so I had to guess."

Without warning, he pulled off the wet tunic he was wearing and threw it aside. Ailsa gained another glimpse of his bare chest and the cords of muscle outlining his torso, how it tapered from broad shoulders to a trim waist. Shadows danced between the ripples fingering his abdominal wall, pushing her gaze lower until she skimmed the low hanging trousers skirting the V shape of his hips. It was a pity she didn't mend him a pair of pants as well.

He pulled on the homespun shirt and looked it over, seeming neither amused nor repulsed by her work. "Ailsa, this is…"

"Awful, I know. Odin's eye, why did I think your arms were so long?" She finished for him as she assessed her own work on his body. Though the colors were perfect with his complexion, the shiny black fabric and gilded stitching matched the color scheme of his hair and his eyes.

"What's this?" His fingers ran over a detailed spot on the lower left edge.

"The sun," she mumbled. Tiny suns were littered throughout the bordered edges, the only feature she had been quite proud of. "Because you are *Sólskin*."

His eyes flickered to hers, disregarding the stitching and the unequal cuts, even the sleeves that pooled around his wrists. No, the look in his eyes was one of sincere gratitude. A tenderness that stripped away the bane in his stare. "No one has ever made me anything before. Thank you, Ailsa. I love it, truly."

"Only because you have no mirror to see yourself right now." Her mouth suppressed a grin despite how ridiculous he looked.

"And if I did, I would love it even more. In fact, I do believe this is my new favorite shirt." He pulled on the leather vest he wore over his tunic; the covering flattered the poorly made shirt.

Ailsa turned to gather her things, feeling more embarrassed the longer she looked at him. "You do not have to mock me, Vali. I know it's terrible."

He snatched her hand in his and stole back her attention, stroking her wrist with the rough pad of his thumb. The tiny motion was enough to send her thoughts into disarray. "You misunderstand me. I sincerely *love* it. And I shall wear it every day unless it starts to smell, and then I will wash it and wear it again."

"You will look ridiculous wearing the same thing every day," she said, smiling.

"I've been known to be quite unreasonable." His lips curled into a one-sided smirk. "How are you, Ailsa? I'm so sorry it took me this long to get back. The giants didn't bother you too much?"

Ailsa slipped out of his hand, despite the pull of her flesh to remain close. Each breath she took pulled her closer until she was practically suffocating from his proximity. "I'm fine, Vali. In fact, I slept great the past few nights without an elfin snoring in my ear."

Vali scoffed. "I do *not* snore."

"You do, like a bear. But I find it to be one of your more endearing qualities." She carefully assessed him in the low lighting, looking for signs of a difficult journey, but his skin was flawless, if not a little wet. "How was your trip to Asgard?"

The tension returned in his shoulders, filling high to his sharp ears as he took a large breath. "Crawling to Odin for help is probably on top of my list of most hated experiences. I hope I never have to go back," he spat. He turned to sit in the only chair in the corner of the room. His leg spread wide as he rested his head against the sweating walls. "I.... met your father by the way."

Ailsa pressed a palm against the wall for strength, steeling her expression. "You saw him? In Valhalla?"

"Yes." His voice was dry of emotion.

Her chest shuddered off a burden she didn't know she carried. She knew her father was destined for paradise. He built his life around the Ostman Law, based his every decision off a personal code of honor. But hearing he was at peace with the honorably slain, filling his eternal days with battle and feasts, it was a comfort she needed to make peace with a darkness inside her heart. A darkness that once felt like anger but now appeared more like guilt. "What about my sisters?"

"I did not see them if they were there. I would have searched Folkvang, but I ran out of time. I had to leave before Thor realized his hammer was missing."

She dipped her chin in a nod. "I understand. Did you seek my father out on purpose? I find it hard to believe you stumbled upon him by accident."

Vali stared at the floor. "I went looking for him. I had questions." The easiness in his voice was gone, the muscle in his jaw locked rigid.

"And?" she probed him to continue with the tenuous arch of her brow.

He fidgeted in his seat, stalling, trying to find the most delicate words like she were made of glass, and he might break her if he said the wrong thing. But Ailsa had known cruelty enough to have thick skin and a pliant heart. He looked at her finally and spoke, "Would you want me to tell you the truth, even if it would only serve to hurt? Even if your father made me swear not to tell you?"

"Of course," she said. "Do you believe I cannot handle harsh matters? After all we've been through, do you think me fragile?" And why would he care to protect her heart? After all, he owed her nothing. He was not responsible to guard her from the pain of truth.

The ghost of a grin flickered on his lips. He shook his head once. "No. You're like the flowers that grow in the deep folds of the mountains. Lovely and fine to look at, yet able to survive the harshest winters without wilting. Utterly resilient."

Ailsa leaned against the wall and hoped the shadows hid her smile. It was the first time he called her lovely. "And here I believed you thought me an orchid—impossible to maintain and difficult to keep alive. But you are stalling. Tell me what my father said."

He explained her family's ancestry, the first shieldmage and the Blessing of the Berserker—a euphemism for what was really a curse. She was silent for a long time after he spoke of how he promised her to Nikros and paid off Erik to disappear. She knew her father had unparalleled wealth and power among the clans, but she didn't realize just how easy it was for him to control her life. Her future.

"I am *sick* so they could have *magic*," she muttered.

"Ailsa, I—"

"Don't," she broke him off. She didn't want his pity, to hear him apologize for telling her the truth. Had her sisters known the price of their powers? Did they think it was a mercy to lie to her? To mask a curse as an illness.

"And Erik didn't leave me by choice," she whispered to herself. Knowing Eurik, he would have traded his own son for that amount of gold. Erik would have never had a choice. While the idea was satisfying, it didn't make her feel any different about him. He had been her entire life until she finally experienced what else the world had to offer. Suddenly, his influence on her heart was much less significant, much smaller next to giants.

Vali's brows jumped despite his unenthusiastic frown. "He had a choice, Ailsa, and instead he was selfish. You should not chase after a man who puts a monetary value on your heart."

"I chase no man," she said slowly, closely studying his reaction. His eyes betrayed no hint of emotion, but his knee bounced to the rhythm of her unsteady heart. She was starting to learn how his body translated his thoughts. How he smoothed his palms across his thighs when he was anxious, bit his cheek when he was holding back a truth, bounced one knee when he was excited, two when he was worried. And how his shoulders fell when he was crestfallen, how drooped they had been when he left four days ago.

She asked him, "What would you have done? If you were starting a new kingdom in a new land and someone offered you an empire worth of gold to stay away from me? You cannot believe he didn't take the better half of the bargain."

He shrugged a shoulder. "If you were mine, I'd be selfish too. But in an entirely different manner. I'd shove your father's gold so far up his ass, he'd be coughing up coins."

The mental image made her laugh despite her anger, but something about the sober look in his eyes told her he wasn't jesting. She sighed, her gaze falling far away as she thought of her father and Erik, of all the men in her life that had her as an option, yet never chose her. "Why is everyone else allowed to be selfish but me?" she asked no one in particular.

"Is there something you want, Ailsa?" She looked at him again, and he wore a conniving grin, the one he put on right before doing something despicable.

Her gaze fell to his chest, watching the rise and fall increase with speed, matching the rate of her own. "Yes."

The affirmation pulled her toward him, and she was no longer in control of her strides as she crossed the small cell to where he sat, stepping between his legs. His grin fell and he sat straighter as she looked down on him. Her hands found themselves on his shoulders, tight with strain beneath her touch. Perhaps she could think of herself, for once. Damn the rest of the worlds who thought she should choose differently.

"I need to be honest with you, Vali," she said quietly, fumbling with the jagged neckline of his shirt where the stitching didn't take.

He stared up at her, the sunshine gone from his gaze, veiled by an overcast to leave them dark and dangerous. "What is it?"

"I didn't make you a shirt because you tore up your old one for me. Skiord already gave you a perfectly fine shirt to replace it." She took a steadying breath before continuing. "Where I am from, a woman will make a garment for a man if she is… interested in him."

"Interested?" The word came off his tongue painfully slow. "Can you clarify what that means exactly?"

She squinted her eyes at him in scrutiny. "Do I need to spell it out for you, Vali?"

"I want to be sure you're saying what I… *hope* you are very shrewdly implying." His hands lifted from his thighs to the crest of her hip bones, and she was powerless as they pulled the words from her lips.

"I've had a lot of time to think about the past few weeks. I have decided that I cannot fault you for killing my family. Once I understood your world better, listened to your story, and the politics backing your heinous motivation, my heart softened toward you in a way I cannot quite explain."

"Are you saying," he said each word methodically, "that you don't hate me anymore?"

Her fingers nestled into the nape of his neck where they caught lingering drops of rain. "I only hate that I feel drawn to you when I know I shouldn't. I hate that I think about you when you are gone. But most of all, I hate that you were fated to be my enemy, and yet my heart was destined to want you."

He shut his eyes briefly, weighing the enormity of her honesty, the implications of her words and their effect on his feelings. They flickered open. "And now? Do you still want to stab me?" His voice was dry in his throat, and he craned his head to lean into her hands.

"Aye, sometimes I do." She smiled. "But I want to do other things, as well."

"Well, I'm sure we can work something out."

She pulled a stray hair out of his face, adoring the way he looked at her. The way he hung onto every word and waited patiently for her next move. How his hands bruised the skin over her bones in a way that felt admiring, beseeching, wanting. "Are you sure you don't want to give this fine shirt to your lionheart?"

She smoothed her hands down his shoulders and slanted her head, pretending to think over his offer. "No," she finally said. "Erik has a much larger physique than you. Much more muscular. This would never fit him."

"Oh, *right*. He's just layers of more man than me."

"Precisely. I'd have to make another shirt and I'm afraid I'm all out of fabric. Guess I'm stuck with you."

His upper lip snarled, flashing a row of white teeth she recalled like to bite. "How…" he croaked. "How does a man in your world respond to such a gift?"

"If he does not feel the same, he gives the shirt back or burns it. If he accepts her advances, typically he will give her purple flowers in return."

Vali flicked his tongue over his teeth in thought before his eyes lit up with the intensity of a hundred suns. The storm in his eyes suddenly cleared. He held up a single finger. "One moment. Don't move."

"Vali you don't—"

But he was already out of his chair and rummaging through his discarded cloak in the hall outside her cell. He pulled a small package from within one of the pockets and brought it back to her, placing the rolled leather into her hands.

"Would lavender count?"

Ailsa shot him a confused look before untying the package and unrolling it a few inches to peek inside. She discovered pouches of dried herbs, the same ones she kept stocked in her bag. The same ones she was running out of. She bound the roll with the leather fastenings. "Where did you… How?" she asked, shaking her head in disbelief.

"Idun's garden in Asgard grows every plant in creation. I had the goddess point me toward the herbs."

"These are herbs from *Asgard*?" she asked, regarding the contents of his gift like they were made of gold. "Vali, this is… You don't understand what this means to me."

"I just wanted to make sure you had enough until we reached Alfheim."

The feelings flooding her heart quickly dried up with understanding. "You mean until you give me to Odin." She took a deliberate step back, hoping her heart would follow.

Vali winced. "No, Ailsa, that is not—"

"You are only good to me because of what I carry." Her fist tightened around the herbs, but her eyes were locked on something outside the cell, refusing to look at him.

"*Stiarna*," he spoke her name like a prayer, pleading. "Do not twist my words and distort their meaning. I want this shirt more than anything."

"But?" her voice sighed the word.

"But nothing! I want your gift. I want you, Ailsa. And I don't know what to do about the Tether or Odin or the dark forces that seek what is inside you. But I vow I will do everything in my power to keep you safe and to protect you from all of it."

"What if they cannot make a new Tether?" she asked with tears festering in her eyes. "What if Odin takes me away… or worse. Accepting my gift will make things more complicated for you, Vali. Acknowledging this connection we have could ruin the lives of everyone in your realm."

"Then why did you make me this in the first place? You have taken away my choice as quickly as you gave it to me." He was about to take off the shirt until he saw the hurt in her eyes, the way she blanched from his rejection. He dropped his hands, defeated on every side. "I have never once chosen anything in my life. But I would choose you, Ailsa, if you let me. There are no strands of time where I would not choose you, no matter how they unraveled in the end."

"I am dying, Vali." Her words cracked. "Wherever this thread unwinds, it will not go far. You must know that."

"I thought I knew many things before I met you." He stepped closer to her, no more space between their chests, her thighs brushed his knees. She let him put his hands on her jaw to study the flush crawling down her neck, the way her skin raised beneath his feather-light touch and spread like a wildfire down her spine. "But now all my principles have been reduced to this single truth: that not even the fates themselves know what tomorrow will hold. So I will choose what makes me happy today, and that is you."

"Why?" she asked. It was then, with that question, she finally saw him. The same determined man that stood on her shores that dark night in Drakame. The one who would stop at nothing, give anything, to get what he wanted. "What can I possibly offer besides a massive headache?"

"What do I offer you besides danger and dungeons?" he challenged.

The air was thin, barely tangible enough to carry her words. "What a pair we make, ruining each other's lives."

He laughed a hoarse sound, shaking his head and sending small drops of rain across her cheek. His lashes lowered as he stared at her lips. "Please, keep ruining me, Ailsa."

She lost her breath as his head dipped. He pinched her lower lip between his. The gentlest of kisses that moved mountains from their pillars in the earth and burned new stars in the sky with its heat.

The testing weight of this kiss was enough to wreck her. His lips were softer than the silk she snatched between her fingers, than the skin she explored all those nights ago. Her hands crumbled the delicate fabric of his new shirt as she pulled him down from where he staggered above her, his body tensed before melting, filling the spaces between her curves. The distance between them disappearing. He molded against her like another half, a piece of her she didn't realize was missing until it had been found.

Ailsa snatched his lip with her teeth, eliciting from him a delicious hiss. She pulled away slightly. Her teeth raked slowly across the thin flesh as she watched as the elfin smirked, pulling the rest of his lip from the snag of her canines.

"Is this one of those scandalous advances you warned me about?" His breath was warm against her cheek as his nose trailed her hairline.

"Oh, sweet Vali," she murmured. In one fluid motion, she flung him hard against the wall behind her and pulled the blade from her waist. The unexpected shove sucked a grunt from his still parted lips. She ran the edge of his jaw with the knife's edge, following the curve of his neck and over the vein in his neck. A month ago, she would have bled him out. He certainly deserved it. But as he looked down at her with hooded eyes dark with desire, any lingering malice was pushed away. "If we weren't in a dungeon next to a shit-bucket, I would pin you against the wall by your hideous shirt and show you all the bad things I can do."

"You are *not allowed* to ruin this shirt."

"Oh, but it will be fun. I promise you will like it."

He leaned his head forward despite the blade at his throat to catch her lips. With a whisper of pressure, he parted her mouth, slipping a hot tongue along her teeth and stealing her resolve with each vanquishing stroke. The knife slipped from her grasp to pull him close by his wet hair.

Gone was sweet Vali. His gentleness burned away with the brazen longing of their kiss. His fingers smoothed around her stomach to pull her close by her waist, shoving his knee between her legs. Vali rose like the tide, and she fell into him like a shipwreck, drowned by his lips and the hands that gutted her with every devastating blow.

Their kiss was chaos, a storm of tongue and teeth competing for dominance like lightning dueling with thunder. The guilt she experienced in the wanting was purged away in the having. He was where her destiny lived and breathed, where it met its match in a perfectly flawed man that was as much of her enemy as he was her desire. He was the best mistake she'd ever made, a gloriously selfish indulgence that took from her as much as it gave back.

She rocked her hips against the tense muscles of his thigh, and Vali carved his fingers down the harsh curve of her hip to hook adept fingers under a knee. She sighed into his mouth as a tension coiled inside her core with each grinding push against his counterpressure, the throb in her hips matching the compelling race of her pulse. It was like they'd done this a hundred times. He knew exactly where to touch her, how to kiss her, how to feel her to heighten the sensation building between her legs.

A coarse noise slipped from his throat as he stroked the length of her thigh, gently rocking his own hips to the rhythm of hers. They were no better than animals, seeking a primal need from the other with no concern about the consequences. Knowing only the rush of a matched need, the power of paired pleasure. The ridge below his belt pressed against her stomach as he pulled her writhing body against him. The evidence of his size made her sigh a breath against his lips, burning her blood hot with want. Her hands dove down his chest, searching for the opening of his belt to feel him--to know him.

"Ailsa," he said, stopping her hands with his. "Not here, not yet." His voice was as strained as her self-control.

She slipped from his knee, realizing just how little she had breathed during their kiss. She broke their connection, too starved of air to continue, and backed away from the elfin until her legs met the small chair. Her weight collapsed into the seat, feeling the ache in her chest soothe with every labored breath. She looked at Vali, but he did not regard her with pity or concern. He simply brushed her hair from her face, leaning his weight against the wall behind her.

"I took your breath away, didn't I?"

She managed a laugh despite the sting in her lungs. "I'm

sorry," she said between breaths. "I guess the moisture down here has affected me more than I realized, and I've been without my medications longer than normal. I promise I have more stamina than this."

"Even though I'm sure you are inexhaustible, *Stiarna,* I think we should take things slow." He shifted the front of his pants. "For both our sakes."

"Slow is good." She cleared her throat when her breath finally regulated and asked, "Was it… to your liking?"

The elfin's brows rose an inch before taking her hand in his. He slid the sleeve of her gown slightly higher, revealing the line of rune marks on her forearm, and kissed each one reverently before answering. "Very much so."

His bruised lips traced the sensitive skin under her arm, pausing only to taste a staggering pulse with a flick of his tongue. The simple kiss was a sensual form of worship, and she realized something terrible. Something impiously selfish, imagining her sister and her father's faces looking at her with accusation in their phantom eyes. "Am I a bad person for wanting something so selfish, Vali?"

"Why would you ask such a thing?" When she didn't answer, he squeezed her hand gently, releasing her shame with persuasive fingers. "Do you regret our kiss?"

"That's the thing," she said. "I don't regret it at all. I expected to feel guilty if I acted on my feelings, but I feel strange. For the first time in my life, I feel free." As she spoke her confession, the ghostly images of her family faded from her thoughts, her soul at peace once more.

"This is going to change everything, isn't it?" she said.

Still kneeling before her, he looked at her with bright eyes that lit the world around them on fire. "I'm counting on it."

33 Ailsa

Seela and Ivor were waiting outside the boat when they traveled back to the river. The pair sat together on the grassy part of the bank, basking in the heat of the midday sun that finally peeked behind the disordered clouds and dried the flooded earth. The sound of Skiord's horse throwing mud behind his trail made them both snap to attention.

Ailsa slipped from the horse's back before the mare could even come to a complete stop. "Ivor!"

The wolven met her halfway in a familial embrace, pressing her face against her cheek. "Ailsa, thank the gods you are okay. Vali took his sweet, precious time getting you back."

"Never mind the fact I did end up getting her back," he grumbled as he passed them.

"Wouldn't have had to if you wouldn't have lost her in the first place," Ivor muttered against Ailsa's head.

"Oh, stop. Both of you." Ailsa slipped from her wolven's arms and gave Vali a look of warning. Ivor was the only family she had left, and she expected him to do his best to have a diplomatic relationship with her at the least. "Do you need to return the horse to Drieger's hall?"

"No, she knows the way back," he said as he slapped her rump and sent her flying up the path toward the mountain.

"I am happy to see you are well, Ailsa. Thrym isn't the most respectable of the giant lords, and I was worried about you. But you are radiant as usual." Seela approached behind Ivor.

Ailsa smiled her way, pleasantly surprised at her compliment. If she was close enough to Vali to be blood bonded, she wanted to remain on her good side. "Thrym's reputation must be as bad as his card skills. I managed the giants just fine, but I don't think I'll be stopping by for a visit anytime soon."

Seela nodded knowingly before her eyes caught on Vali. Her brows narrowed. "Where did you get that shirt? You weren't wearing it when you left."

Vali smoothed the wrinkled places over his stomach with a casual hand before pulling his vest apart to show off his new garment to Seela. "It was custom made. Though the seamstress thought my arms were much longer than they are, I find her eye for detail impeccable."

Seela's lips turned down into a frown. "Who is this seamstress?"

Vali glanced at Ailsa, silently inquiring if he was allowed to tell her. They hadn't discussed taking whatever this was between them to a public level.

"I made it for him," she finally said. Ivor stiffened against her before shoving her away like she was on fire.

"You *what?*" Ivor hissed.

"I made him the shirt," she repeated with a defensive tilt of her chin. Though, it did nothing to help Seela understand.

"You made him a shirt?" she asked. The look on Ivor's face made her disgust plain. "How could you, Ailsa? After everything he's done—"

"I'm sorry, can someone explain to me what the big deal is?"

Seela asked. Vali stepped beside her and mumbled something in her ear, explaining the significance of her gift and why he was wearing it. Seela's eyes widened with understanding, her lips fighting a grin.

"Oh," she only said.

"It's different now," Ailsa explained to her wolven. "It's not like I didn't try to fight this, Ivor. I wanted to hate him. I intentionally pushed him away every time I felt something other than animosity. But it just… happened."

"What *happened*?" she asked her.

Her eyes shifted to Vali for a beat, who had neither spoken for her nor made the indication of doing so. This was her choice to make alone, what she would tell all of them. Because what she would say next would seal them both to this bond by her public confession. Make it real. He only nodded in encouragement, gave that same twisted smile that was destined to be her demise.

Ailsa shrugged weakly. "I fell for him."

Ivor scoffed and turned her back to her, unable to face what felt like a personal betrayal to the wolven who had become her family. "What would your father say? What would your clan say to you courting the man who slaughtered their families?"

"My father," she scoffed, rolling her eyes. "I will never let him influence my choices ever again. How many times in our history has a woman been married off to an enemy as a peace deal? War is not personal, Ivor. And I probably would have committed the same horrible things he has if it meant saving my world and my people."

She shook her head with a heartless laugh. "You make excuses to justify his crimes. But he is a murderer—"

"I am a murderer! I killed a Vanir when he shot Sorrin

down. Will you hate me as well, or do I just have to kill people *you* care about?"

"That is different—"

"It is not!" Ailsa shouted. "This thing inside me isn't choosing sides, Ivor. The road behind us is littered with bodies of every race and realm and the devastating sacrifice of those who gave their lives so that this power would not fall into the wrong hands!" She stepped in front of her friend—her family—to make her understand how seriously she took her situation. "In the end, which one of us is actually right or wrong, good or evil? Are we all not just trying our best to exist and make our mark on the world? Each day my lungs get worse, I need my herbs more often, and I can literally feel my end coming soon. Am I not allowed to live my last days the way I *want* to live them?"

The wolven went quiet, her shoulders drooping in defeat. She spoke quietly, "Will he put your well-being before his realm? Before his family and his people?"

"I cannot ask him to do such a thing," she replied.

"Then he doesn't deserve you." She turned her face to Vali and glared at him, even as she continued to speak to her. "As long as he treats you like a pawn, you will never mean anything more to him. He is deceiving you with false affirmations of devotion like he has deceived you about everything else. Do not come crawling to me for help when he gives you to Odin." She pushed past Ailsa with a harsh brush of her shoulder, knocking her back a step. Her bitterness palpable in the bruising blow.

"Well, now that we have all the crew back together, shall we continue the last leg of our journey?" Seela broke the uncomfortable silence.

Ailsa turned away from them all, wiping tears she wouldn't

let them see. She had guessed Ivor would be upset, but nothing this severe. The throbbing in her shoulder was a poor competitor against the pain in her heart. A hand smoothed down her spine. "Are you okay?" he asked in her ear.

She took a breath to lock away the tears fighting for release and nodded. "I'm fine. Let's not waste any more time."

THE BOAT RIDE was agonizingly quiet as they pushed upstream toward the Highest Branch where Alfheim sat above all the Nine Realms. The weather was perfect for once. The skies were clear with patches of clouds to shield them from the glaring sun. Vali rested for the first time in days with his head in her lap. She combed the shaggy length with her fingers, at bliss from the ease of it all.

While they traveled, Vali further explained the political disputes among the fae and the division the forbidden practice of sedir had caused in his land to prepare her for what she might see. The elves weren't the types for violence or civil debates, but the darkness bleeding over from Frey's power was corrupting the Light inside each of the fae, replacing it with something stronger, something difficult to resist once a piece of it was experienced. The problem with sedir was its strength, as was the reason it was so tempting to those with a form of magic that came from the life of the land.

"You seem pretty powerful to me. How does sedir compare to your magic?" Ailsa asked.

Vali's ego flourished with the smallest of smirks. "I am more powerful than most fae because I am part Aesir. I have the immortality of a god, and the power I have access to in my blood is deeper and richer. I can manipulate the natural world as well as control objects through my will alone.

"Full-blooded elfin draw power from the world, not their blood. It is weaker, like a shallow pool compared to an ocean. Sedir is like another well they can draw from, one that is bottomless. One can have the control of a god without the blood. But if fae magic is considered light, then sedir is darkness. They both cannot exist simultaneously; one soul cannot serve two masters. This is the source of the division among my people."

"Will the Dark Elves not be angry when Frey leaves and you forbid sedir from the land?"

He shrugged. "Alfheim is a land of Light, and they can go to Vanaheim if they wish to continue practicing it."

"What about me?" she asked. "Do I not carry sedir inside me?" The weight in her lap shook with disagreement.

"You carry Gullveig's power and the secret knowledge of sedir. It is not the same. You do not have black magic inside you, but the source of it. Knowledge is far more powerful than any kind of magic."

"Then why can I use it? What about all those times I let it slip?" she asked.

He leaned his face into her palm, his breath warm. "Possibly because Gullveig's knowledge *is* her power. It is what gave her the ability to manipulate the very strands of time, to create life and take it away. She somehow tapped into the secrets of creation before the birth of the Tree of Life. One must first understand the laws of nature if they wish to break them."

"But she didn't want to break them. Odin forced her?"

"Yes. The god is obsessed with knowledge, and he does not enjoy it when others know more than him."

Ailsa chewed the inside of her cheek and looked up at the

sky covering the Realm Between Realms. "I'm going to end up just like Gullveig. But I won't know how to come back to life like she did. Odin is going to destroy me."

Vali sat up suddenly like something had bit him and looked at her hard. "He will not. And if I must travel to the Lowest Root of the Tree and drink from Mimir's well to figure out how to separate this power from you, I'll do it. Until then, the runes on your skin hide you from him. He cannot see you until you are physically placed in front of him. That gives us time to find a new way."

Ailsa eyed the black marks lining her forearm as they disappeared beneath her sleeves. Odin had nearly killed himself to learn the ancient language of runes and the ability to read them. The only one beside Gullveig, the original author, could translate the combination of swirls and lines written across her body. "I wonder what else they do," she wondered out loud.

"Other than attract trouble?" Ivor spoke from across the boat. "Perhaps there is a rune there that makes a person blind to other's shortcomings."

Ailsa scowled at her but said nothing. Instead, she stared off into the distance and watched the landscape pass around them. Vali sucked a sharp breath but remained quiet, and she was grateful for the rare appearance of his self-control.

Seela pushed the boat toward a seemingly random place on the shallow bank. The river was thinning as they pushed upstream, and in the distance, Ailsa could spot a towering waterfall sourcing the iceless river. Mountains whose height alone would be impossible to climb stretched beyond it, hiding the sky with the multitude of peaks.

"We travel the rest on foot, I'm afraid. But we should be able to reach the gates of Alfheim before nightfall. Unfortunately, you won't be able to see the realm in the daylight, but it is imperative we get out of the wilderness. Sightseeing will have to wait." Seela organized her pack as they stood on the shoreline. "The trees will warn our enemies we are almost home. And I will not feel safe until we cross the borders of our realm."

Ailsa nodded in agreement and stepped closer to Vali.

"You still have the dagger I gave you?" he asked.

"Of course," she said, patting her leather belt to prove it.

"Good. Keep your voice down and try not to say any names. Stay in front of me. You too, wolfie."

The wolven muttered something but complied. Seela led the group along the tree line until they came upon a path leading to a dirt padded road. The miles seemed to pass without her noticing, not when the company was more agreeable than last time. They walked without speaking, fearful the trees would hear them and stir, but Ailsa was not afraid of them like before. They brought her back to Vali when she was lost. If anything, the trees were on *her* side. She felt indebted to them.

It was warmer here despite traveling north. A thin sheen of sweat coated her skin beneath the heavy fabric lining the gown the giantess donated to her. The dress was a deep red, reminding her of their youngest daughter's hair. Beautifully structured but meant for colder climates.

She wiped her brow and reached for her tankard. A few drops fell from the spout, teasing her parched tongue with barely a sip of water. She cursed under her breath, feeling the fluid in her lungs thicken as she sweated off the rest of her hydration.

"Let's stop," Vali muttered. "I need to refill her tankard."

"This is the fifth time in the past hour," Seela groaned. "We'll never make it home before sunset at this rate."

"I'm sorry, it's just..."

Vali interrupted her with a placating hand behind her neck. "The Highest Branches are closer to the sun and sky. The weather is warmer and understandably more difficult for your condition. It's fine, *Stiarna*. I'll fill your tankard as much as you need."

His commander choked on air. "Oh, you have pet names now? Gods below, I liked it better when she despised you." Seela rolled her eyes. "*Stiarna!*" She mocked. Vali only smiled at her back as she walked away from them.

"Don't mind her," he said.

"I never do." Ailsa offered him a feigning smile before taking a long swig of her full tankard. The motion sent her off balance, staggering to the side and suddenly becoming very lightheaded. "*Burning Hel*, is it getting hotter?" She clawed at the neckline of the dress, suddenly feeling smothered and her skin set on fire despite the cover of shade. Heat washed from her head to her feet, pooling in her bloodstream.

"What is happening?" Ivor spoke as Ailsa fell to her knees. The wolven caught her before she ate the dirt.

Ivor dragged her deeper into the forest and placed her on the cool earth, but it did nothing to ease the heat. It was like she had been placed inside a furnace and it was scorching hotter by the second. Her fingers fumbled with the laces of the bodice, desperate to be free of the bindings cinching tighter around her waist. Her breath came through noisy gasps, sinking the skin beneath her collarbones as every muscle in her chest pleaded for air.

"Get it off!" Ailsa managed to scream.

Vali didn't hesitate. He snatched the dagger from her belt

and used the blade to split open her bodice and form slits in the sleeves to rip apart with his fists. He slipped the dress free from her body until she was in nothing but her undergarments.

"Odin's fucking eye," Vali mumbled as he watched her skin come to life. New runes were being branded into her skin. An invisible paint brush stroked red lines across her chest before glazing a flaming orange. Ailsa writhed against the earth, unable to take a deep enough breath to verbalize her pain into screams. Not enough fluid in her body to form tears.

"What do we do?" Ivor said, noticing the fresh runes.

Ailsa in her agony only knew she had to get rid of the marks. She needed to stop this hot iron digging into her flesh and searing through her existence. Although the markings were carved into her chest, she felt the pain bleed into every pore of her skin.

She was burning alive, but the flames were inside her.

She snatched the blade from Vali's hand and staggered away from them, crawling on her hands and knees to hide within the shadows of the trees. Ailsa brought the tip of the dagger to the newest rune still being formed and sliced through the intricate triple swirl. The incision ruined the symbol, and her blood quenched the branding heat.

Until another one started the pain all over again.

She sliced the fresh one burning over her stomach, this time cutting deeper than her desperation.

"Ailsa!" Vali shouted as he watched her practically butcher herself. But as soon as the agony ceased from the interrupted rune, another one started. No matter how many slices she made across her skin, whoever was doing this was determined to keep it up as long as she had bare skin available.

She dug her hands into the earth and looked up at the trees

as if they could help her. She begged them to stop this, to hide her.

"Help me," she mouthed. The forest answered.

The blood must be willing.

A crow flew down and perched on a low-hanging branch, watching her struggle with its veiled gaze.

"Who's doing this?" Seela spoke somewhere behind her, worlds away.

Warm blood trickled down her arms, and she staggered to her feet to approach the bird where it perched. It was like the day in the woods when she was lost, the black crow watching her, guiding her back to the right path. Ailsa stumbled toward the tree and reached to steady herself.

The moment her bloody hand touched the smooth ash, her vision was swallowed by darkness.

She awoke inside a dream, or the fabrications of one. The place her spirit had manifested was far beyond the place and time of the Tree. The space where nothing lived and yet where everything was born. On one side, a world of fire and lava. On the other, and a frosted landscape of mist and ice.

The First Realm.

Ailsa stood between them, the birthplace of life itself. Her mind was there, but her body had not followed. She didn't recognize the form she controlled as it hurtled through the vision, operating on its own accord. This form was bare, singed as if she had just crawled from the ashes of a bonfire.

She has returned to us, a voice whispered from the void beyond where she stood. The voice from the Tree.

Risen from the ashes a final time.

Her blood is not willing.

It can be convinced.

"Hello?" she said with a tremble, shaking her voice. The voices hushed like they'd been caught in a private conversation. "Where am I?"

Shall we show ourselves?

It is the only way.

A shadowed figure emerged from between the opposing realms. A woman shrouded in a cloak of darkness. Her face was hidden beneath a shroud.

"Who are you?" Ailsa asked.

The hood tipped up and the face was that of a woman with skin like moonlight. Her hair black as pitch and eyes sewn shut. The woman smiled at her, as if she could *see* Ailsa. Truly see through the sealed flesh and into her very soul.

"You're the blind crow," she said. "The one that's been following me."

And you are the Last Daughter. We were trying to write your name and finish the binding of your power, but you interrupted our ceremony.

"Last Daughter?" She shook her head, disoriented. "What do you mean? This power is not mine to bind with."

Do you think it is not yours because you were not born with it?

"I don't understand—"

You are Ailsa of Drakame. The power inside you has been passed down between eons and creatures. It was once Heid, then Gullveig. Now it has passed to a mortal by the promise of your ancestor.

Ailsa took a retreating step back. "Why? What do I have to do with Gullveig?"

You are *Gullveig. As Gullveig was Heid.*

She shook her head more aggressively this time, her steps still recoiling from the figure. "I am Ailsa, no one else."

Your family asked for help long ago, and now you must pay it back for the gift we gave them. Surely you know about the blessing. The Last Daughter will bind with the ancient power and keep it safe. Fate has chosen you to do this, Ailsa.

She threw her hands up in exasperation. "This is payback

for the blessing? I must shoulder this burden and do what with it exactly?"

Keep it from Odin. He will destroy the world in his endless quest for knowledge.

"He only wants to bring Baldur back."

The woman frowned. *Odin will not stop with Baldur. A god with the power over fate is the most dangerous creature in all of creation, Ailsa. Jomeer tried to warn your father, but he would not listen, and he burned her like they always burn the witches. But the flames only burn our flesh, not our spirit. We still live on.*

"I do not want this! I do not want to have this power. I just want to go back to my little clan and live what little years I have left in peace!"

Those are no longer your choices. If Odin gets his hands on the Tether—

"I don't care about Odin!" Ailsa was screaming now, her small voice booming across time and space.

Be careful who you trust. The snake is coiling before it strikes, the wolf is sharpening its teeth. Learn the truth, Ailsa. The dark may appear to be afraid of the light, but it is the darkness that decides how far the light reaches. Seize your darkness and make the light tremble.

"You aren't making any sense! I am not a witch!"

Neither were the last ones with your power, and yet they were burned all the same. Trust your heart, Ailsa, while you still have it. We will give you one more chance to accept the power and the fate tied to its responsibility. But we will not risk Odin getting his hands on you. The balance of the blessing in your blood, the curse on your breath will claim you before he does. When you are ready to complete the binding, finish the rune. The hooded figure turned its back to her.

"Wait!"

But the crow was gone. Fire and ice mixed in front of her

and hissed a foul smoke in the air. It surrounded her form, thickened until she could not see.

She closed her eyes and let the darkness seize her, too tired to fight its appeal.

Claim the power. Break your curse, Last Daughter.

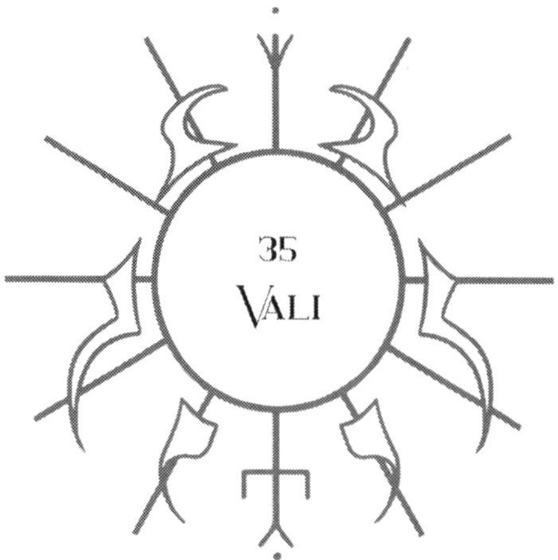

35
Vali

Seela arrived with the horses just moments after sunset, relieved to find Ailsa was still alive. She brought half a legion of the Light Army with her, and Vali wrapped Ailsa's bare body with the remnants of her gown. He pulled her close to his chest once he mounted his steed, monitoring her pulse every second they traveled into the realm of the elves.

She was dreaming. Her lips would move as if she were speaking with someone, pausing to hear their reply, before wordlessly speaking again. Her skin was still bleeding where she lacerated the runes, soaking through the dress and seeping through the thin material of his shirt. He would heal them with his magic just for the laceration to spill open again.

He had never seen anything like this, but his mother had lived for hundreds of years. Surely, she would know what was torturing Ailsa and how to fix it. If not, she would bleed out all over him, across the very shirt she expressed her affections with. He would lose *everything*, both the Tether and Ailsa, what was and what could be. Their number of potentials dwindled by the second.

Vali felt home as soon as he crossed the border, inhaling the magic in the air like a perfume and let it scourge his body with power and life. The Palace of Light was sparkling in starlight. Alfheim was so close to the sky in the Highest Branch that the cosmos appeared within reach, as if he could reach above his head and gather the constellations in his palm. The stars were tenfold brighter here and illuminated the landscape now shaded with night.

They neared the gilded gates carved into the shape of the bending bows of ash trees, and the surrounding cavalry encouraged the gatekeepers to swiftly open the doors and give them passage, allowing Vali to charge right through without question or pause. He spurred his horse to quicken her strides, speeding the mare through the line and galloping past the army to lead the way toward the castle.

Even at night, the Palace of Light manipulated each beam of starlight. The castle's countless spires were crafted entirely from stained glass, painting the land in a thousand broken colors. As the sun and moon moved across the sky, their light would hit the towers at different angles, and the glass would catch the rays making colors change, darken, lighten, forever moving across the world and coloring a new picture into the realm's rolling canvas.

The view was enough to distract him from the wetness spreading across his chest, but not enough to slow him down.

Vali had not seen the inside of his own castle for half a century, yet everything appeared the same. The furniture, the gold-plated wallpaper, the skylights lining the rooftop, leaving only the need for a few scattered wall sconces to light the foyer —it was all the same as he remembered it. The night staff startled as he burst through the front door, Ailsa limp in his arms and covered in her blood.

"Send Lady Rind to the hospital wing immediately!" he

shouted at one of them—all of them—successively as he charged up the foyer steps and toward the eastern side of the castle where the healers resided.

The wing was empty when they entered. He picked a bed and threw her on top of the ivory linens and began gathering any supplies he could find. The bedside table held a sink and a drawer full of freshly cleaned cloths and tinctures he could not name or place their use.

He tried to clean the excess blood from her skin but more pooled and replaced what he wiped away. She had four large gash marks, one above her left breast, one across her stomach, a slice down her forearm, and a short tear across her thigh. But Vali didn't know how to close any of them, and her skin had already paled several shades beyond its normal honey shade.

"Vali!" His mother's voice was a solace. He looked up to find the feminine version of himself trailing a group of healers, her chamber robes sweeping behind her. She rounded the four-poster bed to hug him, but he held out his arm to keep her at a distance. He was covered in Ailsa's blood, and he had no interest in grand reunions just yet.

"Mother, it's wonderful to see you, but this cannot wait. Ailsa is the Tether and for some reason I cannot heal her. She tried to cut the runes before they formed, and now she won't stop bleeding. She's going to die if we don't find a way to close her wounds!" The words fell out of his mouth, and he hoped she could find their meaning somewhere in the mess.

"Let me see," she said. Her raven hair was pulled into a long braid down her back as she leaned over Ailsa, her nimble fingers pressed the edges of the laceration together and assessed them with a power he could not see with his eyes. "God's below," she muttered under her breath after a time.

"Her blood is not willing. It's rejecting the Tether—she is rejecting the Tether."

"What does that mean?" he asked.

"It means the power is trying to bind to her, but she isn't accepting it. I'm sorry, Vali. I don't understand how, but she is in a fight for her life beyond our control. With a force of nature I cannot manipulate."

"No," he whispered stubbornly. He sank to his knees next to her bed, barely feeling the sharp sting in his bones as they struck the floor. "This is not what the Norn told me. This cannot be it. I will find another way, another potential."

Three healers stood on the other side of the bed, quickly soaking cloths with a clear liquid before pressing them to her wounds. Their efforts were futile. The pale pavers beneath the bed were now speckled with crimson stains. The sheets were already soiled. His mother placed a soft hand over his shoulder. "I'm sorry, my son. We will cleanse her with the waters and hope it helps. But she is the only one controlling her fate now. You must let her fight this battle alone."

Ivor and Seela trickled into the wing, the frosty blue of the wolven's eyes now diluted with despair as her eyes found Ailsa lying on top of the sheets. The runes on her skin were now black and dormant. Quiet. But her blood still oozed from the wounds across her body, made by the blade he had given her.

"Why are you all just standing there?" she demanded as she approached the foot of the bed. "Help her!"

"There is nothing we can do but wait," a healer spoke for him.

"You *gargan*! Snake! I've seen you heal your own wounds, Vali. Heal her now!"

"Ivor, he cannot. Don't you think he's tried?" Seela spoke softly behind her.

"She is dying, and he is doing nothing!" Ivor spat at him, her hatred on full display. "She's just another failed attempt to you, isn't she? You're probably already manning another crew in your head to search for the next Tether. Her life meant *nothing* to you!"

"You need to leave," Seela tamed the fire in her voice with a forceful shove. Vali heard her struggle as she managed her out of the room, encouraging the guards from their post to assist in subduing the wolven.

Vali was lost for words, void of fight. Everything he had ever wanted, the things he thought he could never have, were there right in front of him. In a single moment, they had been ripped away, along with the one woman who offered him the potential for a thread of happiness—cut just as it was starting to weave into his life.

The healers covered her with heavy blankets after binding her wounds and left the group. His mother mumbled something about returning in the morning,

He reached into the bed and cradled her limp hand in his own. Her icy fingers made their own runes upon his palm, forever claiming their place with the invisible markings made by the slip of her lifeless fingertips.

"Even this close to the heavens, the night is dull without you, *Stiarna*. Do what you must. Do what you have to *live*."

Her pulse beat a slowing rhythm against his thumb.

If he had a heart, it would have shattered.

36
Ailsa

The morning glare burned her tired eyes awake.

Ailsa shifted in the bed, but her body was heavy, like her limbs were tied to sacks of grain. Her lips were parched, and her skin was freezing despite having been nearly burned alive the night before. But her breath was easy, and her chest was light. She smelled familiar herbs staining the air with their earthy scent.

When she opened her eyes, she was in a place she had never seen before. A bed with a sheer canopy draped over each side, giving her privacy from the bodies stirring beyond the white veil. A window poured light across the fresh linen sheets she was tucked beneath. The stained glass masked her sheets with various shades of greens and golds in the shape of a sun.

Alfheim.

They had made it. She looked around for her crew but didn't find a single fae she recognized. She was alone in a bed surrounded by strangers who hadn't noticed she was awake—until one of them pulled back the gossamer curtain.

"Oh!" the woman yelped in surprise. She was dressed in dark green robes and held a glass pitcher filled with water that shimmered in the unfiltered sunlight. Her face was a deep umber that framed her sharp features in a beautiful picture. She broke out in a wide smile, revealing a row of white teeth. "You're awake! Dallia, go find Master Greer! And someone needs to tell the High Lady and His Grace!"

An obscure figure behind the opposite curtain drew back the covering to peek at her. Before Ailsa could gain a glimpse of the curious elfin, she took off.

"Would you like some water, Miss Ailsa? I've just bought a new pitcher. Your companion, Ivor, just came back from the river to fetch you a fresh batch of our healing waters."

Ailsa nodded and accepted the cup from the healer. Once her tongue was pliable enough to form words, she tried to speak. "Where is she? Or Vali? Seela?"

"The wolven was threatening to kill everyone with her teeth, so she had to be locked in a room, but she has since calmed down after you lived past the first night. I think I saw her in the gardens with Commander Seela not too long ago."

"First night?" she asked, skeptical. "How long have I been here?"

"Four days," someone spoke from the foot of her bed. A white hand pulled back the canopy. "I am Master Greer, the head healer. It is a relief to see you awake, Miss Ailsa. Would you mind if I ran a quick assessment to evaluate your status?"

Ailsa shook her head at the woman whose white hair had been nearly shaved down to her skull. Harsh teal eyes glowed against her pale complexion. Her years were not marked by the ageless appearance of her skin, but the trained eye and calculating hands that studied her like a specimen.

"Can you wiggle your fingers and toes?" she asked after pulling back the covers. Ailsa attempted the feat with a sluggish response. Greer nodded in satisfaction. "You lost a lot of blood, but once you start eating you will gain strength, and we have tonics that will help speed up your recovery."

"Can you put the covers back?" she asked as a shiver ran over her skin.

"Of course. Dallia, put some blankets by the fire and give her a warm one once they are hot." Dallia, the obvious healer's assistant, nodded and disappeared once more. "Has the High Lady been summoned?"

"Yes, she has." A woman with skin like a marble statue floated into view. Ailsa's breath caught at her beauty. Something was familiar about her, from the straight, ink black hair that spilled beneath a gold circulate. Her face was set into an impeccable bone structure that resembled someone else she knew. But her eyes were all wrong. The dark centers were hard on her, lingering over her face as they scanned her body, now hidden beneath the sheets.

"I'm Lady Rind," she said. "It is with warmest sympathies to find you well, my dear. I thought my son was going to lose his mind along with his heart." Ailsa's eyes widened, connecting the semblances. It was obvious this was Vali's mother.

"It's a pleasure to finally meet you, Lady Rind." She somehow found words to speak through her nerves. "I'd greet you formally, but the blood has not returned to my hands yet."

"I still have most of it on my shirt if you'd like some of it back," another voice manifested beyond the curtain. It pulled back to reveal Vali, his hair messy like he had just returned from a long ride, his cheeks pink from windburn.

Ailsa couldn't fight the beaming grin crossing her cheeks when she saw him. "I told you I'd ruin that shirt."

"Mmmm, you also promised I would like it, and I definitely did not appreciate watching you nearly die." His hand slid beneath the blanket and clasped her own, and he was gloriously warm. She wished he would slip his whole self beneath the sheets and cover her with his heat. "How are you, *svåss?*"

Beloved.

Ailsa glanced toward Lady Rind to assess her reaction to such a term of endearment. The regal woman betrayed no surprise in her gaze nor a sign of disapproval. She looked back at Vali, the exhaustion in her bones overflowing into her voice. "I feel like I just came back from the dead. And… I think I possibly did. You won't believe the dream I had. Where I've been."

Memories of the First Realm came rushing back. The space between fire and ice, hidden in a deep place long forgotten by the rest of the realms. If she tried hard enough, she thought she could still smell the burning brimstone combined with the cold sting of snow. The Crow's warning echoed in her mind, reminding her of a choice still needed to be made. One that would decide her very life.

Vali sat on the edge of her bed, propping his knee on the edge and never letting go of her hand. "What happened?" he asked.

She wanted to tell him everything, but something held her back. The whisper of the Crow's phantom in her ear, reciting its demands.

Odin cannot have the Tether.

One more chance to complete the binding.

Break your curse, Last Daughter.

Vali promised he would protect her from Odin, but what power did he have against the Allfather? What authority did he have to fight the fate marred into his flesh? She could not ask him to choose between her or his realm, his family.

She chose her words carefully, only admitting enough to not count as a lie.

"There is a Crow who watches over the Tether. It has been tempting me to release the power into the realms all along. The perils we faced on our journey, the lightning that struck you and nearly killed you, they even tried to write my name in rune language to force the binding of the power to my soul. Each time I bit off a taste, I used a piece of its magic, like it was testing me to see if I was a good match. But this last time I interrupted the binding, and it pulled me to the First Realm to... warn me."

Rind stepped behind her son, the pair wearing mirrored scowls of concern. Vali squeezed her hand gently. "What warning did it give you?"

Ailsa let him deduct his own conclusions based on the knowing look she offered. "The curse will take me soon. We must finish this bargain with Odin quickly."

The color in Vali's cheeks paled a morose shade. "That isn't a warning, Ailsa. That is a threat."

Ailsa nodded once. Her gaze dropped to avoid the pain brimming in his eyes. "One we should heed before it is too late."

"But that means you will die!" His jaw opened and closed, trying to conceptualize the idea. "How can you be okay with this?"

She silenced his building argument by rubbing her thumb in small circles along his palm. "I've been dying my whole life, *Sólskin.* I am not afraid. You must keep your deal with Odin so we can save this realm and you can be free. That is the reason you took me all this way, correct? You must complete your purpose before the curse takes me or this will all have been for nothing."

"To Hel with Odin!" he cursed. "No one writes my destiny

but me, and I choose *you,* Ailsa. I'll skin these runes off my chest to keep you—"

"What you want will not change my fate. Stop thinking about the future for once, Vali. I am here now, and we are together. Let what we have be enough." Her voice broke even as she spat the words from the most bitter place of her heart.

Lady Rind slipped away, sensing this was no longer a conversation that involved her. The healers pretended to be captivated by their laundry. Vali's gaze settled on her like a heavy stone on her chest. "But we barely had any time…" he could hardly whisper the words.

With a great effort, she sat up from the support of the pillows to close the distance between them. Numb hands stroked his face, stealing his warmth. "Remember what you told me in Thyrm's dungeon? Vali, a day being your *sváss* was better than all the days before it. And while I still draw breath, I will seize every moment I have with you."

He kissed her softly behind the gossamer curtains, her tears brining the sweetest lie she ever told. "Then let's get you well, *Stiarna,* so I may give you all my moments."

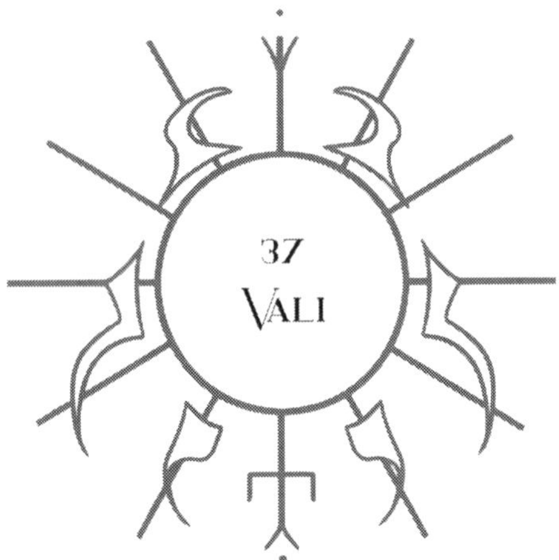

37
Vali

"Odin knows you're here, Vali. I see his raven flying day and night over our land. You need to decide what to do with her."

He followed his mother into her private chambers after making sure Ailsa had eaten something and taken her tonics. Greer had all but thrown him out of the hospital wing, insisting she needed rest, and he reluctantly submitted to the healer's demands only after vowing he would promptly return afterwards, whether she was resting or not.

He was hooked on seeing her alive, addicted to her breath and her movements. Watching her die was starting to wear on him, pulling him deeper with every close call and fainted pulse. His blood used to reach for her, but now it craved her. Being apart for a moment irritated him to the point of genocide. He understood what his mother was asking him, the hidden question dangling between her words.

"I cannot keep her from Odin, but I also seem unable to let her go." The runes pilling down his back cheated against the desires of his heart. Just thinking about deceiving Odin made his skin crawl. "I need to speak with him. I need to see if we can come to an arrangement, if he can heal her or take the power without—"

"Odin will not care about her life," Lady Rind said. She stood near a towering window bordering the balcony. Beyond the twisted metal was a long stretch of Alfheim. The dwarves' mountains shadowed in the distance, their peaks invertedly pointing to the underground realm.

"Then we lie to him," he decided. "We stir up trouble with the Dark Elves and Frey, start a civil unrest, create a diversion—"

"That will buy you time Ailsa does not have," she interrupted whatever bullshit he was about to come up with. "The girl is dying, and no amount of your caring will stop it. Do not dishonor her wishes and what she has been through just because it feels beyond what you can bear. You will endure this just like every other suffering you have been through."

He didn't want to speak of this anymore. Twice he had almost lost her and each time it ripped away a piece of him that would never grow back the same—like a scar on his soul. If he lost her a final time, there wouldn't be anything left to resemble who he once was. "If you truly believe that, then maybe you don't know me at all."

The weight of his mother's gaze lessened on him significantly. She pushed off the window to sit next to him on the velvet couch, placing a warm hand on his shoulder. "I hate to ask this of you, Vali. But I'm afraid we don't have another choice if we wish to save this realm. We must give her to him. Odin is getting desperate. With every solstice, the Allfather becomes more anxious to bring Baldur back from Helheim and prevent the ending the Norns have prepared for him. If we play this right, we can use his desperation to our advantage.

Perhaps we can get more out of this deal than previously arranged."

Vali slipped a long sigh and leaned back in his seat. "What did you have in mind?"

"Your name in the stars, Vali. So, no god can ever rule you or me ever again."

38
Ailsa

"Where are we going?" Ailsa asked, not bothering to hide her excitement. She'd been locked in the hospital wing for almost a week now regaining her strength and resupplying her blood stock. When Vali told Greer he was taking her out to the gardens for the day, she knew he had other plans in mind.

Vali hated gardens.

"Do you think you're strong enough to carry a short blade? Not a long sword, of course, but perhaps a hand and a half?" he asked as they rounded the corner from the hospital wing.

"I think a short sword would make me feel like myself again," she beamed. With a spark of hope, she added, "And maybe some trousers?"

He pulled her down a stairwell leading to a darkened depth. "I'll see what I can do," he replied with a wink.

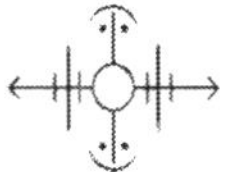

An hour later, she was walking across a portico supported by green glass columns. The walkway ended at what Vali named the Convocation, a towering building with breezeways lining each floor. The structure extended high above them. A worn stairwell wrapped around the building all the way to a flat top.

"You aren't afraid of heights, are you?" he asked before escorting her up the stairs.

"No," she replied carefully. "But I am afraid of falling to my death." A quick glance over the edge of the stairs was enough to make her stomach lurch. Nothing below them but the beginnings of a sea and sharp rocks.

He pulled her to his side, opposite the edge, and vigilantly helped her up several flights of stairs. He made no conversation, listening to the rate of her breathing to adapt his pace against it. An effortless type of thoughtfulness.

When they made it to the top, Ailsa climbed over the side of the roof, discovering a flattened pad crowning the Convocation. She smoothed a hand over her braids, the knots tight like fishbones against the sides of her skull, as a fierce wind tore against her. Vali took her hand in his and pulled her to the center.

"What are we doing here?" she asked.

Vali craned his neck and soaked in the light of the sun. He took a deep breath, inhaling the breeze rolling off the cerulean sea behind him, before answering. "I'm going to show you Alfheim. Well, some of it anyway. I want you to understand why I was so desperate. Why I did things I will forever regret."

"You know I do not fault you, *Sólskin.*"

"Yes, but I put my hands on you," he said quietly. "And I will despise that memory for eternity."

Ailsa rubbed her throat absentmindedly and nodded, feeling the phantom of his hands around her neck. "Aye, and I stabbed you. Three times." Her eyes fell over the unseen marks beneath his shirt. The wounds hadn't even scarred, but she remembered their placement well. "Our relationship didn't exactly start out on the best of terms. But Vali? If you ever do that again, I will do more than just stab you. I will rip you apart and burn the pieces. Probably feed you to my wolf."

He squeezed her waist in succor. "You don't have to worry about that, my fierce one."

Ailsa glanced down at her hip, noting the familiar weight of the blade sheathed against her thigh. "Why the weapons? Are you expecting trouble?"

He grimaced, squinting in the glare. "sedir attracts dark creatures like trolls and demons. I just want to make sure you have something to defend yourself with should we come across them. It's strictly precautionary."

Ailsa nodded slowly and continued to glance around. "And what are we doing here?"

He smiled like he had been waiting for her to ask such a thing. He threw his head back and whistled a sharp cry and it echoed across the world, carrying far beyond where the mountains rested.

"Why did you—" she started to say, but was interrupted by a deep, rustling sound above them. Ailsa stretched her neck toward the source, shielding her eyes against the sun, and startled as a bird with a wingspan three times as long as her body height flew overhead.

"*Freya's tears,*" she whispered. The bird circled around them before landing gracefully on top of the roof. There was a blur of earthy brown feathers flecked with black streaks before it settled, but once the golden-brown plumage of its nape came into focus, she placed the bird easily from her memory.

An eagle.

Though, the eagles in Midgard weren't nearly this large, nor did they wear saddles. Vali crossed the distance between him and the bird, reaching into his back pocket to grab a wafer and gave the expecting creature its treat.

"This is Elísar," Vali said as he fumbled with the harness around the eagle's chest. "He will be our steed for the day." The bird shifted on his talons, each one the size of the dagger strapped to her thigh, to give him better access to the straps. She watched the elfin tighten the fastenings before smoothing his hands up the bird's neck, whispering sweet nothings against its downy feathers in a language she wasn't familiar with.

"Should I be worried?" she asked, circling the pair under her own assessment. "You only pet me like that in the dark when no one's watching."

Vali's gaze flickered to hers over the eagle's back and smirked. "I feel like there is a challenge poised somewhere in that comment."

She shrugged one shoulder. "I do not control how you interpret my words, *sváss.* Can I come closer?"

He walked around the eagle and pulled her in front of him. "Just do what I do. Eagles are usually well-tempered, but this one is very attached to me. He's been known to bite the hands of other riders."

Ailsa swallowed as he pushed her near the eagle's head. He stood behind her and slid his hands down the back of her arms, gently guiding her limbs to stroke the creature's head. "Vali…" she mumbled as the beast eyed her hand with contempt glossing his dark eyes. He whispered something she didn't understand, and the bird relaxed, bowing its neck so she could stroke the silky feathers lining its massive skull. Vali's fingers threaded themselves in the spaces between hers, his chest rising against her back and matching the rhythm of her own.

"What did you tell him?" she asked.

"I told him you are a friend," he said. "And to behave, because I really like your hands."

She ignored his brash statement as the bird lowered its body completely flush with the rooftop, his wings spread wide behind him. "What is he doing now?" she asked.

"He's letting you mount him—"

"We are going to ride him?" she asked in alarm.

"We are going to fly him," he corrected. Vali brushed past her and sat in the wide saddle. He held out his hand for her, motioning for her to join him, but she hesitated. There were some chances taken which were reckless and exciting, and then there were things which were reckless and exciting *and* foolish all at once. She believed this experience might fall somewhere in between those categories.

"Trust me, Ailsa. You will not regret this," he said. His dark green cloak filled with the breeze and fluttered behind him, showing off his solid frame so confidently postured on the back of the beast like he had done this a thousand times. Everything about him drew her in, from his outstretched hand that challenged her courage, to the look in his eyes that tempted her heart.

As long as he looked at her like that, she'd follow him anywhere.

She inhaled the salt from the sea and drank in the confidence overflowing from the elfin before taking his hand in hers as she slipped into the saddle in front of him. Her hips rested on top of his, and if she hadn't already felt him harden for her during his late-night visits, she would have blushed feeling his size press against her backside. "You're going to enjoy this, aren't you?" she asked over her shoulder.

His hands smoothed around her waist to hold her snug against his chest. "You have no idea," he whispered in a voice so rough it was practically a growl.

Not true. She had a good idea how pleased he was.

"Slip your legs into the stirrups and I'll tie you in. I don't need them." She did as he commanded, letting him buckle her into the saddle until she was as much a part of the eagle as his wings.

"Ready?" he asked. She gripped his forearms now wrapped around her middle and nodded reluctantly. He gently kicked the eagle and spoke to him in their secret language, and the bird lurched into action. Ailsa held her breath as the beast stalked toward the edge, perching above the world as it came to the drop off and paused.

"You must swear to me something," he spoke in her ear.

"Aye?" she said breathlessly, unable to tear her eyes away from the jagged rocks far below them now.

He put a hand beneath her chin and forced her gaze to look up at him, where all her fears seemed to cower from the light of their shimmering brilliance. "Don't close your eyes, Ailsa."

She sucked in a thin gasp of air and spoke against his lips. "Never."

He heeled the bird's chest and they fell over the edge.

A violent gust tore against her face, tears blurring her vision as cold air stung the corners of her eyes while a shrill sound formed in her throat. She dug her nails into Vali's arms as the bird fell face first along the edge of the Convocation, the drop both terrifying and thrilling and stealing any substantial thought in her mind.

Vali held her tight against him, his thighs tense in the

saddle as he pressed himself against the eagle in preparation for what came next. Without warning, the bird twisted and unfurled its full wingspan, catching the air and riding the breeze blown from the sea at their backs. With a few powerful strokes, the bird ascended high over the landscape, suspending them somewhere above the cloud line and rendering the world below insignificant.

A nervous laugh slipped from her chest as her heart settled back into a regular rate. "That was..." she gasped, unable to finish and lost for words.

"Breathtaking?" he drawled.

She nodded fervently and peeled her fingers from the thick fabric of his sleeve. Crescent moons from her nails wrinkled the black shirt. But if she nicked him, he said nothing. He kept his hands on the small of her waist as she stared across the endless stretch of realm that was Alfheim, taking in a new world that reminded her so much of her own if she would've had the chance to explore it.

The land was green beneath them. Meadows covered in a rainbow of wildflowers carpeted the earth until it met the hilly terrain against the mountains. They passed over a waterfall as they neared granite peaks, and Ailsa noticed a group of fae riding long oblong discs, using them to ride the fall straight over the edge and into the deep green pool below.

"Fall riders," Vali explained in her ear above the roar of the wind shifting around them. "It's quite a fun sport, though I'm not any good at it."

They continued to travel along the line of mountains, deeper into the horizon. Ailsa turned to him to ask, "Where are we going?"

"Do you remember when I told you how the black magic

was destroying the land? Well, I'm going to show you. You need to see it for yourself."

She returned her gaze ahead, letting go of the saddle to adjust the fitted sleeves of her cloak that gathered beneath leather gauntlets. Vali noticed her chill and pulled her cowl against the wind, shielding her skin. She nestled her head into the crook of his neck, relaxing against him. A thousand feet above the world and seated between his straddle, she felt more at home in a completely different realm than she had in her own village. This journey with the elfin proved home was not a place, but a state of being. And she found this sense of rest in the elfin at her back, pressing his lips to the hood lining her temple. Vali was her person and her place, her greatest adventure she wanted to explore as long as she could.

The eagle shifted his wings as they descended to their destination. From their position in the sky, Ailsa noticed a hard line in the land. A world of life and unyielding landscape on one side, a stark contrast to the fleshy remains on the other. The beastly bird dropped in a heart wrenching fall somewhere between them both, where a powerful river separated the divergent worlds.

When they landed in the middle of a field in the untamed wilderness, Vali helped Ailsa out of the saddle and pulled her by the hand through the waist high grass. The eagle took off into the sky, leaving them stranded in the quiet forest bordering the river.

"A bit off the beaten path, Vali." She struggled through the underbrush as they made their way to higher ground.

"We must. The dark elves are now camping on this side of the river. What once was used as a border between the Light and the Dark is now obsolete. They have enchantments that keep their camps hidden from the sky, so I wanted to make sure we didn't accidentally land near one." He placed a hand on one of the trees for support and the veining beneath the bark came to life, responding to his presence with a golden glow that bled throughout the tree and colored the dull leaves gold.

"Vali!" she exclaimed as she watched the phenomenon.

He looked up and gave the canopy a small smile, unsurprised. "The land is alive here, Ailsa. As it is in your world and the Realm Between Realms. But Alfheim is called the Land of Light for a reason. Light lives in every living thing in our realm, connecting us all." He let go of the tree and the light faded until the leaves were mossy green again, and the trunk was bare and quiet. He proceeded into the depths of the forest; a gold sheen of floating sunshine followed his steps.

She took this time to watch him in his environment, to admire the way his world reacted and worshipped him. The trees seemed to bend toward him as he passed, the air sparkled with an iridescent haze. He was like a god amongst devoted patrons, adorned by Light and revered by all of creation.

He turned over his shoulder in a silent query, wondering why she wasn't following. But she was too invested in the scene of him against the backdrop of lush wilderness. He passed a hand through his hair, combing back the length so it fell down his neck. The motion pulled her stare to the sharp points of his ears. His eyes were a bright contrast under the shade of the branches, intense and consuming as he returned her appraisal.

"Is everything all right?" he asked.

She nodded and stepped closer, basking in his attention. Where the world seemed to bow to him, he looked only to her. "Aye," she answered quietly. "I was just admiring the view. You are beautiful, *elskan min.*"

His jaw clenched as she neared him. Her hand slipped

beneath his heavy cloak to feel the rigid muscles under his shirt. “Do you mean it? When you call me yours,” he asked.

“I’ve never called anyone that before.”

“But is it genuine?” he breathed. “Do you want me to be yours?”

She lifted her stare to meet his own. “With everything I am, Vali.”

He leaned forward and kissed her gently. A single, sweet kiss that when broken left her longing for more. “I have an idea,” he said with a raspy quality, “if you’re up for a side adventure.”

“What do you think?” She winked, having an idea what this detour would entail.

A deep sound ripped from his chest before pulling her past a line of trees, where the canopy was so thick above, the only light came in the form of sunbeams filtering through the small spaces between branches, forming spotlights on the forest floor. After pushing far enough into the woods, he stopped, turning to her.

“I know we haven’t had much private time since we arrived,” he said, his hands returned to her hips. “And those curtains in the hospital wing beds don’t exactly keep out intrusive stares.”

“We’ve had fun, though,” she reminded him, sliding her own hands up his chest and over his shoulders. “I’ve enjoyed learning more about you on a deeper level, Vali, and your hands can be quite stealthy when they need to be. But…”

“But?”

Ailsa smirked. “But I cannot wait until we have a bed behind a door, so I may know you *more.*”

“Perhaps you don’t have to wait,” he said, smiling. Vali let go of her to reach both hands to the ground, where he mumbled whispered words of an unknown language.

The ground beneath his palms streaked with gold, veining across the earth like a web of a light. New green ivy burst from the dirt, covering the root mottled ground with soft foliage. A bed of soft leaves and crawling vines, and each layer wove together to create a thick blanket of greenery. Each strand of vine was illuminated by a vein of golden light, until Vali stood and disconnected himself from the earth, and the woods darkened once more.

Ailsa felt her cheeks grow hot as she stared at the bed he made from the earth itself. The elfin watched her, assessing, trying to gauge her feelings on the matter through her reaction alone. He said, "If you don't feel comfortable, we don't—"

"Take off your boots, Vali."

He did so with little hesitation, and a wild grin stretched wider across his lips as she did the same. She stepped in front of him, deliberately positioning herself between him and the grassy bed, and fingered the cloak off his shoulders, letting it fall to the earth behind him. His face leaned down to snatch her lips, forcing their eyes shut as he blindly felt for the laces of her tunic, her pants, anything that bound her from his sight or his touch.

She snatched her hands in his hair as he undressed her slowly, as she could force herself to do nothing but focus on the trails of his fingertips against her bare skin. Leather and flax slipped from her body, allowing the cool woodland air to engulf her, chill bumps running down her skin. His hands immediately transitioned from her top half to her pants, sliding them free as he traced the curve of her spine all the way down, gripping her ass on the way up. The only barrier she wore were the white undergarments he was rubbing against his palms, creating an agonizing friction, but not where she needed it most.

"Gods below, Ailsa," he breathed against her mouth. "You are fucking exquisite." She loved the way he said her name, how it sounded so rough in his throat. But his hands—those large, persuasive hands—just kept tracing her body and pooling heat lower in her stomach.

"Your turn," she murmured, kissing the corner of his mouth. Her nails caught the bottom of his shirt and ripped it over his head, tossing it to the side. Her fingers were greedy, reaching for the waistband of his pants until he stopped her. Those sweet hands now the enemy. The smile fell from her lips as she made a sound of defiance, only amusing him with her frustration.

"Not me, not today, *sváss.* I will not have you in that way until I've tasted you, until I have earned that privilege," he declared. Vali leaned forward and muttered in her ear, "Now, get on your back and let me adore you."

"This isn't fair," she groaned, even as her traitorous feet followed his command, retreating to the mossy pile of layered ivy.

"Punish me for it later. But for now, do as I say," he said. When her brow arched in a warning, he added, "Please. Do this for me, please."

She let her body relax on the soft earth. Ailsa couldn't hide the way her skin shivered as he watched her. The slightest shift made his eyes dart to the movement. And she could have sworn his golden gaze was glowing, that it couldn't have been a trick of the light now that they were sheltered beneath the thick canopy. He regarded her like a feast, the way he licked his lips and surveyed every inch of her, as if wondering which part he would savor first.

"Vali," Ailsa whimpered, growing impatient, feeling suddenly very bare and alone without his heat around her. "What are you waiting for?"

He finally climbed on top of her, claiming her mouth and silencing any complaint still fresh in her mind. Her thoughts were muddled as he settled between her legs, kissing her with an intensity that made her ache for him all the more. Desperate to relieve the tension, she bucked her hips against his hard body, finding friction anywhere she could.

He broke their kiss to slam her hips back into the ivy. "Bad *svåss.* Did I tell you to seek your own pleasure? Do you not trust I will take care of you?" With his hands so close to that hot place at her apex, she thought he'd finally relieve her in some way, but instead, his hands drew up her stomach, ripping the band covering her breasts. An approving groan ruptured from him as they hardened, exposed to the woodland air.

"You will stay still as I worship you, Ailsa. Or I will prolong your suffering."

"Filthy fae." She exhaled through her teeth, arching her back as he palmed one breast, pinching the sensitive peak.

"Heathen." He smiled.

"I will have my revenge later, Vali." A frustrated breath slipped through her lips as his tongue darted against her cold flesh.

Her soft skin slipped from his teeth with a gentle nip. "And as the god of vengeance, I look forward to it." Finally, *finally,* his opposite hand dipped beneath her hips, between her thighs. Vali could not hide his rapturous grin as his fingers slid over that point of tension, where a wet heat was already soaking through her undergarments. With a single swipe, he ripped them to her ankles, flicking them to the side with a flip of his wrist. His gaze glanced at her reaction, assessing her disposition to seek her consent before he pushed her knees to the side and displayed her—all of her—to himself. But Ailsa did not shy away from his inspection, instead she pushed up on her elbows to view him better.

"Vali?" she said when he didn't move.

His chest was heaving faster than she'd ever seen it race before. A golden haze seemed to burn around his body like a halo as he gradually lowered his head between her legs, as if waiting for her to stop him. His fingers gently probed that small nub, shooting pleasure straight through her core.

"Vali!" she gasped, and she felt the breath of a snide laugh brush the wetness between her legs.

"You are so beautiful, Ailsa," he said, before kissing the inside of her thigh reverently. Sharp teeth followed tender lips, biting at her skin. He draped a leg over his shoulder, his mouth so close until…

A sprawling pleasure climbed within her as his tongue split her in two. She fisted his hair as she cried out, writhing against his face. Vali sucked and lapped, used his mouth to inspect every line and nerve, pushing her further up a slope and toward the edge of bliss. His thumb replaced his mouth as he used it to dive inside her, fucking her with his tongue, tasting the deepest point of her arousal.

"*Sólskin,*" she spoke his name, something between a plea and a praise.

He pulled away for a moment, licking the leftover desire from his lips as he stared at her, the wildest look in his eyes. "You taste like starlight and paradise," he rasped before adding, "fucking delicious."

Ailsa laughed through her shuddering breaths. "What does starlight even taste like?"

His lips tipped into a smirk that made her toes curl. "Do you want to know? Because I can show you."

He dropped her hips and crawled on top of her, dipping his face to kiss her, so she could taste herself on his tongue. An adoring sigh replaced her exhale, but the heat in her hips was agitated from the loss of him. She returned his attention back to them with an exuberant grind against his hardness, wrapping her legs around his waist.

"I haven't forgotten, my fierce one," he said with a wink. "Are you ready for the big finish? Or shall I draw this out a little longer?"

"Vali, please!" Ailsa dragged her nails across the broad muscles of his back so hard he winced, a pain so pleasurable his cock twitched against her.

His merciful fingers returned, rubbed the ache away as she begged with her body. "Well when you ask so pretty, *elskan min,* how can I say no?" His finger dove inside her, deep and thrusting, stretching her before adding another. Ailsa arched against him as they curled against a spot that sent her thrashing, trembling, tipping over a point of no return. A low sound flew from his chest, echoing her sharp ones, feeling him shake against her as she rode his hand harder.

She cried his name as she fell, tensing around his fingers as she climaxed for moments that felt like lifetimes. And Vali held her against his chest as the last waves rolled through her, washing away the remaining tension and leaving her body peacefully still. When Ailsa's heart returned to a steady pace, she smoothed a hand over Vali's chest, slipping behind his neck to pull his cheek to her lips.

"Gods, Vali," she said. "That was… that was amazing. I've never felt like that before."

He leaned his forehead against hers, a glazed look over his

eyes like he was half-drunk. "I feel like I should be thanking you."

Her brows furrowed. "Why? You didn't even—" her eyes fell to his waistband, where something opaque glistened across his abdomen. Her gaze circled back to him, wide with astonishment. "You did!"

Vali laughed, rolling to his back to stretch. "That is how much I am attracted to you, *sváss.* You don't even have to touch me. Your pleasure is my own foreplay." She nestled against his side and shut her eyes, listening to the sounds of his breath in the hollow trunk of his chest. "Never underestimate your power over me, Ailsa. There is nothing stronger in all the realms than the way I feel for you."

His confession pulled her lips into a smile. "For once, fate has been kind to us, bringing us together." Her fingers memorized the inky lines on his skin. "Was there something you wanted to show me? Before we carved out this little detour."

He nodded against her head. "Yes, but it can wait a few more minutes. Hold me until then. Please."

"Okay," she whispered. Meanwhile, she watched flickers of light fall from the canopy, like snowflakes made of sunshine. The trees were veined with Light again, the leaves on every branch shades of gold and orange. The world around them suddenly bright and gleaming, alive because of the man at her side and what she did to him.

Alive because his Light burned all the brighter. And it burned because of her.

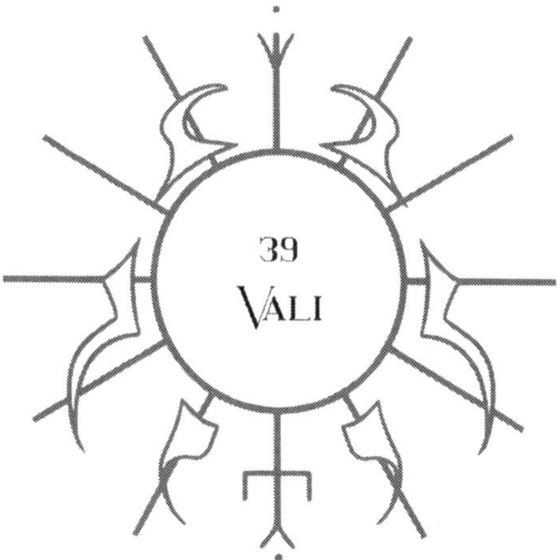

39
Vali

Vali could still taste Ailsa in the back of his throat when they emerged from the woods. He didn't think he'd ever be able to wash away her scent from his skin, the way she marked him as she came around his fingers. The scratches she drove into his back. She had hardly touched him at all, and yet his release was powerful enough to illuminate the entire forest with an ethereal light.

He wanted nothing more than to bury himself inside her, to connect with her on a level so deep they would become one in every way that mattered. But something flipped inside him today when she called him her own, a shift beneath his skin when she claimed him in the ancient language. Like the night on her shores when the Tether called him, but a thousand times more intense. A visceral urge so powerful, he felt as if it would tear him apart.

They heard the river before they came across it—the power of rushing water splitting over jagged rocks, the turbulent stream flowing uninterrupted through the earth. A bridge made the only path to the other side. It was a thin walkway, allowing no more than a horse or two to pass at once.

Observing the way her gaze studied the landscape, he explained. "This is a long-forgotten section of the river, not used as much as the one outside of the Haven, but it flows directly from the Well of Selsnar and supplies the land with Light. All life in Alfheim stems from our wells alone, and Selsnar sources the elfin world on the opposite side of the river. The other well, Mirrenal, sources everything on this side. Both are permeated by the sun shining over the Tree."

She slanted her head in thought. "Your wells source the life in this realm similarly to the wells sourcing the Tree?"

He nodded. "Correct. But we have different wells because the fae require a different life source than the gods and mankind." It was known all the fae were godless, or once were before Frey was introduced to this realm. Odin was never quite pleased with the idea of the fae realms living outside of his influence.

"What is the Haven?" she asked.

"It is another kingdom on the other side of the river, the one Frey claimed as his temple when he first arrived in Alfheim. The dwarves were its original dwellers. They hand-carved every hall and every room into the mountain. It's there, just a half a day's walk that way." He pointed toward a distant peak hazy with afternoon glare before tugging her hand. "Come with me a little further. I want to show you the other side."

She followed him over the slick stone forming the bridge and Vali ignored the cracks running rampant throughout the foundation, focusing instead on the solid hand in his own and the desolate world they approached. As soon as her feet stepped off the bridge to the other side, Ailsa slipped a gasp, horrified at what she found.

Death.

The ground was barren of grass, just the ashy remains of fruitless soil. The trees were withered, not a single leaf still clung to the bones of the branches nor a color existed other than black or grey in the decrepit wilderness.

He watched her slowly pace to the edge of the boneyard, reaching a hesitant hand out to feel the product of darkness in a world so once full of beauty. Vali followed her, showing her how nothing came to life beneath his touch now. The Light in this land was gone.

"This is what will become of the entire realm if we do not get Frey and his Vanir magic out of here. Whatever the darkness of sedir effects, the Light will not touch it," he explained.

Ailsa took in the sobering scene quietly. "Why do they continue to practice sedir if this is what happens to the land?"

"Because they don't care," Vali shrugged. "They believe the world will grow back as it does in Vanaheim. But they don't understand that Light is not just a source, it is *the* source. Snuff it out and life will cease to exist here."

She turned to him, her hand absentmindedly running over the markings hidden behind the neck of her cowl. "And we have the ability to stop it from spreading just by giving me to Odin?"

"Frey leaving is our best chance," he said. "At least then, my mother and I can retain control of Alfheim and we can ban the practice of dark magic and hopefully one day restore this part of the realm."

She gave him a solemn nod, her gaze falling somewhere far beyond him. "I just have to live long enough for Odin to take me away," she mumbled. "We should move up the feast just in case, while I'm feeling well."

"Ailsa, that's not," he trailed. But she cut him off with an affectionate hand on his chest.

"No, Vali. As much as I want to spend each one of my last days with you, we need to fix this. Last week was a close call, and we cannot afford another one."

He shook his head, unwilling to consider it. "I promised I wouldn't let him take you. I will think of something else. Just give me time, *svåss*."

"That was a vow you should have never made me," she stepped away, removing the comfort of her touch, the pain in his chest ricocheted against all the empty places inside him. "And one I should have never bound you to. There are forces against us too strong to fight, Vali. We cannot wage war with destiny and win."

"So this is it." He gestured widely to himself. "You're giving up on us—on me!"

"I'm doing this *for* you, Vali! Do you think I want to leave you?"

His fingers raked through his hair, pulling at the roots to externalize his frustration. "I think you are taking the easy way out," he said too harshly.

Ailsa's eyes hardened into a chilling glare. "*Easy*?" she spat. "I'm the one who has to die, Vali!"

"Yes, and I'm the one who must *live!*" he roared, the bitterness rising too fast to shove back down. She would die and he was the one who would have to survive every empty day that followed.

But when he saw her eyes brim with tears, his anger lashed back into himself. His words a double-edged sword, bleeding them both. His head fell, shaking in shame. "I'm sorry, Ailsa. I know you're doing what's right. I've just never felt so..."

"Helpless? Aye, Vali, I know exactly how you feel." Her steps were quiet as a doe in a meadow as she approached, slipping her hand around the clenched fist at his side. "Let's go home. Before we both say things we do not mean."

He nodded in agreeance, bringing her hand to his lips in a grazing kiss. *Home.* Not her fjord but his kingdom. "Of course. Let's go back to the other side, though. I don't like Elísar flying over to this side. It's dangerous—"

Before he could finish, a sound barreled through the tree line, crashing through the rotten trunks and sending debris flying across the riverbank. They turned to find a hideous creature standing on the edge of the barren forest. A massive beast with grey, sloughing skin sunken into bulging bones and a broken log poised in its right hand.

"Is that what I think it is?" Ailsa shrieked beside him.

"Yes," Vali hissed, "a troll."

"We can't bait it across the bridge, there's no way it can hold the weight," she spoke as the troll's red eyes bounced from him to her, debating which to lurch after first.

"Cross the bridge, Ailsa. I'll take care of it, but I need you out of the way," he whispered.

"Like Hel I'm leaving you to fight this alone."

"Ailsa—" he growled, but the troll had grown impatient with their banter. With a deep wail it sent the log down between them, splitting them apart. Vali rolled to his feet and looked over at Ailsa through raining drops of earth as the troll lifted his club. She was already scrambling to stand upright, her hands unsheathing the weapon at her thigh.

The troll swung the club straight for her, and she only had time to spin to the side and dodge his swing with the grace of an assassin. While the beast was distracted, Vali thrust his great sword into the fleshy meat of the troll's thigh, a crippling blow that sent the creature down on one knee.

It roared into the sky, a furious boom that trembled the

ground beneath his feet. In an angry reply, it swatted him with his hand instead and caught his cloak, and the troll lifted him by the cape. The beast growled in delight and reared back to swing the log toward his dangling figure caught helplessly between its fingers.

It shrieked suddenly as something whizzed by Vali's head. He looked up in time to see a gilded dagger jutting out the beast's hand, the same one Ailsa always kept at her side. The troll dropped him to shake out the splintering blade, and as he shook the stars from his vision, he saw Ailsa approach from behind.

She lashed at the creature's ankles, tearing at his calves and the tendons lining its heels. A green liquid sprayed across her face as she relentlessly attacked, and Vali was awestruck at the skill in her fight. To see a woman as small as her, barely passing the troll's kneecap, stab the beast where it hurt the most and spraying her skin with its boggy blood—it drove him mad with want.

He snapped out his trance and vaulted to his feet to assist her. The troll groaned from the pain she dealt before kicking its back heel, the force throwing Ailsa until she landed on her back some feet away, skidding across the soft earth.

"Ailsa!" he shouted, not tearing his eyes away from her body until he saw her move. The troll turned his attention back to Vali, and the elfin lunged to the side to dodge another swing from its club.

"I'm okay!" she gasped. Satisfied, he danced in front of the troll, dodging the quick hands of the beast until he had its full attention and slicing the thick skin until its forearms were disfigured with gashes.

It was growing tired, and the superficial wounds made it angry and desperate. The troll swung clumsily in his direction and stumbled to the side. Creatures born from darkness were immune to enchantments, but the world around him still answered his call. Vali swung his blade over his head and lunged towards its wrist as it swung past him. His magic willed the blade to cut with the force of a falling tree, and the sword cut clean through a meshwork of skin and tendon and bone.

It wailed a wet howl as his fighting hand was dismembered from its arm, blood spurting from the severed site. Vali slipped in the oily liquid and stumbled while trying to retreat, and the vengeful troll used his only hand to snag him before he could stand, his body now wrapped in its giant fist.

The troll squeezed, and Vali felt the air push free from his lungs, the blood surge to his head as the beast crushed his ribcage. Just before the headrush made his insides collapse, a little figure climbed over the troll's soldier. A breathless Ailsa sat perched on the crest of its arm like a raven, her figure so light and stealthy it didn't even feel her.

She banged the creature on top of his bald head with the hilt of her blade. It gave a startled cry before turning its triple gaze on her. She spat in one of the eyes before thrusting the sword deep into its neck, cutting clean through a field of blood vessels.

The troll uttered a strangled choke, his grip loosening, before falling with a shuddering *thud* across the earth. The world became quiet once more, and Vali hurried to his feet, pushing free from the dead weight of the troll's fingers. He looked across the bank but did not see Ailsa, nor did he hear a single movement besides the hissing waters of the river.

Panic closed his throat, and he scrambled over the beast to find Ailsa on the other side, sprawled across the earth where she landed from the troll's fall. Vali ran to her, dropping his sword to lift her in his arms. A thin trail of blood leaked from her lips.

"Ailsa!" he shook her. She moaned from his rouse, but it hardly made him relax. She was not wakening, her eyes remained shut and her muscles were limp. He looked to the river just yards away from where he held her and dragged her close, knowing its healing waters would be enough to heal the concussion.

He cupped the water between her lips, running his fingers down her throat to make her swallow. And after a few agonizing minutes, her eyes fluttered awake.

"Thank the Light," he murmured, stroking the tangled mess of her unbound braids.

Ailsa shifted in his arms. "Did I get him?" she groaned.

Vali laughed, feeling oddly light after a great weight released from his chest. "Yes, Ailsa, you got him. You killed a troll."

"Good." She smiled, a peace settled over her features. "My father always said *fight like you are already dead.* But I prefer to fight like I cannot die. And in those brief moments of fighting, I am immortal, and it feels good."

"You are made of steel, *sváss.*" He kissed her forehead before pulling back. "I'm going to carry you back across the bridge, and you *will* stay awake until we get to the hospital."

"Master Greer is going to kill you," she said.

Vali grinned. "Good thing I have you to protect me."

She beamed up at him, her smile filling the hole in his chest with its perfection. "Always, *elskan min.*"

40
Ailsa

Vali stayed with her that night, convinced it was a *necessary precaution* to have someone there in case her head injury revealed the worst of itself in the late hours of the evening when no one was around. But her body felt fine owing to the healing waters of the river. Drinking directly from the source proved to heighten its effects and mitigate her symptoms. She remained in a deep sleep until something disturbed her slumber—a nip at her shoulder. She swatted it away without opening her eyes.

"Not now, Vali," she mumbled as she rolled to her side. Just as she was about to fall back asleep, something sharp lanced her palm.

Wide awake now, Ailsa shot up and discovered the offender was not an elfin but a falcon. Its black talons curved into the linen sheet she clutched to her chest as it cocked its head at her. Its beady eyes held a hint of intelligence not belonging to a normal bird.

"What—"

But as she spoke, the bird flew through the sheer curtains

surrounding her bed and departed through the hospital's only exterior door. A door she knew had been shut before the healers left for the evening. Vali was the only other soul in the room, resting in a bed he had pushed next to hers as his body sprawled like a sea star beneath the covers. His snores muffled the sound of the bird's flutter.

The bird danced through the entry, hopping on its talons as it peeked around the door.

Just what I need—another damn bird's attention. She fell back onto the pillow and pressed her eyes shut, determined to ignore the falcon and the attentive eyes disturbing her rest.

Until it snagged her exposed side with its sharp beak.

She jerked against the pinch, and Vali choked as she roused him. She glared at the bird, but it only fluffed its wings like a shrug and quietly flew from the room in the same direction as before.

Once the elfin had soothed back into a steady, albeit noisy rhythm, she gathered a thin blanket on top of the bed and wrapped it around her shift. If there was no chance of getting rid of the little beast, she would just have to see what it wanted. Whatever concerned the falcon, it obviously did not desire to include Vali in their private meeting.

The nights were colder in Alfheim, even colder than in Jotunheim, as the sun drifted far from the Highest Branch. Her breath fogged white against the star filled night as she stepped onto the balcony overlooking the western side of the castle. The tile was damp with dew from the sudden change in temperature, from the warm day to the freezing night. Ailsa crossed the balcony in search of the falcon, realizing too late the bird was not a bird at all.

Cold fingers wrapped around her mouth to muffle her scream.

"Hush, it's all right. I'm not here to hurt you, Ailsa. I just want to speak in private," a voice dripping with venom spoke in her ear. The sound was convincing enough to cease her struggle against the solid body subduing her thrashing.

With his hand still over her mouth, he asked, "If I remove my hand, do you promise not to scream and wake up Vali? I have something very important to ask you—and you alone."

She heaved a flustered sigh and nodded. Her assailant slowly peeled his fingers away from her lips as she spun around, placing a face to the voice. It was a man slightly taller than Vali, with fair hair long and slicked back, bound in a low ponytail. His eyes were a fierce green, bold and cunning. A thin smile slithered across one cheek.

"It is a pleasure to meet the cause of all the gossip in Asgard." He gave a small bow. "I am Loki, god of—"

"Odin's fucking eye," Ailsa gasped.

Loki's stoic expression crumbled in perplexity. "Um, no. Not quite. I was going to say god of mischief but—"

"I know who you are," she laughed, silencing the sound with a hand over her mouth. Her laughter died when she noted the nick on her hand. "You made me bleed."

"Well, it's hardly my fault you sleep like a troll." He leaned against the glass railing tinted a seafoam green. "And sleeping quite close to Odin's least favorite son, I see. He will not be pleased to hear of this recent development."

"I thought the Allfather could see everything. This should hardly surprise him." She leaned over the railing some feet away, staring into the sky and wondering if he was looking down on them even now.

"You are the one thing in all of creation he cannot see. The gold witch made sure he could never find her magic, not by his own means, anyway. That is the greatest power of all, if you ask me."

"To be concealed?"

"To hide. Just as Fenrir has hidden from him all this time somehow."

Ailsa wrangled against the smile forming on her face. "You mean you wish you could just do this sometimes?" She made an obscene gesture toward the sky, and Loki's eyes lit up with delight.

"Oh, I'd do that to his face," he said, mimicking her offensive sign. "Followed by a few words not appropriate for your delicate, feminine ears."

Her breath sang between her teeth in pretense. "I have words in my vocabulary that would make even your greasy hair curl." She cleared her throat to end the banter. "Why are you here, Loki? And why are you wearing a coat of feathers?"

He regarded his cloak made of the same feathers as the falcon. "Oh, this? This is Freya's coat. Allows the wearer the ability to fly anywhere in falcon form. I'm quite envious of it."

Ailsa's brows kissed. From the legends, she was told the god could shift into anything he desired. "Can't you just shapeshift into a falcon?"

He rolled his grassy eyes, like this wasn't the first time he had been asked such a question. "Yes, I can, but it's not the same, and I enjoy taking things from Freya. Speaking of the goddess," he reached into his coat and pulled out a glass jar topped with a lid. Inside was barely a gulp full of a golden liquid. "I also brought something else of hers."

Ailsa stepped closer to look at the jar. "Is that—"

"Freya's tears, straight from the source." He winked before tucking it safely back into his coat pocket.

"What are you doing with her tears?" Ailsa asked warily. She took a guarded step back.

Loki grinned a demoralizing smile. "Did you know Freya's tears have unmitigated healing powers? One could even argue they can extend a mortal life span to even that of the fae." He watched her as he spoke, but Ailsa steeled her expression. Leaving him to only guess at what she was thinking, the ideas connecting in her mind.

"Why are you showing me her tears?" she asked, clarifying his intent.

"Because I have an offer for you." He stepped closer; the mossy tail of feathers skimmed the beaded floor. "And you would be wise to consider it."

"Coming from the Trickster himself," she retorted. But Loki shook his head.

"This offer comes from all the Aesir. I am just the messenger. The gods are granting you divine healing from your condition—"

"How does Odin know I'm sick? I thought he couldn't see me."

"Vali let it slip during his visit. He inquired one of the Norns about how to help you and extend your thread. It was not within his power, but it is within *ours.*"

He took out the jar and held it out for her to inspect. Ailsa took the tears from his fingers, feeling the ending to all her shortened breaths, the answer to all her struggles within the palm of her hand. She shot him a careful look. "What do you want in exchange?"

"Come with me now to Asgard," he simply said.

"Now?" she exclaimed. Her mind raced with the consequences of this alternative. "But then… But then the fae would lose their end of the bargain, and Frey would never leave. Odin would be getting everything he wanted without having to pay for it."

Loki shrugged. "But you would live, Ailsa. Is that not what you've always wanted? The ability to run without fainting. To walk without getting short of breath. Think of the mountains you could climb, the world you could conquer if you were well. All that was unfairly taken from you, now just a sip away from having."

Ailsa stared into the cup, knowing his argument was rooted in a well of truth. All she ever wanted was to live a life to the fullest and a body able to do so. She was entirely deserving after the suffering she endured her entire mortal existence.

"After all," Loki spoke quietly, "what do you owe the elfin? This is not your world. Not your fight."

She *owed* him nothing, yet he had taken everything from her. He had taken her family, left her orphaned and alone with no hope for a future beyond the adventure that would soon come to an end. He had been unkind, negligent, left her in the hands of giants, and she had cooperated this entire time just to please him. Just to help a man who had done nothing but steal.

But he had also saved her from a loveless future, a path promised to an unkind shieldmage in her small corner of the world. He expanded her map, stole her away from a meaningless path and presented a passion for life she would have never found on her own, gave her a purpose beyond living for the next breath. And for once she was not defined by her illness but by a power inside her she alone was destined to carry, so that an entire realm could be free of the oppression of darkness.

Yes, he had taken from her. He had stolen her heart, and perhaps that was the cruelest thing he had done. The most illicit of his crimes. One he would feel the punishment for the rest of his extended life.

"I drink this, and I will be healed?" she asked the god. "And then we will fly back to Asgard?"

"I'll even let you wear the coat," he grinned.

She brought the glass to her lips and threw her head back, letting Freya's tears forever dry her own.

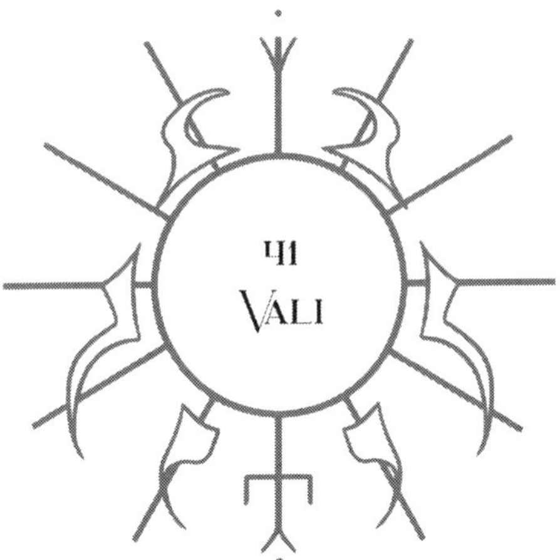

41
Vali

Vali watched helplessly behind the ajar door as Ailsa spoke with the god of deception, every word a dagger to his chest. Even he knew Loki's offer was too good for her to pass up, but it didn't ease the hurt. It did nothing to push down the unwarranted anger rising in his throat, inches away from spilling through with a hateful scream. The icy feeling of betrayal washed over him as she brought the cup to her mouth and drank the tears.

Then thawed away as she spat the golden liquid back into the god's face.

"If Odin thinks for a second he will get out of this bargain with the elves, he is mistaken. I will leave with Frey when the last of the gods' influence is purged from this land. And do not ever try to tempt me again or use my illness as a weakness. Do I make myself clear, *Loki Lord of Lies*?" she hissed, and gold streaked across her lips as she spat the words. The sureness of her voice, the easy scowl she wore as she devoured Loki in her gaze. It was a devastating kind of beautiful. It reminded him of the day he arrived on the shores of Drakame, how she once looked at him with such unapologetic hatred.

How far they had come.

"You'd rather die for a fight you have nothing to do with?" he asked, wiping his face.

"I'd rather die than betray those I love," she corrected.

Vali couldn't hold himself in the shadows any longer. He pushed the door aside and stormed across the balcony, Ailsa's eyes widening with surprise as they crossed him. She barely had time to let out a small yelp before he took her face in his hands, kissing the lips she parted in surprise. He pressed her soft body against the railing, bending her at the waist over an unending stretch of Alfheim meadows.

He tasted the sweet tears of the goddess as he threaded his tongue against hers, adoring the way her breath sucked in when she discovered how hard he was for her. She pulled him closer like an accepted challenge. This woman who held the world in her hands, a promise of unnumbered tomorrows, and let it all go because of her devotion, her loyalty, her vow.

Her love.

Those once impenetrable boundaries she'd been chipping away at finally shattered.

"I suppose that's a *no*, then," Loki muttered.

She swallowed his growl with the sweep of her tongue. Her hands were hungry, sliding down his chest to stroke the tangible length of his desire as she wrapped a leg around his hip. They had explored each other every night since she awoke, a delicious dance of asking and daring, waiting for the other to take them both past the line of no return. But only tonight did he feel the readiness in her touch, the yearning in her kiss.

"This is escalating quickly," the god said. "I'm going to go ahead and leave, but if you change your mind—"

Vali tore his face from the vector of her kiss, his eyes hazy with murderous plans as he interrupted Loki with his stare alone. Without another word, the trickster wrapped himself in the cloak and folded into the image of a bird before flying off into the night. His last foul screeches echoed across the realm.

Ailsa was sitting on top of the ledge, her linen shift pulled high around her hips. Her eyes were low on him, hooded behind a lusty veil. She dangled her long, bare legs and pushed a disheveled lock of wavy hair behind her ear, knowing just how to bait out his savage side.

"The gods must think I'm a fool if they sent *him* to convince me," she said with swollen lips.

"You *are* a fool," he said. His hands fell over the bony prominence of her knees. "Loki may be a trickster, but nothing he said was untrue. Why would you deny the tears and the promise of a long life? They practically ensured you would survive the Crow's threat."

She wrapped her arms around his neck and skimmed her words against his lips. "Because there is more to life than existing. And now that I know you, I don't want to live a single day without you. Much less doom your world with my selfish wants."

"Your health isn't selfish, Ailsa."

"Would you rather I have drunk the tears and left with him? Taking the hope of the Light Elves with me?" She pulled back, confused.

Vali swallowed against the rough edge in his throat. His words weren't coming out right, his gratitude falling short. "Of course not. But your happiness is the most important thing in the world to me. To Hel with the rest."

"Don't say that," she snapped. "You cannot speak like that as a future High Lord. This is your realm, your people. Act like it."

He nodded tightly and averted her gaze, struggling to

swallow the truth. "You would have been perfect at my side. As my Lady."

She smiled and leaned against him, fleshing her body against his chest. "I will *always* be with you, *Sólskin*. Tell me, have I not marked you forever? Or do I need to carve my name across the runes on your chest."

"I have something better in mind," he whispered. "Be my *Fraendi*, Ailsa."

Her eyes flinched, and he thought for a moment she would refuse him. But her jaw only opened and shut, not accepting but not denying either. "Aren't the fae exclusive for life? Once you choose a *Fraendi,* you can never have another one?" she asked.

"Yes, but that changes nothing."

"It changes everything!" She slipped between the railing and his hips to distance herself, retrieving the damp blanket cast aside across the pavers. "I will not take away your one chance for a *Fraendi* just to die and have you to walk the rest of your days alone."

"I won't though, you don't understand…" Gods below, he couldn't say the right thing if he tried, and he was trying his best to convince her she was all he wanted. But if she refused to be his *Fraendi* because of this, the truth would have damned him for good.

"You deserve a real mate," she whispered while looking away from him. "One you can share a life with, not mourn over."

"What I *deserve* is to have you for the rest of my life, and if the only way I can have you is through a mark on my skin, then so be it. You were my first choice, and you will be my last, *svåss*. I have not wanted anyone like I want you for the last century, and I will not for the next!"

She clutched the blanket and faced the door, her back to him as her shoulders rose with indecision. Her chin floated above her shoulder as she asked, "*Fraendi* have a mark?"

He brushed the strap of her shift aside and kissed her cold skin. Chill bumps trailed from the placement of his lips down her spine, disappearing beneath the satin. "Yes," he answered. "Life mates share a mark completely unique to each other, a personal rune written in their combined blood. When they consummate the bond, the blood turns black, branding the skin forever."

"Vali," she breathed. Not *Sólskin,* but his name. It rolled as blissfully off her tongue as the first time. She wanted to say yes. Ailsa had no problem turning a man down, to break a heart with a single word, stab them in the chest while wearing a smile. She knew her mind as well as her heart, but something about this decision made her uncertain.

His lips moved to her neck, where a bounding pulse raced an allegro beat beneath his tongue. She opened for him, letting her head fall to the side so he could taste the curve of her throat. He spoke again in the absence of her words. "If you don't want me, if you don't want to be my *Fraendi,* just say it. But don't take my choice away because you think you know what's best for me. Ailsa, *look* at me."

She spun around sharply on her toes, her hair fanning around her shoulders until it rested down her back. When he met her gaze, her eyes were a deep ocean that drowned him away, almost making him forget his words. "Since the moment I first saw you on the shores of Drakame, my blood has sung for you. Every part of my being reaches for you day and night, and I thought it was because the Tether was my destiny, because the runes on my skin demanded it. But it is not the will of gods that calls me to you, Ailsa, it is the fates themselves. My entire existence, I thought my purpose was finding the Tether. But now I know it was really finding *you*."

Her palms skimmed his chest, tracing the coded runes with a distracted gaze. "But how do you know it is me you will always want? How do you know you won't regret me when I am gone?"

He could tell her heart was convinced, but her head needed more. Needed to hear the words he had been holding back for longer than he realized. "The fae only have one mate for life because there is *only* one mate fated for them. There will never be another who crosses my thread that will fit quite as seamless as you do. We were destined to find each other. And..." Vali cleared his throat, summoning the rest of his courage to say the words. "And I am so inherently in love with you, Ailsa. Every bone in my body, every drop of my blood, every breath I breathe, it loves you. That's how I know you are my *Fraendi*."

Her mouth lifted in the beginning of a smile. "Are you sure?" she asked, giving him one last chance to turn back.

"With everything I am, Ailsa."

Her lips trembled as they parted, a decision made in her eyes that dominated the hesitation in her heart. "Where's your knife, *svâss*?"

42
Ailsa

Ailsa lingered in the doorway separating Vali's bathing room from his bedchambers, waiting for him to return from the Light Palace library. She requested he retrieve the Futhark, the scroll of Elder Runes of the old language that had been passed down from the gods to all beings at the beginning of creation. She knew most of the script by heart, having written protective runes on her family for years. But his search bought her time. Time to think and time to process.

She wanted him more than a soul could want for another. But could she do this? Nearly at the end of her thread, and fate chose this moment to send her the love she'd been waiting for. If her life was written as a song, the worlds would think their story a tragedy.

But even with the promise of numbered days limiting their time left together, Ailsa wouldn't want to spend them with anyone else. When he asked her to be his *Fraendi,* when he said he *loved* her, her heart almost shattered with reprieve. She had been happy enough just enjoying the last week with him, exploring Alfheim, seeing where he trained, learning all his favorite foods, and hearing his childhood stories.

But this… His mate? It was something she didn't know was possible, and now that it was, she wanted nothing else than to mark him forever. To give him a piece of her to carry forever. And if he wanted her in return, then that was enough to give her peace over the decision.

So Ailsa moved toward his desk at the far side of the room, finding ink to write with and a piece of parchment to practice. And while she waited for Vali to return from his futile search, she designed the rune that defined their story, the hope they found in their tragedy, and a love so powerful that not even fate could destroy it.

The black jagged lines that would soon be written into their flesh, embodying a saga of sunshine and starlight.

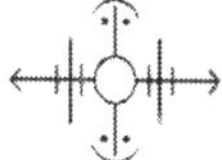

"I SEE YOU STARTED WITHOUT ME."

Ailsa looked up from her work to see Vali holding her requested text. He threw the old scroll to the side where it landed on the bench at the end of his bed, seeing she no longer required it. She gave him an impish smile. "I'm sorry. I just needed some time alone. I hope you don't mind."

He combed his hair back with his fingers, pushing loose wavy strands out of his eyes. The lazy movement was still somehow sensual on him. "Of course not. I needed some time as well, it turns out. I kind of threw this on us both rather quickly."

"Having second thoughts?" she asked, hiding the potential disappointment in her voice.

His smirk showed itself. "Definitely not."

Ailsa held up the final draft of their rune, her fingers now stained with ink. "Good, me either."

His grin stretched wider as he strode to where she sat and took the parchment from her hands, studying the rune himself. She watched his golden eyes flicker over the intersection between the markings of sun and star, branching from the rune of eternal love and rooted in faith and strength. It wasn't particularly complicated or long, but Ailsa thought it fit them.

Vali dropped the paper from his gaze slightly, just enough to lean forward and kiss her long and hard. One of his hands slipped beneath her crown of braids, combed the length of the free-flowing tresses cascading down her back with his fingers. He broke their kiss to mutter, "It is perfect."

That raw edge in his voice made something primal lurch in her heart. She licked her lips, mouth suddenly feeling dry. "You pick where it goes."

His brow arched as his gaze raked over her body still sitting in the round desk chair. His chest purred a sound of pondering. "That's a hard one. There are so many divine places on your skin where this could go." He pulled her out of the chair to stand in front of him, his fingers brushing back her hair over her shoulder, where his lips kissed the curve of her shoulder.

"I like here," he whispered into her skin, though his hands were searching for other possibilities. Ailsa bit her lip to quiet the sigh of appreciation his touch drew.

With a feather weight of pressure, his fingers skimmed over her left breast, tracing the outline of the rune over her heart. "Maybe here," he murmured in her ear.

Her eyes fluttered, fighting to shut and surrender to his sensations. "That's a good spot," she managed to say.

Vali mumbled his agreement, but his palms dipped lower

and stopped at her hips, gathering her night shift between his fingers to push it high over her waist. She was about to ask what he was up to when he knelt and pulled her closer, trailing kisses above her navel. "How about here, where you stabbed me the first day we met?"

Ailsa giggled and pushed him back. Her flesh remembered the last time his mouth had been so low. A fresh heat pooled between her legs when his breath brushed her middle.

"Fond times," she breathed, combing his hair with her fingers.

"For one of us." Her shift fell back over her hips as he took her hand in his. Still on his knee in front of her, he placed his lips on the back of her wrist. Then smoothed over the spot with his thumb as if to seal it there forever.

"Here," he finally said.

"Our hands?"

He nodded, rubbing her knuckles across his soft lips. "So it will always be seen. So I will be reminded of my *Fraendi* with everything I do."

Ailsa took his face into her hands and pulled him up from the floor. "Then so be it. Show me what is next, *Sólskin*."

He took her into the next room, where the hearth mirrored into the sitting area on the other side of his bedroom. In front of the fireplace was a bowl and a sheathed dagger, both sitting on a cot of blankets and pillows.

"Just in case we do not make it to the bed," Vali explained. He sat in front of the fire, the parchment still in his hands, and laid out the rune sketch between the golden bowl and the matching dagger. She slowly lowered herself to sit across from him. Her heart beating an unsteady beat in her ears, hiding the tremble in her fingers by fisting her hands.

"Is something wrong, Ailsa?" Vali asked.

She offered him a reassuring smile and shook her head. “Just nervous.”

He picked up the dagger and pulled it from its sheath. The only thing brighter than his smile was the reflection of the flames on the blade. “Me too,” he said. “I’ll go first if you’d like.” When she nodded, he took the tip of the dagger and dragged it along his index finger, wincing slightly at the pain. Ailsa watched as the skin peeled open and dripped blood into the small basin.

As it collected in the bowl he spoke, “The rune is born from the combination of our blood because it is a sacred part of our bodies. Together, it binds what used to be two separate threads into one. And from its joining, a new rune is created along with our new thread.” When he was satisfied with the amount in the bowl, he grabbed a hand towel and wiped his finger clean, healing the cut in the process with his magic.

“My turn,” she said, feeling a bit giddy. “But I need you to make the cut. My hands aren’t steady.” She was shaking worse than her breath and hoped he didn’t interpret her trembling with fear. But Vali only cradled her hand in his large palm, pressed his thumb to still the base of her ring finger, and quickly made a sharp cut along the side.

She flinched but bit back her cry as the blade sliced her deep enough to spill her blood and join his own in the basin. He milked her finger to speed up the process. “Usually,” he said, “this would be done as a ritual in the Temple of Light for all to see. My mother will not be pleased with me when she hears we kept our ceremony intimate.”

“Then why aren’t we going to the Temple?”

“Because I don’t want to share this with anyone else. And I know everyone will have an opinion about our decision. Before they talked you out of it, I wanted to seal the deal.” His mouth turned up in a smile as he grabbed the hand towel and wiped her finger.

"You are devious, *elskan min.* And I will not go down with you when Lady Rind finds out." But Ailsa was glad he chose to keep this private. It felt too special to share with anyone else. Too pure to allow the world's opinions to taint this moment.

Vali appeared as if he were going to kiss the slice, but instead sucked her entire finger into his mouth, and Ailsa could hardly breath as he slipped his hot tongue along where the cut ran. When he released her finger, the wound had disappeared. Her skin was completely healed and free of pain.

"Thanks," she said, wiggling her hand. "Now I draw the rune on your hand?"

"And I'll draw yours," he said, outstretching his arm to give her the best angle.

Ailsa took a steadying breath. The air in the room suddenly heavy and thick as she dipped her pointer finger into their blood still warm in the basin. Everything seemed to slow into silence around her until the cracking of the fire was worlds away, and the sound of her heavy breath was all that grounded her to this place in time.

"Ailsa?" she heard Vali's voice split the quiet consuming her. She looked up from her focus on his hand to the sunlight in his eyes. They were forgiving and warm, a feeling she wanted to wrap herself inside and never forget. "You know we don't have to do this. I love you no matter what."

She took his hand in her free one and brought a bloody finger to his skin. "I know," she whispered, and completed their rune like she was painting his soul instead.

When she was finished, Vali briefly admired her work before moving on to her. No hesitation, no time for pause, his finger sure and steady as he drew their mark on the back of her hand. As he came to the final line, he spoke, "I take you, Ailsa Ledgersdóttir, to be my *Fraendi,* to be the flesh of my flesh and the blood of my blood. To bind my thread with yours and walk eternity with you. For to me you are the sweet whisper of the tides and the secret in the starlight. I love you now, and I will adore you always."

A jolt ran through her wrist as he spoke his vow over their mark. She spoke them back, hoping to seal this connection between them and begin the next tale of their story, to continue their saga. "And I take you Vali, Son of Rind, High Lord of the Elves, and demigod of revenge and redemption, to be my *Fraendi*. The one I will love until my last breath and beyond, for all the eternal years that follow. I will forever seek to know who you are and love you like a mystery, sharing with you every sunrise and sunset, every happiness and sadness. Because I love you, and I will never stop."

He squeezed her hand back, and Ailsa felt the charge between them, a strange sensation humming inside their bones where they clasped. "It is done," she whispered, feeling her eyes brim with tears.

"We did our part, yes." Vali smiled. "It is up to the fates now, *svåss.*" He tugged her arm to pull her closer, claiming her lips in a reverent kiss. Ailsa parted his mouth with her tongue, deepening their connection as she crawled into his lap, straddling his waist.

"I say we take fate into our own hands tonight." She let go of his shoulders to slip her night shift over her head, leaving nothing to separate their skin except the thin undergarments Ailsa still wore and the cursed pants still hiding all of Vali from her sight. But that would change tonight.

Before the male could get distracted with her own body, Ailsa pushed him hard on his back. Surprise marked his grin as she used their positions to loosen the ties around his waist. Heat bloomed in her hips as she brushed the suggestion of his arousal with her fingers, needing to see him, needing to feel him inside her and know him fully.

Vali did not stop her this time, only relaxed against a pillow as she pulled the drawstring free and shoved his pants lower. "You are mine tonight, Vali," she said as she pulled his cock free. The fae lord hissed as she stroked him once, already alluringly stiff and rigid for her to prime. "Fortunately for you, I am feeling quite impatient."

And she already felt a slick coolness between her legs as she stroked her center along his shaft, grinding her pleasure out to please them both. Ailsa used both hands to pump his length against her, feeling hard veins full beneath her thumbs. So thick around her fingers, she squeezed him from his base to the tip, his cock already spilling a bit of his release. She gathered the small bead with her thumb and brought it to her lips, where she rubbed it like a balm across her mouth before licking his seed away. His eyes locked on her as she tasted him, savored him as she rolled his essence across her tongue, moaned at the salty-sweet taste that made her grip on him tighten—begging for more.

"I've wanted to taste you for so long," she purred.

"Fuck, Ailsa," he choked out, his head falling back as she rubbed the tip of his hardness against her swollen entrance. "That feels incredible. Every inch of you is perfect." He was torn between watching and writhing. Every push of her hips against his base threw his head back and a worshipful moan from his chest.

He reached down and ripped her thin underwear from her hips, tossing them in the fire. The evidence of her own desire covered him in a wet heat. Ailsa felt him kick off his pants and bend his knees, place his hands over her hips bones to feel the motion of her body, to pull her down harder against him. She let out a shaky breath, practically dripping from the want coiling into something more frenzied between her thighs.

"Ailsa, I am burning for you," he said between panting breaths. And she ached for him as well, the tension between them building like a ball of snow pushed down a hill, gathering speed and force, threatening a sweeter crash, the steeper the slope.

"Shall I have all of you at last, Vali?" she asked in a voice that sounded foreign to her own ears. The male beneath her only rocked his hips against her hands in reply, his face strained, the muscles in his neck taut like bowstrings ready to snap.

"Yes, my love. Please," he finally begged.

Ailsa shifted to her knees and guided his shaft where she needed it. Vali didn't move himself, even as she slowly lowered onto his cock, letting her walls stretch and accommodate his size, appreciating how much he filled her. When she felt certain she could take him, she slammed her hips down, sheathing him completely inside her.

"Ailsa," he groaned her name, and she wanted to hear him say it like that again. "Gods, you feel so good." Without waiting any longer, he slowly nudged into her, inch by inch, penetrating her impossibly deeper.

Ailsa felt pure pleasure splinter straight through her, reducing her to flesh bound by seams this goodness was quickly unraveling. Feeling his eyes trace her body, she removed the lace band covering her breasts, letting the heat from the flames in the hearth burn a new fire beneath her skin. Inviting him to touch her. And the male gladly accepted her invitation, running rough palms over their sensitive buds, building more sweet friction. He worshipped her with adoring hands that pinched and claimed and squeezed so hard, his fingers left red marks on her skin everywhere he dragged them.

She leaned over him, placing her hands on his chest and eased her hips back and forth, matching his rhythm, her partner in this dance of desire. He stared up at her, frustrated moans of need muffled behind gnashed teeth. The fire next to them burned violently as Vali's eyes began to glow again. A shudder ran through her nerves as his movements against her increased in pace, force bordering on unrestrained.

Without resistance from herself, Vali pulled her down to his chest and flipped their positions, so her head was resting against a soft pillow and her body was covered with his.

"You are bad, *Sólskin*." she teased, snapping her legs around his waist. Her fingers snatched the soft blanket beneath them, solidifying herself as he claimed control.

"And you are perfect," he murmured. His next thrusts were merciless. A building sensation veiled her vision like the waves of a wrathful sea. She was falling apart as quickly as her world was settling into place. Became undone as her heart was made whole. Each erratic surge of his hips into her center pulled her deeper into the depths of ecstasy until the world was drowned away and all that existed was Vali. Her mate. *Her Fraendi.*

The sounds he made only undid her faster until she was moments from release. Ailsa pulled him close, dragging her nails into his shoulders, arching her back as an explosion of pleasure shattered her into fragments. He reached his climax just as quickly, emptying into her as every muscle tight in his back shuddered into an exhausted stillness. His only movements were the final rolls of his hips as he milked the last ounces of pleasure into her, and she took it all, savoring every drop of him as he spilled his devotion into her.

"Ailsa," he panted into her ear, his head dipped low before his body collapsed to the side. "Gods below, you are incredible. That was—"

"I know," she whispered, curling herself into his warmth. "So amazing, I wonder if we could ever simulate something that good ever again." Her finger made lazy circles across his stomach. The blood on her hand now nearly black in the firelight.

A deep laugh resonated from his chest. "Give me a few minutes, *sváss,* and I will ease all your concerns."

Ailsa shut her eyes and listened to his steady breathing and waited for him to fulfill his first vow as her *Fraendi.*

And Vali did.

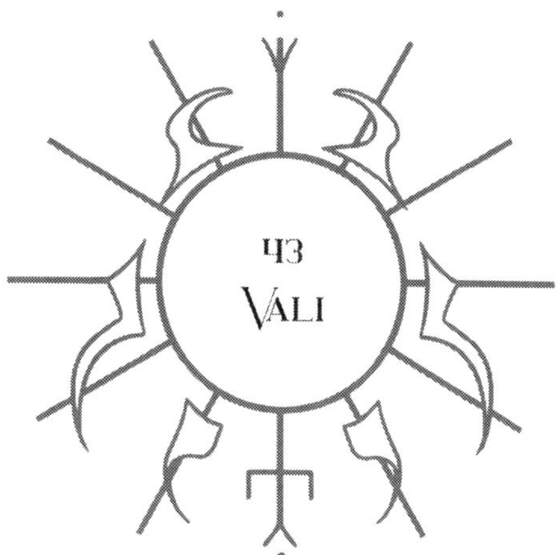

43
Vali

The next morning, Vali awoke in his own bed in his private chambers. The sunrise gently provoked him, peeking through the dark green curtains lining the wall of windows opposite the bed. A fire still kindled in the hearth from the night—morning—whatever time he finally closed his eyes.

"How long do you reckon before they come looking for me?" Ailsa asked in a voice rough with sleep. He turned to find her on her stomach with a pillow beneath her shoulders, the satin sheets pooled at her waist. She was as bare as he was, though gloriously elegant as though she was poised for a painting. Her hair flipped and curled loosely across the creamy pillow sheets.

He smiled and stretched, feeling the tightness of a fresh rune across the back of his right hand. When she accepted the title of his *Fraendi,* he brought her back to his room. A hospital bed was hardly the place he wanted to commit such a ceremony, and he wanted privacy in the morning. To see her radiant in his own sheets, drunk off pleasure, and satisfied into a deep slumber. He wanted this image, in this bed, carved into his memory. Her ghost would haunt these sheets until the end of their days.

"I'm sure Seela will be banging on my door any minute—"

"*Vali!*" a voice shouted in the drawing room beyond the door of his bedroom. Vali groaned and his head fell back against the pillows.

"Did we lock the—"

Seela burst open the bedroom door and sauntered into the room with a wild look on her face. Her violet eyes were full of panic. "Vali, wake up! Ailsa is missing and—" her voice cut off as Ailsa sat up in bed, covering her chest with the sheets.

"Good morning, Commander. Do the kitchens have breakfast ready? I'm *starving.*" She smiled at the elfin, who stood in the doorway gaping.

"Gods below…" Her cheeks colored a deep shade of scarlet. "Did I just walk in on—"

"Yes, you did. Would you mind waiting outside, Seela?" Vali's morning voice was hoarse from a very long night.

The commander visibly paled. Her gaze darted everywhere except the bed. "I really hate being your blood bonded sometimes." She turned sharply on her heel and slammed the door on her way out.

Ailsa's small body shook the bed with her silenced giggles. She twisted in the sheets until she was on top of him, every inch of her skin warming the place she melted against him. "Good morning, *elskan mín.* Did you sleep well?"

"I barely slept at all, but you already knew that." He smoothed his fingers over the subtle arch in her back, formed by her position resting against his chest. The fullness of her breasts filled against him as she sighed, and Vali shuddered beneath her. Her body was a source of both pleasure and pain, the purest form of torture destined to be his undoing.

"Did I?" she grinned innocently. "Who kept you up all night, sweet Vali?" Her fingers combed back his tangled hair, traced his profile with a pointer finger, and traveled down the valley of his chest.

"My *Fraendi*," he said. The simple word made her ocean eyes surge with pride. Her hand slipped lower, following the dusting of hair training down his stomach. Vali tensed as she skimmed his length. The simple motion made his hips lurch off the mattress and press into her palm.

"Did your *Fraendi* please you?" she asked.

Vali could only nod. His words caught somewhere from his chest to his lips. She squeezed him, relishing as he writhed beneath her, drugged from her power over him with a single touch.

"Would you like her to please you again?"

The morning sun gleamed against her hair, highlighting the gold strands threaded within the rich brown waves. Her skin was soft against the satin as it slid from her waist. She had a finesse about her movements, a confidence in her ability to please him that made her all the more erotic. She sat over him, clothed in nothing but draping sunlight and a sublime afterglow.

"Gods below," he whispered. Daunted as he took in how her body looked in the light. "You are—"

"Skinny? Sickly?"

"Mesmerizing. The most beautiful being I have ever seen."

Her fingertips skimmed the lines across his chest, the story of his destiny, the markings a map to his *Fraendi*. "How would you like to be pleased, my lord?" she asked.

"Your mouth will do, heathen," he muttered as she rolled her hips, enjoying the sounds she pulled from him.

"Filthy fae," she whispered, sliding lower.

Voices carried beyond the door, joining his commander waiting for him beyond a thin layer of bedroom wall. "I think we have more company in the drawing room," he breathed. But he no longer heard them as she kissed the tip of his shaft, stealing his every awareness until she was the only thing that existed.

"Good." Her tongue swirled around his length. "I hope they hear what I do to you. Open the doors, Vali. Let them all hear me worship you like the god you are."

His fingers ceased combing her hair for a second to snap the windows and the doors open to his balcony, where beyond sat the sprawling kingdom city. The icy sting of the morning breeze whipped her back and she arched between his legs, shivers gently thrashing her body. The cold breath of the morning contrasted her hot mouth. Through the harsh light of the glaring sunrise, Vali watched her take control, squeezing the base of his shaft with her hands while she slowly began to suck him, diminishing him into a mess of carnal compulsions.

He shoved a pillow behind his head to watch her. His fingers tangled in her hair. Their rune mark, her lips around him, the pleasure scourging through him every time her cheeks hollowed, and her sounds of appreciation vibrated his cock—he wouldn't last long. Every thrust she took him deeper, surrounding him with wet heat in her tight, little throat.

"You take it so well, *svàss*." His eyes shut, fighting the urge to fist her head in place and pump his hips against her face. She convulsed around him with a swallow, and he almost spilled right then and there. But she eased off, tempering her movements as his hips twitched, noting how close he was just to draw out his torture just as thoroughly as he had done to her.

Gods, he had fallen. Hard. And the longer he fell and the steeper the stakes became, the more he wanted this forever, believed something this good deserved a fighting chance. The Norn once said he had a choice, but nothing about Ailsa was a choice. This pull in his bones, this attraction originating deep from his marrow—it was not a choice of fate.

It was destiny.

His knees jerked off the bed as reached his peak, a roar muffled through his teeth as he spilled into her, the merciless surge of molten pleasure as she swallowed every drop of him, skillfully extending the finality of his pleasure with her tongue. Her hands continued to stroke him as his hips thrashed with the final waves of his climax, and he caressed her hair as he panted her name, his chest starved of substance.

She crawled over him wearing a victorious smirk like a conqueror. Her skin glistened in a sparkling sheen of sweat despite the morning chill. "Vali?" she said. "You can no longer be called *heartless*."

A soft smile crossed his lips as he ran his fingers languidly through the length of her hair. "Why do you say that?"

"Because you have mine, and for the rest of my days, it will beat for you." She nestled her nose into his neck.

He held her a bit tighter, and for a moment, the threads of fate were meaningless. Life gave them a timeline, but weren't they all just a thread cut away from an untimely death? Not one of them knew how many days numbered their strings, and it all could be snapped away in the next hour, the next second. As long as he drew breath, he would challenge the potentials.

"Ek elska þik," he whispered affectionately in her ear. And *gods below* it was as easy as breathing.

She smiled without opening her eyes. "I love you, too."

Ailsa asked to meet Ivor in the gardens after being cleared by Master Greer. She informed the healer she had been thoroughly assessed and checked off by Lord Vali, thanking her for all her help and the staff for their dedication to her rehabilitation. Greer gave her little objection, only a few discharge instructions and a curt smile.

They walked in silence for a few minutes, weaving through the trimmed hedges while Ailsa tried to find the right words to explain to the wolven the events of the night prior. Ivor had made her disapproval of Vali clear, avoiding him at all costs, leaving every time he entered a room. And Ailsa feared how she would react when she noticed the mating rune on her hand.

"How are you feeling? You look well." Ivor broke the silence first. Her voice was even, betraying no hint of knowing.

"I feel better than I ever have in my life," she admitted.

"Can't imagine that. You hardly slept last night," the wolven remarked. Ailsa stilled and shot her a side eye, but discovered Ivor was staring straight ahead. Her face a solid mask barren of feeling.

"You heard about last night?" Ailsa winced.

"*Everyone* heard," she replied dryly. "Not to mention you've wreaked of his scent since you returned from the river. And I swear to the gods, if I ever have to hear Vali's name again, I will bash my own skull into the headboard."

Ailsa felt a hot blush crawling up her neck. She didn't realize they had been *that* loud. "Are you upset with me?" she asked.

Ivor paused in front of a statue made of a polished white stone. The figure was a man who resembled Vali, a raven perched on his shoulder and a tree branch dangled in his hand. "I am disgusted and a little annoyed at having my sleep disrupted, but I love you like a sister, Ailsa. I also know you don't have much time left, and as you said in Jotunheim, you deserve to live your days how you want to live them. No matter how much I disapprove."

"That is… Not what I expected you to say," she replied, skeptical despite her wanting hope.

Ivor shrugged. "I would be lying if I did not share your admiration for elves. They can be quite charming—"

"Seela, you mean?"

Ivor spun a lock of silver hair around a black nail. "Aye, we've spent a lot of time together recently, especially after you decided to court Vali. She speaks to me like I'm a person, not a… not an abomination. Not something to hide away like the wolven I am."

Ailsa's heart snagged in her throat, a rush of guilt flooding her chest. "I'm sorry, Ivor. I didn't even know you felt that way. I've been so consumed with my own life, and I've been negligent to my best friend. My family."

"True friends don't fault the other when they are busy *living*."

"Well, I hope you keep that thought in mind, because I need to tell you something." Ailsa had been holding her palm over her right hand, hiding her secret engagement under the guise of a casual stride.

Ivor straightened, sensing her unease like it was spilling from her scent. "What is it?"

Ailsa hesitated, biting her lip, and decided it was best just to rip the scab off the sore spot and let it bleed a fresh wound. She held up her hand and wiggled her fingers, showing off the intricate rune with a proud smile.

"We are *Fraendi*."

Ivor's eyes widened, locked on her hand. She stumbled away, retreating from the rune like it was causing her personal pain. Her face transformed from shock, to confusion, to a head shaking denial. Ailsa had expected her reaction, prepared herself for the lashing she would receive and the wrath of her wolven. But she didn't expect the murderous glare Ivor delivered like a weapon. Her icy gaze struck her cold in the heart.

"What have you done?" But the words were accusatory, not a question. Ailsa clutched her marked hand to her chest.

"I love him." She wielded the truth as her only defense.

Ivor's chest heaved like a sea in a storm. "You didn't have to *mate* with him! Do you even understand what it means to be his *Fraendi*?"

"Aye, of course," she murmured. Though, Ivor could tell she was lying from the weakness in her assertion.

The wolven responded with a joyless laugh. "Seriously, Ailsa? What do you think it means? If *Hjartablóds* can sense each other and heal their bonded with their blood, what do you think the bond of a *Fraendi* would do? The fae's deepest and most sacred bond!"

Ailsa's heart pounded like it was trying to escape the cage

of her chest. Perhaps she should have asked more questions about this bond before she jumped into it, but she was so consumed by his words, how he wanted her, and she chose to be selfish for once in her life and take something that shouldn't belong to her. But by the way Ivor was pacing, she judged she had made a very rash decision without having all the facts.

The wolven paced in front of the statue and raked through her silver hair with clawed fingers. She had kept up the practice of filing them since they left Drakame, keeping them sharp. And Ailsa had never questioned why. But the anger seeping out of Ivor made her hold on her shift loosen, distracted by her frustration. It had been nearly two months since she had let her wolf out, and Ailsa feared she couldn't hold it inside any longer.

"Ivor, you need to calm down!" She approached her with an extended hand, but when Ailsa skimmed her shoulder, the wolven reared back and clawed her face. A blur of gray hair and umber skin and visceral growls.

Ailsa fell back across the pavers lining the path through the maze of shrubbery, holding the soft part of her cheek where her claws shredded the skin. A burning pain lanced into her bones, feeling the poison of a wolven's claws sink deep into her flesh. Blood trickled between her fingers from the grazing wound. Her sister's betrayal stung worse than her assault.

"Ailsa," Ivor whispered. "I'm sorry I didn't mean..." But Ailsa's shock dissolved into fury, and she stood to her feet without listening to another word.

"I understand you are angry, that this must seem like I'm being reckless and foolish. I knew you wouldn't support *us,* but I thought you would always support *me.*" Ailsa turned to leave, unable to look at the woman she once knew or the stranger she had become.

"You don't understand what you've done!"

"Then explain to me the crimes I have committed!" she shouted. "I am so *tired* of everyone keeping secrets from me!"

"Do not act so blameless, Ailsa," she spat. "I know you lied to Vali about what the Crow told you. We both know you are keeping the truth from all of us—"

"How do you know what the Crow told me?" she asked.

"It doesn't matter! Nothing matters anymore, you've ruined everything!"

"Ivor!"

"You bound your threads together becoming his *Fraendi*!" Ivor hissed at her. Ailsa stiffened, her heart speeding impossibly faster until it felt like it would burst.

"What?"

Ivor took a steadying breath to soothe her anger. "Your fates are tied together now. If you die, he dies."

Her vision tunneled. This wasn't happening. This couldn't be true. Vali wouldn't keep something like that from her, he wouldn't bind his life to hers knowing their timeline. The air suddenly was thin and unsatiating, her legs tingled until they were completely numb and unable to support her weight. Her knees buckled, and she fell on her backside, her stare a thousand miles beyond where she sat.

But he *had* told her. Just not outright. He told her their threads would be one, but she hadn't the reasoning to redact something like this. She'd never in her wildest deductions believe he'd tie himself to her fate.

"No..." she whispered. The salt from a single tear stung the torn flesh of her cheek.

She heard Ivor kick a rock across the pavers in frustration, her breath still heavy. She neither helped her nor spared her another minute of her time. "I have to go," she mumbled.

Ailsa watched her as she turned away and left in the opposite direction of whence they came. She stared up at the ivory statue of her *Fraendi,* a storm of emotions all competing for dominance in her heart. No longer did her decision affect only her. She had to tell him the truth, the complete truth about what the Crow told her.

This changed everything.

"Ailsa?" Seela's voice cut through the quiet. But she could not turn to face the commander. Not when she probably thought of her as the most selfish creature in the Nine Realms, unknowingly dragging her *Hjartablód* down into the pitfall of death.

"Ailsa, look at me! What happened?" Seela crouched in front of her and assessed her wound with wide eyes. "Who did this to you?"

"I'm so sorry," was all she could say. "I didn't know, I swear. I didn't know about the *Fraendi* bond." More tears followed the leader until her cheeks were damp. Seela wiped the diluted crimson streaks with the back of her shirtsleeve.

"Why are you apologizing?"

"He didn't tell me our fates were bound together now…"

"Oh, Ailsa," she said. Seela smoothed a hand down her back, remaining quiet for a while. Letting the silence wear away the shock. "Do not apologize for something so beautiful. The fact Vali chose you means your bond with him runs deeper than choice, than life itself. Some elfin wait lifetimes to find their mate! Don't you understand how much this means to him?"

"But he's going to die!" She was sick just thinking about it.

"How do you think he felt when you told him about the Crow and the threat of your death?"

"Probably just like this," she admitted weakly. She understood what Seela was saying, but she still felt this was a blind-side. He should have been honest with her. "Is that why… you were so mad at us this morning?"

"What—no!" She flinched. "Vali is like my brother. I don't ever want to catch him post-sex ever again! And please refrain from… pleasing him while I wait in the next room." A shiver rippled down Seela's spine, and she shook it off, making Ailsa's lips betray a ghost of a smile. "Come on," the commander beckoned as she stood up. She held out her hands to pull Ailsa to her feet. "Let's go get your face fixed and then we'll find Vali. But Ailsa?"

"Aye?"

"Please don't be too hard on him. Yes, he kept a major part of the bond from you, but this only proves he loves you more than life itself. For the sake of the little time you both have left, don't ruin this for him."

When Ailsa sat with Erik on her final night in Drakame, she had only asked for a love that rewrote the stars, for someone who would look past her early death and love the person beneath the illness. Vali did *more*. He had known the consequences of this bond, and he still tied his thread to hers without a second thought.

Who was she to choose his fate?

She nodded and embraced Seela in a tight hug, the elfin stiffened in surprise before timidly returning her embrace. "Thank you, Seela, you are a good friend to us both."

The commander walked her back to the castle while blood still oozed from the three lines on her cheek. She brought a hand to her face and skimmed the torn flesh, the breeze drying the sticky liquid and tightening her skin as she spoke. "You know what I'm curious about?"

"What is that?" Seela asked.

"How did Ivor know about the *Fraendi* bond, and why did

she say it ruined everything?" She had been too shocked to question the wolven before she fled, but it troubled her heart.

"I don't know, but I intend to find out when I see her again," Seela replied.

Ailsa looked behind them in the direction where the wolven disappeared, but she was long gone.

"Aye," she said. "Me too."

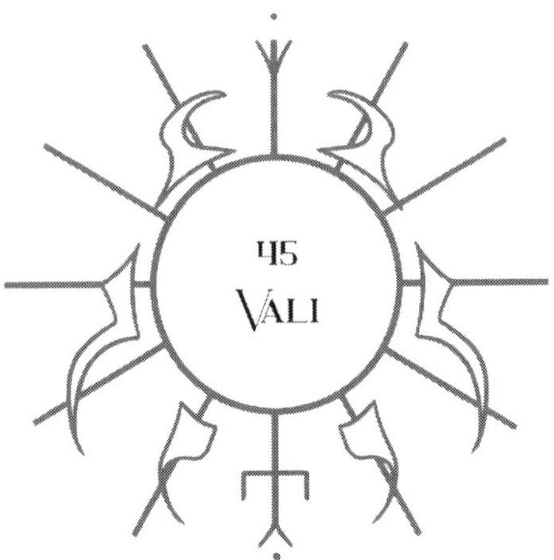

45
Vali

His mother could hardly look at him when she saw the mark on his hand, heard the announcement from his lips.

It hurt him to know she didn't approve of his choice, but that was why he made it without consulting anyone. There would always be someone who disagreed, someone who would try to talk him out of his decisions. This was one he needed to make for himself. Alone.

His only choice.

"Maybe we shouldn't give her to Odin," his mother said softly. "Perhaps we can appease the Crow and keep her from him, and the curse will not claim her."

"The Dark Elves are nearly on our doorstep, Mother. How will we stop them? How will we get rid of this dark magic from our land? You cannot care about Ailsa's death now just because I am tied to her," he said.

"I always cared, Vali. But I just got you back," she said before her voice broke. Vali swallowed the guilt her tears formed inside him. She was meeting with him to discuss the progress with the Dark Elves until he spoiled their meal with the happiest news of his life.

"And I barely even got to know her, though she seems lovely." She painted a stoic smile across her face like the High Lady she was and dried her tears with the fold of a napkin.

"She is lovely," he said. "I couldn't fight the pull she had on me, Mother. I thought it was the Tether calling me, but all along it was her. She was destined to receive the ancient power —I was destined to find it. Our paths were meant to cross from the beginning of time."

She gave him a curt nod. "I am happy for you. You deserve this more than anyone. And you will have a small ceremony before the feast—"

"Mother…" he groaned.

"You *will* give me this, Vali!" Her voice shifted from a smooth stream to treacherous torrents. "Just a few people, and a fifteen-minute ceremony with you in the High Lord robes so I can see you in them at least once before–" her voice cracked "–before it happens."

Vali conceded with his silence, sensing this a fight that wasn't worth winning. He was supposed to inherit the throne when he had completed this deal with Odin, but that wasn't going to happen, it seemed. "Can we move on to the reason for this meeting?"

Lady Rind cleared her throat and sat straighter before handing him an envelope with a broken seal. He unfolded the note and read the scribbled writing of the latest scouting report discussing the local movements of the Dark Elves in their camps near the border dividing the realm.

"They left?" he asked. His brows kissed in perplexity. "Why would they draw back now? If anything, I expected them to grow more hostile closer to the feast."

"And they were," she admitted. "They pushed all the way to

Traz, just a day's march east of here. I thought we were going to have a war when the Aesir arrived, but every single encampment was called off this morning. I messaged for you as soon as I received the raven."

Vali twirled a crystal glass between his palm in thought, watching the legs of the wine drop like tears around the base. "How did you keep the Dark Elves out of Valinor all this time?" Not that he was surprised the Palace of Light had been maintained by Lady Rind and protected from the dark forces attempting to overthrow the Light's authority. But half a century was a long time to subdue a force growing exponentially as the years passed.

"I gave them the Haven and the river that supplies it. It was a peace deal. But when they heard you returned with the Tether and were going to complete our bargain with Odin, they broke the treaty and attacked the eastern villages. They are strong, Vali. The sedir in their blood has completely washed away the Light they once carried, and it serves a master of inexhaustible strength, no balance for what it takes. While we run our well dry trying to fuel our magic, they overpower us without tiring. And I fear they are posing for their final siege."

"Then we move up the feast," he argued. "Tell Odin he has two days to take the Tether and Frey and all his minions out of Alfheim. But I will be going with Ailsa, and I will stay with her until the curse claims her."

"He's done us one better," she winced, pulling out another envelope. This one with the golden seal of the Aesir. "He's coming tonight."

Before he could swallow the news, Seela burst through the double doors leading to their private lunch. Vali stood, sensing her dissent in the specific way she carried herself. "What is it, Seela?"

"When were you going to tell her?" she practically shouted. "How could you not tell Ailsa what the *Fraendi* bond *meant,* why it is practiced in the first place, so the fae don't have to live a day without their other half?"

"You told her?" he groaned. This was not the way he wanted her to find out. He didn't want her to find out at all.

"No, Ivor told her, right after she slashed her face open!"

The glass in Vali's hand shattered, spraying the ivory rug with dark crimson droplets. "I've had it with the wolven. I've been patient and respectful, but if she put a hand on Ailsa, I will gut her and use her pelt as a fucking coat."

Seela nodded her head toward the door. "I brought her back to Greer. She's stitching her up as we speak."

Vali cursed and turned on his heel and paced the room, taking his frustration out on the rug. "Where is the wolf now?"

Seela passed a hand through her hair and shrugged. "No idea. She left Ailsa in the gardens before I found her. Your bond must now connect me to her since we are technically blood bonded, because I could sense she was in trouble. I've never felt like that before, not with Ailsa."

"I felt strange earlier but I… I didn't know what it meant." He looked at the mark on his hand and sighed. He knew so little of the benefits of their bond—other than the physical act of creating one.

His mother stood from her chair. "I'm going to the hospital wing. We have much to prepare in a few hours, and I expect you to stick to your word despite the circumstances."

"What?" Seela inquired. Vali explained his mother's demand for a unification ceremony and the commander lit up with delight. "Oh, absolutely! Lady Rind is right. We'll go get Ailsa ready and you just meet us at the castle temple at dusk."

Vali balked, his face draining of color. "The Allfather is coming *tonight* and you both are worried about a wedding?"

"We have mead, and we have meat. That should more than flatter the Aesir gods and their churlish appetites," his mother said. Clearly, she was not eager to see his father again, but Vali didn't press the subject. "You are much more important, my son."

"I don't trust the Aesir—"

"Vali, enough," Lady Rind spoke. "As long as we honor our side of the bargain, they will honor theirs. Odin is a lot of things, but he is not a liar."

"He sent Loki to Ailsa's bedside last night!"

His mother remained quiet as he explained how Odin tried to slip out of his side of the deal. It was the first time the Aesir showed their deceptive side to the fae, but not the only instance Vali felt an unsettled feeling deep within his gut. And he had a good inclination they would try to get their way again.

Lady Rind hardly flinched, her expression turning stone from a practiced history of being High Lady. "Be in the temple at dusk. But wear gloves. We have the upper hand knowing something Odin does not, and your bond with Ailsa might work out in our favor if they have something up their golden sleeves.

"Fine." He threw up his hands in surrender. "But I expect Seela to tighten security around our border. I want every guard keeping an eye out for the wolven. Make sure she doesn't get close to us tonight. If she returns, I want her locked in the dungeon." There was something about tonight that bothered him. Too many players moving themselves at once.

The timing of these events all coming to a diabolical head. "And I'm going to tell Ailsa all this myself, so both of you can wait in her chambers."

"Watch out world," Seela teased behind him as he passed. "Vali's got a *Fraendi.*"

He looked over his shoulder at her and did not return her smile, because in his mind, it wasn't a joke. It was the most dangerous threat in the universe.

46 Ailsa

Ailsa soaked in a large iron tub nearly the size of her entire washroom in Drakame. The elves had a strange, convenient way to source their water from a tap, heating the waters with their magic that made her inevitably relax despite the events of the night looming just outside the salted waters.

She had been unable to tell Vali the truth about the Crow's warning, and it shamed her. She could save both their lives—but at what cost? She saw the land with her own eyes, the monsters infesting this world. How could she damn the lives of thousands just to save the fates of two?

It was too late.

Odin was already on his way to Alfheim, coming to claim her. Destiny was breathing down her neck. They had already begun the process, and there was no going back. Even now she could hear Lady Rind bark orders at the palace staff as she soaked in the bathroom connecting to her chamber—from the floral decorum of the temple to the placement of the guards by Seela's arrangement, she listened to the muffled commands inside the solitude of her bathroom if only to distract herself from her guilty thoughts.

Vali found her in the hospital, where Master Greer shot him a scolding look as she threaded the stitches on her face. Their healing magic could not be used on wolven poison, as she had recalled when Ivor attacked Vali all those moons ago, and her face had to be treated the *mundane* way as the elves liked to say.

It's time, Vali had first said when he saw her, and she understood his meaning by the sorrow in his gaze. She'd never seen his eyes appear so dark.

Tonight, she would be wedded to an Aesir and then handed over to one like livestock. It was all happening much faster than she anticipated. Her timeline with Vali suddenly dramatically shortened. The weight of it all made her sink lower in the tub, pulled down by the shriveling thread of her future.

A knock tapped gently on the bathroom door.

"Come in," she called.

Vali poked his head through the door before slipping inside, shutting the frosted glass door behind him. "How's your cheek?" he asked as he approached the tub, pulling a stool with him to sit near her head. His thumb stroked the stitches in a careful assessment.

"They burn, but I'll be fine. You know, my people believe it's bad luck for the groom to see his bride before the ceremony."

A sharp breath sang between his teeth. "Like luck matters right now."

She gave him a sad smile in agreement. "Why didn't you tell me, Vali?"

His fingers stroked the warm water and formed ripples on the surface, but his stare was far away. "Would you have refused me if you knew?"

"Possibly," she admitted. "But only because I love you and

would never want you to die for me."

"I am part god. Who knows what will happen? But I made peace with my decision the night I asked you to be mine." His clipped words informed he was finished speaking on the subject. "How do your lungs feel?"

She shook her head. "I feel great. I know the Crow said the curse would end me soon, but I don't feel bad at all."

"Perhaps the Crow was lying," he said, hopeful.

Ailsa chewed on the inside of her lip. "Perhaps." She reached an arm from its submergence and stroked his face with a wet thumb. "Did you come to join me, *elskan mín?"*

Vali's eyes lowered to the transparent water, and he smirked. "My mother is in the next room, so I'll have to take you up on that offer at another time. I actually came to tell you Ivor returned."

Ailsa sat up in the bath, disturbing the rose petals floating on the surface. "She's back? Did she say anything to you?"

"Only that she wishes to meet with me and discuss something in private."

Ailsa's mind wheeled with ideas; none she could manifest into meaning. "Just you?"

He shrugged. "That is what she asked, yes. If you don't want me to meet with her, I won't. I was about to throw her in the dungeons when she asked for my personal audience."

"No," Ailsa shook her head. "No, you should speak with her. She needs to explain herself, how she knew about the *Fraendi* bond and why she reacted the way she did." She brushed the seams of her stitches absentmindedly. "She doesn't deserve the dungeons. Be kind, Vali. She's been through a lot and I… I haven't been the best friend to her lately."

Vali grunted, the sound of reluctant agreement, before standing from the stool. He helped her out of the tub and wrapped her in a thick ivory towel. But not before wrapping himself around her bare frame, sliding his hands down her lubricated skin and kissing away the salt from her bath.

"Vali," she whispered, hoping he heard the plea in his name. From the way his hands lingered in low places, he did. She pressed her hips against his length, feeling his consensus.

"Yes?"

"Please, stay. Don't go yet."

He bit the inside of his cheek and sucked a breath, a chip in his resolve. Ailsa leaned closer and kissed his neck, sucking his skin between her teeth to nip him. A shudder ran through his body as she shattered the rest of his determination. "I need you to make me forget this is happening, to feel you instead of this fear. I need *you*, Vali."

"We must be quiet," he whispered

"Are you reminding me or yourself?" she asked, grinning. "I believe you are the noisy one between the two of us."

His brows danced, the wicked look in his eyes returning from the woods. "Only because I have not taken you from behind yet, *sváss.*"

"Empty words," she slipped the towel from her shoulders. "I thought you were a man of action."

He silenced her baits with a kiss, the momentum shoving her back until she felt the plush rug lining the vanity. Breaking away, he said, "I am not a man. Have you forgotten?" Vali spun her around and slammed her back against his chest. His hands roamed her skin, and she relaxed against him, watching his reflection in the mirror as his palm cupped her breast and his opposite dove low. Part Aesir, part fae, a being of myth and legend. Vali was no mere man—he was her god.

Ailsa bit her lip to silence the whimpers triggered by his touch, how his skin felt so hot compared to hers now cold from the bath. His fingers slowly circled her center, the small ministrations glacial and priming. Her head fell against the bend of his neck, eyes fluttering close.

"No," he commanded in her ear, halting his hands. "Keep your eyes open. Watch me as I take you, Ailsa, and keep those pretty lips shut." Only when Ailsa opened her eyes did his hands move again, and she found him smiling, enjoying her frustration. His nose traced her hairline and peppered it with kisses.

She bucked her hips, rolling them to his rhythm, finding him equally aroused behind her. She wanted to feel him, reaching up to settle in his hair as it was the only accessible portion of him when he was so flush behind her.

"You're so soft," he whispered. "I could touch you all night."

Ailsa shook her head. "Tonight is not enough. A moment is never enough. Only forever will do with you," she muttered between breaths. The grin fell from his face, and his hands hesitated. Vali pressed a bruising kiss to her temple, his eyes closing for just a breath.

"Bend over and put your hands on the vanity, *svǽss,*" he said quietly.

She did as he requested, feeling the absence of his hands as he untied the front of his pants. She spread her legs a little wider as he freed himself, each self-stroke of his shaft sent a shiver of want in her core. Through the mirror, she watched him pull a chair closer to them, his eyes never leaving the place she left spread on display.

As he straightened, his cock came into view behind her. Hard and stiff and glistening with his own desire triggered by her body alone. Seeing him now as a reflection, the size of him compared to her hips, she marveled at how he had fit inside her before.

His hands returned to smooth around her ass, climbing over her hip bones to dig in firmly with his fingers. "Remember, my love, do not make a sound, other than those cute little squeaks you make," he whispered. She nodded vigorously, biting her lip in anticipation.

He eased his hardness against her throbbing center, sinking his length against her heat, before propping his foot up on the chair beside them. Ailsa tipped her hips back, guiding him where she needed him, just as the tip of his shaft buried into her. A muffled groan eased from his chest. She could only gasp to hold back her moan of praise as he plunged inside with a single, devastating thrust. Impaled on his length, splitting her with pure pleasure and pressure, every push of his hips delved impossibly deeper until Vali was just as much a part of her as her heart or her spirit.

Ailsa's hands sprawled against the cold marble surface of the vanity to better grip herself and solidify herself against his thrusts, now unhindered and frenzied. There was no time for gentleness. The frustration of their situation communicated in the way he made love to her—hungry and brutal. Treating each encounter as if it would be the last time.

His jaw clenched, a starved look in his eyes as he watched her face in the mirror, her body as it writhed and quivered. Her fingers knocked glass bottles in their search for an anchor, and the perfumes rolled off the side of the vanity, crashing to the floor successively and splintering the quiet.

Vali's eyes went wide at the sound, and Ailsa suppressed a giggle with her hand. His hips stalled to pull out of her, and he yanked her up by her shoulders. "I thought I told you to be quiet?" he snapped in her ear, though even he was smiling now.

She shrugged, running her hands behind his neck. "I don't know what you're talking about. I haven't made a sound." In a fluid move, she kicked his foot off the chair and spun around to face him. She fisted his shirt and shoved him into the seat. His legs spread wide as she straddled him, the expression on his face enthusiastic about the sudden position change.

"Such a heathen," he said into her neck, kissing the rune marks inked there.

"Yes, but you like it."

His voice dropped into a husky tone. "I *love* it."

His confession made her hips move on their own accord, slipping him back inside her where he belonged, where she wanted him forever. He caressed her backside before turning her head to the side with his fingers around her jaw. Another mirror, this one full length and reflecting the image of her sitting over him, her bare figure on top of his sprawled one. Every muscle in his body had gone slack as she rolled her hips along his length. Something about watching herself please him, the erotic motions she made, the way his reflection adored hers, it only exacerbated the sweet tension building between them.

Her fingers threaded into his hair as his head leaned back, eyes shut as he fell completely under her spell. His teeth gnashed together to hold back breathy moans, the grunts as he reached the peak of his climax and spilled, jerking inside of her as she came undone with him. Ailsa buried her face into his neck to keep from crying out, every wave of bliss surging larger than the last until her release eased into small trickles of ecstasy.

"I love you. Gods, I'm so in love with you, Ailsa," he said. This time he did not whisper. "Forever will only be enough with you."

"I love you too, Vali. Tonight, let's make our own forever."

He pressed a long kiss to her forehead. "Forever," he echoed.

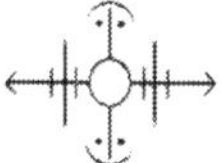

THEY DRAPED her in fine silks the color of a sunset—a gradient of golds and deep reds bordering on a deep shade of orange. Seela attempted to braid her hair how she liked it, with the fishbone pattern against her skull and the rest flowing in loose curls down her back. Lady Rind made sure the stitches were hardly noticeable, painting her face with powders that shimmered against the candlelight, a striking match to the brilliance of her flowing gown.

Her ceremony dress was revealing. The elves cut their gowns to show off the elegant curves of the feminine figure, and Ailsa's gown was no different. The neckline cut out the valley of her breast to her waist, where a gold belt tied the draping gown and flattered her shape. The rune marks shielding the power tethered to her soul made a line down her chest, centered by the sheer fabric. Each leg had its own slit, allowing her to walk effortlessly.

Vali's mother adorned her with her personal jewelry, a row of gold bangles on her gloved forearms, a long necklace dropping with the neckline of her gown with a ruby dangling on the end, and a red gemstone ring she used to tie it all together. When they were finished, they both assessed her like she was a piece of art and they were artisans, and Ailsa felt radiant, beautiful, and priceless.

"I am so happy Vali found you, *elskan*. You are so beautiful, inside and out. I only wish I could have gotten to know you fully." Lady Rind's voice floated on a shaken breath. She stepped closer to Ailsa and placed her hands on her shoulders. "The *Fraendi* bond is a significant thing to have. I myself still have not found my own *Fraendi*, but it fills me with an unparalleled joy to know my son has found his. Especially with a woman as strong as yourself."

"Thank you, Lady Rind—" Ailsa's voice broke under the weight of his mother's kindness. It was too much; her admiration was misplaced. She was not strong, nor did she deserve someone like Vali. She sure didn't deserve his fate.

Seela hugged her from behind and squeezed her waist just to make her feel worse. They knew she was taking their Vali, and still they accepted her with open arms. And she didn't even have the decency to be honest with them. That she had the power to stop this all from happening, she would just doom the rest of the realm in the process.

It was a heavy burden to bear, and she was weary of carrying it. For a moment, she was glad this was coming to an end.

"Thank you, both," Ailsa said. "Where I come from, not many would welcome a girl like me into their families. Especially not under these... circumstances. You deserve to hate me, and instead you're treating me like... like—"

"Family? Because you are." Lady Rind spoke the word for her. She twirled a piece of curl that had fallen over her shoulder. "We could never hate you, Ailsa. You did not choose your destiny no more than Vali chose his, but you *did* choose to face it together. Besides, it isn't over until your threads are cut. Until then, I will love you like I have you forever, and I hope you'll do the same."

"Of course," she smiled.

Glass shattered behind them, Ailsa and Rind jumped at the sound. They turned to find Seela gaping, her hands loose in front of her where they had once held a hand mirror. Ailsa couldn't see her face from her posture, but by the rigidity in her stance, she was disturbed by something.

"Seela?" Lady Rind spoke with caution. "Is everything all right?"

The commander seemed to snap back into herself, turning her face to expose a bright smile. "Just perfect. I'm going to go check on Vali," Seela offered. "Gods know he's never on time for anything. We'll meet you downstairs."

THEY WAITED near the temple doors—and then waited some more. Ailsa was growing flustered. Had Vali really been this offput by the ceremony to be so late? The Aesir would be arriving anytime now. The sky was already bruising as the sun fell behind the mountains. Ailsa stood behind the painted glass lining the outer sanctuary, watching the world mute under a dark filter.

"Something's not right," she whispered to herself. Vali was nothing if not a man of his word. If he regretted this ceremony, he wouldn't have said so from the beginning. He wouldn't have kissed her the way he did in the bathroom. He wouldn't have left her waiting.

"Lady Rind!" A guard approached them, his chest panting as if he had just run clear across the castle. "We cannot find Lord Vali."

"What do you mean you cannot find him?" Ailsa shrieked.

The guard's silver eyes darted from his High Lady to her, unsure who to address. "Commander Seela has had every room and every inch of the grounds searched, but he's not here. She was wondering if Miss... Lady Ailsa knew the last place he went."

Ailsa bit her lip. A worry that felt more like fear struck her heart, and she had trouble settling the thoughts in her head. "He... he told me he was going to speak with Ivor. Did no one see him return?"

The guard did not answer, and his silence told her everything she needed to know. Her chest heaved with a panic so thin her voice was shrill as it skated across. "He's been gone for hours! No one has bothered to look for him since he left?"

Lady Rind clutched her arm, and Ailsa felt the strength of a mother's fear in the simple gesture. "Send every patrol to walk the perimeter of the kingdom. Wherever he met Ivor, it wouldn't have been within city limits. He wouldn't let the wolven anywhere near Ailsa," she commanded as quickly as she reasoned. Her face never faltered despite the fright tensing her grip. "Keep the castle guards at their post. We don't need the Aesir finding out about this. We will resume the feast like normal. Tell Seela to give us updates when she receives them."

The guard gave a curt bow and turned on his heel. His dark green cape flowing behind a body stocked with light gold armor. Ailsa's hand fell naturally to her thigh, lifting the sheer draping just enough so that the gilded hilt of Vali's dagger caught the torchlight and sparked a fire inside her bones. She wore it as a nod to her own culture's tradition, a trading of blades between the two families. Although he had given her his dagger on the first day they met instead of today, it was something to don as a homage to their fated union.

But she would use it if she needed to. And if Ivor was involved in his disappearance—if she betrayed her—the wolven would pay.

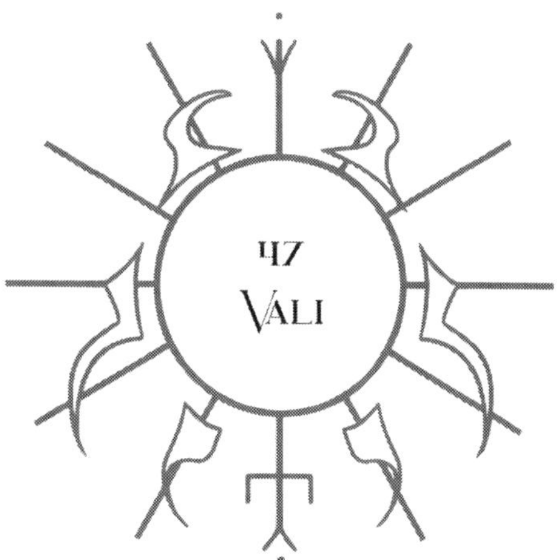

47
Vali

Vali groaned awake, feeling a cold floor against the back of his head and a pool of blood soaking through his hairline. It was black as pitch wherever he stirred, and it smelled of piss and vomit. Every move he made sent a scouring agony through his veins.

"You're finally awake." A flame struck to life, purging the room with a soft glow of light as Ivor tossed a match into a pit. The logs caught quickly, dry despite the moisture hanging heavy in the air.

It all started flooding back to him. Riding out to meet Ivor past the kingdom line, the pack of wolves that tore him from his horse. It was a mottled memory, but the bite marks all over his body reminisced the event in painstaking detail. He tried to stand but discovered a weight to his body that was over cumbersome. He was pinned to the ground, drained of magic and strength.

"What did you do to me?" he gasped.

Ivor stood from where she sat next to the pit. "We broke all your bones and then drained you of blood. Can't use the power of the Aesir if it's spilled across the pavers."

"Why? Why are you doing this?" He spoke through gnashed teeth, determined not to show the wolven an ounce of his suffering.

"You got in the way, Vali. You were supposed to deliver Ailsa to Alfheim, but we didn't expect you to get this far. To fall in love. Certainly not bind your life to hers."

Dread rolled inside the crypt of his chest at the mention of her name. "We?"

She paced around his body, her steps wading in blood like they were rain puddles. "The wolven. Though we do have a notable ally helping us with our cause. Care to take a guess?"

He was definitely not in the mood for guessing games. "Frey?"

"The Volva," she whispered excitedly. "Turns out they hate Odin almost as much as we do. He's made many enemies on his path to becoming all-knowing."

Vali grimaced as he tried to stroke the flames of his magic alive, but it was quiet inside his bones. Never had he felt so hollow. Like his body was sleeping and he was watching inside a dream. "What does any of this have to do with Ailsa?"

Ivor crouched where he writhed, smiling pleasantly. "Ailsa is at the center of everything, isn't she? Everyone wants a piece of her."

"Funny, you almost sound concerned."

"Oh, I am concerned. You see, I've been watching Ailsa all my life. I was given the job to protect her until the line officially ended with the death of her sisters and she became the Last Daughter. I was the good little companion while we traveled so the Volva could keep an eye on our movements. I even nudged the Drieger brute and revealed your identity. The Volva helped speed things along with a helstorm storm, but you two are simply resilient."

"You pretended to be her friend—"

"I pretended nothing!" Ivor spat. Her smug smile finally fell. "I *love* Ailsa in a way you never will, and I will do anything to keep her safe. Something you do not have the ability to claim. I am not the villain in her story, only yours."

"You betrayed her!" he shouted, his voice scraped his voice raw.

"I am *saving* her! Everything I have done on this journey, the events that led us here, has been to guide Ailsa to where she needs to be. And when we arrived in Alfheim, I passed intelligence under the guise of gathering water from the river. We gathered our number with the Dark Elves and prepared for the final attack on the castle, but then Ailsa explained you were now *Fraendi.*

"We *were* going to finally kill you, Vali. The Dark Elves wanted your family dead, to overthrow the Tyranny of Light so a new era could descend on Alfheim in exchange for the Dark Elves' secrecy. Ailsa would be captured and handed over to the Volva, so Odin could never get his hands on the power trapped inside her. We are still going to kill you, but now we must kill you *carefully.*

His mind tried to process what she was saying. All the pieces were fitting together, all his questions answered at once. "I thought the wolven left Alfheim when Odin sent Frey to rule the land?" he asked.

"Not all of us left, just some. Just enough to breed a resistance and protect what is ours." She stood and crossed the room back to the fire pit, grabbing an iron pole. "We are done hiding, Vali."

"We?"

Ivor's lip curled over serrated teeth. "The witches and the wolves."

She stepped on his arm. The toe of her boot hammered his wrist against the ground. She hovered the blazing iron above the back of his hand before continuing. "This is so much bigger than your little realm, Vali. Soon, you'll understand just how small of a piece you were in his game for power. How your very destiny was built on a lie." She drew a symbol with the pointed edge of the blazing rod.

"Ironic, isn't it? She did all this to save your realm, but your realm was never in danger. Odin knew this, too. He knew Frey's magic was not the problem. He used you and your mother's desperation to find the perfect seeker for his Tether. But this darkness is not spreading because of sedir, Vali. Your world is dying because there is no Light in the waters to source its life. Because the Light is afraid of something far darker than black magic, something far stronger."

Vali could barely speak as she dug deeper into his flesh, relishing in his paralyzed agony. "What could be stronger?"

Ivor laughed and granted him a moment of pause as she lifted the rod from his skin. "What is the only being the Light is afraid of? Who is the only one who could chase away the sun?"

A new pain swelled in his chest; dread stuck to his ribs as he tried to gasp. His lips managed to mutter, "Fenrir."

Ivor looked down at him and smiled, a torch now poised in her right hand. "That's right, Vali. You led your mate into a pack of wolves, and this den is out for Aesir blood."

When Ailsa imagined her last hours, it didn't include sitting at a feast with literal gods.

She was seated next to Vali's mother at the head of the table. Odin and his son Thor sat on one side, accompanied by a few others she did not recognize. They sat beneath a glass dome, the stars blinking down at them from their home in the sky. Her eyes drifted to Thor's waist, discovering his hammer had been returned, and she wondered about the fates of the giants she had grown fond of.

Frey sat to her left. His golden hair was braided long down his back. The skin of his chin was smooth and barren of stubble. His hands were delicate and almost feminine as he cut his meat with a fork and knife, unlike Thor whose fist seemed to be constantly filled with something. Ailsa winced as she watched him devour an entire pig by himself, the bones carted away by a servant to make room on his plate. The spectacle ruined her appetite.

An awkward silence settled the room when they were finished before Odin spoke. "Where is Vali?"

"Did you need him for something?" Lady Rind asked. "I believe this arrangement was strictly between us, Odin."

"I've heard the rumors, Rind," he replied. "I am surprised he wouldn't see her off. I know my son has been quite… *taken* with the vessel."

"My *name* is Ailsa. And I am not a vessel, I am a woman." Ailsa's outburst startled even herself. Odin only looked at her through his one good eye, but his glare was intense enough to challenge her newfound confidence.

Frey cleared his throat next to her. "Are you ready to leave Alfheim and see Asgard, Miss Ailsa? Even the mortals we accept into Valhalla and Folkvang do not get to see the God's Realm. You will be the first." he said. His voice was higher than she expected from the towering man. Softer than the silky drapes of her gown.

"No," she replied, and stared at her untouched plate of food.

"I'm sure your displeasure wouldn't have anything to do with a certain Son of Odin."

Ailsa didn't need to so much as turn her head to know Loki had sauntered into the room. His emerald robes swept the floor in a regal display. "Never fear, Ailsa darling. Once we find a way to get this ancient power out of your silly little hands, you can run right back to Vali. Well, if you survive it. How are your lungs, by the way?"

Ailsa's nails made crescent moons in her palms. "Has anyone ever told you, you're a condescending little shit?"

Loki bristled as he hovered near an empty seat, gesturing to himself in feign offense. "Me? *Never.*" His conniving smile curled on his lips. "Asgard is going to eat you alive, girl."

"Then I'll make sure it chokes."

Frey coughed on his drink, concealing a giggle.

"I'll ask once more, and if I don't get an answer, I will leave without honoring my end of the bargain." Odin was not here for food or banter. His eyes settled on Rind, who barely looked his way as he spoke.

"He is not coming," Lady Rind answered.

Odin's fist slammed on the table. "Why not?"

"Because he did his duty to you, Odin. He doesn't have to hand her to you on a silver platter. The Tether is right in front of you. Why do you care for my son?"

Ailsa felt the tension like a wave of heat from a bonfire. Odin was out of his seat in a second, a meaty fist pinching the High Lady's throat. She clutched his arm, her eyes spilled tears.

"Let go of her!" Ailsa shouted, not caring she was ordering a god. "What is wrong with you? Just take me and leave already!"

"The day I bend to elves is the day Fenrir claims me at last," he spat as he spoke. "If I make deals with you, all the realms will think they can cheat me out of favors. That power *belongs* to me, Rind. As does Vali since the day you let me write my runes on his skin."

"You were never going to help us," Rind gasped.

"I'm a god of my word," he murmured. "I will take Frey from this land, but I never said it would restore your realm, nor will it stop the darkness from spreading. I will continue to use *my son* to lead the fae in my name. Even if I must mark every spare inch of his skin, he will serve me. So be it, your kind will never be godless again."

Just as the High Lady's lips were blanching a shade of blue, Ailsa felt a burning pain in her hand. She leapt from her seat in the chair, pulling off her glove to watch the back of her palm grow a vicious red. She wailed as it bubbled before her eyes, blisters forming from a fire she could not see.

"Vali!" she whimpered, clutching her wrist and the rune mark being scorched. "Gods below, he's being burned alive!"

Odin released the High Lady to approach Ailsa. She staggered away from him before he could snatch her. "Where is Vali?" He demanded to know.

She shook her head, fighting to ignore the pain reaching up her arm. "I don't know, honestly. He went missing only hours ago!"

Odin mumbled something about *doing everything himself*. He lifted the patch covering his eye, revealing a hole puttied with soft skin. The spot glowed a white light as the god looked for Vali. His all-seeing eye replaced the physical one torn from its socket long ago.

"He's not burning," he mumbled. "He is in a dark room, but I smell a great amount of blood and burning flesh. There is a woman there, dark skinned with silver hair. Do you know her?" Ailsa lied with the shake of her head, apparently not convincing enough. "I don't believe you, but it doesn't matter. I'll find another way to rule this realm. You're right, Rind, I don't need Vali anymore."

"Please, Odin," Ailsa beseeched him. "If you let him die, this power will be lost, along with the one who was fated to find it in the first place."

He stepped closer, his eye twitched. "Why?"

She held up her hand and wiggled her fingers. Odin scowled and snatched her wrist before she could withdraw, holding the burning mark close to his face in assessment. He threw her arm back down like it had offended him. *"Fraendi!"* he murmured. Thor, one of Vali's many half-brothers, choked on a bone he had accidentally swallowed at the news.

"That's right," she said, smiling. "If you leave Vali to die, then you will *never* get your hands on this power."

Odin interrupted her with a derisive laugh. "Then we had better make this transfer quickly before he does."

Dread hung from her shoulders, heavy as a pelt of fur. Her footsteps retreated, a soft sound against the cold tile floor. "No!" she shouted. "I will not let you have it, not when Vali needs you… needs us!"

"Concerning your choices, Ailsa, you have none in my realms. You are a mortal. Weak, small, *sick—"* He was on her before she could retreat. His grip ensnared her forearms as the runes across them glowed gold—a warning to them both.

"Let me go," she hissed. Odin yanked her aside, throwing her to the floor in front of a god with one arm—Tyr, the god of battle. Her gaze lifted to see him reach for her, pulling her against his solid frame until she was flush with his chest and trapped by the fortified cage of his arm.

"Bring her outside. I need her close to death for this to work, and things might get bloody," Odin ordered him.

Ailsa struggled against his embrace despite her futile efforts. She looked back at Odin, her voice tired from being helpless. But a touch from the god of battle awakened the warrior dormant in her spirit. "We *worship* you, Odin. My clan, my family, we honor you with our lives! Through our laws and our actions, we count you as revered, and this is how you treat me? And your son! How can you do this to the ones who did nothing but serve you until the end?"

Odin locked his jaw. His anger against her dissolving, a shade of tenderness struck his blue eye. "Everything I do, everything I strive to know is for the purpose of protecting Midgard and all the Nine Realms, Ailsa. You think me cruel, but you don't understand the big picture. But you will see soon enough. And I will make sure your people know what you've done for them."

Tyr pushed her towards the exterior doors, and the Light Elves watched her with sorrow as she was dragged from the feast. Lady Rind was screaming her protests, but Odin silenced her with a flick of his fingers, her voice stolen by the will of his power.

The rest of the Aesir gods stood from the table, where they had enjoyed the display over the remnants of the feast and followed leisurely behind. Ailsa was about to give up her fight against Tyr's grasp when the ground started to tremble beneath her flats. A silence fell, the Aesir's taunting laughter died as the rest of the room felt the rumble gently shaking the hall.

Thor unsheathed his hammer at his hip, the runes enchanting the magical mallet glowed an iridescent blue.

"Giants!" Thor shouted. His gaze darted over the room, searching.

The rumbling ceased, though it made the quiet more sinister. The gods stood with their weapons in hand, a stance of defense, and waited for the giants to show themselves. A flicker of movement grabbed her attention from the top of the dome, and Ailsa had no time to warn them all before it happened.

The glass ceiling shattered.

49
Ailsa

Tyr shielded Ailsa with his body, and as the last shards fell in a delicate sprinkle, Ailsa crawled from beneath the god's dead weight. He was alive, of course, but the weight of the dome had fallen upon them all, rendering the gods incapacitated.

She was the only thing that moved, her limbs carefully pushing against the glass shards that caught the delicate wrappings of her gown and snagged the threading. Her forehead was bleeding where she hit the tile, preceding Tyr's tackle. She didn't know why the god saved her, only that she was grateful he did.

The crunch of footsteps accompanied her own as she struggled to her feet.

"Ailsa?"

Drieger stood across the dome, a large mallet in his fist, and a group of giants behind him. His empty fist glowing a green flame, the same color she noticed peaking the dome right before it detonated into countless pieces. His expression on her was one of pleasant surprise.

"Drieger, what are you doing here?" She dusted off the dust of rubble and crossed the sparkling ground, the debris catching the starlight in a beautifully chaotic picture of desolation.

"You didn't hear?" he said dryly. "The Aesir tricked us, went to my brother's hall with Thor disguised as Freya. He then killed them all when he touched the hammer. Every single giant at the wedding. Dead."

Ailsa gasped. Her heart broke to think of Thrym murdered in his own hall by the same hammer he used to blackmail the gods. "Was your family there?"

Drieger shook his head. "No, Skiord was ill, and the weather in the valley was turning for the worst. I made us all stay home."

She neared him where he stood with the rest of the Jotun. "I'm sorry," was all she could say.

He nodded solemnly. "We heard the Aesir were leaving Asgard to come here, so we took the opportunity to strike back for revenge. Tell Lady Rind we are sorry for damaging her home, but it was necessary. Where is Vali?"

Ailsa looked down at her mating rune, which was now numb but blistering a hideous sight. "He's in trouble. Do you think you could help me once more, Drieger?"

"What do you need?" he asked.

"Time," she looked across the landscape leading toward the distant mountains. "As much of it as you can give me."

Drieger smiled and clutched the mallet in his fist, his blue knuckles turning white. "Well, we didn't plan on leaving just yet. We'll keep the gods busy, Ailsa. Go help your elfin."

"Thank you!" She slipped past them, following the entrance from the destroyed gathering hall where the giants lined up waiting to take their revenge. She ran as quickly as her breath allowed, ignoring the wheeze inevitably building in her throat as her feet flew across the portico leading to the Convocation.

"Ailsa, wait!"

She stumbled to a stop and turned to see Frey approaching her, his braid now unbound in long, golden waves. His robes floated in the vicious night breeze, sticking to his body, revealing the outline of his breast and curvy hips through the thin garment.

He noticed where her eyes traveled. She asked, "I thought you were—"

"I am both Frey and Freya," he said, catching up to her. "A god and a goddess, worshiped through different names but the same deity."

"And you switch back and forth between identities?"

He nodded. "Yes, though I am generally referred to by my masculine title. There is power in a man's name, but Freya gets to have her fun when matters exceed a man's authority." He waved a hand dismissively. "But I am not here to speak about myself. I am here to help you."

"Why would you help me?" she asked. "You're one of *them,* one of the gods."

Frey shook his head. "No, Ailsa. I remember being as much of a pawn in Odin's struggle for power as you are now. Surely you know my story?"

She did. Frey and Freya were traded by the Vanir to the Aesir as an exchange of hostages to maintain the peace between the god tribes. But Ailsa maintained her guard. She no longer trusted so easily.

She nodded and Frey continued, "Gullveig was my sister, my mentor, and my closest friend. When Odin burned her, he burned a piece of my loyalty with him. Her power is inside you, and Odin will stop at nothing until he has it. But he cannot take it if you bind it to your soul."

"I do not want the ancient power," Ailsa protested. Her breath was heavy in her chest, drowned by the fluid in her lungs exacerbated by the stress of the evening. She wouldn't last much longer without her medicine, but there was no time with Vali in danger.

"That is why you are the best one to control it. You've tasted it, have you not? You've let it out in spurts and glimpsed the knowledge of the original power and have done things your mortal hands could never accomplish. The fates sent you the power for a reason, made you a Tether so you would carry it into your destiny. It is threaded into your life's spool to be your ending or your beginning. It is your choice, Ailsa." he said. His eyes glanced at her hand. "Your rune mark is fading. Vali is dying. You can still save him if you leave now."

Ailsa's gaze fell to the world beneath them, her heart torn in so many pieces. "But how will we save Alfheim without Odin's help?"

"There is more than one way to fight for something. Always remember that."

She looked down at her hand, the back now blistering, the ink lighter than it had been before. Tears burned her eyes, blurring the corner of her vision. "I don't even know where he is or how to complete the rune!" she admitted, finally realizing she was in way over her head.

"Look down your bond. It connects you always. As for the rune, you already know how to make one. Remember, the blood *must* be willing. Make my sister's sacrifice worth it, Ailsa."

Make all *their sacrifices worth it.*

Her father, Marrin, Lochare, Sorrin, her clan, the elves, so many bodies littered the trail for this power to be with her, to come to her. For their sakes, she would make their deaths worth something.

Starting with her next choice.

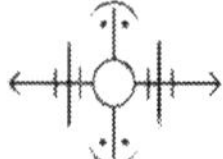

Her whistle screamed into the night, carried across the realm by the shifting wind that tugged her gown like a sail inhaling the gust. Elísar remembered her as he descended on top of the Convocation and let her mount his back. The saddle was cold between her thighs without Vali's heat behind her.

She quickly buckled her legs into the straps, her fingers trembling from the frigid night air. Ailsa focused on the rune once more, just to be sure of the right location, before kicking off the eagle and forcing it to charge over the edge.

A string of curses left her numb lips as they caught free air. She would never get used to the rush, never tire of the thrill of flying. She stood high in the saddle, feeling more comfortable the second time around, as the eagle spread its wings and ascended over the earth.

"The Haven, Elísar," she spoke to the bird in plain language, praying it would understand through the pleading strokes of her palm against his neck. "We must go into the mountains, to Haven. Find Vali!"

The bird shifted its wings to the west, and Ailsa shuddered a chilled breath of relief. Somehow the bird sensed her desires, and they flew above the quiet world where Vali was calling to her through the inky veins on her hand. She reached for the dagger at her thigh, the icy metal stung her skin with cold.

"I'm coming, *Sólskin.*"

Vali had known pain before, but this was a type of suffering he had only just been introduced.

When Ivor was through branding his body with the iron, tracing the runes on his chest and melting his skin to the hot metal, she brought a torch to his hand and set the skin on fire. Being drained of blood, he was powerless against her torture. Unable to so much as lift his head and see what was coming next.

"What's taking her so long?" Ivor hissed.

"There was trouble at the Light Palace. Giants, it seems."

Vali clenched his teeth, the only thing he could move besides the rise and fall of his chest.

"That won't stop her," Ivor decided. "And Frey already said he would help—" A sound rocked the world above them, sending a sheen of dust trailing from the ceiling. "What was that?"

His captors assessed the sound with still breaths.

"Grab the prisoner, Finn. The witches have arrived."

A low growl slipped from the receding darkness before Vali felt the wolf's teeth in his shoulder. But the chords in his throat were shredded thin from heavy breathing and swallowed screams, and he had no voice left to cry out. His body slid easily across the slick tile as they dragged him from the room.

A small victory.

He smelled the night crisp against his throat. The contrast of air burned his nose and chilled the blood still oozing down his airway. They brought him outside, where voices muffled together in a chorus of disorder, unable to discern words hidden by other words. The wolf dropped him on the granite face of the mountainside before a figure loomed over him. The face concealed beneath a hood and a shadow formed from the moonlight.

"Vali, Vali, Vali," it sang. "Look how far you've fallen."

"Nerissa," he muttered with distaste.

"Hello, darling. Have you missed me?"

He spat a mouthful of blood that persistently pooled in his cheek and hoped it met its mark. Judging by the way she jerked out of his line of vision, his trajectory had been accurate.

"Tie him to the stake. When the Tether comes, we need him ready to burn immediately in case she tries to do anything noble. Where is the Great Wolf? He should be here by now." She spat the order at the witches around him. Their hands clawed at his skin and stirred alive new pain from the shifting of his broken bones.

When they were done, he opened his eyes and found they were in an empty courtyard overlooking the valley outside of the Haven, a castle built into the mountain itself and carved by the river bordering just south of where they stood. If he could make it to the waters, he could be restored. But the river was a long way to travel with a snapped femur, and he had two of those.

Frey's domain towered above and loomed a shadow across

the valley, exaggerating the eerie glow of torches held by each Volva witch before him. It appeared half the coven was here, waiting for the source of their ancient power to show itself so they could take it, or watch him burn along with Odin's last hope.

"Death by fire?" he asked Nerissa. "Didn't you already try that?"

She smiled with a wicked twitch of her lips. "I made a mistake last time. The runes are in your flesh not your heart, but once I burn them away, so will their protection over you fade. And you'll be just like the rest of us." She stepped close, her nose in line with his. "Vulnerable."

His breath was raspy in his throat as he returned her glare. "If you kill me, you'll kill her too."

Nerissa's face betrayed a flinch. If she carried any ounce of care for him still, it slipped the moment he spoke of his bond with Ailsa. "I know. But it is better she dies if she refuses to do what we say." Nerissa spoke as the witches poured an oil over the kindle beneath his feet, spare drops speckled bare skin where his clothes had been torn.

"And what will you ask of her?" he asked.

Nerissa looked away, searching the shadows lining the valley as if they would answer instead. "I will not be the one asking questions, Vali. What happens from this moment on is out of my control."

Vali's breath quickened. "What do you mean *out of your control*? Are you not the one orchestrating this? Was it not your idea to kill me all those years ago? Do not pretend you are not here to finish what you started."

Nerissa growled, and for a moment he thought she would set fire to the kindle beneath his feet regardless of killing his mate. "Don't flatter yourself, Vali. I am here because the wolven required the services of the Volva and we are here to claim our payment. No longer will we have to hide in the shadow of the Tree or be ruled by spinners of fate. With Ailsa we will recreate the worlds how they were originally designed to function. But for a new universe to be born, this one must burn."

Vali's eyes widened with understanding, and he cursed himself for not seeing this sooner. The wolven were not acting on their own, they did not hide in Alfheim because it was their home. They came here to hide from the divines, in the only godless realm in the Tree.

His silent wonders were answered as a door leading to the stone courtyard swung open. Out stepped a towering figure of a man with silver hair flowing down his shoulders. Vali had never seen this man before, but the frosty eyes that studied him were familiar, as was the hatred they burned him with. They glazed over his body pathetically tied to a pyre near the mouth of the court. The fists balled at his sides were lined with long claws; his skin was grey, like he hadn't seen the sun in a century.

This wasn't just another wolf. This was *the* wolf. Standing before him was the demigod, Fenrir.

"Nerissa, love," he spoke as the moon draped his half-clothed body in light. The man was stacked with muscle, shadows hung inside each cord and chiseled rivet. He reached for the witch, and she came to his side, slipping her hand between his treacherous claws. "You have outdone yourself this time."

"Oh, just you wait, Great One. It's about to get better."

"Look at the sky!" someone shouted. Every head followed the command, and Vali saw a black figure descending above them. Silver moonlight filtered through eagle feathers. A lone rider on Elísar's back.

"No," he whispered. "Ailsa, no." He shut his eyes and willed her image away, hoping it was anyone else. Hoping it was anyone except his *Fraendi* circling lower now toward the tip of the landing. But even with his eyes closed, he felt her. Her presence was now like the very breath in his chest, a natural need that was unbearable to endure when it was taken away. So familiar, she was now an extension of himself, another half to render him incomplete when she wasn't there.

The beast landed at the end of the strip of granite, and Ailsa dismounted in a storm of gilded gossamer, her gown flowing behind her as the valley wind inhaled her skirts. They whipped in a graceful dance behind her, her hair swept away from the sharp angles of her exquisitely crafted face, only blemished by a trail of blood sourced from her temple. The runes dipping down her neck, between her breast, and disappearing beneath the silk burned orange with a fiery rage. She looked like a goddess, held herself like a queen, and the quiet anger activating the glowing runes was hardly the most dangerous thing about his *Fraendi*. It was the look in her eyes that never showed a flicker of fear, even as she met the stare of the most dangerous demigod in the Nine Realms.

"Vali!" Her gaze finally found him, and her stoic expression fell apart with heartbreak. "*Sólskin*… What have you done to him?"

"Broke a few bones so he couldn't run. Drained his blood so he couldn't heal. He will be fine as long as you cooperate," Nerissa said, her voice moving as she stepped around the pit.

"Who are you?" Ailsa hissed.

"Me?" Nerissa stepped in front of him now, flipping her

hair over her shoulder. "I'm the girl who stole his heart. I'm sure you've heard lots about me."

"Not really." Ailsa's voice was bittersweet. "Where is Ivor? And who are all you people?"

The wolves stalked from the darkened places of the terrace. Their stormy coats bristled with a sensed threat. Ivor slipped between them, her chin high and hands relaxed at her side. Ailsa unsheathed the blade at her thigh.

"Hello, *systir*," Ivor spoke first.

Ailsa only bared her teeth at the wolf. "You are not my sister. My family wouldn't betray me in such a way as you have."

"Your father lied to you and forced you into marrying a swine, uncaring if you died early as long as you kept his family line revered. I am *helping* you—"

"You're helping yourself," Vali hissed behind her. Ivor spun her head over her shoulder to glare at him. "Tell her Ivor. Tell her the real reason you went to her all those years ago in the Aelderwood, how you've been leading her into a den of wolves this entire time. Remind us all who you really serve."

The wolven shrugged. "I am not ashamed I protected Ailsa her entire life until she received the Tether. Nor will I apologize for not letting her fall into Odin's hands. If Odin gets his hands on Gullveig's power, he will be able to free the only god who can kill—"

A low growl interrupted Ivor, and the wolven balked to the side, aware of her mistake. "Great One, I apologize, I did not mean to—"

His growl lowered from a warning to a threat, and Ivor fell quiet. The half-god stepped around the pulpit and into view, Ailsa's eyes tearing from the wolven to the Great Wolf himself. Her grip on the useless dagger tightened with the slight twitch of her fingers. "Who are you?" she asked. Her voice solid and steady, though Vali sensed her fear through their bond. When she was this close, he found he could sense everything she experienced.

Fenrir's breath was heavy. He watched her thrust the blade outward as he stepped closer. "You know who I am, Ailsa. Especially considering you hold the key to my undoing."

Ailsa only swallowed and lifted the dagger a little higher as she said, "Fenrir."

The Great Wolf nodded. Witches and wolves stepped aside, pressing their backs against the obsidian railing to give whatever was about to happen some space. Vali squirmed against his bindings, but his strength was gone, left somewhere back in his holding chamber.

"Well, if you wanted me dead you would have killed one of us by now. What do you want with Vali?" she asked.

Fenrir rolled his bare shoulders back, baring his chest to appear even larger than he already was. "You are right, I do not want you dead. Ivor has told me of your curse and the witches have foreseen your last hours. Your end is near, Ailsa. Which is why it is imperative we bind this power to you before you die, so the power is not lost again."

"And if I refuse?"

Fenrir shook his head. "You will not refuse. Because I am going to keep your mate in the same chains his father bound me with, and I will not set him free until we have successfully destroyed Odin and the rest of the gods. Then you can have him back."

Ailsa's eyes rolled with the flutter of her lashes. "I am so tired of being threatened into taking this power. I'd rather die than be used to destroy realms. Don't you realize I was prepared to die before this? The best part of being cursed is learning how to accept death, not fear it."

Fenrir threw his head back with a laugh that echoed across the valley. He glanced at Nerissa, who was standing off to the side, and nodded. "I believe I can make you fear death, Ailsa."

Vali could only watch with dread as the flames sparked the wood beneath him, time slowed into crystal clear still frames like he was a spectator to his own execution. The hiss of ravenous flames drowned away the sound of his *Fraendi's* scream.

51
Ailsa

The flames swallowed him like they had been starved for a century. Ailsa's heart stalled in her chest as he burned, his bloody clothes catching fire first and forcing a strangled scream from his lips. The sound split through the night, tore the earth with its pain, etched itself forever in her memory. Ailsa knew she'd never forget it as long as she lived.

Her breath heaved as she tried to call his name, catching on the rawness in her throat until she choked. She smelled the smoke, thick and heavy in her own chest, the heat in her toes creeping up her legs. He was the one burning, but she would go down with him all the same.

"Please," she begged Nerissa. Something shifted inside her, watching him burn. An instinctual urge to protect, a visceral need deeper than her marrow. Whether it was from the rune on her hand or the love in her heart, she realized she couldn't let him go—she couldn't let them both die. "Stop this! Don't do this to him because of me, please!"

Nerissa snatched the wrist still clutching the dagger. "Finish the rune, Ailsa. Save him yourself."

Ailsa glanced from the dagger to the witch, unsure if she

could trust her. Unsure if it even mattered. "You vow this will save him?"

"*Only* this will save him, Ailsa."

Without further decision, she pulled her dress aside on her chest and placed the knife edge to the scarred rune over her heart. Her eyes fell to the sky, glaring into the winking starlight where she knew the blind beast watched and relished. "I'm willing," she hissed to the Crow, and slashed through the scarred skin disrupting the ink.

The runes surged to life across her body, but she felt no pain this time. Only light and life, death and darkness. Surging together until the ancient power wove itself into the threads of her soul, her destiny claimed with the simple cut across her skin. She felt it everywhere, every part of her being from her skin to her blood, the very sustenance inhaled in her lungs charged with a living force that both set her on fire and drowned her away. And she could breathe. Each rise of her chest was no longer a fight but a natural movement, effortless and satisfying. Her body was no longer filled with fluid, and she felt alive and strong.

But Vali was still screaming somewhere beyond her body and the sudden sensations pulsing a new life in her veins. She heard Nerissa at her side whisper something and the flames ceased, leaving only a charred man tied to the stake.

"Vali," she spoke his name with hope this time. Ailsa pulled him from the stake before the wolves could get any closer, ignoring the heat from the fire still fresh on his skin. He was hot everywhere she touched, his eyes were shut, the skin of his cheeks black from smoke. "*Sólskin,* wake up." She held him to her chest, feeling the rune on her hand fade as his own was shriveled and scorched. The heartbeat in her own chest slowed with a painful throb.

They were dying.

"What do I do? How do I help him?" she whispered to someone—anyone who could help.

The familiar voice in her mind answered, *If runes are born from blood, what do you think rewrites the threads of fate? My knowledge is inside you now, Ailsa. The power to change the past and lay a new future is at your fingertips. Listen to your heart, it will know what to do.*

She dipped her fingers in the bleeding flesh above her heart, where the rune binding herself to an untapped power was carved into completion. She wet the pads of their tips and rewrote Vali's fate like ink across a blank page. That whisper of knowing echoed inside her flesh, like the voice of her spirit nudging her inclinations, moving her hands until they were drawing symbols across Vali's excoriated skin. She covered the old runes Odin marked into his body, writing over his past to make a new future, a new destiny that would belong to him and him alone.

Her eyes had never seen these symbols before, but her spirit knew them, *felt* them. They faded into his skin as soon as she was finished with one, disappearing so that none would ever see the forbidden language of fate nor be able to copy their scriptures. Each one replacing a darker one written by a god with the power to control flesh, but not fate.

She saw their threads in her mind, woven together like a braid, the edges smoothing back together from their fray. The witches whispered around her, but she paid them no attention. She now held a power they had no knowledge of, one that had been suppressed since the fall of Gullveig over a century ago. Only once their threads were bound into time once more did her fingers stop tracing his chest.

Ailsa opened her eyes she didn't realize had been shut,

gaining witness as Vali took a gasping breath. His body renewed before their eyes, every inch of discolored skin now creamy and smooth. His chest now bare, unmarked, a blank canvas for a new future. The sunset of his gaze found hers and brightened the hazy valley with their life.

"Ailsa," he whispered. Her name, both a request and an affirmation. He sat up in her arms and pulled her into his chest, kissing her with the heavy weight of his relief and the fierceness of his passion. He pulled away when he sensed something different about her, his eyes falling over the crimson stain bleeding through the sheer fabric of her gown.

"You did it," he only said.

She swallowed and nodded, pulling her gown aside for him to see the new rune formed above her heart. "Does this change what you feel for me?" she asked.

His lips turned up in a slow smile. "No, Ailsa. Never that."

A giddy laugh broke the fleeting moment of relief, reminding them both they were hardly safe yet, only experiencing the bliss found in the eye of a storm. Ailsa looked up to see Nerissa and Fenrir watching them, her face glowing with pride. "What did I tell you, Great One? I promised I would return the power to you. Now that you have it, you cannot be stopped. Odin will fall." He kissed her hand appreciatively, never tearing his eyes away from Ailsa.

"I will not help you destroy the Nine Realms," Ailsa spat, pulling Vali closer.

"I do not need your *help,* just your submission." Fenrir looked to the south, where the Palace of Light stood somewhere behind the nightly fog. "Maybe I should pay Odin a visit since he's in the neighborhood."

"Vali," she whispered without moving her lips. The wolves and witches now distracted by her performance, chattering amongst themselves. "We need to get out of here before they chain you." Stories said Fenrir could break through any chain until the dwarves crafted a metal with the contrasting ingredients of life itself. If the wolf couldn't break them, Vali would be helpless.

"Even I cannot hold off a coven of Volva, Ailsa. But we will not go down without a fight. I'll create a distraction while you grab your blade." The blade she had dropped when she cut him from the pyre.

"When?"

The scraping of metal against cold mountain answered her inquiry. Vali's gaze widened on hers, his hand abandoned her waist to spread a palm across the granite. "Run to the top of the steps and don't look back. I'll be right behind you." His lip slipped beneath his teeth, her first warning a sharp whistle.

The shudder of the mountain side was the second.

She threw herself away from him in the direction she believed she had tossed the dagger. Rows of teeth glistened in the corner of her vision, viscous snarls behind them. Nerissa shouted something at them both, but her voice was swallowed by the cracking stone beneath their feet, a deep sound that reminded her of breaking bones. She looked back to see the jutting end of the courtyard crumbling to pieces, the wolves and witches who stood there fell into a mess of granite and ash.

"*Go*!" Vali shouted at her. Clutching the dagger, she took off toward the double doors sitting high over several clusters of stairs. A wolf lunged at her, but she evaded its attack, swiping the dagger across one of their eyes to force it back. Blind and bleeding, it whimpered away. Vali used the wind to push the rest of them back, pressing the wolves against the railing as he dealt with Fenrir.

A great roar shook the stone floor once again, and Ailsa turned to see Fenrir had shifted. Living up to his namesake, the Great Wolf was at least five times the size of a normal wolf. Her head was nearly the size of one of his fangs. He lunged at Vali, jowls snapping and narrowly missing the elfin as he leapt aside.

"Vali!" she gasped, but she was too far to help him even if she could. Another wolf sprung towards her face, and she barely had time to lift her dagger and sink it into its chest, falling on her back against the cold pavers. She pushed the dead weight off her chest, now looking up at the night sky. The sight above made her pause.

Eagles.

An entire fleet of them circled above, their wingspans covering the starlight and masking the night. One swooped down and clawed a wolf, tossing it over the side of the mountain where its sharp wails echoed far across the mountain range. The wolves scattered, forgetting Ailsa as more eagles plunged. Nerissa was busy saving witches falling from Vali's rockslide, giving Ailsa the opportunity to run up the stairs as Vali commanded.

She looked down on him from the steps she had ascended in the time he gave her to escape. He gained no ground with the Great Wolf, thick saliva strung between his teeth as he snapped his jaws and kept Vali on the defensive. The eagles noticed the elfin's struggle and a group of them dove toward the wolf, tearing at his hide until the beast was writhing against their talons and thrashing his massive head in an attempt to reach them. Vali fled while the beast was distracted, not breaking his stride until he met her on the landing.

"Let's go, while they're preoccupied." Without stalling, he snatched her upper arm and pulled her back into the castle, but a force wrapped around her ankles and yanked her back out of his hand. Ailsa hit the floor with the slap of her hands against the stone, dragged by her ankles down the stairs. The planes of her face hit the jagged edges of each step. Lightning struck down from the sky and rubble rained in front of her face, concealing Vali from sight.

Nerissa flipped her on her back as she clawed against the magic pulling her back into the courtyard. She heard Vali's voice, but it seemed far off, getting smaller as if he were speaking through a wall. "I should kill you for what you've done to my witches!" she shouted, looming over Ailsa. With the flick of the witch's fingers, Ailsa felt the air coaxed from her chest. "I showed you mercy, I gave you power over fate and helped you save your lover, and this is how you thank me? No, Ailsa. You will pay for this, even if we must lose our collateral in you."

Ailsa's vision mottled. A heavy weight pushed down on her chest, even as she used all her effort to take a breath. She swung at the witch above her with the dagger still in her fist, but the move was clumsy, and Nerissa barely moved aside to dodge it.

This was it. This was how she would die, at the hands of a vengeful witch with her *Fraendi* far from her touch. She wondered if Vali could feel the burning ache in his chest as well, if the blood in his eyes blurred everything out of focus, if he felt the end.

But the enchantment was suddenly broken. Ailsa took a gasping breath of air and discovered a wolf with its jaws around Nerissa's throat, the witch screaming in pain as poison from its teeth slipped into her bloodstream. The wolf tore something from the witch's throat, looking up at Ailsa with crimson saliva dripping from its jowls. But that frosted gaze she knew anywhere.

"*Ivor,*" she whispered in shock. Why would she save her now, after all the wolf had brought her through? But Ivor only snarled, baring her teeth at her before she barked. The sound was so menacing it had Ailsa scrambling to her feet.

"Thank you," she said, before turning on a heel back up the stairs where Vali was shifting through the defaced mountain rubble. He cleared a boulder from the path with his magic, and his figure came into view. Those golden eyes glowed like a beacon against the ash smeared across his cheeks and dusting his matted hair.

They made it through the doors and ducked inside the castle, where an unsettling quiet swallowed the hammering pulse in her ears. Vali's hand was tight around her own, pulling her down deeper into the castle. The floor sullied by a trail of blood.

"Where are we going?" she asked breathlessly. Her heart demanded they slow down, but her fear pushed her beyond the limits of her body.

"We need to get out of Alfheim," he only said.

"But how?"

He had no answer, and Ailsa understood. It didn't matter how, only that it must be done. There were one too many gods in this realm looking for her. With the runes still marking her skin, she must still be hidden from Odin, and hopefully from the Volva and Fenrir as well. Perhaps she could mark Vali similarly and hide them both from prying eyes.

They burst through the doors leading to a great hall, one empty of furnishings but not unoccupied. Lines of elves dressed in black armor, glistening like wet tar against the lit chandelier hanging above, poised ready to attack. The front lines joined shields, the back cocked arrows. The stretching of their strings the only sound in the room.

"Dark Elves," Vali whispered. He held up his hands in surrender, stepping in front of her.

"Lord Vali," one man broke the front line to approach him. Vali straightened at the formality, like he had forgotten he was the heir of this realm. The soldier approached them with a slight nod of his head in respect. "There were rumors of Fenrir hiding in the mountains, but we had no idea the wolven were working with the witches. Only today did the Great Wolf show himself after Frey left for the Light Palace."

"Are you saying the wolven were behind our war?" Vali asked.

The soldier nodded. Ailsa admired the intricate design carved into the metal of his helm, covering a blanket of scarlet hair. "They used us. Took advantage of the animosity between the Dark and the Light Elves to distract us from Fenrir hiding somewhere near the well. We knew using sedir wasn't the reason our realm was dying, but we didn't have any other explanation to prove otherwise." His eyes shifted over Vali. "But I think you have seen the truth with your own eyes."

Vali nodded just as a shudder rocked through the palace, sending a sheen of dust trailing from the high ceiling. Ailsa squeezed his arm and said, "As grateful as I am this civil dispute between your people is resolving, we kind of pissed off half a coven of Volva. Can we get out of here now?"

The soldier placed a hand on his pommel and gave her a soft smile. "Our swords and sedir are yours, Lady. We can fight them off so you can get to the Light Palace."

"No, the Aesir are probably still there. I need to take her to Vanaheim; it is the only place safe for her," Vali briefly explained, pointing out the runes marking her skin and the ones that had disappeared from his own. The only expression the soldier disclosed was the growing whites of his eyes.

"We can make you a portal to Vanaheim."

Ailsa startled, slipping a gasp. "You can do that?"

His smile widened, sensing she was impressed. "Have you ever seen the Volva traveling by foot across the tree, Lady? How else would they travel once summoned? Yes, sedir allows you to travel great distances, but a portal all the way to the Lower Roots will take many of us. We must start now."

He turned back to his men and gathered a few of them on the dais where Vali and Ailsa were waiting. She turned to her elfin. "But what about Seela? And your mother. Do you feel safe leaving them all behind with the Aesir behind their walls and now Fenrir at their doorstep?"

He shook his head and held her closer. His chalky skin was rough against her cheek, warm in all the places she was cold. "I will make sure we send word of what happened here to Seela and my mother. Seela may venture after us or stay to defend her queen. Either way, it is her choice." His fingers lifted her chin to angle her face toward his. "We will return, Ailsa, I vow this. I will not let my realm fall to Fenrir."

"But for now?" she asked.

He sighed and lowered his face to graze her lips, pulling back only a breath to speak against her mouth. "For now, I will take you to Njord to keep you safe. He knew Gullveig and perhaps he can help you learn more with this power you have claimed. Though, you seem to have a good grasp on it already."

She pressed her lips together to hold back a choking sound. "I'm sorry, Vali."

"For what?"

"For making you leave. For making you choose." He was only leaving to protect her, and she felt ashamed for being the reason he had to leave behind his land while a tyrant still raged and threatened the safety of his people.

He took her face in both of his hands, wiping a stray tear with his thumb. "*Stiarna*, do you not realize what you have done for me? Have I not made it clear how much I am beholden to you?" He placed her free hand over the left side of his chest, where deep beneath the layers of skin and bone was a steady beat against her palm. A place once barren, empty for half a century, now filled by his *Fraendi*. A part of him born from her love and her sacrifice.

"You have a heart!" Her words trailed a sigh, followed by a nervous laugh.

He smiled the kind of smile that showed teeth, a sight so pure it felt misplaced in this room. "I have you, *sváss*. And while this heart in my chest still beats, I will fight for us and our future. Whatever we face next, we face together."

The doors leading to the Great Hall shook against a pounding force, causing Ailsa to snag his shirt in her fist. They were running out of time. But the Dark Elves appeared nearly finished with their portal, a dark cloud shimmering atop the dais and tossing her hair with its own violent gust. Shadows wrapped around them and swallowed the surrounding hall, and she shut her eyes against the portal sucking them into a void, a cold place between stars. Wind tore at her gown, her hair, tried to pull her from his arms, but she held firm.

Quicker than a breath, than the space between her racing heartbeats, the disorder was replaced with quiet. The Great Hall had become a beach beneath a night sky, dark waters lapped at her toes. This place was so familiar it tugged at a closed off place in her heart, the scar of an old wound not yet completely healed.

But this was not Drakame. She was still far from her home

and deep into the heart of another strange land, this one far darker and colder than the ones located among the Highest Branches. Vali's shoulders fell as if a great weight had been removed from them but remained still beside her, even as the waves stung icy pools at their feet.

"Finally, the fates have worked out something on our side," he said.

"This is Vanaheim?" she asked. He finally peeled himself from her arms and looked around, nodding.

"Yes. As you know, this is one of the lower realms in the Roots of the Tree. These waters may look like an ocean, but this is one of the three wells that feeds the Tree. I can fill you in on the geography later." He held out his hand to pull her up black sand. "We need to get to Njord's sanctuary before nightfall."

"Before nightfall?" she echoed. "What would you call this?"

Vali's smile was ladened with sadness. "A bright day in the realm beneath the Tree. Come, Njord must know we're here already."

Ailsa took his outstretched hand and followed him up the coast leading to the seaside castle. Her bones were restless from the abrupt cease in chaos, her thoughts still reeled with images of Fenrir and Nerissa, of Ivor tearing out her throat. All they had learned this day, of the darkness originating from the Great Wolf and the threat on the Nine Realms now alive with his resurrection.

She could not enjoy this moment of peace, of the salty breeze cool through her tangled hair nor the warmth of the hand clutching her own. Not when so much was still left undetermined. Not when she alone could stop Fenrir from destroying the worlds.

Ailsa could not face a god herself and win, but she knew

one that could. If Baldur was truly their last hope, then she would deliver him to Odin herself. And once this was over, she would embark on her next great adventure with her *Fraendi* at her side. And she would go home at last, wherever that was in the end.

"*Sváss,* I haven't had the chance to tell you how beautiful you look tonight," Vali said, squeezing her hand.

She smiled, throwing him a sideways glance. "You should have seen me outside the Temple of Light. I assure you, I was much more desirable before I flew across Alfheim and fought your ex girlfriend."

"You're right, I should have seen you." His strides stop suddenly, half turning to face her. "I am sorry we didn't get a chance to complete our ceremony, Ailsa. I hope you know I wanted nothing more than to swear my oath to you."

"Vali, do not apologize, it wasn't your fault." She smoothed a hand over his cheek. "I'm just glad you are safe now. The only oath I want from you is that you will never scare me like that again."

She felt his smirk against her palm. "Of course, *Stiarna.* I have something for you, by the way. I was supposed to give it to you tonight but… things didn't work out. I am pleasantly surprised it didn't fall out when the wolves dragged me across the castle."

"What is it?"

He guided her hand between them with his own, his opposite pulling something out of his pocket. Her heart arrested when she felt the cold metal slip around her fourth finger.

A ring.

Ailsa assessed it in the failing light, and Vali produced a bright orb with his magic so she could see the ring and all its details. Runes etched the surface, ones she recognized. The same markings on their hands written in repetition around the edge. A saga of sun and stars.

"Vali," she whispered, "why did you—"

"I remembered you said something about your mother's ring being inherited through your family's generations. I wanted to give you another to pass down for yourself, for the legacy that we will build together if you will still have me." His magic dimmed, leaving only a faint glow shining in the sliver of space between his hand and hers. "I know it doesn't replace your old one, I know it's not your mother's—"

"You're right. This one is mine," she said with a soft smile. "This one is *ours*. Thank you, *Sólskin*."

She placed the hand with the ring inside his palm, and together they continued to walk up the coast. Understanding crept up on her like the warmth of a spring sunrise. Though they were thousands of miles from a friendly soul or familiar place, she knew she didn't belong anywhere else.

For the first time in her life, Ailsa was home.

EPILOGUE

ERIK

Erik faced the final night of his three-day journey deep into the heart of the Aelderwood. He carried a sacrificial offering over his broad shoulders. The goat's throat soaked a thin line of blood down the sleeve of his tunic. The clan leaders did not agree with what he was about to do, and they demanded he stray far from the village to protect Drakame from any collateral damage. But Ailsa had been gone for nearly six moon cycles, and he was desperate to get her back.

His last moments with her were not the kind he liked to think about. His temper had once again gotten the best of him. His lack of control only rivaled that of his father's, and he never wanted to be like that man. He remembered the hurt in her eyes when he snapped at her, when he said things he didn't mean, the way she looked back at him one last time as she left with the fae. The memory so clear, it was like it happened just yesterday. The guilt was still fresh, as if no time had passed at all, and his shame ate at him day and night.

Erik needed to know if she was alive and what had befallen her after the night she left her home with that man—no—that monster with yellow eyes and godlike power. Nikros had ordered him to wait, but he had done enough waiting these last several months. He hadn't even traveled home, breaking his vow with his promised bride and undoubtedly shaming his family name by ignoring his duties as clan leader.

But he didn't care. He needed answers, and tonight he vowed he would have them.

He placed the offering in the center of a stone altar, using the blood from the puncture site to draw runes the town seeress instructed him to scribe on each stone surrounding the sacrifice. He then grabbed a torch and set the bed of bramble and sticks on fire, burning the dead goat and watching the smoke curl to the heavens, calling the dark forces who would not deny a man as desperate as him.

Erik's lips used the old language to call the witches, and to his surprise, they answered.

"Well, hello there, handsome," a soft voice spoke behind him. Erik spun and found a woman draped in black robes emerging from the shadows spacing the trees. Her dark hair spilled over one shoulder while her blood-red lips curled in a smile. "Tell me, why is a pretty boy like you calling upon the Volva?"

"Answers," he said. "A woman was taken from me by a man from another world. I need to know if she's all right. If she is, I want to save her and bring her home."

"Of course, a woman." The Volva witch licked her lips with distaste. "And do you have something of hers I can use to track her location? I cannot find a soul without something they have touched."

Erik dug into his cloak and pulled out a note she had written him before his father all but dragged him across the Great Sea. The one he replied to like a coward, breaking off their relationship so his family could start a wealthy empire in the Westlands. He had chosen his family over her all those years ago, but he kept her words. The last ones that belonged to him.

The witch snatched the letter from his hands. She brought a blade to her hand and cut her palm, letting blood bleed across the faded ink. Erik winced, but said nothing as she ruined the note, only watched as the witch's eyes widened. Her breath hitched in surprise; a smile curled again on her porcelain face.

"This woman you seek, she is alive," the witch said. "But she is not in this realm. If you wish to bring her home, you will need a bit of sedir to assist you with your quest."

"I will do anything," he replied. His heart thundered against his ribs, praising every god he could think of. Ailsa was *alive*.

The witch sighed and thought for a moment, crumbling the note in her palm until it disintegrated into crimson ash. "There is a man who guards her. If you wish to save her, you must kill him first. I will give you the power to cross realms and a weapon that can slay gods, but you must repay me with your blood. When the time comes, I will find you, and you will do as I say. Even if it cost you Valhalla. Even if it costs you everything. Do you understand the consequences of this bargain, mortal?"

Erik nodded before his mind could convince him otherwise. It was his fault she was out there and held captive by a demon. It was his job to find her and bring her home. He could not live the rest of his days carrying this shame in his heart. "I understand. Help me find my Ailsa, and I will be at your service no matter the penalties."

"Good." She beamed. "This is going to be a beneficial partnership for us both, pretty boy."

She held out her bloody hand, and he took it. Lightning shot through the place they connected. The light sensation of snakes crawled beneath his skin, swirling up his arm no matter how hard he tensed. When the witch released him, the discomfort ceased. He pulled back his sleeve to find red lines covering his forearm. Markings he'd never seen before.

"They are blood runes," she explained. "So you cannot go back on our arrangement. They will give you the power to open the portal separating Midgard from the Tree. In your satchel, I have placed a dagger forged from the mines of Svartalfheim, the only blade that can penetrate fae skin, and a map of the Tree leading you to your woman. Do not speak of our deal to anyone else, especially Ailsa. If you do, I will end you using those runes."

Erik nodded, still examining the red lines across his skin. "Thank you," he muttered. "You don't understand how much I want to see her again."

"Trust me, Erik, I know *exactly* how you feel."

Hearing his name from her lips forced his gaze back at her, but the witch was gone. Leaving him only to wonder about her meaning. He picked up his satchel and unfolded the rolled-up map she had somehow placed inside, skimming over various lines running over the Tree of Life toward a red dot marking one of the Lower Roots.

"Vanaheim?" he whispered. "What in Odin's eye are you doing down there, Ailsa?"

Erik took a steadying breath before strapping his new blade next to his old, feeling more hopeful as the gilded handle chilled the clammy flesh of his palm. He had the map, the magic, and now the means to kill the elfin who had taken everything from him. The embers of his rage flickered anew, the memory of those golden eyes burned a fresh fight in his heart.

He would find Ailsa and bring her home, even if it destroyed him.

GLOSSARY

This story contains many names and places from Norse Mythology, most of which I chose to Anglicize for easier read-ability. With that being said, some of these terms may appear differently in other works and retellings. Below I have listed a glossary of people and places included in this story. For my research I used the *Prose Edda* by Snorri Sturluson, translated by Jesse Byock by Penguin 2006. I also used the *Poetic Edda,* translated by Benjamin Thorpe by Corundum Classics.

Aesir- One of the two tribes of Norse Gods. They reside in Asgard and are associated with war and knowledge.
Balder- son of Odin. Known to be the strongest and best of the Aesir. Loki became jealous and tricked the blind god, Hoder, into killing him.
Bifrost- the rainbow bridge leading to Asgard
Fenrir- the giant wolf, son of Loki and Angrboda. Fated to devour Odin at Ragnarok

Frey/Freya- brother and sister in Norse Mythology, come from the Vanir tribe. Associated with fertility.
Frigg- wife of Odin. Goddess of fertility
Gullveig- a mysterious witch, also known as the "gold witch." According to the Völuspá, is known to be the source of conflict between the Aesir and the Vanir
Heimdall- the watchman who guards the Bifrost. Son of Odin.
Hel- the goddess who rules the underworld, Helheim, where those who died of sickness or old age reside. She is the daughter of Loki and Angrboda. Half her body is rotten flesh.
Jormungand- the Serpent of Midgard. Circles the world and is fated to be freed during Ragnarok. Son of Loki and Angrboda
Jotun- the race of giants, enemies of the Aesir.
Loki- a trickster figure, father of Fenrir, Jormungand, and Hel. Can shape-shift and often uses his ability to cause mischief.
Norns- most powerful entities in the universe. Weave the tapestry of fate beneath the World Tree. They create and control fate for all beings, including the gods.
Odin- Also known as the Allfather, he is the highest of the Norse gods and has two ravens that circle the worlds.
Ragnarok- the final battle between the gods. Many of the Aesir gods are predicted to fall, but out of the ending of the old world, a new one will be born.
Skuld- Norn who weaves the fates of the future
Thor- god of sky and thunder
Tyr- god of war whose hand was bitten off by Fenrir.
Valhalla- a literal translation of "hall of the slain" where warriors who died in battle reside. Watched over by Odin. Each day begins with a battle in preparation for Ragnarok and ends with a great feast.
Vali- son of Odin and (in Norse Mythology) the giantess, Rind.

Was said to have been created to seek revenge for Balder's death.

Vanir- one of the two tribes of gods. Reside in Vanaheim and known for their association with wealth and fertility

Volva- a seeress. Usually female practitioners of magic and foretell events.

ACKNOWLEDGMENTS

First and foremost, I want to thank you, the reader, for picking up this book and giving an indie author a chance. This was a passion project from the very beginning, and I hope you enjoyed the journey as much as I loved writing it. Writing a retelling based off of mythology is something I took very seriously, because I wanted to make sure the core parts of the stories belonging to Norse Mythology remained true while also giving the reader a fresh adventure and fun experience.

While my FMC is a true heathen, I am definitely not, and I want to thank God for giving me this opportunity to be a writer and live out the dream He placed in me at a very young age. He put a fantasy lover heart inside me the day I was created, and I am grateful for the doors that opened these past few years to allow me to pursue this dream.

Thank you as always to my husband, Kennon. For picking up the financial slack and working extra, for helping me manage our toddler so I can get some quiet time on the weekends to write, and for supporting my dream without the guarantee I would be successful at it. I couldn't have done any of this without you, and I love you so much.

To my editor, Brittany Corley, I cannot express how much I appreciate your friendship and your counsel. It is safe to say this book would not exist if it weren't for you and your constant encouragement. From beta reading, to agreeing to edit, to reading this book 1000 times, you have been here from the first draft to the last, and there are no words to express how grateful I am to you.

Thank you to my beta readers: Brittany Corley, Bryony Stout, Brianna Payne, Phoebe, Emily K., and Lora. You all gave me amazing advice and feedback concerning the early parts of the story and it would definitely not look like the story it is today without each one of you.

To everyone who has read ARCs, posted on their social medias to hype my story, taken the time to write reviews, message me about the book, and have supported me in your own, individual ways, thank you from the bottom of my heart. I never expected to find such a welcoming community, and I am so grateful you all have embraced me so openly.

And to the sweet lady I spoke with at Renn Fest last year, thank you for pointing me in the right direction concerning research materials and for sharing your beliefs with me. I hope I see you again one day to thank you in person, and to share the story that you inspired.

ABOUT THE AUTHOR

Alexis Menard is a fantasy romance author and happily ever after enthusiast. She lives in Hammond, Louisiana with her husband, toddler, and two dogs. She graduated from Southeastern Louisiana University in nursing. She enjoys long walks through the Renaissance Fair, reading smutty romance into the dark hours of the night, and wine nights with her "Finer Things Club." She hopes to enrich the lives of her readers with worlds they can both escape in and take with them long after the final chapter.

MORE BOOKS YOU'LL LOVE

If you enjoyed this story, please consider leaving a review. Then check out more books by Midnight Tide Publishing

A KINGDOM OF FLAME AND FURY

BY WHITNEY DEAN

At ten years old, Raven was mysteriously willed to be the next ruler of Seolia, a kingdom nestled within the realm of The Four Kingdoms. Orphaned as a baby, she has spent fifteen years ruling over a kingdom she believes she did not earn all while hiding secrets: she possesses dark magic and she thirsts for blood. Now at almost twenty-five years old and with a sudden addiction to stealing life, Raven must fight through her new procured darkness to save her soul, but when a mysterious stranger arrives in her kingdom, she starts experiencing vivid dreams that detail who she truly is. As she slowly starts to unravel her story, what she uncovers at the end of the spool will change the course of her life and her kingdom forever.

A Kingdom of Flame and Fury is book one in a steamy and thrilling new fantasy series: The Four Kingdoms

Made in United States
Orlando, FL
19 March 2023

31214681R00248